P9-EMR-509

Rough & Tumble

Rough & Tumble

Mark Bavaro

St. Martin's Press
New York

This book is a work of fiction. However, I have used the name of the Giants and the names of other NFL teams to enable me to establish a setting for my novel that is familiar to football fans. This novel has not been endorsed nor sponsored by the New York Giants. Although the principal character in the novel bears certain resemblances to me, all of the other characters, teams, and events portrayed in this novel are the products of my imagination or are used fictitiously. None of the players, coaches, or other football personnel referred to in this novel are intended to portray actual people or teams.

Printed in the United States of America. For information, address St. Martin's Press, 175 Fifth Avenue, New York, N.Y. 10010.

www.stmartins.com

Library of Congress Cataloging-in-Publication Data

Bavaro, Mark.
Rough & tumble / Mark Bavaro.—1st ed.
p. cm.
ISBN-13: 978-0-312-37574-4
ISBN-10: 0-312-37574-3
1. Football players—Fiction. 2. New York Giants (Football team)—Fiction. 3. Football stories. I. Title. II Title: Rough and tumble.
PS3602.A9735R68 2008
813'.6—dc22

2008020440

First Edition: September 2008

10 9 8 7 6 5 4 3 2 1

For Pop

Acknowledgments

I'd like to thank my wife, Susan, first and foremost. She was the catalyst in the chain of events that led to this current publication. Until she took control of things, this book was sleeping quietly in its grave in our basement. It was she who dusted it off and brought it back to life. Without her, I never would have found my wonderful agent, Alex Glass. His excitement and enthusiasm made me a believer once again. Through Alex, I met editor extraordinaire Richard Marek. Not only did Dick edit my manuscript into readable shape, he taught me lessons in writing that I would not have learned in a lifetime of classroom lectures and exercises. My gratitude to him cannot be overstated. Dick, you truly are the Cadillac of editors. As a result of Dick's work, this manuscript caught the eye of a very sharp editor at St. Martin's Press named Marc Resnick. After some great edits of his own, *Rough & Tumble* assumed its final form.

Thanks to Robin Bavaro, Eddie Jesser, and David Nyhan.

Through my sister I met Eddie, and through Eddie I met David. It was David's memo concerning the original manuscript that made me dare believe I might one day be a writer. I wish I'd had the opportunity to thank you in person, Mr. Nyhan. Until we meet again, rest in peace.

Thank you, Gary Larabee, for your editorial work in the early years. Thank you, Uncle Donald and Mike Pope, for your technical advice.

And finally, thank you, Holly Martin, for a word of encouragement you probably don't even remember giving. It may have taken a long time to germinate, but the seed you planted in me twenty-six years ago in Freshman Seminar has finally bore fruit.

As I've known all along, very rarely is anything accomplished on your own. In my athletic life I was surrounded by great coaches and teammates. Nothing I did on the field would have been possible without them. In my short writing life, the situation hasn't changed. This book would not have been possible without the above-mentioned people. If it were appropriate, I'd give you all a hug and a slap on the ass.

One

"H slot out Z-Motion Sixty-two Semi Y-Hook Z-Flag on two, on two!"

Jogging up to the line of scrimmage, I repeated the jumble of code words instructing me to run ten yards upfield, stop, turn around, and wait for a pass. It used to be the kid with the best arm in the neighborhood would simply tell me, "Run a curl. Joey, run a post. Teddy, go to the corner. Billy, go deep. And the rest of you guys stay in and block." That was when football was a game. After eight years in the National Football League I knew what I was doing at the moment was anything but a game.

"Blue Fifty-two! Blue Fifty-two!" shouted Dan Ramsey.

Ramsey was our backup quarterback. He'd taken over when golden-boy Ron Hanes broke his leg. Ron was the team's franchise player, the highest-paid guy on the New York Giants. We'd made each other famous over the years as one of the best throwing/catching tandems in the league. He threw the balls and I caught them. But he'd gotten hurt back in September and was out for the season. Ramsey filled in admirably. Hell, we'd all been performing admirably without Ron. Somehow, his absence made us all play better. With five games left on the schedule, we were 10-1. With any luck, we'd improve to 11-1 after beating the Philadelphia Eagles, whose defense was now staring me in the face as I assumed my three-point stance as the Giants' tight end.

"Set!"

The Eagles sucked. They'd only won three games all year. That didn't mean much. Regardless of records, our meetings were always a toss-up; more like rumbles than games. So it was no surprise we found ourselves trailing 21–14 in the fourth quarter.

"Hut!"

Crouched in my stance, the fingers of my right hand pressed into the artificial turf of Philly's stadium, while the other hand rested on my left knee. My blue-and-white sock drooped below my calf, and I ran my fingers over the long scar across my kneecap from last year's surgery. It was raised and bumpy and ran like a diagonal zipper from one corner of my knee to the other. Although twelve months had passed since my ligaments had been torn to shreds, the injury was still fresh in my mind. The pain accounted for that. But the injury didn't worry me. It was just the latest in a long string of mishaps. I'd already overcome a dozen surgeries to various parts of my body with no problems. It was going to take a lot more than a bum knee to slow me down. Although a lot of people had thought my career was over, I proved them wrong. My knee recovered just enough, and I was now playing as well as ever. Hell, the way I felt at the moment, the end of my career was nowhere in sight.

"Hut!"

I bolted from the line of scrimmage. Groggins, the linebacker before me, swung his elbow at my head, then wrapped his other hand around the back of my shoulder. My breath shot out unexpectedly as his taped hand slapped my spine and stuck to me like glue. I tried to avoid him. My job was to run a pass pattern, not to get tangled up with him. But the price of being a good tight end in the National Football League was no free releases off the line of scrimmage. The harassment was a sign of respect. I took it as a compliment.

"Get your fuckin' hands off me!" I yelled, regaining my breath.

"Fuck you, punk!" he replied.

"Fuck you, bitch!"

And so our conversation continued from our previous fifty plays. Churning my legs into the turf, I chopped at the linebacker's arms with my fists and elbows. Despite the pain, my knee felt good. The Butazolodine I'd taken at halftime was kicking in. Prescribed mainly for horses, the anti-inflammatory worked wonders for me. I couldn't play without it.

Fighting my way off the line of scrimmage, I thought to myself, I love this game. Not because it was fun. But because it made me whole. I'd been playing football since the fourth grade. It was who I was. It was all I was. I was respected because of it. I was known because of it. And most important, I was paid because of it. It was my job and I was good at it.

Cracking the linebacker's forearm with an elbow and shoving my palm into his chin, I wondered if I would ever achieve the same satisfaction from another profession. I guess I'd never know, because I planned on playing forever.

"Banjo! Banjo!" the 240-pound prick holding my jersey screamed as I broke free of his grasp. He was communicating with his middle linebacker. *Banjo* was a defensive code word meaning I was about to be handed off like a baton in a relay race from one man to another. As Groggins's fingers flicked from my jersey and he fell to the ground, I ricocheted into freedom. Unmolested, I stole a quick glance at my surroundings. Bodies were everywhere, each consumed with his personal opponent. Chaos seemed to reign. But in fact, it was all carefully planned and rehearsed. As expected, the Philadelphia middle linebacker appeared directly in front of me ready to assume the package his buddy was delivering.

The middle backer was about two inches shorter than the six-foot-four-inch outside backer but at least twenty pounds heavier. He moved awkwardly compared to the grace of his teammate, but because his job was to fill holes and stand his ground at all costs, he was an even more formidable foe here in the middle of the field where there was little room to maneuver.

Ramsey expected me to be ten yards over the center in about one and a half seconds. My pass route demanded discipline and timing. Like a baseball player running the bases, I couldn't leave the baseline. There wasn't any room. But even if there were, I couldn't ad-lib. The only path to my assigned spot went straight through this new prick.

As Groggins's hand left my jersey, the middle backer stuck his head into my chest. Until I was farther downfield, I was fair game to these headhunters. My ribs bent inward at the blow, and my shoulders nearly met on the other side of his head. He hit me so hard his face mask touched my spinal cord. My breath exploded like a popped balloon, and I spit my mouth guard out with the force of a bottle rocket. He'd gotten me good, but I'd seen it coming. This, at least, gave me time to plan my countermove.

Even as his head displaced my lungs, I grabbed the back of his shoulder pads with one arm and, like a swimmer, swung my other arm over his head. With a tug of his shirt and a twist of my body, I shimmied past him and let his forward momentum take him to the ground.

Adhering to the imaginary baseline of my pass pattern, and trying to regain my breath, I continued to my designated spot ten yards deep into the defense. It only took three unimpeded strides to get there, and when I did, I planted my feet firmly in the turf and turned around.

The ball met me in the exact spot that the middle backer's helmet had just vacated. It had been no more than a brown flash in the bottom of my eyes, but my hands rose instinctually to meet it. The sound and feel of the ball as it *thwacked* into my hands told me it was a completion before my eyes confirmed it. Holding it now like a potted plant I'd just purchased from a nursery, I was met from behind by a blow to my back. The force buckled my knees and nearly popped the ball loose from my grasp. It took every fingernail I had to hold on to it. The hit had been hard, but not hard enough to take me down. It must have been delivered by a defensive back. Whoever it was, I felt him slide down my legs. Before he could grab my ankles and trip me up, I tucked the pigskin into my belly and turned upfield. For the first time since I'd left the line of scrimmage, I could see farther than a few yards in front of me. I began running for my life.

Philly had been triple-teaming me, I realized. Groggins, the middle backer, and now the defensive back had all been assigned to prevent Ramsey from throwing to me. With the other Eagle defenders chasing Giant receivers all over the field, they weren't even aware that I'd caught the ball.

The end zone was forty yards away and only one Eagle stood in my way: Demetri Rivers. From the look of things, he was the only man with a chance of making the tackle. A smile came to my lips. Of all the Eagles I could've faced, Rivers was my first choice. Not because he was giving up forty pounds to me, but because I hated him. He was a cheap-shot artist, known around the league as "Dirty" Rivers. Like a hunter who gathers pelts for his wall, Rivers collected the cartilage and careers of opposing players. As a football player, he was average. But as a hitter, he was dangerous, especially after the whistle when you weren't looking.

Over the years, I'd absorbed a multitude of his blows, most of them aimed at my back, kidneys, knees, and lower spine. Never had he hit me head-on, and never had he struck the initial blow. He was a scavenger on the football food chain, joining feeding frenzies only after the prey had been disabled. His shots were usually the third or fourth delivered and were executed not with the intent to tackle, but solely to inflict as much damage as possible.

The sight of him standing there on the twenty-yard line made me drool. For the first time since I'd known him, the responsibility of making the tackle had fallen squarely on his shoulders. He couldn't jump on the pile this time. Instead, he would have to create it.

Like a shark smelling blood, I strained to get to him faster. He did nothing to hasten our collision, but simply stood there waiting for reinforcements. I hurried to get to him before any arrived. I could see his mind calculating our size difference: 210 pounds of still weight versus 250 pounds of rolling fury. Those figures couldn't have boosted his confidence.

We needed a touchdown to tie the game. I knew one little juke to Rivers in the open field would accomplish this. But I also knew the opportunity to run him over might never come again.

"Look at him!" a little voice in my head suddenly yelled into my ear. "Bury him! Make him hurt! Make him pay!"

The voice was persuasive. But I'd never needed much prompting to hit someone. Leaning forward, I pumped my legs faster and harder, my arms shooting back and forth like pistons. I felt I could punch them through steel, and indeed, I intended to punch them through Rivers. The football became a distraction, and in my rage I thought of dropping it. I didn't, though. I wanted to put Rivers out of the game, but I hadn't completely lost my mind.

As I came within range of my target, Rivers stood still. The whites of his eyes expanded like two carnations blooming in time-lapse photography. The moment of impact was upon us. I lowered my head, leaned forward, and abandoned all chance of advancing to the end zone. I was sacrificing a touchdown to satisfy my blood-lust. I would deal with our head coach's disapproval later. Besides, in his heart, Lou Gordon would understand. He'd drafted me because of my temperament. Eight years on the front line had only intensified it. I was going for the kill.

The last thing I saw as I braced for the hit was the sardonic grin of the dirtiest player in the league. At the last instant before contact, Rivers moved his body out of the line of my main thrust. He'd been baiting me all along the way a toreador does a bull. Using his head as a red cape, he ducked away at the last second and with his helmet went for his own kill shot, his intended target all along—my knee.

The two hit brutally hard. The foam rubber of my knee-pad did little to absorb the blow. It might as well have been made of tissue paper. I felt as if I'd run full speed into a knee-high fence. The impact was swift and intense. My leg cut out from under me, and my forward momentum turned into a nosedive. With no time to twist or turn or even extend an arm, my face mask drove straight into the turf, past the threadbare carpet of Veterans Stadium, and into the cement foundation on which it lay. My brain sloshed inside my skull like the yolk of an egg.

As I lay there, I was sure of only two things. One, I had come half a footstep away from blowing out my once-already-blown-out knee. And two, I had squandered the chance to score a touchdown that we desperately needed.

Watching the clouds float overhead, I smelled something vile beside me. Dirty Rivers was on his knees, holding his head in pain. I glowed with satisfaction until I realized his situation wasn't serious. A headache was a small price to pay for nearly ending my career. That I'd attempted to end his was inconsequential.

He looked back at me with disappointment in his eyes. "You're a lucky prick, Fucillo," he said. "But don't worry. I know which knee it is, and I'll get it before the day's over." There was malice in his voice and determination on his face.

My rage intensified. That little bastard. Hiding behind that helmet, cloaking his criminal behavior in the game of football. He disgusted me. The little voice in my head returned. "Rip his head off!" it whispered.

I struggled to my feet to go after him, but a referee came up behind me.

"Don't even think about it, number eighty-four! Give me the ball and get back to your huddle."

"So you heard what he said?" I asked.

"Give me the ball and get back to your huddle."

Rivers began laughing.

"C'mon, ref, that's bullshit. The guy's trying to take out my knee. Get him off the field."

"Just give me the ball and get back to your huddle."

"At least throw a flag."

"Ball, please."

"You worthless piece a'sh—"

"Watch it, Fucillo. The only one who'll be getting a flag is you. You ain't no choirboy yourself. So quit whining and just play the game."

The ref ripped the ball from my hands and ran to spot it at the nearest hash mark. I watched in disbelief and fury. As the referee, he's supposed to regulate on-field behavior, but instead does nothing but blows whistles and spots balls. What good was he? Why was he even out there?

"You're pathetic," I said to him. "If you're not gonna do anything about that dirtbag, then I'm gonna!"

He tapped the yellow flag in his back pocket with his fingers as a warning.

"You throw that flag and I'll kick your ass," I said.

I'm not sure if he heard me, but Rivers did.

"C'mon, Fucillo. You know you ain't gonna hit no ref. Now go to your huddle, boy, and get the play. My helmet's got an appointment with your knee."

I made a move for him. He was only ten yards away.

"Dominic!" Ramsey yelled at me, stopping me in midstride. "The play's over. Let it go and get in the huddle."

Oh, right, the game. I reeled in my anger for the moment and returned to the huddle. Ramsey called the next play.

"Two Flood F-Peel Eighty Max X-Post Z-In on one, on one!"

"Break!"

The only word I needed to know was *max,* which stood for "maximum pass protection." That meant I stayed on the line of scrimmage to block rather than run another pass route. Thank God. That last play took a lot out of me. I looked forward to the chance to catch my breath.

"Green eighty! Green eighty! Set, hut!"

Springing upright, I waited for Groggins to rush the passer, but he just stood there, waiting for me to run a pattern. It was a standoff. Neither one of us felt moved to improvise. We simply stared at each other and enjoyed the rest.

It was a nice moment until I saw Ramsey's pass fly into the hands of the Eagles' middle linebacker, who intercepted the ball in the flat. With no one in his path, he began running toward our goal line. Suddenly, my vacation was over.

As the fastest Giant among the pursuers, I had the only shot at making the tackle. I dodged two defensive linemen, then came up on a wall of linebackers escorting their buddy to the end zone. Wedging myself into the pack, I tried to make a grab at the man with the ball. I got a hand on him but Groggins rebuffed my effort. The middle linebacker raced unmolested down the sideline. It was all over but the end-zone dance. Meanwhile, Groggins wanted to disengage from me and go celebrate with his buddies. No way, I thought. I held him tight. The impending touchdown was going to bury us, and I'd be damned if the guy I'd been battling all day was going to dance on our grave.

We continued to run downfield, pushing, shoving, and grabbing each other's jerseys until I ran him out of bounds and body-slammed him to the turf. He hit the ground hard and I landed on top of him with an elbow to his neck for good measure. Instinct and experience told me he wasn't going to appreciate that. So I rolled onto my feet with raised fists and prepared for action. But Groggins got up and resumed his trip to the end zone without giving me a second thought.

There I was, ready for a fight with no one to hit, when suddenly a green flash of an opposing jersey traveling at high speed appeared out of the corner of my eye. It was heading right at me. Dirty Rivers. He may have been coming over to gloat or to taunt. He may have been trying to take another shot at my knee. His intentions mattered little at this point. I didn't hesitate. In an instant, my fists were cocked and loaded, and as soon as he got within range, I fired a solid right hand into the heart of his Adam's apple. He dropped like a rock, gagging. For a second, I wondered if I'd broken his windpipe. I didn't feel bad about it. I just wondered.

I didn't have much time to reflect, for as I stood over that choking asshole, a metallic *ping* against the side of my helmet distracted me from my thoughts. A bright yellow flag, tied at one end around a neat little ball of BBs, bounced off my head and sailed through the air on its way to the ground.

"Personal foul! Number eighty-four!" I heard someone scream.

I looked toward the voice. The same official who only a moment before had told me to "quit whining" was pointing his finger at me in condemnation. The nerve of that bastard! He knew what Rivers was all about. Couldn't he see I was defending myself? My rage overflowed. The Philadelphia crowd was going wild over the touchdown, which all but assured an Eagle victory. The noise was deafening. The ref was barely audible. Blood rushed to my head, the stands started to spin, Rivers's choking grew distant, and all I could see was the ref's finger wavering in slow motion, inches from my face, provoking me, as his deliberate and guttural voice mouthed the words again in an obvious gesture of overkill: "Perrrsonalll Foulll! Numberrr eightyyy-fourrr!"

What happened next wasn't my fault. I told the son of a bitch what I'd do if he threw that flag.

Two

Monday morning was dreary in the Meadowlands of New Jersey. The sky was overcast and gray. Thanksgiving had come and gone, and we were licking our wounds from yesterday's loss to the Philadelphia Eagles.

No one acknowledged my birthday as I entered the stadium to get my ankles taped for the day's workout. I didn't expect them to. No one even looked at me. Or maybe I never looked at them. We played football together. That was the extent of our relationship.

Half-awake zombies roamed through the myriad connecting rooms that our locker room comprised. There were a dozen sections in all, ranging in use from constant to none. In the circumference of the stadium, the succession of rooms ran the length of roughly a quarter of the oval, while maintaining a symmetrical width of no more than twenty yards. Day in and day out we worked, ate, and frequently slept in these subterranean catacombs dug from the reclaimed grounds of the surrounding swamplands. Every day the smell of ill health permeated the place. Perpetual moisture, coating anything and everything within its gray cinder-block walls, reminded us that only a few years earlier we would have been standing in the depths of mud and water.

Official team meetings would not start for another hour. Still, every player was present in one condition or another, taking care of assorted maladies. Standing in front of my locker, I pulled off my jeans and hung them on a hook. The gray shorts and T-shirt remaining on my body were standard locker-room attire. A fishnet bag hanging on the hook beneath my jeans contained another pair of clean shorts and another clean T-shirt. Those were my clothes for tonight. I hadn't done a load of laundry or bought a new pair of underwear in years.

As I looked around the room, I saw various large men in gray shorts like mine bump slothfully, in some cases drunkenly from the previous night's debauchery, into walls, stools, and each other as they made their way through the snakelike configuration of our workplace. It was no small feat to conquer sore muscles post-game-day. But when the guilt and shame of a defeat were added to the mix, our coordination looked downright pathetic. The low mood in the locker room matched perfectly our location in the bowels of the enormous arena where nothing ever dried out, not even the dirty carpets we slept on between meetings.

To me, however, this place was as cozy as home, and I, along with fifty-three of my teammates, would've chosen it any day of the week over a bright, clean office building. All of us had been playing football since we were kids. *Comfort* was not a word often used in our world. Such accommodations were commonplace to us. Of course, being young and stupid helped. Twenty-five was the average age of the team. We didn't know any better. A handful of guys had survived into their thirties. But they were an oddity—relics from a past generation. Today, I was joining them.

"Happy birthday, Dominic," I whispered to myself, invoking a habit I'd learned from my grandfather. The birthday boy should hear that phrase at least once, he'd told me, even if it has to come from his own lips. Today would be my first day of football as a thirty-year-old. I should have known hard times were coming.

Jimmy the trainer sprayed my ankles with an adhesive mist designed to help tape stick to skin. The spray was cold and trapped every piece of dust in the air onto the hairs of my lower calf as they floated by. My ankles crusted over with film. Jimmy placed two pieces of greased gauze on top of my foot and heel to prevent tape cuts and blisters. Before he could slap the first piece of tape around my ever-swollen ankles, however, the team physician, Dr. Bedrosian, motioned for me to see him in the examining room. The doctor's room was a door removed from the primary training room and was in reality no more than a utility closet that he'd commandeered some years ago. It was barely large enough to accommodate the medical table, flexible lamp, and knee-high stool he used for medical checkups. His requesting my presence was not unusual. It was routine to look over injured players every Monday morning after games. Although I hadn't sustained an injury in yesterday's game, last year's knee surgery required me to visit "the closet" every Monday morning as if I had.

The memory of that six-hour operation was still fresh in my mind. Thanks to my phobia of anesthetics, I'd been awake for every minute of it. It was my longest surgery yet, and my recovery was still ongoing. The operations on my shoulders, jaw, hands, and feet were minor in comparison. Those were two-hour walks in the park compared to this all-day sucker. The number of power tools used to slap my knee back together was extensive. Saws, drills, hammers, staple guns . . . the same type of tools my grandfather and I had fiddled with down in his basement when I was a boy. He'd been a barrelmaker's apprentice in Italy, but after arriving in America his carpentry skills were limited to fixing broken furniture for neighbors and friends in between his jobs as a factory worker. He'd taught me how to hammer and saw and drill, and as I watched Dr. Bedrosian during those six hours on the table, I realized he could have been fixing the leg of a chair or couch just as easily as my knee. The three two-inch screws remaining inside me, which showed up on every X-ray taken of my joint, were reminders that except for a diploma and a sterile room, my grandfather might have fixed me just as well as Dr. Bedrosian had.

The procedure appeared to have been a success, and although the pain never really subsided, I was able to return to the field of play. I was playing as well as ever, but my performances were coming at a greater expense. Every game hurt a little more than the last, and every week the recovery time took a little longer. Even the anti-inflammatories, which I was now dependent on, worked only sporadically. Their only consistent effect was the stomachache they produced whenever I took them. As the season progressed and I took more of them, the pain in my gut nearly matched the pain in my knee. Sometimes I'd have to choose my pain for the day, not having the strength to endure both. With my name permanently on a list of subhealthy players, checkups were regular, daily treatments were mandatory, and X-rays, bone scans, and MRIs were frequent. But all this was fine as long as I continued to play.

Dr. Bedrosian looked agitated when I squeezed into the examining room and hopped up on his table.

"Avascular necrosis," he stated firmly.

"Huh?"

"Avascular necrosis. It's a disruption of blood flow to your bones. As a result the bone dies, decays, and disintegrates, leaving nothing in its place but a big hole."

"Sounds gross. What about it?"

"You've developed it. In your lower femur."

"You're kidding, right?"

"I wish I were, Dominic."

Happy birthday, I whispered to myself again.

"Hold on, Doc. I just played a game yesterday. How bad can it be?"

"Very bad. In fact, it couldn't be much worse. You got a hole the size of a quarter in your knee. Look at this bone scan we took in July. See that black spot at the end of the lower femur?"

He held up an eight-by-ten X-ray in front of a neon-lit chalkboard hanging on the wall. The light illuminated the transparent piece of black plastic, and I could see the bone structure of my knee joint.

"Yeah, I see it," I said, pretending to know what he was talking about. Twenty other black spots looked exactly like the one he was pointing to.

"Well, *that* spot is nothing to be concerned about, and that's why nobody noticed it back in July. But take a look at this picture from September."

"Yup." Still no difference as far as I could tell.

"And now look here, at the bone scan we took last week. See how much it's expanded?"

This time, the black spot he pointed to did, in fact, stand out from the others. Enough so that even I noticed it. "Yeahhh . . ."

The black spot from July had grown from the size of a dot to the size of a quarter. As he said, it seemed to be turning the lower part of my thighbone into a dark hole. The sight disturbed me. Twenty-five cents never seemed like much before, but now it resembled a fortune; one that I was about to lose.

"What does this mean?" I asked, knowing I shouldn't. I didn't really want to know too much about it. My knee felt fine, that's all that mattered. Knowing *too much* about anything prevented me from employing my strongest ally: ignorance. Ignorance had allowed me to stay in the game when my injuries should, by all rights, have ended my career long ago. Ignorance kept me focused on my job. All I needed to know was the contents of my playbook. Tell me whom I had to block. Tell me which route to run. Everything else was a distraction.

"This means," he said, pointing to the X-ray, "that you have a hole in your knee. The knee is weight-bearing, and it's just a matter of time before it collapses. It could happen a month from now in the middle of a game, or it could happen tomorrow walking down the street."

"What then?"

"A knee replacement, of course," he said matter-of-factly.

Knee replacement? The last I heard, knee replacements were for eighty-year-old men. I was no genius, but even *I* knew you couldn't play football with a knee replacement, not even in the backyard with your kids.

"Wait a minute." I shook my head defiantly. "Are you telling me this is the end of the line?"

"Well, no, Dominic," he said at first. "But, yes . . . No, I mean . . ."

The look of horror on my face made Doc choose his words carefully. He wiped his beaded forehead with a monogrammed handkerchief and ran his slender fingers through his thick, black, curly hair. I liked Dr. Bedrosian. He was a good man. His real job was chief of surgery at York Orthopedic Hospital in Manhattan. His patients there were mostly weekend athletes and those of the elderly persuasion. Fixing their ailments was not as exciting as returning elite athletes to the field of play, but getting them back to work or back to the nursing home had made him a rich man. Compensation from the Giants, on the other hand, came mainly in the form of fringe benefits: access to the locker room, sideline passes to the games, inclusion on the road trips . . . As a rabid Giants fan, these were as important to him, if not more, than the business he garnered from the working world as a result of being the team's official surgeon.

"I'm not saying your career is over," he said finally. "Not yet anyway."

His resolve eased my panic.

"But," he continued, "this is a serious problem. Your career doesn't have to end today, but it will very soon. The only way to fix your knee other than a replacement is to have a bone graft."

"What's that?"

"A procedure where we take some bone from your hip and fill in the hole that's developed in your knee."

"Okay, let's do it," I said eagerly.

"It's not that simple. Once we do it, you're looking at over a year's rehab."

"So?"

"So, think about it, Dom. That means you'd miss the rest of this season as well as all of next year. I'm sure the club will pay you for the rest of this year. But next season calls for the biggest salary of your contract. I doubt they're going to pay you that kind of money to sit on your ass and ride an exercise bike."

I'd never thought about it that way. My contract was not guaranteed. No NFL contracts were.

"Besides," he said, "once we perform the surgery, I could never, in good conscience, give you medical clearance to play with a bone graft in your knee."

"But you said this wasn't the end for me."

"It doesn't have to be the end *just yet.* As long as you don't have the surgery, you can keep playing."

"You mean I can keep playing with my knee, shitty as it is. But as soon as you fix it, I'm finished?"

"Pretty much."

His logic was stupefying. "That makes no sense."

"I know it sounds strange. But this is a strange injury. The avascular necrosis means your career is over. The surgery date simply marks the day it officially ends. That's why I said you can keep playing until we fix it. As long as it doesn't collapse, you should be fine. Your knee's held up tremendously so far this season. Chances are good that it will continue to do so."

Sure, I thought, chances are always good when someone *else* takes them. I wondered if he'd be so enthusiastic if we were talking about his knee.

"Look," he said, his Giants fanaticism showing, "we're ten and two right now. We're going to take the division. We might even secure home-field advantage throughout the play-offs. With the way we've been playing, reaching the Super Bowl is practically assured! You're having an all-pro year, and if you made it this far, I'd say you'll probably make it the rest of the season. It's a risk, I know, but after what happened to Hanes, we need you now more than ever. Once you have the surgery, you're done. Why not finish out the year before calling it quits? It'd be one heck of a way to go out. Think about it: walking away with a Super Bowl ring!"

The Super Bowl ring sounded good. It was the *walking away* part that worried me.

"Of course," the doctor said, resuming his professional persona, "it's strictly up to you. I can't sway you one way or another. I've told you the facts. Now it's your decision. I'll abide by whatever you choose."

He folded his arms and raised his head toward the ceiling in an air of indifference. But I could see him straining to read my mind. If he could have read it, he would have seen a man in denial. This was just a bad dream, I thought. I must have dozed off on Jimmy's training table, and any minute I'd wake up to fully taped ankles. But the more I stared at my feet hoping to see some tape on them, the more I could see Dr. Bedrosian out of the corner of my eye, waiting for an answer.

I couldn't believe he was laying this much on me first thing in the morning. I was still blowing out the candles on my imaginary birthday cake, for crissakes. Did he really expect me to give him an answer that would so drastically affect my future with only a minute's time to think about it?

I balked at the audacity of the man and considered giving him no response at all, but I knew that wouldn't do. I had to say something. He wouldn't allow me to leave until I did. I delayed a moment and watched him sweat. It might've been my decision, but it was *his* ass on the line. Coach Lou made a habit of blaming the doc for injuries. If I opted to quit, Doc would have to break the news to the head man and face the abuse by himself. The last time he did that (when Ron Hanes broke his leg), Lou tipped over Doc's examination table and nearly tied the flexible lamp into a bow tie around his neck.

I waited another moment to think further, but really, I'd already made up my mind. X-rays or no X-rays, I'd just played yesterday. How bad could it be? I wasn't about to voluntarily end my own career. Besides, as much weight as Dr. Bedrosian's opinion carried, his word was far from final. Nobody's career ended, or began for that matter, unless the head coach, Lou Gordon, gave his blessing. Medical clearance was by no means objective. If Lou wanted to give me a chance to rehab from this impending surgery, he'd force Dr. Bedrosian to give me medical clearance if and when I recovered. Staying on Lou's good side was imperative. If I wimped out and elected for the surgery now, he'd cut me as soon as I got out of post-op. If I gutted it out the way Doc wanted me to, I'd better my chances, in Lou's eyes, of staying on the team. Doc was asking the question, but I knew it was Lou who was waiting for my response. So I gave Doc the answer he wanted to hear, and really, the only answer any of Coach Lou Gordon's players would have given.

"You're right, Doc. We are havin' a good year, and I don't want to bail on the team now. My knee feels pretty good, so let's just keep goin' and see what happens."

The doctor smiled and sighed with relief, if not for the sake of the team, then for the opening of the vise grip that had just released his balls. "I think you're doing the right thing, Dom. We have a great opportunity here. You wouldn't want to miss a chance at the Super Bowl, would you?"

"No, I sure wouldn't," I answered, although I figured he was speaking more for himself than for me.

"That's the spirit! Besides, a Super Bowl ring would make a nice wedding gift for that fiancée of yours . . . Emma, isn't it?"

"Yeah, Doc . . . Emma. Yeah, I'm sure she'd love something like that."

Emma was my girlfriend, not my fiancée. We'd been going out for a few years. She couldn't have cared less about a Super Bowl ring. Or football, for that matter. That's why I liked her. That, and her killer body of course.

"Emma, that's right," Doc said with an enlightened look on his face. "How's she doing by the way? I haven't seen her in a while."

"Oh, she's doing great," I lied. "She's been real busy with her law practice. Hasn't been able to make it to many games this year."

"Well, you're a lucky man . . . besides this current bad news, that is. She seems like a very nice lady, and a lawyer to boot. You two have a bright future ahead of you."

"Thanks, Doc. It should be a good one, for sure."

I hadn't seen Emma in months. We'd had a fight back in August and hadn't spoken since. She was still my girlfriend as far as I was concerned. We were just having communication problems, that's all. I was planning on fixing things when the time was right. Until then, I was ignoring her as though she were an injury. "Thanks for the reminder, Doc," I thought to myself. "You've been a wealth of information this morning."

"Again, I think you're making the right decision to keep playing," Doc said, picking up his next patient's chart. "There's a risk, no question, but I believe it's a risk worth taking."

He'd gotten what he wanted. Other players were waiting to see him. My time was up.

Practically shoving me out of his office, he closed the door behind me as if to say, "Nice doing business with you. All sales are final." With the cold metal of the door up against my hindquarters, I was back in the training room watching my teammates tend to their various afflictions. I was more than willing, I thought, to lay my body on the line yet again for these guys. But one of these days, my body was going to fail me, and I knew it. Strangely, however, their anticipated approval, if they had known what I'd just consented to, as well as the actual approval in the eyes of Dr. Bedrosian, seemed to make it all worthwhile. Clearly, it was the wrong decision to make regarding my health and well-being. But then my health, and well-being, rarely figured into any of my decisions when it came to football.

As I resumed my place on Jimmy's taping table, Ron Hanes, our injured quarterback, came hobbling into the room. Dark-haired, small-nosed, with a deep-chiseled jaw, he bore the scars from nearly two hundred NFL games and hundreds of quarterback sacks. One scar ran from his right nostril down to the crown of his top lip. The work of a blitzing linebacker, I'd heard him say. Hanes was tough, but he was still a quarterback. He wasn't ever going to put a hurting on anyone. And like most quarterbacks, his main concern was himself. That's why I didn't like him. For Hanes, his quarterback rating came first. Winning and losing came second.

"Hey, big'un. How's the wheel?" he said, lighting a cigarette and exhaling in my face.

"Not bad. How 'bout yours?"

"Leg's awright. It's the cast I can't stand. The itchin's drivin' me crazy, and it smells like a pile o' horseshit. My wife won't come near me, and the kids run away when they hear me clompin' into the house. It's been real peaceful, though, I'll tell you that much. Never had so much time to myself in my whole life. And when I wanna have a good time, I just grab a coat hanger, stick'er on down there, and scratch away. Man, it's better'an sex!"

He took another drag off his cigarette and chuckled. I eyed him suspiciously. His stopping to talk to me was out of character. We weren't friends, and now that he was out of the lineup, we weren't active teammates. When he was playing, my health mattered greatly to him. Having the best hands on the team, I was his favorite receiver. A throw to me was a near-guaranteed completion. Completions gave Ron a high quarterback rating. And a high quarterback rating spelled M-O-N-E-Y. Contracts, endorsements, appearances, and a future in the broadcast booth were riding on every one of his throws.

"Well, that's good," I said. "I thought you'd be goin' stir-crazy by now, not playing and all—"

Ron's eyes quickly darted up and made me stop in midsentence. To suggest, even innocently, that he was no longer a useful part of the team was an insult as grave as debasing his mother. I knew this of course, and my question was hardly innocent. But he was the franchise. As long as his throwing arm remained intact, he could break every bone in his body and still be all right. His place on the team was secure, and he knew it. But the mind plays funny tricks on an athlete when he's injured, especially when he sees someone else doing his job, and doing it as successfully as his replacement, Dan Ramsey, was. This had to be bothering him. But I was surprised at just how much.

"Hell no, big'un. I ain't goin' crazy," he said through a forced smile. "This is the most fun I've had in a long while. For the first time in ten years, I'm eatin' right and sleepin' through the night. When I wake up, my stomach's not all twisted in knots 'bout the game we just played or the one coming up. And best of all, I still get my paycheck every week."

Yeah, I know, I said to myself, I saw your new Mercedes in the parking lot.

"Last Sunday I filled a Gatorade bottle with bourbon and Coke," he continued, "and sat on the sidelines while you guys ran around like a bunch of chickens with your heads cut off. I never realized how stressed-out everyone gets about these goddamn games. When I'm playin', I'm so caught up in what I'm doin' that I never noticed it before. Maybe it's cuz I'm just as wired. But yesterday, I felt like the only sober guy at the party. And let me tell ya, I was *hammered* by the third quarter. Everyone assumed all these strange personalities. It was like an episode of *The Twilight Zone.* Look at James Moze, sitting in that whirlpool over there. He's practically comatose from wherever the hell he was slinking around last night. But during yesterday's game, flames were shootin' from his eyes. If he'd a had a knife, I swear he woulda been hacking people to pieces. He may be the best linebacker in the league, but from what I saw yesterday, he could just as easily be a mass murderer. Thank God I had that bottle to keep me company. It made the whole thing look kinda funny instead of scary. But it made me wonder . . ."

He paused.

"About what?" I asked.

" 'Bout what the hell some of you guys are gonna do when it's all over."

I stiffened. "Whatta ya mean *you* guys?"

I knew what he meant, though. Ron Hanes was a Giant and would always be a Giant. Hell, we had so many old quarterbacks from previous eras hanging around the front office doing public relations work, you'd think they'd never turned in their cleats but just had their lockers moved upstairs. Instead of shoulder pads and helmets, of course, they now had suits and ties hanging on their hooks. Hanes belonged to this elite club. There was always going to be a place for him in this organization. He may have been on injured reserve at the moment, but he'd be back in action as soon as the cast came off. That was a given that didn't apply to the rest of us. For lesser athletes, IR was the equivalent of death row. Even when players managed to successfully come back from IR, they were labeled *injury-prone.* Damaged goods. It was only a matter of time before more "durable" bodies were found to replace them. This discouraged players from reporting injuries and often hastened premature returns to the field of play. This, in turn, led to further complications of the original injury and possibly even newer, more serious ailments, which would before too long result in someone else sitting at your former teammate's locker.

Hurt players' comings and goings were a way of life in the league. Injuries, more than anything else, determined the length of NFL careers, the average one lasting barely three and a half years. That's why the acronym *NFL* was known in the locker room to stand for "not for long." The best advice pertaining to injuries in this injury-riddled sport was this: don't get them.

"Listen, Dom," Hanes said, continuing his line of reasoning. "There's only two places for personalities like I saw on Sunday. The football field . . . and prison. Unlike prison, there ain't no lifers in football, only short-timers. And that means every year there are hundreds of crazy *muthas* who get kicked out of the game and wander the streets. You can't act out in public like you do in here. Not without getting into some serious trouble. You guys have an outlet for your aggression now, but what about when it's over? Whatta you gonna do then?"

He looked at me with the air of a philosopher exposing a flaw in the system. Although he was expecting an answer, I just stared at him, wishing he'd go bug someone else. Goddamn injured guys. They had too much time on their hands.

"Gee, I don't know, Plato," I said disinterestedly. "I'll keep that in mind next time I'm shovin' some guy's face into the dirt, though."

"Don't be a wiseass with me, rookie!" Hanes shot back with a little aggression of his own.

Even though we'd been playing together for eight years, he was quick to remind me that he'd played without me for two years prior to that. When I arrived as a rookie, he was already an established star. As far as he was concerned, the situation hadn't changed.

"That attitude of yours is exactly what I'm talking about," he said. "'Shoving some guy's face into the dirt.' Listen to yourself. You sound like some high school punk who thinks the whole world revolves around his stupid games. You think you can do anything you want and get away with it because you play football? I got news for you. You were the most zoned-out player on the field yesterday. Forget about James Moze. *You're* the main guy I'm wondering about after football!"

My mood changed from lousy to worse at the mention of my behavior the day before. I hadn't forgotten about it. I was just ignoring it, the way I'd been ignoring Emma.

"I was into the game," I said, defending myself and wondering why people were reminding me today of things I was trying to forget.

"Hah!" He laughed. "You were *out* the game, you mean! What in the world possessed you to attack the referee, son? And I stress the word, *possessed.* Thank God you didn't kill him!"

My face turned red with shame. My behavior had been embarrassing, not to mention disturbing. That's why I was trying to forget it.

All twelve tables in the training room were now occupied, and everyone was busy getting taped over, iced down, heated up, or stretched out. The activity took place in the silence of a postgame defeat, and every word from Hanes's mouth ripped through the air like a clang from a bell. For entertainment, Hanes and I were as good as it got. Everyone waited for my response as if it were the next line in a soap opera. But I couldn't think of anything to say, so instead I shifted my frustration to the nearest subject who would take no offense.

"Owww! Jimmy, what the hell you doin'? You know I don't like my ankles taped that tight!" I barked.

"Just be glad you're getting your ankles taped at all," Jimmy said. "You and I both know you can't touch the referees. You crossed the line."

Jimmy had started taping my ankles as soon as he'd sensed I wanted nothing more to do with Hanes. Strips of tape flew off his roll over and around my bare foot in a blur. With a stick for a body and a big, round head, Jimmy was the furthest thing from an athlete you could imagine. He looked like a human lollipop. But next to Dr. Bedrosian, he was the man most responsible for keeping me on the field. If it weren't for him and his rehab program, I would never have made it back from last year's knee surgery.

"See!" Hanes shrieked triumphantly, pounding me with a good ol' boy slap on the back. "I told you, big'un! You were *out of control*! Even Jimmy admits it. I came over to calm you down, but your eyes were craaaazy and you kept screamin' at the ref, 'I'm gonna kill you! I'm gonna kill you! I'm gonna fuckin' kill you!' Then you started cryin', an' kickin', an' throwin' yer helmet like my four-year-old at the fair when I won't let 'im get cotton candy. Lou didn't know what to do. He looked around for someone to restrain you, but when he saw that no one was gonna go near you, he just turned around and put his headphones on and called the next play. Hell, you weren't even supposed to be out there. When you get ejected from a game, you gotta go straight to the *locker room*! It was a good half hour before the head referee had the balls to come over and tell you to screw."

"No way. I went to the locker room right after the play," I insisted.

"Hey, believe what you want," Jimmy chimed in. "When you get the letter from the commissioner, you'll see."

"What letter?" I asked.

"How long you been in the league, son?" Hanes resumed his paternal tone. "The commissioner of the NFL is deciding, as we speak, whether or not to suspend you. And *more importantly,* he's deciding how big your *fine's* gonna be. The fact that you refused to leave the field after you were ejected is gonna cost you *big-time.*"

Hanes's eyes lit up at the talk of a fine.

"Hey, Fucillo! I got some mail for you," a voice said from across the room, as if on cue.

I didn't have to look up, I knew the sound of Red's—the equipment manager's—voice. Everyone did. It sounded like a tuberculosis patient coughing up pieces of lung with every word. A relic of a man about sixty years of age, but who looked ninety, entered the training room, pushing a rolling hamper filled with jocks, socks, and a box of mail.

"It's from the commissioner," he managed to spit out.

He handed me a saliva-specked envelope and continued on his way, muttering, "Goddamn filthy animals."

I held the letter he'd handed me up to the light, searching for a postmark. There wasn't any. Someone from the commissioner's office on Park Avenue must have hand-delivered it to the locker room this morning. Its sudden appearance caught everyone's attention as though a sunbeam had burst into the room and dispelled the gloom of yesterday's loss. Everyone's mood rose substantially at the sight of a player in deeper shit than himself.

"Open it up!" someone yelled.

"Yeah, man, open it up!" I heard again, as one by one men on tables covered with electrical wires, submerged in ice baths, or plastered with tape grew impatient at my dalliance. I would rather have saved the letter for later when I had more privacy, but I feared a hostile intervention from the mob. So I opened it and began to read.

Mr. Fucillo,

First and foremost, let me state, for the record, that your behavior in yesterday's Giants-Eagles game, November 28th, was an embarrassment to all who are connected with the National Football League. Malicious contact with game officials has never been, nor will ever be, tolerated by the leaders of our great league. Such behavior demands substantial and swift disciplinary action. Nothing would please me more than to suspend you indefinitely without pay. The integrity of the game deserves nothing less. Unfortunately, the visual evidence available to me does not justify such punishment as nothing shows conclusively that it was you who knocked the referee to the ground. That being said, film footage, as well as broadcast tapes, clearly show you aggressively and violently grabbing *the referee's shirt. Film evidence also captures your irrational refusal to leave the field after being ejected from the game. The fact that you remained on the Giants' sideline long after being told to leave only adds to your incredible display of bad sportsmanship. Accordingly, I have determined that you should be assessed a fine of $50,000. Consider yourself fortunate. By copy of this letter, that amount will be deducted from your paycheck by the Giants' management, who will in turn forward it to this office.*

Sincerely,
Commissioner Arthur Brutole

My heart dropped like a rock into my stomach. Fifty thousand dollars? That was a big chunk of my salary!

Hanes, who had replaced his cigarette with a wad of chewing tobacco, grabbed the letter from my hand and began to read it aloud for the viewing audience. He talked like a sportscaster doing play-by-play and highlighted all the passages he thought most interesting.

"'An embarrassment to all who are connected with the National Football League'! . . . Suspension! . . . 'Disciplinary action'! . . . 'Bad sportsmanship'!"

And finally: "'*Fifty thousand dollars'!*"

I sat frozen on the taping table in disbelief, too shocked to stop him.

"Fifty grand!" Hanes repeated. "That must really hurt, tiger." Money always got his attention. "Hell, big'un. You might as well be playing the rest of the year for free! Hee, hee!"

My head was swimming. Within a matter of fifteen minutes, I'd been reminded of my estranged relationship with Emma, discovered there was a hole in my knee, learned my career might soon be over because of it, and realized the days of being paid to play football might already be behind me.

Hanes leaned on his crutches, waiting for me to say something. No wonder he was stalking me this morning. With all his friends in the front office, he must have known the letter was coming. I looked at him and saw the bulge in his lower lip where he'd packed an oversize wad of Skoal. An overwhelming urge to punch it down his throat came over me. But I managed to suppress it. I wanted to at least say something. Something hurtful. But nothing came to mind so I decided to just stare him down. Then I realized that if I looked at his shit-eating grin for too long, I'd clock him just the same, so I turned away and focused on Jimmy instead.

"Jimmy! Will you please watch what the hell you're doing! I already told you, the tape's too goddamn tight!"

Jimmy just kept taping, the way he always did, unfazed.

"You better watch that temper, Fucillo. Someday it's going to *cost you,*" Hanes cracked.

Laughter filled the room. My whole world was crumbling and my teammates thought it was just one big, funny joke.

Over in the corner Jeb Watkins, our kick-return specialist and team ladies' man, sat with two ice bags under his hamstrings. A third was nestled onto his groin. His hamstrings were sore from yesterday's game, his groin from last night. Leroy Wilkins, our noseguard, laughed into his cereal bowl, his back wired to an electric-stimulation machine. His muscles twitched rhythmically to the pulsating current. Every so often a power surge jolted him, sending milk splashing onto the floor. Next to him, Derek Jones held the morning paper before his face. A few minutes ago, he'd been chuckling at the funnies; now he laughed only at me. And Charles Rosen, our pass-rush expert, found Hanes so amusing he stopped scanning his fan mail for admiring letters. At his feet were discarded requests for autographs. Apparently, they hadn't been accompanied by the proper amount of adulation.

With the exception of James Moze, who was still comatose in the whirlpool, I was the only one in the room without a smile on my face. The big linebacker continued to soak in the tub, staring blankly at the cinder-block wall, fully submerged in his own thoughts. Great, I thought. My teammates consisted of laughing hyenas gnawing at my rotting carcass and one on-again, off-again drug addict jonesing for his morning line of coke.

These were the guys I risked injury for every day. Hell, these were the guys I'd already sacrificed parts of my body for, many times over. And what did I get in return for my efforts? How did they repay me? With ridicule and indifference, that's how. Worst of all, Hanes, who would never have to live through a day like this, laughed the loudest. A vision of him, ten years from now, still throwing touchdowns and making millions of dollars while I sold meat door-to-door wearing an old game jersey, flashed in my head.

He began to crutch away. The anger from yesterday's game returned. My temper was about to blow. Maybe Hanes was right. Maybe I did have an anger problem.

Ahhh. Screw him, I thought. What the hell did he know? I stuck my untaped foot out in front of me and caught his left crutch as he went by.

"Oh, jeez. Sorry!" I cried as genuinely as I could. Ron tumbled to the ground and rolled head over heels. "Are you all right?"

He hit the carpet hard but appeared to be okay. He didn't answer my question, however. Apparently, he'd swallowed his wad of tobacco and was too busy coughing it up to answer.

See, no anger problem, I thought. At least I wasn't the only one not smiling anymore. Besides James Moze, that is.

Three

Ignorance truly is bliss, I thought as I immersed my head under the hot water falling from a spigot in the shower room. Only a half dozen guys were in there with me lathering up and rinsing off, and the five showerheads on each of the three walls seemed like overkill. But Mondays were quieter than the rest of the week and so were the showers. The schedule for today was structured for only a couple of hours of light conditioning, light weight-lifting, and heavy doses of postgame ice and treatment. After these requirements were met, everyone was free to add on as he pleased—in the weight room, out on the field, in the film rooms, or on a trainer's table. Only a few of us overtimers remained. Apparently, none of us had anywhere to go. I knew I didn't. Late Monday afternoons were always a relaxing time and I tried to enjoy them.

Yet, this Monday had lost its luster. I couldn't believe all that had happened. A day ago, I was fine. Ignorant of my knee. Ignorant of my punishment by the league. Ignorant, yes, and fine. But after speaking with Dr. Bedrosian and reading the letter from the commissioner, I was no longer ignorant. I was now enlightened. Enlightened and miserable.

I had stayed in the showers for a long time, enjoying the warm water, and no one was left in the bathroom when I was done. Mine was the only face I saw in the wall-length mirror above the row of sinks as I toweled off. No one bumped and jostled me as I stood there. No one combed his hair over my shoulder. And no one reached into my sink from behind to rinse off his toothbrush. A late Monday afternoon had no sense of urgency or shortage of space. I could stand in place and look at myself as long as I wanted. Or until Red, the equipment manager, kicked me out for the night.

It wasn't out of admiration that I looked so long. Normally, I didn't give myself a second glance, other than to make sure nothing was hanging from my nose. But on this afternoon, I studied my face particularly hard because it seemed to belong to someone else.

After three-quarters of a season in a football helmet and countless hours in windowless and dimly lit film rooms, my skin had lost its olive complexion. I was paler than a sick albino. My bedroom eyes, as Emma liked to call them, were now hollow. And my proud Roman nose looked merely hooked and oversized. Even the scars on my chin and forehead, which Emma found endearing, were now exposed for what they truly were: defects. I looked old, tired, and worn.

After my talk with the doctor this morning, I realized I could see myself *too well.* My flaws had been revealed as plain as day, and my demise was now a foreseeable reality. Every step I took, I half-expected my knee to collapse.

I thought back to my first car. A beat-up, old Chevy Malibu that I'd driven in college before pulling up to Giants Stadium as a rookie. Even though the car was on its last legs, I continued to drive it well into my career. Sure it made mysterious noises and rattled at times, but if I ignored them long enough, they usually went away. Not until a mechanic revealed its condition to me did I begin to have a problem with the car. After going in for a routine oil change, he informed me that the rear axle was cracked, the carburetor was shot, and the tires were balding down to the steel belts. It was a safety hazard, he said, and refused to give it back to me. I didn't protest. I couldn't drive it once its problems had been exposed. Such knowledge made them impossible to ignore. As soon as the mechanic opened his mouth, the Malibu's career was over. But unlike that mechanic, Dr. Bedrosian was hell-bent on keeping my corroding chassis on the field. Somehow he thought I could keep rolling. Rolling long enough to finish the season. Maybe even long enough to get him a Super Bowl ring.

I thought of this analogy as I shaved my ugly face. I didn't mind Doc wanting me to take that chance with my knee. Hell, I would've begged him for the opportunity if he'd never offered. I guess it just bothered me somewhere deep inside that he and I both cared so little about me that he was actually giving me what I wanted and that I was jumping gratefully at the chance to accept it.

"Hey, Dom," a voice said, breaking my concentration.

Startled, I turned to see James Moze coming out of the sauna, a towel wrapped around his waist. The life had returned to his face since his morning soak in the whirlpool.

"Hey, Moze."

"How's your knee? Looked like you were hurtin' yesterday."

"It's all good, man," I said, having no desire to talk about my knee. "How's your head? You looked like shit this morning."

"Ho-ho. Dude, I don't even remember last night. Whatever happened, I hope I had fun cuz this morning I was in a world of hurt."

James Moze was as intense off the field as he was on it. The same dimensions as myself, he glistened with sweat, as last night's poisons poured out of his body and ran down his muscular frame.

He was as old as Ron Hanes; together, they were the elder statesmen on the team. Unlike Hanes, who ordered everyone about for his own gain, Moze demanded everyone's best efforts for victory. Wins and losses meant everything to him. And he meant everything to our defense.

"I don't know how you do it, Moze. Football's tough enough without beating yourself up off the field as well."

"Ain't no big thing, man. Just having some fun, s'all. Besides, I seen you nursing a hangover or two before."

"True." I laughed. "I'm not one to talk."

"Hey, you wanna go out tonight? Penrod's got a great night lined up."

"Thanks, but no. I'm having dinner in Connecticut."

Sammy Penrod was a main character on the periphery of the Giant world. He was always skulking around outside the locker room, hosting golf outings, charity dinners, tailgaters, and fundraisers. All noble functions, I'm sure. And James Moze attended every one of them as Sammy's personal friend. But I didn't trust the guy. He seemed like a sleazebag to me. When I arrived in town as a low-round draft pick, he had merely shot me a passing nod while latching onto the more promising rookie prospects. I wasn't worth his time back then. But as the years passed and I became a pivotal member of the team, his advances grew. Offers of dinners, nights on the town, blind dates, even steep discounts on jewelry, clothing, and cars, were constantly being thrown my way. As a rookie, I might have succumbed to his temptations, but as a veteran I'd grown wiser. Through the years, all I ever saw were guys doing favors for him, showing up at his charity events and postgame tailgaters, where he reveled in their company. I never saw him do anything for them, which led me to believe that whatever they were getting in return wasn't meant for the public eye. Besides, I saw how he treated "his guys." Like property. And I saw how they, in return, bowed to him. The sordidness of their relationships was apparent to me. But whatever my teammates were doing with him was their business. They were full of testosterone and cash. I realized they weren't Boy Scouts. But I wanted nothing to do with Sammy Penrod. I took care of myself and dealt with my own problems. I expected everyone else to do the same. I just knew Penrod had his claws into these guys in an unholy way, especially James Moze, and I made damn sure those claws never found their way into me.

"C'mon, Dom. Sammy's a lot of fun. He can open any door you want."

"You're James Moze, man. Can't you open your own doors?"

"Sure. But it's a lot easier with him. He's got all the connections and does all the legwork. I ain't got time for that shit. More time to party, bro. Plus, there are some things I can't, or shouldn't, be getting for myself, if you know what I mean."

James's reputation as a drug user was universal. He'd spent last off-season in rehab after one too many DUIs. Apparently, it had no lasting effect.

"I don't want to know about that shit, Moze."

"You don't have to, dude. You won't see anything you don't wanna. But come on out. Sammy likes you. He's been bugging me about hooking up with you for years. Give him a shot. We're hanging at The Club. A stable of models is supposedly waiting for us. Those chicks are for real, bro. No effort required."

"No thanks, man."

While I enjoyed a drink or two as much as the next guy, I preferred to partake in establishments where I was less likely to catch hepatitis.

"All right. But I know you ain't seen Emma for a long time. A night out might do you some good, relax you a bit. After your meltdown yesterday, I think you need some sort of release." He laughed.

My behavior yesterday was inconsequential to him. The defense was his only concern. He never crossed the line. Neither did I.

I smiled. "Seriously, I'm good. But thanks for the thought."

Moze was a piece of work. He was a great teammate. A total team player. On the field or in the locker room, there was none better. But outside the stadium, it was a different story. Because I didn't hang out with him, my only knowledge of his activities in the real world came from newspaper reports chronicling his fuck-ups. He was good for a couple of bar fights, breakups, and drunken episodes of public misconduct a season. Like my hollow knee, he was only a step away from imploding.

"Suit yourself, Dom. You're a good man. But ain't nothing wrong with having a little fun once in a while."

His lifestyle wasn't my idea of fun.

"I have fun my own way."

"Shit, man. You've been tearing up the league for the last eight years and I ain't never seen you out on a dance floor. You could have this town by the balls if you wanted. Instead, you're wasting the best years of your life eating dinner up in East Bumfuck, Connecticut." He shook his head disapprovingly. "But do what you gotta do. I'm going uptown to enjoy the fruits of my labor. Just don't bother me in the morning when I'm recovering in the whirlpool."

He laughed. I laughed, too. Maybe he had a point. I wasn't much fun. But to me, this job was too hard to act like a college frat boy. Talent came naturally to Moze. After the work I did to maintain my skills—workouts, training, conditioning, studying, surgeries, rehabs, and treatments—I didn't have energy to party.

"Look, Moze. Go tear up the town. Thanks for the invite, but I don't wanna go, especially not with Sammy Penrod. I don't like him."

"I don't blame you. It's probably best you don't come anyway. He's in a real shitty mood. That loss in Philly hit him harder than it did us." His eyes widened.

"Whatta ya mean?"

"Nothing, bro. Forget it. He's a big fan, that's all."

"Hey, knock yourself out," I said, rinsing the last remnants of shaving cream off my face.

"Oh, I will, my friend. You can count on that. And by the way," he said, assuming the moral high ground with a twinkle of irony in his eye, "I missed you at Mass yesterday."

"Shit, that's right."

Yesterday's Mass was another thing I'd been ignoring. Despite Moze's reputation for debauchery, he was a practicing Catholic, during the season at least. We were part of a handful of guys who attended the team Mass before games every Sunday. I'd been so caught up in preparing my knee to play the Eagles that I'd lost track of time. When I arrived for the service, it was over. It was the first time I'd ever missed a pregame service. My grandfather, if alive, would not have approved. He'd instilled in me the routine of going to church every week. Regular attendance, he'd said, warded off bad luck, like a superstition. I'd been living by those words for years. Unfortunately, there was nothing holy about my attendance. I believed in God, but what mattered to me was the physical act of putting my ass in the pew. That's what made the superstition work. Missing Mass yesterday added one more plate to the barbell of bad karma that was beginning to crush me. No wonder my life was falling apart so suddenly.

"You're a sinner," Moze teased. "Well, I'm off to spend my spiritual collateral on some fine young *thangs*." He threw his towel on the floor. "Maybe you should stay home after all and say some Hail Marys and Our Fathers."

Maybe you're right, I thought. My lungs tightened. Breathing came hard. Missing Mass was big. Ignoring it wouldn't help. I was going to have to make up for this breach of routine. Looking in the mirror, my face seemed even uglier now that it was clean-shaven.

Four

While the rest of the players returned to their homes in the New Jersey suburbs or ventured into Manhattan for some action, I jumped onto the New Jersey Turnpike and guided my Chevy Monte Carlo north toward southern Connecticut for my habitual dinner in Saugatuck at my buddy Salvi Rossini's restaurant.

Tonight, of all nights, I could especially benefit from some good food and friendly company. Halfway over the lower deck of the George Washington Bridge, however, I realized that I'd left my playbook in my locker. Such an act was punishable by a thousand-dollar fine. I'd no choice but to turn around. I couldn't afford another fine right now. Besides, I shouldn't have forgotten the book in the first place. I may not have always studied it, but Coach Lou's rule was to bring it home every night, no matter what. Despite my shortcomings as an employee, I followed Lou's dictates to the letter. Everyone who wanted to stay on his team did the same.

Lou was the only coach I'd ever served with such obedience. The man made me yearn for his approval, for his respect. I loved him like a benevolent commander. He'd taken a chance on me when no one else in the league would. An injury record the length of my arm, combined with a reputation for unruly discipline, had made me somewhat of a football leper in the annual spring draft. Only Lou, acting on the advice of one of his scouts that "this kid's not for everyone, but you'll love him, he's tough," had the courage to pick me in the face of prevailing wisdom. Aware of this from the beginning, I'd done everything in my power to validate his faith. For the last eight years, I'd hardly missed a day of work, had never been the cause of scandal or rebellion, and was as subservient to him as I'd been belligerent to my college coaches. There was nothing I wouldn't do for him, including running into brick walls, which, judging from my medical records, looked exactly like what I'd been doing since I'd arrived here. Although chances were good that he'd never know about my leaving the playbook, I would. And that's all that mattered. Salvi was just going to have to wait, and so was my growling stomach. It was a small price to pay for peace of mind.

I was only ten minutes away from the stadium when I made my discovery, but the U-turn and evening traffic delayed my return for an hour and a half.

The stadium lot was empty when I arrived. Everyone had left. It was depressing—I'd never been here this late on a gameless Monday night. The eerie stillness of the place raised doubts as to whether the locker room was still open. This was the one night of the week that Lou allowed his staff to go home before midnight. Despite his reputation as a workaholic, even Lou realized his coaches needed to have dinner with their families sometime. Assistant coaches weren't allowed to stay even if they wanted to. Still, I was confident that one person would be there.

Family obligations, such as weekly dinners, were never attributed to Red. I'd never stopped to think if he had a family, and apparently, neither had the front office. Just because Mondays were shorter and less intense than other workdays didn't mean we kept the locker room any cleaner or used any less laundry. Someone had to mop up after us. Guilt or shame did not arise at the thought. Neither did gratitude for his services. At the moment, I could only hope that we'd left such a mess that he'd still be cleaning up and would be able to open the door for me. That's about as much thought as I gave to Red. That and how much of a miserable prick he was.

We'd see Red only twice a day, once in the morning and once at night. In the morning he'd make his rounds, passing out the mail with the day's wash. At night, he'd retrace his steps, collecting the dirty laundry and trash that we'd left lying about. It only took one glance to realize he was perfectly suited for his job. At five feet two inches tall and a girth of equal distance, he possessed an uncanny leverage for scooping up debris from the floor. In eight years, I'd never seen him lose his balance, get light-headed, or complain of back problems. Although he spent most of his time in the laundry room, he reeked of body odor rather than detergent, and his clammy skin, an ashen gray, matched perfectly the color of the underwear he cleaned every day.

Red had a filial attachment to all team-issued fabrics, including jocks and socks, and was under the impression that every piece of equipment in the locker room belonged to him. He grew enraged if we mistreated them in any way, which in his eyes we did merely by wearing them. After reclaiming his loved ones and tucking them gently into his washing machines and dryers, he would soothe his wounded pride with swigs of whiskey from a jug he kept between his machines. The label on the bottle said WHISKEY, nothing else. He'd been drinking it for as long as he could remember, or I should say, for longer than he could remember.

Next to the bottle, rumor had it that he kept a loaded shotgun at the ready. Why he would do such a thing, I couldn't say. There had been no break-in attempts at the equipment room for as long as I'd been around, and last I heard, stained jocks held little value on the sports-memorabilia black market. No one knew why he kept it there and no one asked. He wasn't the kind of person you sat down with to discuss such matters.

Despite my disdain, I was anxious to see him. Knowing he might be down there on such a deserted night gave me comfort, for a foreboding had come over me as I stepped out of my Monte Carlo in the parking lot. It grew as I descended into the darkened tunnel beneath the stands.

To my surprise, there were no security guards. No stadium workers, either. The silence spooked me. Skulking along the oil-stained cement, I looked over my shoulder with every step. It didn't matter that I'd spent the majority of my last eight years walking this exact path. Tonight, the stadium seemed foreign and hostile. The equipment room, where I hoped Red would be, appeared to be my only sanctuary. In a near panic, I began running toward it.

Within seconds, I arrived, my heart racing and my lungs tight. I pounded on the steel-reinforced door like a madman. The stadium shook in reply. Hurry up, Red, I thought. No answer. I could hear his machines running. He was in there. I banged again, but with my foot. The stadium shook again. Still no Red. Four other doors opened into the locker room beside this one. I made my way toward one about thirty feet away. Just as I was about to bang on it, the door I'd just been at flew open and flooded the tunnel with light. A figure spilled out of the equipment room and shouted drunkenly into the night, "Who's out there?"

It was Red, and he was holding his shotgun.

"For crissakes, Red, don't shoot! It's me, Fucillo!" I cried, instinctively jumping behind one of the steel girders that supported the eighty thousand seats over our heads.

"Fucillo?" he slurred. "What the hell are you doin' here?"

"I-I need to get into the locker room. I forgot something!"

Red hesitated before speaking again. I believe he was considering whether to shoot me. After a few moments of nervous silence, he said, "Awright, c'mon in, but watch yourself. This thing's loaded."

There was disappointment in his voice. Apparently, he was not happy with his decision.

"I'd appreciate it if you'd put down the gun first!" I shouted from the safety of cover. "What are you doin' with it anyway? There's nothin' in that room but jocks and socks!"

"Screw you, Fucillo!" he shot back. "You're all the same, just filthy animals."

The tunnel was so quiet I could hear the strands of phlegm breaking and snapping in his lungs as he breathed. I could also hear the hurt and contempt in his voice.

"I'm sorry, Red. You just scared me, that's all."

"Well, you scared me, too! No one's come knockin' on this door, *at this hour,* in over thirty years."

Who would want to? I thought. We tried to avoid Red during daylight hours, never mind at night. This nocturnal encounter absolutely petrified me.

The only time we interacted with him was when an equipment malfunction forced us to. And even then he'd deny 90 percent of our requests. Everything you needed, he'd say, was given to you at the beginning of the year: one pair of gray shorts, one pair of socks, one gray T-shirt, one jock.

Once, I had gone to him for a new pair of socks after mine had become frayed. He disappeared behind his cage with the torn pieces of cotton and never returned. After waiting awhile, I was forced to go to meetings. When I came out a few hours later, I saw the socks on my locker stool, full of stitches. He actually sewed the damned things!

Getting anything new from him was impossible, unless of course you paid for it. Everything had its price. At times during games a player might come off the field with a broken shoelace. If he called for Red's help, Red would show up dangling a new one in front of his face, refusing to hand it over until the player promised to pay for it in cash after the game. And Red never had to worry about collecting. There was no way to beat him. He determined what shoes you wore, what kind of pads you got, the size of your pants and jersey, and what sort of helmet protected your head. On top of this, he was alone every night in the locker room with control over all your equipment. If you crossed him or reneged on a payment, even by accident, you could find yourself going into next week's game suited up in a pair of the kicker's shoulder pads, a suspension helmet (they stopped making them in the sixties), a jersey or pants or both that were either too loose or too tight, and a pair of Johnny Unitas, black, high-top specials.

"What the hell you doin' here so late?" Red growled, turning his back toward me and going back through the equipment-room door.

"I just need to get something outta my locker."

The door closed behind him. I pulled the handle and stepped into the equipment room. Red was working away as if nothing had happened. The shotgun remained in his hand, but he still managed to move piles of clothes effortlessly. The noise of the washing machines filled the air, a stark contrast to the stillness of the tunnel.

In one corner, just out of sight of the wire-meshed cage, a small desk sat with a three-legged stool in front of it. The word RED was painted on the seat. It must have been brushed on decades ago. The blue paint was faded and chipped. The top of his desk was cluttered with papers and tools. Wrenches, screwdrivers, hammers. There were a stapler, scissors, magnifying glass, transistor radio, pens, pencils, and one framed photograph of a plain brown brick building, three stories high, with what looked to be the spire of a church in the background.

Next to the desk was a cot with a worn pillow at its head. It was perfectly made. A blanket and a crisp white sheet were tucked neatly at the corners. Above the desk were a half dozen nameplates hanging on the wall alongside more tools. The nameplates were of the same type that hung over my locker. Some of the names were vaguely familiar, but not all.

"Don't worry about your playbook, if that's what you're here for," Red shouted over the whir of the washers and dryers.

His words startled me. I'd become entranced with his home.

"I hid it under your pads so's no one would see it. I know Lou's a stickler for that sort of thing, and after your letter this morning from the commish, I figured it'd be a bad time for you to lose another thousand bucks."

His thoughtfulness stunned me. "Why would you . . . I mean, how come . . . ," I tried to spit out, before just saying, "Thanks, Red."

"No problem," he said quietly.

"I still need my book, though. Can you open the cage door? I'll only be a minute."

"No can do. You know the rules. No one allowed in the locker room after hours."

"C'mon, Red. It'll only take two seconds. I won't be able to sleep tonight if I don't have my book."

"Nothin' doin'. That cage opens for no one. Besides, you don't need your book anymore. If you don't know your plays by now, it's time to retire."

You don't know how right you are, I thought.

"It's true. I don't need the book, but I'd like to take it home anyhow. I've never forgotten it in my entire career. Not once."

"Don't worry about it. Go to Salvi's and relax. No one will know you forgot your book. I'll make sure."

I couldn't tell if I was mad or grateful. "Awright," I said reluctantly. "I guess I won't worry about it. But wait a minute. How d'you know I was going to Connecticut tonight?"

"It's Monday, ain't it?"

"Yeah, but . . ."

"Yeah, but nothin'. I know a lot more than you think, Fucillo. We all have our habits. Some might say secrets. They're impossible to hide. All it takes is a good pair of eyes and keen set of ears to figure 'em out."

Secrets? "I'm not hiding anything. Going to Connecticut every Monday night is no secret. I just didn't think anyone knew about it, that's all."

He kept picking up armfuls of clothes and shoving them into the machines. I could see his smirk grow wider. My gratitude was waning fast.

"So how do you know?" I asked, eyeing him curiously.

He was feeling pretty happy with himself. He put the bottle of rotgut to his lips and took a long, slow pull as if it were an oxygen mask and he were underwater. A small trickle of the amber fluid ran from the corner of his mouth onto his gray shirt. He didn't notice.

"Eyes and ears, Fucillo. Eyes and ears," he said with a burp.

As though that solved everything, he returned to his work. I began to move out into the tunnel.

"Hey, Dom!"

"Yeah?"

"You can't play this game forever, ya know."

"I try not to think about *that,*" I said cockily, as though that day would never come.

"Well, that's the problem. You guys live in a fantasy world. One day this will all be gone and you'll be wondering where the hell it went. Don't think those jerks upstairs in the front office are gonna help you. As soon you're no use to them, they'll be through with you. Believe me. I've seen it. I've been here for thirty years and I'll be here long after you're gone." He paused. "I like you, Dominic. I like the way you play. But I think it's time you grew up."

He scooped up a pile of neatly folded shorts and walked through the wire-meshed door. The door clicked shut, and he disappeared into the main body of the locker room.

As I walked slowly back toward my car, foreboding mugged me again. Maybe it was the doctor's words from this morning, or Red's words just now, or maybe just the solitude of the tunnel. Nothing I could put my finger on, or name. I just felt weak. Weak and vulnerable. When I reached my car in the parking lot, I peeled out as fast as I could.

As I drove, my fears diminished with every growl of my stomach. The prospect of hot food and cold drinks calmed me. Soon, I was able to laugh at my cowardice and threw the memory of it out the window along with the toll money at the George Washington Bridge. By the time I'd crossed through the Bronx and approached Salvi's exit, all that remained in my consciousness were pangs of hunger and an overwhelming desire to slake my thirst.

Five

The Point Restaurant sat just off I-95 about thirty miles north of Manhattan at the junction of two heavily traveled neighborhood roads. The diagonal intersection formed a triangular island of land that stood isolated between the rivers of cars that whizzed by on either side. This island was the home of Salvatore Rossini's eatery.

Famous for miles around, the Point stood benevolently amid the rush of traffic like an inviting haven from the busy world. Neon lights from its sign beckoned weary travelers and encouraged them to quench their thirst and fill their bellies.

More than forty years old, it was as prestigious and permanent a landmark as the small municipality's town hall. In fact, according to local lore, the Point was the political nerve center of the community, the place where the town was really run.

The small village of Saugatuck had seen many changes over the years. Once a grimy mill town populated by Italian immigrants, Saugatuck's need for space, both residential and commercial, had transformed the town entirely. In the seventies and eighties, a building boom had hit the area with such force that the old generation of Saugatuck laborers had evolved into a new generation of skilled workers, builders, and entrepreneurs who took full advantage of the opportunities that had escaped their mothers and fathers. But the core of the town remained solid and intact, even as it was slowly surrounded by the upper-class homes that so many Saugatuck laborers had built for the overflow of executives from New York City.

Throughout the transition, and steadfastly at the heart of this transformed community, sat the Point restaurant, with its long, well-worn bar and its red-and-white-checkered tablecloths. The place had the atmosphere of a commune, and the building overflowed with friendship and familial love. Every time I walked in the door, it was like being smothered with hugs and kisses from my grandmother.

Salvatore lorded over the Point like a caesar at the Colosseum. With a simple flip of his thumb, a patron could be served a drink on the house or a beating in the parking lot. And like the caesars of old, Salvatore's moods followed no logical pattern; the guy he had thrown out the night before could be sitting with him the following day, chumming it up like old buddies. Sipping on a free drink, missing teeth and all.

Salvi had three sons, all of whom were bigger than me. Individually, they were intimidating. All three together, well, they were plain scary. When strangers stumbled into the place, they were always welcomed. The first drink was on the house, and all newcomers were made to feel at home. But four pairs of eyes watched their every move, waiting to pick them up off their barstool and throw them out into the parking lot at the first sign of disrespect (a spectacle I'd seen many times through the years). The oldest, meanest, toughest, and most discriminating pair of eyes belonged to Salvi himself.

He may have been a restaurateur for as long as I'd known him, but the scars on his face, the broken nose, and especially the missing leg all suggested that he'd been engaged in a different occupation in his younger days. I didn't have any concrete evidence to support my suspicion, but that he'd introduced himself to me on the sideline of my first pro game (hallowed ground onto which few civilians were allowed to tread) convinced me that he had connections more powerful than a spaghetti-joint owner ought to have. And when he extended his hand to me that day between plays and invited me to join him for dinner at his restaurant, the invitation carried with it the weight of an order rather than a request.

Regardless of any shady side, I still loved the man because I sensed he had a good heart. Whatever he may have been behind his restaurateur façade did not concern me. He was no different from a lot of the men I grew up with as a child. Especially my grandfather. I didn't ask him about his business, and I didn't ask Salvi. I didn't want to know.

The inviting aroma wafting out from the Point's kitchen exhaust hit me as soon as I got out of the Monte Carlo. It was a beautiful, crisp autumn night. The stars were clear and shone bright as candles. It was hard to believe the season was three-quarters over. The weather would soon turn. You could feel it.

Inside, I was greeted by the same guys at the bar and the same families at the dinner tables as the week before. It seemed they hadn't moved since the last time I was there.

"Hey, Dom, how you doin'?!"

"Great game yesterday!"

"Tough loss."

I sat down at the bar. Salvi's oldest son, Frank, served me up a VO manhattan, half and half, on the rocks.

"Great game, nice catches," Frank said. "But what the hell happened between you and that ref? What'd he do, insult your mother?"

Frank's brother Joey came around the corner as if on cue. "Naww, Frank, he's just friggin' *stunahhd.* Whatta ya expect from a *Gulah-braze*?"

I took a sip of that perfect manhattan and tried to push the episode out of my head. "I'm not Calabrese. I'm *Nah-blo-tahn,*" I said calmly, for the hundredth time.

"No way!" Joey said. "Neapolitan? Not with that hard head of yours. Look at it." He started knocking at my skull with his fist. "You could use it to break rocks!"

I took another sip before attempting to push his hand away. Joey, who weighed 280 pounds, had hands like an orangutan. Wherever he put them, they stayed, until *he* wanted to move them. I managed to free myself, but it was a struggle, and he knew it. He laughed.

"Screw you, Joey," I said, which only made him laugh louder. Not many people could say that to him and elicit such a response.

Joey's other brother, Danny, came out of the kitchen with a plate of fried calamari.

"Hey, Dom, how you doin'? Have some *calamahd,*" he said, placing the platter before me. "Nice game yesterday. You really kicked some ass out there. Next time try hittin' someone with pads on, though."

"Screw you, too," was all I could repeat. I finished my drink and dug into the calamari.

"Where's your dad?" I asked the brothers.

They looked at each other and laughed as though I'd just told the funniest joke in the world. Within seconds I was laughing, too, although I had no idea why. We giggled like kids for two or three minutes before Frank was able to compose himself.

"Well, last night Dad's in here in one of his moods . . . know what I mean? And in walks three strangers. So we tell 'em to siddown and we offer 'em a drink on the house. Everyone's happy, right? These guys seem really nice, they start buying drinks for the bar, everyone's getting along fine, when someone starts talking about the Giants game. Now we're gettin' into a whole *dissersection* of the game, ya know, when one of the strangers says, 'It's one thing to lose, but when you got *mama-lukes* like Fucillo on the field, it's just plain embarrassin'. He's a disgrace to the game. They should suspend him!'"

Frank barely got this out before the brothers burst into laughter again.

"What's so funny?" I said. "The guy sounds like a jerk to me."

"Oh, yeah?" Frank says. "That's just what Dad said before he grabbed all three of them. One minute they're laughing and talking like old *paisans.* The next, he's on top of 'em all, poundin' away. It was the mother of all mood swings. He was so mad. He didn't even bother to take 'em out to the parking lot. He just beat 'em right there on the spot. Look over there. Broke his cane in two."

"He beat all three of them?"

"Yep."

"Why didn't you help him?"

"Well, they weren't that big and besides"—they paused and exchanged mischievous glances—"we agreed with them!"

"Hey, Dominic!" someone yelled from the front door. I turned to see the focus of our conversation limping toward us using a broomstick for a cane and chomping on his trademark unlit cigar. Salvi was in his midsixties. Despite his missing leg, he still carried his weight around 230 pounds. His hair was a spiked crew cut, and his sharp nose, excited eyes, and pointed jaw gave him the appearance of a hawk. A restless hawk, in search of prey, with limitless energy, insatiable appetite, and passion for life.

"Great game yesterday. You really clocked that ref. Attaboy!"

It figured Salvi would be the only one to compliment me on hitting the referee. His sons told me how they grew up watching their father fight everyone and anyone that got in his way. They thought that was how the world was; that every dad took his kids to Atlantic City or to Vegas or to Yankee Stadium to watch a little sports, bet a little money, and get into fistfights.

"That ref must have been *baccalahd* to mess with you," Salvi said, sitting down at the bar. "But you showed him, boy . . . you showed him good!"

"Well, ya know, you're really not supposed to hit the referee. You can get into a lot of trouble for that," I said, trying to temper his enthusiasm for my blatantly illegal and offensive act of poor sportsmanship. "And I seriously doubt that he was drunk."

"Shut up, will ya! You're starting to sound like these twats over here." He pointed to his boys, who gave each other a look of exasperation and in unison said, "We love you, too, Dad."

The boys went back to their business. Salvi turned his attention toward me.

"So are you in trouble?" he asked.

"No, not too much, just a fine, that's all."

"Not too bad."

"Naww, it's only money, right?" I lifted a new manhattan to my lips.

"You ain't kiddin' there. I went to Atlantic City after having dinner with you in Philly Saturday night. I was up ten grand and walked away two g's in the hole. I had a helluva time, though. But whatta ya gonna do? It's only money. Fuhgedabowdit."

Salvi came to every game, home and away, and took me to dinner on the road after Saturday-night meetings. He always got me back for curfew with a full stomach and a wine-soaked head. There was nothing better for a good night's sleep. I knew his words had truth to them. It was only money. A semblance of relief came over me and eased for the moment the pain of the fine. Or was it the manhattans?

"Whatta ya wanna eat?" Salvi asked, situating himself at the bar.

"Nothin'. I'm not very hungry."

"Will you please shut up before I knock you stiff! You sound like a friggin' broad!"

This was Salvi's caring side. I knew he'd order for me anyway, so I always said, "I'm not hungry." The food was in front of me all the quicker.

Angel-hair, loaded with olives, shrimp, basil, and of course garlic and oil was served in minutes. Before I was halfway done with that, Joey brought out three filet mignons sautéed in olive oil, salt, and about twenty cloves of garlic. It was enough to keep any evil spirits, including undesirable personages, at a safe distance.

Every bite eased my pain from the day. Every sip reignited the future that Dr. Bedrosian had seemingly extinguished. This was exactly what I'd hoped my visit to Salvi's would accomplish.

Frank had brought out a nice Chianti for my meal, and as I emptied glass after glass, the day's events were shoved into the back of my mind. Soon I was relaxed and comfortable, eating and drinking with eyes closed, as if lost in a wonderful dream.

"Asshole!" Salvi shouted into my ear.

I opened my eyes to see him yelling at the television above the bar. The local sports was on, showing a replay of me stalking the sidelines after being ejected from yesterday's game. I looked like a wild animal. The sight was mortifying. Even more frightening was that I didn't remember that particular moment. Like a drunken episode, most of the incident had been blacked out. The announcer said a fine was too light a punishment for me, that a suspension was more fitting.

"Can you believe that asshole?" Salvi said again.

I kept eating, trying to ignore the set. "Don't worry about it," I said, trying to calm him down. "You're not supposed to hit the ref, plain and simple. I'm lucky I got away with just a fine."

Salvi bristled at my acquiescence. "You finished?"

"Yeah. It was great, thanks."

"Coffee or dessert?"

"No way, I'm stuffed."

He gave me a look of disgust and ordered a nearby waiter to deliver a couple of cannoli and a double espresso. Salvi was now sitting with me full-time; his patrons had departed for home on this late Monday night.

"How's your knee?" Salvi asked. "It looked like you were limping a little yesterday."

"Yeah, it's been hurtin' lately. In fact, the doctor told me this morning something's wrong with it. It's dyin' or something."

"Whatta ya mean, dyin'?" Salvi looked startled.

"I don't know; dyin', that's all. He called it some Latin name."

"Well, what's the deal? Is it gonna get better?"

"I don't know."

Salvi rubbed his face with his hands, acting as though it were his own knee. He stared at the floor in silence. I could see the wheels turning in his head. Finally, he snapped out of his contemplation. There was such intensity in his face, I thought he was going to grab me by the lapels.

"Jesus Christ, Dom, will you please call Johnny Marotta, you dumb ass!"

Salvi had been trying to get me to call his friend Johnny Marotta for the past couple of years. Johnny was in the pharmaceutical business. Because of my name, and fame, he believed that I could be an asset to his business. All I would have to do would be to accompany him on his rounds, sit down with different doctors, and shoot the breeze about football while he closed the sale. But I couldn't see myself doing that. Hell, I didn't like talking to Salvi about football, never mind a bunch of strangers. Besides, I was still playing. I was relatively young, and I was making good money. Why would I throw that away to be a traveling salesman?

"I told you I ain't doing that. I'm still playin'. I don't need a job."

"You've been playing for eight years. You've been to the hospital a dozen times for one surgery or another. And now the doctor says your knee is dying? You gotta start thinking about the future."

I didn't want to hear this. Not now. Salvi was ruining my beautiful night.

"Wake up," he continued. "It's got to end sometime. Let's face it, your best days on the field are behind you. You're one of the toughest pricks out there, head and shoulders above the crowd, but even the Giants are starting to think about the future without you."

Fine. Let them, I thought. Just because they were didn't mean I had to.

"You seen Emma around?" I tried to sound casual.

"Nope," he said bluntly, delighting in his inability to offer information to a hardheaded prick. "She hasn't been in here for months."

I turned to my refilled espresso. Where the hell has she been? I wondered. She couldn't have just disappeared off the face of the earth.

Emma was the only woman I'd ever gone out with more than twice. She was a beauty, blond hair, blue eyes, and I knew she was special right away. I knew because I was unable to finish the meal in front of me at the time, due to a sudden loss of appetite. That had never happened before. But she wasn't perfect. She had flaws. That's what I loved most about her. Her canine teeth were a little more pronounced than her others and would sometimes get caught on her lower lip when she closed her mouth. I called them her fangs and absolutely adored them. One eye was spectacularly blue, while the other was less brilliant and specked with flakes of green. The contrast made my head tilt when I looked at her, like a dog trying to understand something.

When I first met her at the Point, the maraschino stems from the manhattans had already created quite a pile when she walked up to speak with me.

"You know George Sakowski?" she had asked casually, taking a seat next to me at the bar.

I struggled for control of my vocal chords. "Huh?"

"George Sakowski? You know him or not?"

"Uhhh, yeah, I do. Do you?"

George and I had run together as teenagers. He was my partner in crime, so to speak. The girls we'd pursued "back in the day" were the smoking, swearing, heavy-metal type that suited our lifestyles then. In contrast, this woman at Salvi's was classy, well-spoken, and sharply dressed. She certainly wasn't the type that George would set his sights on.

"He used to go out with a friend of mine," she said.

That was a relief. It would have ruined my opinion of her if she had actually gone out with *him.* Still, I found it hard to believe that George had managed to make time with even one of her friends. I looked at her skeptically.

"Well, she wasn't really a *friend,*" she explained. "She was just a girl I waitressed with one summer in Newport."

"Oh." That made more sense. "But how did you know that George was a friend of *mine*?"

"He used to come into the restaurant. Sit at the bar for hours. Drink. Wait for Susie, my friend, to finish her shift. Sometimes, when things were slow, I'd wind up talking to him. Interesting guy, to say the least. Anyway, one night I found out we had something in common."

"Oh, yeah?" I said, not even trying to hide the puzzled look on my face. "And what was that?"

"You." She smiled slyly.

"Me? How do you figure that?"

"C'mon, Dominic, we did go to college together!" And that's when she hit me with the line that made me fall for her, though her beauty had already brought me to my knees.

"Of course, our paths didn't cross too often. I spent most of my time in the classroom. That's probably why you don't remember me."

"That's funny," I said, chuckling. And true, too. I didn't spend much time in the classroom, and I certainly didn't remember seeing her on campus.

She was something all right. Beautiful, smart, funny, *and* not in the least affected by my postcollegiate position of prominence, if you call being drunk at the bar of the Point a position of prominence. In fact, she was so unimpressed with my sports celebrity that she walked right out of our conversation.

"I just thought I'd tell you that," she said, and headed toward a group of girls at the other end of the bar.

"Wait a minute!" I said in near panic. "Where ya goin'?"

I reached out to grab her, but stopped short as soon as I saw her eyes shoot me a look saying, "Don't even think about it, mister!"

"Hold on," I said pathetically. "I-I don't even know your name."

"Emma."

"Well . . . You, ahhh . . . you wanna go out sometime . . . for a drink or something?"

"We're out now, aren't we?" She raised an eyebrow along with her glass.

"Yeah, of course. But I mean . . ."

"I know what you mean." She smiled. "Tonight I'm out with some friends. But maybe we'll run into one another again sometime."

"I come here every Monday night," I blurted out. "And sometimes more."

She laughed at my eagerness. "All right, Mr. Football Star. Maybe I'll see you around."

That's how it started. First we met every Monday night, then every Tuesday night, and for a while there I was coming to Salvi's almost every night of the week. We got along great. That opposites-attract stuff was true. She was Irish, I was Italian. She was an intellectual lawyer, I was a mindless jock. She was a feminist, and I believed that was fine, as long as dinner was ready when I came home from work. We became serious after a year, but when she confronted me with commitment, I hesitated, and she was gone. Her hot temper got the best of her, and I knew she was too proud to come back after that.

I should have reached out to her, but as the months passed and the season started, I had a life filled with worries. Her involvement only added more. I hadn't given up on her, but there were just too many distractions at the moment, too many things always popping up and preventing me from looking for her.

I assumed we'd run into each other sooner or later. She lived in the area. I figured it was inevitable that we'd meet at the Point and straighten things out. But the second half of the season was already here and she was still nowhere to be found. It was going to take more than a few months for me to forget about her. I hoped with all my might that she felt the same. I could use her help right now. I'm sure she'd have something better to say than "Call Johnny Marotta, you dumb ass!"

As much as I loved seeing Salvi, I always hoped Emma would be waiting for me at the Point. But it was beginning to look as if she never would again.

"She was always a pain in the ass," I said angrily.

Salvi scoffed. "She was the best thing that ever happened to you, you idiot. She was silver and gold."

"Yeah, I know. Where the hell has she been?"

Salvi looked nervously away, as if he wanted to tell me something but couldn't bear it.

"What?"

"Nothing," he said. "Hey, how's Moze doing?"

I was wondering when he'd get around to that subject. Every time we'd have dinner lately, he'd ask that question.

"He's doing okay." It was the only answer I ever gave. Moze showed up for work every day and he played well every Sunday. What more was there to know?

"He's healthy? No problems?"

"He's doing okay," I said again.

He was healthy as far as I knew. He had no football injuries, at least. If he was having other problems, I wouldn't know about them.

"Glad to hear it," Salvi said, as if he was keeping tabs on him.

There was concern in his voice. There always was. I thought it strange, but it wasn't my business so I thought no more of it. Moze was a fan favorite. A lot of people asked about him.

"That guy don't know when to quit though, I'll tell you that much," I said.

"Whatta ya mean?"

"Just that he was sitting in the whirlpool this morning looking like death warmed over from last night. But then just as we were leaving the locker room this afternoon, he was rarin' and ready to go, all set to do it all over again."

"I hear he's been hanging around with some bad people lately."

"Sammy Penrod?"

Salvi looked startled. "Why do you mention him?"

"Moze asked me this afternoon to go out with him and Sammy tonight."

"You didn't go, did you?"

"I'm sitting here, ain't I?"

"Yeah, right." Salvi laughed, realizing his mistake. "Just stay away from that guy. He's a piece of shit." Salvi looked at his watch as if he were late for an appointment. "It's past midnight, you better get going."

Salvi never hustled me out of the Point. But I wasn't offended. Rather, I was grateful for the heads-up.

"Wow, I didn't even notice the time. You're right, I'm outta here."

I was usually gone by eleven-thirty on a work night. I got up off my barstool and gave Salvi a hug and kiss good-bye.

"See you soon, Salvi."

He bristled. "Don't worry about me, you goddamn faggot. You better worry about finding a life outside of that goddamn locker room."

"I love ya," I teased, and ducked just in time to feel the breeze from his broomstick swoosh past my head.

Within a minute I was speeding up the on-ramp to I-95, hyped on caffeine. My mind kept pace with my car as we circled and both raced out of control. Blasting onto the main roadway, I could see the Point below me, the parking lot well-lit and sparse. A Jaguar had pulled in as I pulled out, and now I could see the occupants emerging from the vehicle. From such distance it was hard to be sure, but the two men walking into the Point looked an awful lot like Sammy Penrod and James Moze. I blinked hard to focus, but once I reopened my eyes, they were gone. It couldn't have been them, I reasoned. Moze said he and Sammy were partying with models in Manhattan. Why would they be walking into an empty barroom in East Bumfuck, Connecticut (as Moze had put it)? What did it matter anyway? I asked myself. Moze and Sammy were none of my business. I had my own problems at the moment.

Six

The thump of the morning paper against my motel-room door signaled the end of another restless night. There was a time when I groaned at such a wake-up call, but now even the slightest hint of day brought relief from the nocturnal wrestling matches with my torturous bed. The pile of padding and springs twisted my back into knots, and the thin, fraying sheets never failed to find my ever-present turf burns.

Turf burns were the mark of a player in this league. Anyone who stepped onto the field on Sundays had them. And no matter how well these wounds were covered with Band-Aids and gauze, the linens of my bed undressed them during the night to settle firmly upon my raw and exposed skin. By morning, the two would have melded into one, leaving me no choice but to rip fresh layers of newly formed sheet-skin off my body. The pain cleared my head faster than a cup of Frank's espresso, and the gobs of blood that followed were as interesting to peruse as the morning paper.

I couldn't remember the last time I'd woken up without this morning greeting. In the off-season, I figured. Back before I'd recommenced slipping and sliding on the artificial turf of the stadium.

I use the word *turf* loosely. What we played on was really little more than a green carpet laid over cement. To me that's not turf, that's a miniature-golf course. Sure, it was better than scraping your knees and elbows on the sidewalk, but not by much. That turf peeled away more layers of skin than I ever knew I had. And new skin was slow to grow back. What took a week to heal in the outside world took months in the NFL. Every day involved some type of trauma to your body. New injuries were ever-present, and the aggravation of old ones was a given. There wasn't any time to heal. Ripping scabs off my body every morning along with my sheets didn't help things either. But there wasn't much more I could do. Every day after practice I covered those burns like a field medic in the army, while every night those sheets latched onto my wounds like leeches.

The sun hadn't yet thought about showing its face when the paper hit the door. The hum of traffic buzzing into Manhattan told me the workday had begun. After ripping my sheets off in one quick motion and watching the blood flow for a minute or two, I quickly threw on some clothes and went into the bathroom to brush my teeth. I skipped the shower since I was only going to the locker room. Hygiene was reserved for the end of the day, not the beginning.

This place I called home had been my in-season address for the last eight years. A run-of-the-mill motel, the Regal Motor Court was situated among the warehouses and factories of the outlying meadowlands. Adorned with a crown and scepter and a royal robe, the neon sign out front proclaimed ROOMS FIT FOR A KING. While the rooms were adequate and the facilities relatively clean, I never saw it house anyone higher in status than a court jester or some wandering peasants. Certainly, it was not the destination point of royalty. In fact, I was the only one who ever stepped through his door with a tie on. And that was only on travel days before away games, as one of Lou's "on the road" rules.

But that was not a concern of mine. I didn't care who stayed at the motel or what clientele it catered to. The only reason I stayed there, besides the cheap rates, was its proximity to work. My commute took four minutes, sometimes five if I hit the one red light on the way.

From my second-story window, I had a nice view of my workplace. Local calls were free for monthly renters like me, although I knew of no one in the area whom I would like to have called. And fresh towels and a clean toilet greeted me every night when I came home.

The best thing about the place was that no one ever bothered me. Whether that was due to ignorance or indifference on the part of my fellow boarders, I wasn't sure. But that didn't matter. I lived there in relative anonymity, and to me that was priceless.

In less than five minutes, I was ready to start my day. A zip of my jeans and a quick slip into two untied and worn-out turf shoes and I was out the door.

Before letting it shut, I scanned the room. I always did, just to make sure I wasn't forgetting anything. Without my playbook in hand, I felt disjointed. Out of whack. Confused. The room seemed to feel the same way.

My bed looked like the scene of an animal sacrifice. Bloodstains splattered the sheets. Dirty clothes covered the floor. Two pots sat on a double-burner hot plate in the corner. One side boiled macaroni, the other heated the sauce to accompany it. The latter pot was half-full of old sauce. I'd lost track of when I used it last, but the green mold on top told me it was a while ago. I had tried to clean it the other day, but the leftover sauce clung to the sides of the pot like a batch of dried cement and refused to let go. Maybe someday it would mysteriously take care of itself. The key was to ignore it.

Used Band-Aids and gauze pads littered the room from my turf burns. Each was stained with varying shades of dried bodily fluids. The dresser was home to most of them, along with a multitude of pill bottles, all of which contained anti-inflammatories for my bumps and bruises. Indocin, Naprosyn, Toradol, Butazolodine, you name 'em, I took 'em. The pills were great for my joints, but they did little for my mind. Only Salvi and his wine could tend to that. Although, there was a time when that job belonged exclusively to Emma.

Emma. What a comfort she'd been to me in troubled times. Always there with a calm hand and a cool spirit. Nothing ever got to me when she was around. Not bad games. Not bad press. Not bad seasons. She had a way of deflecting negativity. Her presence brought peace to my world, her love brought fulfillment.

Those were happy times for me. As I looked back, even our last days together were good ones despite the turmoil that eventually led to our breakup. The flash point in that setting was the same as now. The future.

When are you going to get a *real* job? she started asking me out of the blue. Or find a *real* place to live or make a *real* commitment in life, like marriage? Up to that point everything had been fine. She was happy with my job. She was happy with the Regal. She even seemed happy with our relationship, even though we'd never really defined it.

And then literally overnight she turned on me like a strong safety grabbing my face mask from behind and practically ripping my head off. I didn't know where all this anxiety about the future, about us as a couple, had come from, but I wanted to find out. I wanted to make her happy. I liked her so much that I contemplated finding a real apartment for us to move into.

The job issue, on the other hand, was harder to address. I wasn't about to walk away from football. And the marriage thing . . . well, I don't know what that was. Once she got on that *tangent,* she went from being a source of comfort to one of anguish. What did marriage have to do with my needing to improve my bench press or lower my forty time? How was thinking about the future going to help me block defensive ends or catch the ball any better? Why was she so concerned about the future anyway? I'd ask her. Didn't she realize there would *be* no future if I couldn't focus on the present?

Her disappearance told me her answer was no. At the time, I viewed her leaving as a solution rather than a problem. The season was about to start and I couldn't spend time and energy on anything but the game. When she left, I was actually relieved. But, God, I missed her. I missed her all along, but I missed her now more than ever, especially since the future that had so preoccupied her had suddenly blindsided me. At times, I could be stubborn, but since yesterday, I realized her absence weighed heavier on my mind than any thought of settling down with her ever had. I was seeing now, in my desperation, how much I needed her for stability and direction in life. I cursed myself for letting her go so easily.

As I stood with one foot in my room and one foot on the outdoor walkway, an ill wind blew at my back. I realized that I was standing in the middle of a rare November snowstorm. The landscape was covered with the stuff. Odd, I thought. It never snowed this early in the season. And only last night I was enjoying a beautiful fall evening. Today's practice, with this snow and Sunday's loss, was going to be miserable. Just another thing to look forward to, I said to myself.

I let the door slam behind me. Normally, as a courtesy to my neighbors, I'd ease it shut this early in the morning. But they never showed me the same concern. So screw them.

A wave of frustration engulfed me. Looking up into the snow-filled sky, I asked aloud, "What the hell is going on? Why is this happening? What am I supposed to do?"

I stood for a moment, letting the snowflakes land on my face. Rivulets of cold water ran down my cheeks. Snowflakes continued to fall. But no answers fell with them.

Seven

The Meadowlands sits between the Hudson River and the suburbs of northern New Jersey, where, every day according to the dictates of the moon, it sucks in and spits out the excess waters of the North Atlantic. A vast expanse of tidal flats and marshes, it extends north and south the length of Manhattan Island.

Once undoubtedly a pristine work of nature, the meadows, like the rest of the immediate area, fell prey to progress and necessity. Busy roads with nameless bridges crisscrossed this sea of reeds, while commercial and industrial businesses sprang up around and within it.

The abundant waters in its possession had long ago presented too great a temptation to manufacturers in need of a toilet, and before long its ponds and marshes were as exploited and polluted as the rest of its industrialized surroundings.

Numerous cities and towns ringed this tidal basin, one being the small burg of East Rutherford. East Rutherford would be indistinguishable from other such burgs had not its property lines extended around the stadium and my motel. Your basic blue-collar town, it was home to single- and multifamily homes squeezed between multitudes of old factories. Like similar communities, it boasted a Catholic church that rose above the temples of capitalism and which stood in lasting memorial to the faith of its hard-working people.

St. Basil's-by-the-Sea was a block away from the diner where I stopped for coffee. I drove by it every day, yet had never stepped foot inside. Church, for me, took place at whatever hotel we were staying at before games. Visiting priests would facilitate our communion with God in a conference room amid stacked chairs, unsheathed projection screens, and speaker's podiums serving as altars. I hadn't been in a real church in eight years. But because I'd inexplicably missed Mass at the Cherry Hill Hilton this weekend, I decided to forgo breakfast and instead enter the magnificent structure in an attempt to make amends.

St. Basil's was enormous. Old, ornate, and beautiful. It reminded me of the church I'd attended as a child. Both were built of red brick that had grown black and grimy from pollution, and both gave the appearance of old-world cathedrals stuck in the wrong place amid workers' houses and depleted factories.

As I walked up the steps, my grandfather came to mind. He always did at times like these. Every Sunday growing up, the hard-bodied, tough, little immigrant dragged me to Mass whether I'd wanted to go or not. Our church was a block from his house, and along the way he'd ease my pain by tossing a football back and forth between us. He was a sports fanatic who loved any type of competition, especially any sport you could bet on. Horse racing, dog racing, and football were his favorites. His obsession with gambling, along with his failure to fully grasp the English language, kept him, as he put it, "forever behind the eight ball" in his new country (he was a regular at the corner pool hall, as well). It was a lament we heard every weekend at the dinner table, when his homemade wine flowed freely from the gallon jug parked safely on the floor by his feet. He'd been dead for years now, but I never went to Mass without thinking of him.

Only five other people were in St. Basil's this morning, and they all sat together in the front row; a bunch of old ladies, wearing kerchiefs on their heads. A calm came over me as I took a seat in the last row and breathed the sweet smoke of incense wafting down the aisle. The church was cold, but a comforting warmth surged through my body. I'd have liked to believe that the presence of God brought such repose, but I knew better. Ever since football became my livelihood, God had stopped being someone I worshipped and had instead become someone I needed to appease. I counted on Him for blessings and protection. Injuries, dropped balls, missed blocks, blown assignments, players more talented—any of these things, and more, could ruin my career. Perfect attendance at Mass was my way of insuring that the Big Guy was on my side and was working for me. Admittedly, my faith had devolved into a superstitious routine. And I was here to rectify a break in routine this past weekend. One missed pregame Mass in eight years had resulted in the loss of $50,000, the game, and my career, all in one shot. I needed to fix things quick. Leaning back in the pew, I could already feel the weight of the world beginning to lift off my shoulders.

Unfortunately, the weight didn't disappear so much as it shifted to my eyes. Skipping my morning coffee was having its effect. While I waited for the priest to appear, my mind grew foggy. Shaking my head and squeezing my eyelids didn't help. As the bell announced the beginning of Mass, I fell asleep.

With my inner eyes wide-open, I watched as I floated dreamily away from St. Basil's into the heavens above and drifted aimlessly among the clouds. My grandfather must've still been on my mind, because in no time I was dreaming of the last time I'd seen him alive. Standing by his side, I looked at him as he took his last breaths on earth. Pale, gaunt, tattoos shriveled beyond recognition, he'd been sent home from the cancer ward of the hospital to die in his bed. A crucifix hung on the wall. Rosary beads dangled from the headboard. And a prayer card for the souls in purgatory was held tightly in his hands. He was old-school when it came to religion. Purgatory was as real to him as his apartment. As a seventeen-year-old, I wasn't quite as convinced.

"Believe and live your faith," he'd said to me with labored breath. It was the last piece of advice he ever gave me. I remember thinking how odd those words sounded coming from his lips since he'd never lived by them himself. Unless the Bible defined "believing and living your faith" as spending your week's wages down at the track or with the corner bookie on some football game, I assumed he thought he was in trouble. And he certainly looked troubled as he uttered his last words on earth. Clutching the prayer card, he said, "Pray for me," before slipping quietly away.

The pleading look on his face was heart-wrenching. The desperation in his voice, pitiful. I lost my best friend that day, and my biggest fan. My playing in the NFL would've meant more to him than anyone else.

"Believe and live your faith" and "Pray for me" weren't phrases I'd taken to heart. I doubted I was living as I should, and I'd certainly never prayed for him as he'd requested. I was too busy praying for myself. Besides, he was dead. He didn't need my prayers anymore.

"Are you all right, my son?" I heard a voice say. A hand on my shoulder jostled me from my sleep. Looking up, I saw a priest standing over me, his face full of concern.

"Uhhh, yeah," I said, looking around a bit confused and rubbing the sleep from my eyes. Five old ladies walked down the aisle, staring at us over their shoulders. Each held rosary beads in her hands.

"Yeah, Father, I'm okay," I repeated, remembering where I was. "Did I interrupt the service?"

"Not at all. You slept through it from beginning to end." He smiled.

"Jeez, sorry, Father." Inside, I panicked. Suddenly, I realized I'd missed Mass. Again! My attempt at amends was ruined. Not only that, but I may have caused even more damage by disrespectfully sleeping through the service. I came here to win back God's favor. Instead, I think I just pissed Him off.

"That's perfectly fine, my son," the priest said, sitting down next to me, not noticing my inner turmoil. "We were just a little worried about you, that's all."

"We?"

"Yes, myself and the ladies. They come here every morning, rain or shine, to attend Mass and recite the rosary."

"I slept through the rosary, too?" He nodded. Man, I'd been *out.*

"My son, if there's anything you need to talk about, I'm here every morning."

"Thanks, Father, but I'm fine, really," I lied.

"All right, but just so you know, we prayed the rosary for you this morning in the hopes that you might find work." His voice was tender.

Find work? Did I look that bad?

He noticed my embarrassment. "There's nothing to be ashamed of, my son. It happens to everyone now and then. Perhaps if you showered and groomed yourself more carefully, it might help."

I barely contained my laughter. I wanted to tell him that I made more money than him and all the ladies' Social Security checks combined. But I had bigger things on my mind, so I just said, "Thanks for the advice, Father," and got up to leave. What a waste of time, I thought.

"You're welcome, my son, and God bless."

We said good-bye. He stretched his hand over my forehead

and mumbled a short blessing. I walked toward the door but stopped short, remembering my grandfather.

"Father," I asked, turning around, "is purgatory real?"

"Yes, my son. We should pray for the poor holy souls, always. Especially our departed loved ones. They're in a particularly frustrating state. They can't be who they were, as they're dead, and they can't be who they're going to be, as nothing unclean enters heaven. They're stuck between two worlds. They can't go back and they can't go forward. They can only wait, helpless. Only our prayers can alleviate their sufferings. Only our prayers can hasten their deliverance into paradise." He reached into his pocket and pulled something out. "Here you go, my son. Take this as a reminder of their plight. They will be eternally grateful."

As I walked out the massive front door, the cold New Jersey air hit me like an uppercut to the jaw. It was still pitch-black out, and snow the size of golf balls continued to fall. Driving out of the church parking lot, I was sure I hadn't helped my situation any. My only consolation was that it couldn't get much worse. Strange things, I thought, would have to occur for that to happen. But what the priest had pulled out of his pocket was a start in the right direction, for in my hand as I pulled onto the street was the same prayer card my grandfather had clung to in the dream I'd just had.

Eight

I grabbed a cup of joe from the diner down the street before immersing myself in the quiet back roads of the Meadowlands. The panic I'd felt at St. Basil's subsided with the first sip of coffee and eventually disappeared altogether, giving way to the guttural groans and chugs of my aging car. The noise from the Monte Carlo cut through the silence of this wilderness like a giant scythe making sweeping passes through the stalks of the tall marshland grass. I felt I'd been up for hours, but the absence of the sun reminded me just how early it was. My time at church had lasted only forty minutes, and even with my coffee run, it was still shy of six o'clock. I was fully awake, and wholly alone except for the massive silhouette of the stadium looming before me on the horizon.

The place always looked its largest this time of day. Sitting in the flat and desolate meadow, it was a towering monument to the sport of the gods, a cathedral in its own right, a temple of pain and pleasure, of joy and despair. A place where men, women, and children journeyed each week in pilgrimage to fulfill their innermost desires of conquest and victory; to pay homage to their team; and of course, to hate, despise, and curse the evil of the world manifested in the men wearing different-colored jerseys.

The winter storm continued to blow. The car drove light and soft over the snow-padded blacktop, and for an instant I felt as if I were back in my church dream, floating along toward the heavens above instead of the stadium below.

A lone car sat in the deserted parking lot. Judging from the layer of snow on its roof, it had been there for quite a while. I couldn't see the make or model, but its location told me that it could only be James Moze's. That was his spot and had been ever since I'd been coming here. Either he'd arrived before the snow covered the lined spaces of the lot, or his Mercedes had an automatic homing system that led him to the same space time and again regardless of climatic or chemical impairment.

James Moze wasn't just a star on the Giants, he was a star for the NFL. At six feet four inches tall, 250 pounds, and chiseled out of granite, he was considered by many to be one of the finest linebackers ever to play the position. Given the great athletes and warped personalities who'd preceded him, that was saying plenty. He played the game at one hundred miles an hour and rarely drove his Mercedes any slower. The ultimate competitor and consummate teammate, he'd transfer his energy at the end of the workday directly into his nightlife, where he'd become known as the ultimate partyer. With a firm jaw, high cheekbones, and fiery eyes, he radiated energy and oozed violence. Every physical feature of his was sharp. His chin, nose, ears, lips, even his shoulders and elbows and knees, appeared as though he were drawn by a sadistic cartoonist's pen. And like a cartoon character, every action was performed with superhuman strength and vitality, even sitting in a whirlpool in the training room. That's why I'd noticed him yesterday morning during my humiliation. I'd never seen him so preoccupied or less interested in his surroundings. Commanding the room was his specialty, being the center of attention a must. Even without drugs, he would have been hyperactive to the point of distraction. His personality was tailor-made for football. And that in turn made him a hero to a world that would otherwise have rejected him.

Apart from thinking I'd seen him last night walking into Salvi's, I wasn't sure where he went or what he did after work. I knew he didn't go anywhere or do anything beneficial to his game. Besides the cocaine and painkillers, we all knew he had an alcohol problem. In fact, booze-free flights were instituted on our team charters because of him. Lou didn't want him tempted by the sight of us swigging down a few cold ones. It was a nice gesture, I guess, but it only led to Moze's sneaking aboard a bottle of Old Grand-Dad while the rest of us were forced to choke down Gatorade and ginger ale.

Moze was a phenomenon. I don't know how he survived the New York party scene or where he got the strength to have a successful football career. He hardly ever slept, and the times he did were spent mostly in the front seat of his car.

He was never aware of it, but every morning I'd peel myself from the sheets of the Regal Motor Court and sit near him in the parking lot to await the opening of the locker room. *My* parking space, however, was on the fringe of the asphalt, almost hidden in the reeds, while his was the first slot of the front row.

After slithering around the Manhattan hot spots from dusk till dawn, he'd come barreling toward the stadium, going a hundred miles an hour through the empty concrete tollbooths guarding the parking lot. I cringed every time. With little room for error, I didn't know how he hadn't crashed into a booth yet. But then I didn't know how he did a lot of things. In fact, I didn't know that much about him at all. For example, I didn't know where he lived.

In the eight years I'd played with him, I'd never heard him once talk of a house or apartment that he called home. As far as I knew, his only home was the stadium, and his only bedroom was the parking lot.

After performing his daredevil stunt through the tollbooths, Moze would screech to a halt in his parking space and fall asleep in his bucket seat for an hour or two. Then the two of us would sit like orphans locked out of our foster home, waiting in the darkest and loneliest hours of the day for the equipment manager to come and open the door for us, Moze, with his booze-soaked head, the music from the clubs still pounding in his dreams, and me, sipping coffee and trying to attain the same level of numbness without the chemical infusion.

Pathetic, the both of us. Maybe we were just naïve and stupid. Naïve enough to think of this place as our home, and too stupid to realize that no matter how well we played or how many victories we piled up for the organization, they were never going to give us a key to the house.

Indirectly or not, I was a part of Moze's routine and he was part of mine. I felt connected to him because of it, a connection I felt toward no other teammate. But that's no surprise when you share a parking lot together.

I knew Moze's world, like mine, was turbulent. Being able to experience the quietest, most peaceful moments of our lives together was something I savored. Knowing someone else was out there whose life was as meaningless as mine without that damn stadium soothed me and made me feel that I wasn't such a fool for looking upon that arena as my home or upon the game as my reason for being.

On this morning, however, Moze's car failed to deliver the peace and comfort I'd come to expect and instead struck me with a sense of dread. He had beaten me to the stadium. That had never happened before. It was always me who watched *him* show up. But even with my side trip to St. Basil's, the amount of snow covering his car told me he'd been there for hours. That would have meant he left the clubs long before last call. And that was way out of the ordinary. Suddenly, I wondered again about seeing Moze and Sammy Penrod walking into the Point last night as I was leaving. They'd emerged from a Jaguar, Sammy's car. That was even more strange. It was hard to imagine Moze relegating himself to the passenger seat.

Within an hour, the snow had ceased and my coffee was cold. The first ray of sun peeked over the horizon, and Red's beat-up Ford soon followed it into the parking lot. As the aging Grand Marquis slid in the snow, I could hear Red cursing Mother Nature for making this morning's bagel run more miserable than usual. Besides cleaning up our mess, he had to provide a daily supply of fresh bagels and doughnuts for our grazing pleasure. As far as I knew, this duty was the only reason he owned a car.

I watched as he stopped at the twelve-foot-high fence that separated the stadium from the rest of the parking lot and unlocked the giant gate that led into the tunnel below the stands. From there he would drive down the ramp to his parking space just outside the locker-room door, but not before performing *his* morning ritual first.

Red was Moze's alarm clock. Every morning, after unlocking the gate, Red would walk over to Moze's Mercedes and wake him up from his night's slumber by pounding furiously on the driver's-side window. Sometime he'd have to pound for a few minutes, sometimes it would only take a tap, but Red would never leave until Moze was out the door. The sight of these two completely different men greeting the day together always amused me, Moze towering over the diminutive crab-meister, and matching three of Red's choppy steps with every flawless stride of his own. The two never spoke, but walked almost hand in hand toward Red's idling car.

I watched Red trudge through the snow toward Moze's car this morning. The car seemed quieter than usual and Red's fist seemed harder. I got the impression that today might be the day that the window would actually succumb to his wrath. Red must have relished this aspect of his job. Hitting Moze's Mercedes was the only time he was able to abuse and disrespect the player's "stuff" the way he saw us abuse and disrespect his self-supposed own belongings.

Red raised his fist like Moses about to throw down the Ten Commandments, but then stopped and uncharacteristically peered into the Mercedes's window. Instantly, he ran away from the car in a panic, jumped into his still-running Grand Marquis, and sped into the tunnel, plowing a path through the snow along the way. Strange.

Normally, I'd wait until Red and Moze had been in the locker room for a few minutes before showing my face. I didn't want them to think that I was hanging around waiting for them to open the door like some homeless voyeur. But this morning was different. Immediately, I barreled down from my stealth observation post to see what was going on.

I approached the Mercedes apprehensively. The glass that Red had cleared in the window was already frosted over, so I had to clear it again. I could have just opened the door, but something told me not to. In seconds, I pressed my face up against the window to look in. My reaction was identical to Red's.

"Call an ambulance!" I shouted, bursting through the equipment-room door. Red appeared stunned. I must have scared him. He was already on the phone and I heard him say, "Yes, that's right, the stadium. In the parking lot, by the players' entrance. . . . Yes, James Moze. . . . Yes, and hurry!"

He slammed down the phone. "Did you see him?"

"Yeah. What the hell happened?" I said.

"I don't know."

Red brushed past me and ran back up the ramp to the parking lot. I'd never seen him run before. It was all I could do to catch up to him. We arrived at the Mercedes together and looked at each other for a split second before opening the door.

"Be careful!" I said. He opened the door.

Moze's bloody head slumped toward the fresh air. If Red hadn't caught him, he would have fallen into the snow. The sight froze me in place.

"Don't just stand there, give me a hand!" Red yelled.

We gently placed Moze's body back into an upright sitting position. The Mercedes's beige leather interior looked as if someone had sprayed it with blood from a hose. My hands were covered with it. Moze was foaming at the mouth like a rabid dog. A bloody tooth was in the passenger seat. In the back, white clumps of powder sat irregularly in pools of fluid from an opened whiskey bottle on the floor.

"Look at his face!" Red said.

Moze's eyes were swollen shut and his chin had been split open. He looked as if he'd just fought twelve rounds with his hands tied behind his back. Bruises were everywhere. His sharp features were gone. His face no longer had any angles. His head was as round as a swollen balloon. We handled him as gently as we could for fear that pieces of him might fall off.

Looking quizzically at each other, we tried to make sense of the scene before us. What the hell happened? we said with our eyes.

As my shock subsided and I stared at Moze's face, an unexpected emotion crept in. I was *angry*. Although Moze wasn't exactly a friend of mine, he was my teammate. A teammate to whom, as I said, I felt a connection. That was enough for me to believe that this assault, heaped upon him, was somehow directed at me as well. I could tell Red felt the same way. His face was flushed, and his concern had turned to rage.

"Red—" I began, but was cut off abruptly by the wail of the ambulance's siren. Paramedics loaded with equipment rushed out of the truck and inundated the scene, reducing Red and me to spectators. We watched as they assessed the damage, put Moze on a stretcher, and secured him in the ambulance. When they were done, the doors closed, the siren resumed, and the truck sped toward the exit. In less than twenty minutes, the lot was as quiet and as calm as it had been earlier. We stood there, astounded at what we'd just seen. I looked at Red. He had nothing to say. So I spoke up.

"What should we do now, Red?"

"We?" he said, raising an eyebrow. "*We're* not gonna do anything. *You* go and do what you do every morning, and *I'll* call upstairs and let 'em know what happened."

"That's it?" I asked, as we made our way toward the locker room.

"Yeah, unless you wanna call the press," he said sarcastically.

"Well, no. I just thought—"

"Don't think. You do your job and I'll do mine. That's the best advice I can give ya. I gotta go make sure Ward's game jersey is clean for the weekend." He disappeared through the equipment-room door. Bobby Ward was James Moze's replacement.

Nine

Once the ambulance departed, the day shaped up like any other. Routine was the way of the world at the bottom of the stadium, and my teammates would soon begin theirs. Within the hour, they'd swarm the locker room, using ice packs, whirlpools, toilets, trainers, and anything else not nailed down. Images of my going through the day half-taped, half-iced, and half-relieved pushed Moze's plight aside for the moment. There was nothing I could do for him. He was in the hands of professionals. So with no remorse or second thought, I went to my locker, where I kicked off my shoes, unbuckled my jeans, and started my day.

Fallen comrades were common in football. Over the years, dozens of teammates had disappeared (with playbooks in hand) into Lou's office, never to be seen again. Injuries eliminated even more. Parents or wives might be shocked or sympathetic about a player's misfortunes, but his teammates never were. A simple, disinterested "Tough break" was the likely response to a fallen comrade. But that was extremely charitable compared to Lou Gordon's attitude.

If someone went down on the practice field, Coach Lou would blow his whistle and shout, "Riverside!"—signaling the rest of us to turn around and ignore the poor bastard moaning in the dirt. Practice would then resume in the opposite direction, with our backs to the injured party. Once Lou turned his back on you, he'd better not see you again until the end of the day, meaning, you'd better really be hurt and not be taking up his practice time unnecessarily. The same was true during a game. If you couldn't make it off the field under your own power, there had better be medical evidence to justify the use of the injury cart or your teammate's shoulders, or it might be the last time you exited a field with Lou Gordon as your coach.

Injuries were of concern only to the injured. The healthy were preoccupied with the job at hand. Worrying about other people's problems only led to more of your own. So when we looked around the huddle and saw a new face, it was of no concern to us as long as the new face did his job and didn't hinder us from doing ours.

At the moment, I certainly had enough of my own problems without wasting energy figuring out what had happened to James Moze. The guy may have been a phenomenal football player, but he was questionable as a human being. Whatever happened to him was no doubt of his own doing and something he probably deserved. Why should I care? I rationalized. The hustle and bustle of my teammates as they spilled into the locker room reminded me that my own interests would be best served if I went ahead and forgot about the big linebacker.

So far, I had heated up, iced down, ingested a handful of Indocin, and was about to hop onto Jimmy's taping table to be wrapped up nice and tight when Lou Gordon stuck his head into the room and pointed his Coach of the Year finger at me like a loaded revolver. I knew what this gesture meant. Jimmy did, too. He gave a mock look of doom as I did a quick about-face. Obediently, I followed Lou out of the room.

I had a good idea what this was about. I figured Lou was about to officially reprimand me for my ejection from the game on Sunday. It was his obligation to do so. He was my boss after all. I'd take whatever he had to dish out, especially since any reprimand would merely be window dressing. Coldcocking him or anyone else who gave me a hard time was always a possibility for me, and he knew it. So to avoid any incidents, Lou never yelled at me. I did my job and he left me alone. That was our relationship.

I'd only taken this walk once before in my career, back when I was a rookie. I'd dropped three passes in one game and had been summoned by Lou afterward and told to shape up or ship out. I took his advice to heart that day and never gave him reason to point that finger at me again. But Sunday's outburst was reason enough. The same feeling ran through my body now as it did then: I'd let him down, I'd disappointed him.

"Siddown, Dom," he said as soon as we entered his "field" office. (His real office was upstairs somewhere with the rest of management.) Nothing was in this small room but a table, three chairs, and a locker and shower for one. It was as Spartan as Dr. Bedrosian's examining closet. The gray cinder-block walls were unpainted, and I almost didn't notice Red leaning up against one of them because of it. As soon as I saw the decrepit old man, flashes of James Moze's bloody face resurfaced in my mind and replaced any thoughts of punishment Lou might have for me. Immediately, I understood that this meeting was about Moze.

Lou made his way to the other side of the folding table and sat down without waiting for us. In this world of giants that he ruled, he was an unremarkable specimen. Medium height, medium weight, neutral, dull-colored hair, neither blond nor brown, thinning a little on top; he looked like an everyman. I'd seen guys like Lou sitting in

CEO chairs at the world's largest corporations, or behind lunch counters slicing prosciutto for my afternoon grinder. He was void of an accent, or any distinct physical characteristics, and you'd never have known he'd grown up surfing the waves of the Southern California coastline before attending the most prestigious prep schools in New England. He could've slipped into any occupation or settled into any region of the country and never have looked out of place.

Looks, however, were deceiving. Despite his bland appearance, Lou was a remarkable man. What made him so were his words. Lou's strength was his oratory; his weapon of rule, his wit. All it took was one sentence, his eyes cutting and slashing whatever they looked at, and his nostrils steaming like those of a bull seeing red, for anyone to realize that he was born to coach and would neither have thrived nor survived in any other employment.

Lou's criticisms were debilitating. His praise, transcendent. He could get more out of a player with a quip than any other coach I'd ever known. Every word was measured and weighed. And we hung on every single utterance. His phraseology and tone changed from individual to individual. No one was treated the same. No two players were addressed alike.

He once dubbed one of our linemen Dumpling because the player was one dumpling away from exceeding his weight limit. All day long the guy was called and responded to the name. It was done in good humor. No offense was taken. But Lou got his point across without calling the guy a fat slob and breaking his spirit. The name was taken as a term of endearment. It inspired loyalty and obedience, and as a result Dumpling played his ass off for Lou, all the while knowing that one too many dietary indiscretions and Lou would cut that same ass right off the team. No hesitation, no remorse.

I was not immune to Lou's manipulations, although I understood what he was doing. My way of pleasing him was to never arouse his attention. Never require his therapy. After that ultimatum my rookie year, he had hardly addressed me at all. Occasionally to correct or to teach, but *never* away from the field. Not once the pads were off. I liked to fly under the radar screen. That was my personality. Lou knew that. He manipulated me by not manipulating me.

"I guess you know why I called you in," Lou said.

We nodded our understanding and waited. I was expecting he'd want an explanation of what I'd seen this morning, along with the names of the guilty party responsible for Moze's condition. But there was nothing to tell. I thought about mentioning that I thought I'd seen Moze and Sammy Penrod enter the Point together late last night. But I couldn't figure the relevance to Moze's condition this morning. So I kept quiet.

"Did either of you mention this to anyone?"

Red and I shook our heads.

"Good. The media haven't been notified yet, and I'd like to get the story straight before we issue our official statement. James was in a car accident this morning," Lou said assuredly. "He's lucky to be alive. The police say he hit one of the empty tollbooths coming into work this morning. Evidently, the snow was responsible. I heard you were with him right after it happened and that you called for the ambulance. You probably saved his life."

Lou looked only at me. Red seemed invisible to him.

"I just wanted you to be the first to know that he's gonna be all right. And I want to make sure that we're all on the same page. You got any questions?"

I looked over at Red to see his reaction. The thought of Lou calling what I'd seen this morning a car accident didn't sit well with me. For one thing, there had been no damage to the Mercedes.

Surely, Red felt the same. But he stared blankly at the floor and shook his head from side to side like a brainwashed dummy. I, on the other hand, couldn't believe Lou was feeding me this line of bullshit with a straight face. I was expecting answers, not more questions.

"What about all the stuff in the car?" I asked reflexively.

"What stuff, Dom? I just finished reading the police report and there was nothing about any *stuff* in the car."

I said nothing.

"Listen, you know what kind of crazy driver Moze is," Lou said. "Hell, we all know. It's amazing this hasn't happened sooner. The main thing is that he's gonna be all right. He'll be back on the field in a few weeks. Let's just be glad it wasn't more serious. What I need from you is to stick to the facts. You were an eyewitness at the scene. If the media finds out, they might ask you questions. The worst thing you can do is give them ammunition to use against us." Lou emphasized the word *us.* "They've been on Moze's back hard enough this season as it is. He doesn't need anymore setbacks."

What do you expect when you have a checkered past like Moze's? I wanted to say, but didn't. Since day one, I'd heard rumors of Lou covering up for Moze's indiscretions, and I realized that this was shaping up as more of the same.

Lou loved Moze. Prior to drafting him, Lou and the Giants had struggled. They'd been so bad during his first two years at the helm that Lou nearly lost his job. But then Moze came along and changed things. Because he'd discovered Moze on some obscure Midwestern college team when no one else had, and because Moze lit the NFL on fire his rookie year, Lou earned the reputation as a football genius. The Giants became a respectable team after that and Lou became a respected coach. Although he'd always been a good coach overall and had since drafted a team to complement Moze, Moze had legitimized Lou and Lou never forgot that. Neither did Moze forget the man who'd made him a star, and ever since, their relationship had been both ironclad and symbiotic.

Lou would do anything for Moze, the least of which was to lie. In a way, I was jealous of that. I knew that after talking to Doc Bedrosian yesterday, my time of need was fast approaching. Similar protection would be required on my behalf if I was to have any future with the team. I wanted to tell Lou that I'd go along with anything he'd say, as long as he'd go along with me later on.

But I didn't need to say such things. Our relationship may not have been as strong as his and Moze's, but it was tight, especially now that I was risking the integrity of my knee for him and the team. Surely, he'd take that into consideration at the end of the season. Besides, he wasn't asking me to lie. He was ordering me to go along with the official version of events. If the team said it was an accident, it was an accident. Who was I to dispute it?

I nodded in agreement. "Whatever you say, Coach."

Red and I got up to leave.

"Thanks, Dom, I know I can count on you," Lou said, closing the door behind us.

Yeah, but can I count on you? I wanted to say back to him.

Lou had directed the entire conversation at me, never acknowledging the existence of Red. Walking back down the hallway, I heard Red wheeze under his breath, "That was no goddamn accident." Hurt and anger filled his voice.

"Then why were you noddin' your head like a puppy in the backseat for?"

He stopped to face me. "Hey, I wasn't the only one, was I?"

"No, I guess not," I admitted sheepishly. "But if it wasn't an accident, then what was it?"

"Look, whatever happened to Moze was no *accident,* that's all I know for sure. If I've ever seen anyone worked over, it was the guy in the Mercedes this morning."

"Worked over?" I said.

"Yeah, someone was either payin' back a debt or sendin' a message. I don't know which. But whoever did that to Moze knew exactly what they were doin', and the only reason he ain't dead is cuz they still want him alive."

Before I could reply, we turned the corner and were greeted by a row of ceiling lights. The main cavity of the locker room opened before us.

The wide, spacious room was filled with my teammates lounging in different positions before their stalls, talking to one another, studying their playbooks, and making last-minute adjustments to their tape jobs or equipment.

I saw Leroy Wilkins in one corner slurping down his morning bowl of raisin bran. He did this every day without fail. A whole box of cereal and a quart of milk, poured into a mixing bowl the size of a small cauldron. He looked like a Neanderthal warlock brewing up a spell. Stir, stir, slurp. Stir, stir, slurp. It was amazing how much bran this Fred Flintstone of a human being could consume in one sitting, not to mention the two scoops of raisins. But no one asked the question "Where did it all go?" For we knew exactly where it went. And needless to say, it was a good idea to go the other way whenever Wilkins came storming into the restroom with an urgent look on his face.

As disconcerting as the sight of him coming at you in the men's room might be, the sight of him sitting in the corner of the locker room ingesting a vat full of bran brought a measure of comfort and peace to a man's soul. Wilkins's breakfast was more than his daily intake of nutrition. It was his routine. As our noseguard, he was the keystone of the defense, physically and spiritually. James Moze might be the star of the show, the one who made the spectacular plays, but Leroy Wilkins was the foundation upon which Moze stood. As long as the foundation was solid, so was our defense, and so was our team. And as long as he fulfilled his morning ritual, Leroy Wilkins remained solid, even if his stools didn't.

The sight of Wilkins eating his cereal reminded me that the team's problems were bigger than any individual's, and that Red, Moze, Lou, and I were, in the scheme of things, inconsequential. I was part of something bigger than all four of us combined. No matter what might be wrong in our personal lives, everything at the moment was fine because I could see Wilkins shoving a box of raisin bran and a quart of milk down his throat.

Meetings were about to start, so I hurried into the training room to complete my own routine. There, I commandeered Jimmy from some lowly rookie and had my ankles taped at last.

Ten

On the left side of the corridor were three small, separate rooms, one of which had just housed my meeting with Lou and Red. On the right side, running the length of the hallway, was one long room that could accommodate the fifty-three-man roster complete with coaching staff. We gathered there every morning to be briefed by our commander in chief. This was the only point in the day that the entire squad was in the same room at the same time.

The classroom wasn't a place where any of us had ever tasted success, so this was the last place any of us wanted to be. The mere smell of those plastic seats and the noise created when the half-desks were flipped up and down for the hell of it sent chills down my spine. Flashbacks of lectures and exams and marginal grades spilled forth from the dark hollows of my mind. It had been eight years since I finished school, but nightmares of showing up late or unprepared or even undressed for final exams continued to haunt me. The same was true for my teammates.

I don't think I ever showed up for an exam feeling confident or prepared or even on time. Every exam I ever took was not only a test of my knowledge, but also a test of my nervous and digestive systems. Except for the swimming test I had to take as a freshman, I never took a test where I didn't struggle to pass.

It wasn't that I was dumb, because I wasn't (at least *I* didn't think so). It was more that I couldn't sit still in those goddamn uncomfortable chairs. They were too small for me. That, combined with football taking up most of my study time, made my four years of higher learning one long nightmare from which I awoke only intermittently.

The day that I learned I was, indeed, going to graduate was a far more exciting day than the day I got drafted by the Giants. The former signaled the end of one kind of punishment. The latter merely promised the continuation of another.

When I first arrived at Giants Stadium, the sight of the meeting room threw me. School? Again? But I soon realized it was more a case of the room *playing* the part of a classroom than actually *being* one. It had all the trappings of a classroom, but in reality everything that determined a player's fate happened somewhere other than here: the field, the training room, or the streets. Those were the places where actions could make or break a guy. Those were the real classrooms of professional football, with each carrying its own final exam.

Bad performance on the field, too much time in the training room, or deviant behavior in the community could all be construed as failing grades resulting in expulsion. None of these were tolerated, unless of course you were getting an A in the first subject—the playing field.

No, this mock classroom was just a room where players gathered to drift in and out of consciousness and to chew tobacco until it was time to practice. The coaches knew they couldn't keep us on the field for more than three hours, maybe four max, without rendering us useless for the game on Sunday. But at the same time, no way in hell did they want us roaming the streets for half a day with nothing to do.

In the old days, the money the players made was so small that many had to find jobs on the side to support their families. Practice and a short meeting were all they had time for before they showed up for their real jobs. But as the salaries increased, so did the average workday for the professional football player. One-half of this rationale was "We pay 'em more money so we want more of their time." The other half asked, "Do we really want a bunch of really big men, with borderline criminal mentalities, wandering the city streets with cash in their pockets?"

Over the years, meeting time had increased proportionate to the rising pay scale, until we found ourselves sitting bored out of our minds in a pitch-black meeting room lit only by the glow of flickering projector lights and coaches' cigarettes. It was kind of like adult day care, except that game film was substituted for sedatives.

Our meeting room had three folding dividers that could cut up the space into four cramped rooms. We started every workday with a five-minute state-of-the-team address by Lou before breaking up into offensive and defensive units, then into positional groups. Lou's five-minute monologue could last anywhere from three seconds to half an hour, depending on what kind of mood our manic head coach was in. His talks could range from volatile dissertations on previous performances (there was no statute of limitations, he might bring up games or plays from years past), to silent, disgusted glares of contempt with a quick "Let's break up!" or a simple "Offense, defense!" to cap it off. You never knew what to expect from him.

The beauty of Lou was, just when you thought you had him figured out, bam! He'd shock the shit out of you faster than Sybil changing her personality. His erratic behavior kept everyone alert. For me, his instability added a spark of interest to an otherwise dull and mundane morning.

This morning was a particularly tough one to call. I wasn't sure which Lou was going to walk through the door. The caring and gentle Lou? The satiric and witty Lou? The volatile and bombastic Lou? . . . We had one of the best records in the league, but we had just lost a game. I had embarrassed the organization by acting like a lunatic on national television, but I seemed to have escaped a suspension. I had also decided to continue to play despite the ill health of my knee, but we were still without the services of our starting quarterback, Ron Hanes. The preliminary reports on James Moze were encouraging, but the whole situation was still, and would continue to be, disconcerting.

"Siddown 'n' shaddup!" Lou screamed as he burst into the room. Ah, the volatile and bombastic Lou.

I don't know why he was always in such a hurry. As far as I could tell, he did nothing during these morning hours except retreat to his office and study film. He could've left the Meadowlands altogether and not returned until the start of the afternoon's practice. Once our offensive and defensive meetings began in the basement of the stadium, we saw only assistant coaches until it was time to go outside.

Lou took his place behind a podium that stood in the corner for his use only. "Listen up, fellas! I don't know what you fuckin' guys are laughing at!"

This was not a good start to the day.

"You just got your *asses* kicked on Sunday! I don't know what the hell you find so amusing!" Lou stared us all down. "Maybe you're just a bunch of pussies who like being dominated by bigger and stronger men? Is that it?"

Another stare, another pause.

"Maybe some of you like being manhandled and pushed around. Laughed at and embarrassed. Booed and ridiculed right out of an NFL stadium! *Maybe that's it!*"

He glared defiantly with a set chin, pursed lips, and clenched fists. His posture was a challenge to every one of us, individually and collectively, to prove him wrong. He posed for a full minute, silence filling the room, and slowly swept his eyes back and forth from one side of the room to the other. But he wasn't talking to anyone in particular. He was making a point to us all. This was vintage Lou Gordon psychology. He wasn't really mad. I had seen him fifteen minutes ago and he was perfectly fine. If he was as upset as he was claiming to be, he'd have said something to me in his field office. Or at least hinted at it. But again, that would have been personal and this wasn't a personal matter. It was a team thing.

As quickly as his anger appeared, it vanished. He dropped his head between his shoulder blades and hung it there in the deepest and most painful throes of defeat. He was off to an effective start. His biting words cut to the core of our manhood and challenged our toughness and sexual orientation. That did not sit well with us. The laughter that had preceded Lou's arrival quickly turned to looks of outrage and injustice. In two minutes, with a couple of sentences and some penetrating glares, he'd cannon-blasted us out of our complacent midweek, get-through-the-day attitude and cast us into an abyss of fury.

In a game that requires fifteen-second intervals of all-out, kill-or-be-killed passion and emotion, separated by forty-second lulls of peace and nonaction, our ability to jump from one end of the emotional spectrum to the other was essential to our survival in the league. Lou was a master psychologist, no question about that. But his effectiveness was more than doubled thanks to the emotional volatility of his audience.

Where only a moment ago we were lounging and joking, he now had us sitting on the edge of our seats. We were suddenly transformed into attack mode.

"Who does he think he is, calling us a bunch of pussies?!" we all thought.

Lou had us right where he wanted us, on the verge of violence.

But like an attack-dog trainer who fearlessly smacks the raging pit bull on the nose, he was confident that the violent thoughts evoked would never be manifested against him.

He continued to hang his head as if he were at a loss for words. Even though he looked down, I'm sure he could see the fire in our eyes. I knew he could sense the animosity emanating from the men in front of him. You could practically smell it.

He took it all in, weighing and measuring. Only when the time was right would he proceed. His bent-over, exhausted, tired-old-man-at-his-wit's-end, where-did-I-go-wrong, pathetic-father-figure posture was meant to evoke our sympathy and turn our anger inward for bringing him to this pitiful state. Of course it was our fault. We were the ones who had embarrassed him on Sunday. It was time to own up to it. Lou shook his head like a disappointed dad who didn't know what to do with his wayward sons.

"I, I . . ." He searched for the words. "I-I don't know, fellas. I just don't know. I thought you guys were ready. I really did. I thought I'd prepared you to be in this position."

The position he referred to was first place in our division. He lifted his head and scanned the room, a bewildered and confused expression in his eyes. "Maybe it's my fault."

There was dead silence. Our outrage had indeed, just as Lou intended, turned to enmity toward ourselves and sympathy for our leader.

"No, Coach! It's not your fault," we seemed to say through our silence.

A few guys shook their heads, eliciting a small grin from our martyr-general.

The twinkle in his eyes told me that he enjoyed this puppeteer aspect of his job. His ability to manipulate a roomful of world-class athletes, as if our psyches were connected to his handheld marionette, was as important to him as his ability to draw up the perfect play or put together a winning lineup. He absolutely loved it.

I'd been on other teams where winning was not the number one objective. Statistics, personal glory, girls, money, whatever, dominated the thoughts of many of my old teammates. But these guys were Lou's guys. Just as I wouldn't have fit in with any other NFL franchise, so would most of my present teammates have been lost in those chest-thumping groups of glory-seekers and self-promoters.

It wasn't Lou who made us this way. He merely found us. Over the years, we'd been collected from various college and NFL teams and brought together in one place. Lou had before him a group of guys who heard his words and responded like trained dogs. We knew what was going on, but it was exactly what we wanted. None of us could win by ourselves. But together, led by the right man, we could go all the way.

Lou's strained and tortured look continued as he spoke. "Maybe I blew it. I thought you guys could handle being on top. I thought that after all this scratching and clawing to reach the summit, you'd know how to act."

Most of us were ashamed. He was right. He had taken us all the way, from perennial losers to first place. And how did we respond? Like spoiled, ungrateful children. And in my case, like a raving lunatic. We deserved to be punished! In fact, we *wanted* to be punished. It would cleanse our consciences and wash away the stench of Sunday's defeat.

"I guess I was wrong," he said dejectedly.

We joined him in despair. Lou could feel our self-loathing. He knew it was time for the whupping. More important, he knew it was safe. We were beyond reprisals. We would take it lying down like the guilty dogs we were.

Lou stood straight up and began to bellow once again. "It wouldn't be right of me to let you keep going like this. There's gonna be some changes around here starting today!"

The fire was back in his eyes and the bite in his voice. He was now the disciplinarian father who was about to "do what he had to do" not out of malice or abuse, but simply and mercifully for "our own good."

"Defense! You looked fat and happy Sunday. I thought by this point in the season we'd be in shape. I guess not. Sprints after practice for everyone. Offense! That was your most pathetic performance yet. Only ten percent on third-down conversions. That stinks. That stinks like a pile a horseshit!

"Ramsey! Three interceptions? One returned for a touchdown. Son, you won't last long in this league playing like that, believe me."

"Jackson! Five missed tackles? The last one blew any chance for a comeback. Get together with Coach Franklin after practice for some one-on-one tackling drills. You miss another one this season and you're gone!"

Five minutes earlier Lou was on the verge of retirement. Ten minutes ago we were joking around. Since then we had gone from fighting mode to sympathy to shame. Now we were cowering in fear. Lou had resorted to a tactic he rarely used, calling us out by name.

"Derek! Since when does a goddamn offensive tackle call a time-out? Do you wear headsets, son? Do you have Sansabelt shorts on? Do you stay here all goddamn night watching films and drawing up plays? *No, you don't!* Then please tell me why in the world you think you're a goddamn coach? The only person who calls time-outs around here is me, and the last time I looked in the mirror I did not see your fat, ugly face looking back! If you want to be a coach so bad, I can have you home tomorrow coaching the Dubuque High School Cornhuskers or whatever your shitty high school used to call itself! Do you understand me, son?"

Lou was really going now. Each man he singled out slumped in his chair like a scolded schoolboy. Everyone else put his head down like a disobedient dog hoping to be spared the rod.

"And what kind of display of uncontrolled aggression was that?" he said.

Although he didn't mention my name, I knew whom he was talking to. So did everyone else.

"Do some of you have psychological problems that need to be dealt with? If so, just tell me and we'll take care of you in confidence. In all my years of coaching, I've never seen a referee assaulted like that. I certainly don't condone that type of behavior, and I surely will not stand for it! After seeing that game on Sunday, I realized there are plenty of places where some of you would fit right in. *They're called institutions!* And if some of you don't get ahold of yourselves soon, that's exactly where you're gonna end up! Believe me, fellas, the pay's not so good when you're playing football against the Rahway state-prison guards!"

Of course, he was talking to me. But as in my previous eight years on the team, he never spoke directly *to* me. I was the one dog who might, despite my training, bite the hand that fed me.

I stared down the whole time. Though my ankles were covered with tape, most of my feet were exposed. I studied the scars from the previous foot surgeries I'd endured and squinted at the crooked joints of my battered toes. They were all I could focus on. To look at Lou would have been too painful. I certainly wasn't going to look at my teammates. I could already feel their sidelong glances burning holes in the side of my head as they were forced to share the brunt of my admonishment. Lou was right. I had acted like an idiot in the game.

"Listen, fellas," he said gently, shifting gears once again. "This is the best team I've ever coached. The players in this room have what it takes. I know. I've been around a long time. I've seen thousands of players and dozens of teams, and I'm telling ya, you've got what it takes. You guys."

He pointed both index fingers at us.

"You guys, right here, can be *champions*! I can't make the tackles for you. I can't throw the ball for you. All I can do is prepare you each week and draw up a game plan that's gonna give you the best chance to win. But *you* gotta go out and do it. And if you do . . . believe me, fellas, nobody'll stop you . . . *nobody!*"

He finished the last sentence in a hushed voice as if he were fighting back tears of affection. I looked around the room. On a team full of guys with no decorum or manners, not one head slumped. Not one shoulder slouched. Not one back bent. Everyone sat at attention, and every eye glistened with moisture. In fifteen minutes, we had been slapped awake, torn down, ridiculed, shamed, soothed over, and built back up. Now we were being told we were the best. The best ever! God, this guy was good.

"Are we all on the same page, fellas?" Lou asked rhetorically. "Good. Then let's put last week's game behind us and go to work . . . O and D!"

The heated room burst into a frenzy of scraping chairs and folding partitions. Everyone moved at the same time. Lou walked out of the room, the storm of activity swirling about him. He wasn't looking at the crazy scene, but I knew he was watching.

Eleven

In less than a minute, the large space had been divided in two, and Coach Chuck Farrel, our offensive coordinator, had assumed his place in the back of the room, which, upon conversion, was now the front.

"All right men, the big guy's right. If I had to give the speech this morning, I would've said the same thing."

Originally from Midland, Texas, Farrel had a Southern drawl. For longer than I'd been alive, everyone had called him Midland.

Midland was an offensive guru. He'd been coaching for forty years. His offensive schemes had propelled almost every team he'd worked with into play-off contention. But like the rest of us, he was never able to win the big prize. His success had once earned him the chance to be the head coach of his own NFL team. But the only thing he seemed to do right before being fired was to hire a young college coach named Lou Gordon. Lou never forgot Midland, and as soon as he got his own chance to be head coach, Lou hired Midland to lead his offense. In this new power structure, they'd been together for twelve years now, with Midland playing the perfect Gabby Hayes to Lou's John Wayne.

"Like Lou said, let's go to work, men. Lights!" he said, as he fell into the easy chair brought in for his viewing pleasure.

He held a remote control in his hand that reversed the film's direction with the press of a button. This allowed him to view the action backward and forward as often as he liked. I thought it was a neat thing the first time I saw it, but quickly changed my mind the day I watched myself get knocked on my ass, forward and backward, twenty times in a row. Since then, I'd no use for it. But Midland couldn't seem to get enough of it. He was so obsessed with that button, at times I saw him pressing an imaginary one on the practice field, only to be mystified when the reality in front of him refused to play in reverse.

His obsession with film was so intense that it distracted him from the inattentiveness of his players. Once he was in that La-Z-Boy and the projector was running, he didn't care what we did. As long as the film flickered and the world on the screen obeyed his command to run in either direction, he was the ideal coach, filled with words of wisdom and amusing anecdotes. He had a deep, soothing voice, and as I listened to him this morning, I drifted off to sleep, wondering why he hadn't won every Super Bowl to date.

"Dominic, what were you thinking, boy?" Midland's voice cut through my semi-dream-state.

I'd been asleep for a while. My face was glued to the palm of my hand.

"Huh?"

"Care to elaborate, son?"

The game film from last Sunday was rolling on the screen. He had come to the play leading to my ejection, and he was playing it over and over, trying to figure out what had happened. As I watched myself go backward and forward, the play, along with the gut-wrenching regret that followed, returned from the wasteland of my mind and threw itself smack-dab onto the slate that for a brief moment had been wiped clean like a child's Etch A Sketch. The camera followed the Eagle middle linebacker into the end zone after his interception, but quickly panned back to my melee upfield. Disorder reigned. A crowd had gathered around a referee laying unconscious on the turf. Giant and Eagle players pushed and shoved one another. In the corner of the shot, I saw my teammate Derek Jones (all 320 pounds of him) hustling me off the field as he wrapped me in a bear hug.

I thought before answering. Reliving the incident had opened up several wounds I thought had scarred over. But as with a broken scab, the blood and emotions ran more intense than before. I felt sick all over again. I wanted to defend myself. I wanted to apologize. But then I realized, what would it matter? These guys didn't care. They had their own problems. It was over and done with. Ancient history. Move on. In football there's no such thing as the past (once films have been reviewed, that is). Only the present counts. Did I care to elaborate?

"Nahh," I said nonchalantly.

"Okay, big guy. Just take it easy next time. It's only a game."

Midland was a good guy. And with that moment of compassion out of the way, he returned to his routine demeanor.

"Ramsey! What kind of piss-poor throw was that? My grandmother can throw better than you! If you don't shape up, we won't make the length of my dick for the rest of the season!"

"That's not asking for much, Coach," someone in the darkness cracked.

Our practice field was a small, green oasis in a desert of cement. Although the parking lot surrounding the stadium encompassed more square mileage than some small towns in America, the powers-that-be deemed the land so valuable that they could only spare us eighty yards of it on which to practice. For the football illiterate, that's forty yards shy, including the end zones, of a regulation-size field. Not that it mattered. We didn't really need a full-size field to practice on. But considering all the nothingness that surrounded us, I wondered why they couldn't have thrown in the extra forty yards of dirt.

Whether out of privacy or embarrassment, the field was guarded by an eight-foot-high, barbed-wire fence. The fence was covered by a blue fabric that was a cross between plastic and canvas. No one on the outside could see in, and no one on the inside could see out. Only the upper decks of the stadium, the multitude of radio and television towers, and the Manhattan skyline were visible from our confines, keeping us focused on the reason for our existence. We were there to play football, in that stadium, for that city, for the sole purpose of selling airtime to advertisers.

"Rotate those shoulders!" Paulie, our strength and conditioning coach, barked out in his best marine drill-sergeant voice.

Paulie was a miniature version of Arnold Schwarzenegger, with as strong a Mississippi accent as Arnold's Austrian one. He'd competed in bodybuilding competitions when he was younger, but was now content with instructing us how to lift weights properly and how to stretch out every day before practice.

"Small circles!" he shouted.

Stretching eased my mind like no other part of the day. If I looked at it rationally, this was probably the *worst* part of the day, the lull before the storm, the moment of peace before all hell broke loose. This serene façade of team togetherness, featuring friendly banter between the players and the coaches, only masked the real truth—that we were about to embark on a three-hour quest to rip each other apart, while the coaches rode our backs all the way, exhorting us toward violence, belittling us into conformity, and berating us into competency.

"Bigger circles!"

Paulie's voice cut through the vacuum of silence in which we pulled and twisted our tight muscles. No yelling, no whistles, no thudding of pads. No grunting and groaning of men, not even the rush of cars speeding by on the New Jersey Turnpike. And certainly not one peep from the noisiest city in the world on the other side of the river. Nothing but dead, calm silence, interrupted only by Paulie's vocal cords signaling the end of one stretch or the beginning of a new one.

"Bigger . . ."

He coaxed us on. The entire squad spread out in ten neat lines, five across, swinging our arms around in circles. At this stage in my career, I knew enough to seize these peaceful moments whenever they arose and to make the most of them while they lasted. I also had the ability, as did most of my teammates, to fall asleep during a ten-minute break in meetings, even after drinking five cups of coffee, while lying on a cold, hard floor using a pair of cleats for a pillow.

The coaches wandered menacingly through the rows, stopping every now and then to talk to a player or to another coach. For the moment, they were impotent. They had no one to yell at and no one to "coach" just yet. Lou wouldn't allow it. They were going to have to wait for his, and only his, whistle before they were allowed to implement the game plan they had painstakingly drawn up the night before. For as long as the stretch lasted, they had no one to control. No one to manipulate. And no one through whom to vicariously play the game. So they wandered the field aimlessly, looking and feeling lost, denuded of their ability to blow their whistles and have everyone jump at their command. Except for Lou, that is. He could blow his whistle anytime, anywhere, and we would all jump, including them.

"Bigger!"

This was Paulie's shining moment. This was the only time we had to listen to him as a *coach,* and the only time the other coaches got to witness *his* coaching skills.

You'd think playing experience would be a prerequisite for professional coaching, but it wasn't. In fact, to become a football coach, there was no requirement to have ever stepped on a field in full equipment professionally or otherwise. All you needed was a little knowledge and a maniacal love for the game.

That was true with our coaches. They had a fabulous understanding of the X's and O's, of strategy, clock management, play selection, and judging talent. But they had no clue about the physical side of the game. They didn't know what it felt like to stick their head into someone's gut and feel the fire from a pinched nerve shoot down their spine and into their hands and feet. They had never been rendered helpless by a helmet to the ribs and been left lying on the turf, suppressing the high-pitched screams and shrieks that are normally reserved for a wounded soldier on the field of battle. They couldn't fathom the pain and confusion of a reality-altering blow from a linebacker, the kind that turns day into night and leaves the injured party trying to account for the fifteen or twenty minutes of his life he will never remember living.

No. While they had set ideas about the physical stature and proportions of the players they wanted on their teams, they had no idea how to coach the techniques and training necessary to attain them. That's why they'd hired Paulie. He had no talent for coaching football. But he knew exactly how to work and sculpt an individual to the precise specifications put forth by Lou and the rest of those who did.

"All the way now!" Paulie shouted. We all swung our arms in full circles like windmills. I could actually feel the breeze we created blowing across the field.

"Take a seat!"

Obediently, we dropped to our butts and spread our legs. When Paulie said take a seat, we did, no matter what the condition of the ground or how inclement the weather. The morning snow lingered on the field's frozen dirt. Its moisture seeped through my nylon pants. Only a jockstrap insulated my skin. I felt as if I were sitting bare-assed on a block of ice. A few moans of discomfort broke the silence, but not many. At least the snow was clean.

The days of summer training camp were still fresh in our minds. We'd gone through the same stretching routine at a Westchester County college, on a field that served not only as our practice facility, but as a toilet for approximately eight thousand Canada geese. Every morning and afternoon during those summer sessions, and sometimes in between, when Paulie barked "Take a seat!" we had to nestle our cheeks into the softened, squishy goose-shit that littered the field. Obediently, we also lay down on our backs and stomachs and rolled around in it to conduct the stretches Paulie ordered. By the end of those twenty-minute stretching sessions we were encrusted in a batter of shit, ready for deep-frying in the sweltering sun of New York in July and August. Many were the days I cleaned goose droppings out of my ears after practice, or at least thought I did, only to have some leftovers ooze out through the night and leave their greenish skid-marks all over my nice white pillows.

"Partner up!"

Players in odd-numbered rows got up and matched with teammates in even-numbered rows behind them. By this point in the season, I knew enough to remain on my back while the guy in front of me made his way over. Like anything else in the sport, our alignment for stretching was an unchangeable pattern. Once the final cuts had been made in preseason and the team was in place, the way we lined up *that* day to stretch was the way we lined up to stretch for the remainder of the year. No one thought about changing his spot. It wouldn't happen. Lou wouldn't allow it. I'd wound up in the tenth row of the far right line eight years ago and hadn't changed since.

My stretching partner had been coming to me for God knows how many practices as I lay on my back and stared at the sky through the bars of my face mask. It was always a treat if, in those few seconds, I could spot a jetliner leaving a contrail or two against the blue canvas of sky above me. The sight appealed to my sense of adventure and made me realize that, despite the narrow world Lou had created for us, there was something to do other than football. That, indeed, there were places to go and things to be seen besides game film or hotels or other cities' stadiums. But these thoughts were shadowed over by the face of Dan Ramsey as he reached the spot where I was lying and mechanically grabbed my leg and pushed it gently toward my head.

Ramsey had a lethargic and apathetic gait about him that was made even more lethargic and apathetic by Lou's and Midland's expostulations this morning concerning his performance on Sunday. Ramsey was a lot like me. The more you yelled at him, the less he responded. But unlike me, whose bad moods were considered dangerous, Ramsey was only a quarterback, and quarterback retaliations induced no fear. In fact, they were little more effective than what a pouting child might achieve.

Unfortunately for Ramsey, as long as he remained with the Giants, he was destined to languish under the title *second-stringer* and was accorded the same respect given to an unheeded middle sibling. This was his station in life (or at least on the team) and went a long way in explaining his somber disposition.

Ramsey was actually full of smiles and energy when the coaches weren't around. I looked forward to our ten minutes together every day as we stretched one another out, doing things to each other's body that our girlfriends had never done.

"Hey, Dom." Ramsey knelt between my legs and whistled three or four notes from a song that I was supposed to identify.

He picked up my left leg, in keeping with Paulie's command, and pushed my heel back over my face so that my kneecap almost touched my face mask.

"Hey, Hoss," I groaned.

For my entire rookie season, he had stumped me with the theme song from the old television show *Bonanza.* Not until I saw a rerun was I able to "name that tune." Hoss Cartwright, I found out later, was Ramsey's favorite character, so I dubbed him with that nickname. He didn't seem to mind, and after a while the other guys took to it as well. He liked assuming the character of "Big ol' Hoss," especially since he was a skinny ol' quarterback.

"I heard about the fine," he said. "That sucks."

"Yeah, well, it's only money."

He had my leg over my head with my foot almost touching the ground. I recognized the tune he had whistled along with his greeting.

"'Miles from Nowhere,' Cat Stevens," I said quickly.

"Good one."

"They were a little hard on ya this morning, don't ya think?" I added, before he could get back to his original train of thought.

"Fuck'em," he said morosely.

"Don't worry about it. You're doing great and they know it. I think they're just worried about Moze."

"If you ask me, they shoulda worried about Moze a long time ago. How long did they think he'd be able to live like that with nothing hap'nin' to him?"

"I dunno, Hoss, but accidents do happen," I said, not very convincingly.

"Bullshit," said Ramsey, very convincingly. "When you play with fire your whole life, it's not an accident when you finally get burned."

You're right, I thought, but said nothing. Ramsey lowered my left leg to the ground and took up my right one in the same manner. Midland came ambling over with a cigarette hanging out of his mouth and a look of concern on his face. The cigarette was mysteriously glued to his lower lip like some sort of leftover crumb he'd neglected to wipe away. The more I watched it dangle in the damp air of the afternoon, the more I suspected he didn't even know it was pasted to his lip.

"Hey, Fucillo," he said. "How's Jesse James over here?"

He was pointing to Ramsey. Ramsey lowered his head and pushed my leg farther toward my face. His friendly smile was quickly replaced by a full and menacing pout. Midland knew Ramsey was mad at him and wouldn't engage in any conversation with him that wasn't forced, particularly not this type of friendly banter before practice. That's why Midland was talking to me.

"Why do you call him Jesse James, Coach?" I asked, playing Abbott to Midland's Costello.

"Cuz he's stealin'!" Midland cracked.

I laughed, although I didn't get it. What else was I gonna do? Ramsey pushed my leg back until my laughter turned to grunts of pain.

"Hell, *Fuc*illo," Midland began.

He always put the emphasis on the first syllable of my name instead of the second. He'd been doing it for eight years now. I never took the time to correct him. It didn't bother me. Besides, I think he knew anyway.

"Ramsey's been stealin' for years now, haw, haw!" Midland laughed. "Getting paid all that money and never takin' a snap! He's averagin' fifty grand a play for crissakes!"

Midland laughed again. I laughed again, too. But this time for real because he was right.

"Yeah, Coach," I said jokingly. "But he's still gotta put up with your shit, so I'd say he was underpaid."

This was the only time during the day you could talk to the coaches on an equal footing, where no disrespect was intended, nor any offense taken.

"You're right, Dom. But this is a tough game," Midland said, turning serious. "Anything I might say to him is meant for *his* benefit. I will say, though, most of the passes Ramsey threw were good ones. Even those a little off target. Hell, they all could've been caught if it weren't for Dino and the rest of them Venus de Milos out there."

Dino was the nickname we gave to guys who short-armed

catches. No one was above being labeled with that degrading sobriquet. It could fall on the toughest and most fearless among us. Most of the time it wasn't something we could avoid. Short-arming a catch was a reflexive action, like defending yourself from a blow to the groin, or better yet, like throwing a punch with a broken hand. A receiver's mind might not allow his arms to extend fully away from his sides and thus open his midsection to a world of pain. Instead, even though he *thinks* he's reaching out for the ball, his elbows hardly leave his ribs. That results in a man with a thirty-eight-inch sleeve measurement suddenly being reduced to having arms the length of Fred Flintstone's pet dinosaur, Dino; or in extreme cases, no longer than Venus de Milo's arms, which have mysteriously disappeared altogether.

Throughout the entire time Midland stood there, Ramsey kept his head down and manipulated my legs. We had moved to the next stretch. I sat up facing him with the soles of my feet brought together as close as possible into my crotch. I let my knees fall away from my body and felt the stretch in my groin. Ramsey knelt before me with one hand on each knee and pushed my two joints toward the earth while I reeled in discomfort, my privates hanging, clothed but unprotected, in the afternoon air. For an area of my body that was so guarded, I couldn't have been more given over to the man in front of me who pried my legs apart like a giant oyster in search of a pearl . . . or two.

"Well, the key is not to panic," Midland continued, finally taking a drag of the smoking crumb on his lip. "We're sittin' pretty good right now, and if ol' Jesse here hangs in there, we'll be just fine."

Midland patted Ramsey on the head, then moseyed over to someone else he felt he needed to reconcile with from this morning's meetings. Ramsey never looked up nor in any way acknowledged Midland's presence. Maturity didn't run strong in this place where we were paid hundreds of thousands of dollars a year, in some cases millions, yet were still given $25 a day on road trips for snacks, in case we got hungry in between the lavish meals provided free of charge. As soon as Ramsey sensed Midland was gone, he let out a big sigh and a "Screw him" before whistling another three or four notes for me to guess.

"'Communication Breakdown,' Led Zeppelin," I shot back.

"Man, Dom, you are good." Ramsey giggled like a schoolboy. "But I'll stump you before the day's out."

Stretching was winding down to its close. Practice was about to begin. It was amazing to think some people in this world actually looked up to us as role models.

Twelve

All it took was one blow of the whistle, albeit a blow from the *right* whistle, and the calm of the afternoon was shattered. As soon as Lou raised the black piece of plastic to his lips, stretching and kibitzing were officially over whether Paulie had gotten us through the whole routine or not.

Not that Lou's whistle sounded any different from Paulie's, or any other coach's, but something about Lou's shrill was unmistakable, and every player on the field could distinguish it from the "ordinary" whistles, just as a bunch of hounds could distinguish their master's call from any other.

The day became a typical Tuesday. Practice was in full swing. My head pounded. My muscles ached. My lungs gasped for air. And we'd only completed the warm-up phase. This afternoon, my equipment felt unusually heavy.

Perhaps because for the first time in my career I truly felt my days of wearing it were numbered.

In particular, my helmet seemed to weigh a ton. The plastic and steel hat sat oppressively on my head. I'd rarely been aware of its constraints in the past, but today everything about it altered my senses. The two ear-holes muffled the voices and sounds around me. The bars etched a permanent grid onto every scene before my eyes. The tunnel vision created by the shell itself produced a sort of drunken, drug-induced state of perception that lifted me out of the everyday world.

I loved my helmet. Putting it on was for me the same as Mr. Rogers donning his sneakers and sweater after a long, hard day in the outside world. With my helmet on, I was back in my own neighborhood. I felt at home. I felt safe. Inside my helmet . . . I felt like me.

The realization that this skullcap kept me alive on the field of play made me treat it with reverence. The "force-field" effect it created transformed my personality whenever I donned it. I could go from law-abiding citizen to raving lunatic in the snap of a chinstrap. It gave me strength to cope not only on the field but off it as well. Just knowing it was on my head, or even hanging in my locker, provided me with a sense of protection.

I panicked to think I might soon never wear it again. Scenes of a helmetless future crept into my mind. The old familiar questions arose: Where would I go? What would I do? How would I do it? I regained my composure when a small rock ricocheted off my plastic security blanket.

Pinggggg!

My ears vibrated like a bell that had just been clanged. With my head wrapped in plastic, the effect was the same as wearing a garbage can for a hat and beating it with a stick. I picked up a rock of my own and turned around in search of the perpetrator. I saw Ramsey staring at me. He giggled through his face mask.

As soon as he caught my eye, his lips pursed and he rifled off a quick three or four notes. I could hardly breathe, and that goofball wanted to play name that tune. I wanted to kill him, but his playfulness made me laugh instead. Attacking a quarterback in practice was not a good idea. In a lot of ways, it was similar to attacking a priest or a nun on the street.

I weighed my options and realized that the most I could do to retaliate was what he had done so well to Coach Midland . . . ignore him. So I turned away and refused to look at him as he called the next play in the huddle. And I continued to ignore him as we jogged up to the line of scrimmage to execute it.

But Ramsey was not put off that easily. Unperturbed by my silence, he continued to smile. "Well?" he asked, taking his place under the center.

"Well what?" I was never good at giving the silent treatment.

"Name that tune?"

"Go bang yourself, Hoss" was all I could spit out, although the tune had sounded familiar. I had other things to worry about at the moment, in particular, a rookie named Bobby Ward.

Bobby was James Moze's backup, and in Moze's absence he seemed intent on making his new assignment permanent. Although the kid was no Moze, he was a first-round draft pick with enough talent to be a bear in practice. Still in the proving stages of his career, he was an especially dangerous opponent during the middle of the week when all I cared about was recovering from the last game and trying to prepare as gently as possible for the next. Our two states of mind were not in harmony, and unfortunately for me, it was my philosophy that seemed most likely to be altered.

"Bobby," I said, as I approached the line of scrimmage with Ramsey's musical notes ringing in my ears. "Take it easy, will ya? I'm hurtin' today."

"Sorry, Dom, no can do."

His response took me aback. Did that goddamn rookie just say what I thought he said? Ramsey whistled his notes again just before he put his hands under the center. For an instant I heard the whole song in my head, but quickly shook it out. This was no time for games.

"Bobby, I'm askin' ya nice, now. Go easy."

"Strap it up, Dom, it's game day," he said, fire in his eyes.

Well, that young little twerp. The nerve of him. Telling *me* it's game day! He hadn't busted a grape all year. What the hell did this kid know about *game day*? The last *game* he ever played in was followed by a keg party at the local frat house! Things began to spin out of control. My sanity began to unravel. Bobby's obstinacy and disrespect, combined with my fatigue and fear of the future, pushed me right over the *edge* that I'd been so precariously straddling since the beginning of practice. Bad things were about to happen, and I was powerless to stop them. Maybe Hanes and Lou were right about me. Maybe I was headed for an institution after all. These violent thoughts weren't rational, that's for sure. Certainly, none were justified by Bobby's actions. But in my quickly warping mind, Bobby ceased being a teammate of mine.

I got down into my stance and prepared to teach this young punk a lesson. It had to be done carefully. Too much effort would give the impression that Bobby was better than he was. He had to be beaten convincingly while making it appear easy. That's hard to do when every joint in your body is on fire and a storm of emotions is swirling in your head. But I knew that it had to be done. This rookie was breaching all etiquette. It was up to me to punish him like the wayward child he was and bring him back into line for the sake of everyone on the field. It might take ten years' time and a wayward rookie tight end out on some future practice field for him to realize it, but he would eventually thank me.

I settled into my stance, resolved to carry out my mission, but seething that I was forced to do it at all. There was enough on my mind without this extra added bullshit. My career was about to end. My knee was killing me. My paychecks had all but stopped. I couldn't get that goddamn song of Ramsey's out of my head. And now this?

Where were the goddamn coaches? Couldn't they see Bobby was going a hundred times harder than everyone else? Why weren't they telling him to relax and cut me some slack?

Then I realized something that made me even more furious. Lou loves that sort of stuff. He probably ordered Bobby to step up the tempo, figuring I would respond in kind. This way, the kid gets an idea of game conditions on Sunday. That's great, I thought, but why me? Why do I have to be the stick Lou uses to stir up the hornet's nest? Didn't I warrant a little more respect than that? Especially since I'd just made the decision to forgo all concern for my knee by continuing to play for him?

Anger bubbled inside me like a boiling volcano. As Ramsey began the cadence, I could feel hatred spilling out of me. It bubbled upward and onward and prepared to explode in the direction of the young, unsuspecting linebacker who was merely doing his job in preparation for his big debut this upcoming Sunday.

"Hut-hut!" Ramsey barked.

Ramsey had called a pass play in the huddle. But I lined up in a run stance, my weight forward, the knuckles of my hand turning white. Everything about our formation suggested pass, but I knew the rookie hadn't yet learned to look beyond the man in front of him.

"All right, rookie. You want game day? You got it," I said, making a show of digging my back cleat into the turf for traction. Bobby, standing before me, shifted his stance as well, digging in and preparing for a collision. This is too easy, I thought.

At the snap of the ball, I stepped forward, feinting a frontal assault, staying low with my arms cocked ready to unload. Bobby stayed low as well, his weight forward, ready to meet force with force. As our helmets touched, I sprang backward from my initial first step and instead of driving my arms into his chest, I swung my right hand around and slapped the back of his helmet so hard my fingers went numb. Rocky Marciano couldn't have thrown a better right hook. Head slaps had been outlawed for years. Maybe that's why Bobby wasn't expecting one. Too bad for him, I thought, because it really must've hurt. As I threw it, I turned my body sideways and cleared a path for his forward momentum. The force of the shot, in conjunction with his reckless lunge, sent him hurtling toward the turf at the speed of sound. One second he was up, the next he was down. It was actually comical. The laughter of my teammates confirmed that.

"There's your game day, jackass," I said, hardly breathing at all.

Bobby lay motionless on the turf, his head embedded in the mud and snow. He looked dead. But after a second or two, movement returned to his limbs. A glazed look in his eyes was apparent as he turned toward me. I'd dinged him good. But not good enough. Rising to his feet, he tentatively assumed a fighting position, however wobbly his legs. He might've let the cheap shot pass if not for the laughter of our teammates. But the gauntlet had been thrown down, and as our new starting linebacker, he was required to answer it. I waited for Lou to end the matter, but he chose not to. My rage intensified, and before Bobby could even take a step in my direction, I attacked. Swinging, punching, kicking, kneeing, anything I could do, I did. At one point, I even stuck my fingers through his now bent face mask and tried to gouge his eyes out. He crumpled onto the ground in a ball of rookie meat, still half-cocked from the original blow to the head. I saw nothing but his disheveled face. I heard nothing but the sound of my fists on his body.

I didn't hear the panicked shrill of Lou's whistle when it finally blew. I didn't feel the restraining hands of my teammates as they wrapped me in a human straitjacket. I didn't notice the blood dripping from my knuckles (a mixture of both Bobby's and mine), nor feel any pain from the wounds on my elbows and forearms (opened by the plastic and steel of Bobby's helmet, the same helmet that most likely kept him from dying). I don't remember being unceremoniously carted off the field like a belligerent drunk being tossed out of a bar at closing time, either. I wasn't aware of anything at all until I heard the clip-clopping sound of my own cleats tapping upon the cement of the stadium tunnel.

That sound alone brought me back to reality. Every Sunday as I walked toward the playing field, that sound was the only thing I could hear amid the surrounding madness. Waves of fear and anxiety accompanied me, and the clip-clopping sound of my cleats became synonymous with cold sweat and rumbling intestines. These effects, and nothing else, dispersed the storm clouds of practice this afternoon, and I was once again able to see and comprehend the scene in front of me. It didn't take long to realize that I was being escorted back to the locker room by Jimmy the trainer and Derek Jones, who must've felt more like a nuthouse guard than an all-pro left tackle. We walked along in silence, each holding on to one of my arms. And as I listened to the rhythmic beat of my cleats upon the oil-stained cement, a revelation burst forward.

"'It's Howdy Doody Time'!" I shouted, startling both men.

Jimmy and Derek stopped in their tracks. I must have seemed a complete lunatic to them. The look on their faces said as much.

"'It's Howdy Doody Time,'" I repeated, this time much quieter and more to myself. That bastard. I laughed, thinking of Ramsey and the three or four notes he'd been whistling only minutes earlier. Looking at my blood-covered arms, I laughed again. Howdy friggin' Doody.

The locker room was quiet when Derek dropped me off. Eerily quiet. Rarely did I see the place like this. It was as if time had stopped once we'd gone out to practice.

Everyone's clothes hung in his locker, undisturbed. Tape, shorts, trash, and coffee cups were strewn about the floor. Lights burned bright, and my teammate's stools were scattered into various groupings and positions throughout the room, suggesting places where conversations and communal gatherings had taken place. But there were no people. No activity. No life.

I was alone. Derek had returned to practice, and Jimmy had gone straight into the training room. Yet the locker room seemed alive. Like a lonely pet biding its time until its owner's return. Waiting patiently, ready to burst forth with energy and activity at the first sound of approaching cleats.

I took a seat before my locker. My shoulder pads bunched up into my face mask, the strain almost unbuckling my chinstrap. I leaned back to relieve the pressure on my helmet, but couldn't bear to remove it just yet. The shell swaddled my head like the security blanket it was and hid me from the outside world. Like a child hiding his face behind his hands, I felt invisible as long as I wore it. Invisible and safe.

It didn't matter that I'd wanted to, and had tried to, kill someone. It was only a game. A case of overexuberance. All-American fun. As long as I'd acted with my helmet on, it was just "good football."

Gazing into the bottom of my trash-filled locker, my body felt light and tingly, the way it did after a blinding migraine. My eyes jumped from one piece of trash to another, from one pair of shoes to another. I began to relive the incident out on the field. At first, I smirked at the vision of Bobby lying on the ground, blood pouring from his nose and mouth. I even chuckled at the look of horror on Lou's face. That'll teach him, I thought. Trying to get the kid ready for game day at my expense, huh? How's about I hasten the day of his retirement instead?

Self-satisfaction washed over me after the first two or three replays of the incident. But I couldn't stop at a couple of reruns. Instead, like Midland, I kept pressing that replay button. And as I did, the argument for my case unraveled.

The more I saw myself in action, the more concerned I became. Luckily for me, my victim was as big and as strong and as padded as I was. Any damage inflicted had been minimal. But what if it had happened on the street, or at home? What then? Where would I wind up after an incident like that? Would it be like Hanes and Lou said? The penitentiary or an asylum? I shuddered.

Finally, I couldn't take it anymore. Take your thumb off that damn button, I told myself. Enough contemplation. Thinking and football were becoming a dangerous combination. Besides, Jimmy was waiting in the training room. It was time to take care of business. Time to fall back into the routine.

Squeezing my head out of my helmet, I walked toward the training room, peeling off pieces of my uniform as I went. I didn't care where they fell. Red would pick them up later.

"What the hell's wrong with you, Dom?!" Jimmy started as I walked through the training-room door. "What were you *thinkin'* about?!"

"What?" I said in my best Vinnie Barbarino imitation.

"Out there, on the field!"

"Where?"

"G'head, make a joke out of it, peckahead. I'll be laughing all through the rest of the season while you're anywhere but here."

"Lighten up Jimmy," I said with confidence. "They ain't gonna do nothing to me. Not now anyway. Next year maybe, but not now. Not when we're so close to the play-offs and Hanes is out and now Moze is missing in action."

"You're a goddamn idiot," he mumbled, knowing I was right. He began my postpractice routine as he did every day. First he poured a couple of Toradols into my hand and gave me a cup of water. Then he put ice bags on one foot, one ankle, both knees, and one shoulder. He wired my bad knee to an electrical-stimulation machine and did the same for my lower back, which had been spastic lately. Then he left the room without a word. Like Derek, he was needed back at the practice field. Within moments, I was alone again.

Emotion returned. There was nothing to distract me from my behavior except the pain of the ice and electricity. Thankfully, both stung like a bastard, and it wasn't long before they became my only concern. Within minutes, I was transformed into a shivering lump of flesh. Thoughts of Bobby Ward faded.

Minutes creep by when you have frozen water all over your body, and watching the clock hoping for a reprieve only makes it go slower. The first fifteen minutes are always the worst. That's when pain freezes the nerves and the ice begins to feel hot instead of cold. But no sooner do you settle into that hot-ice mode than it's time to defrost. The pain of thawing out is almost worse than that of freezing up. Especially when the pain of a hot shower is added to the mix. Hot water hitting frozen skin feels like a thousand darts finding their bull's-eye all at the same time. Day after day, it was the same routine. You'd think I'd get used to it by now, but I never did. Every postpractice was just as unpleasant as that the day before. Yet, as I wallowed in my agony, I cringed at the thought of life without it.

"Punchin' out a little early, aren't 'cha, Fucillo?" Red coughed, wheeling his laundry basket into the training room. He picked up shorts and T-shirts that guys had discarded on the floor, including the last few items I'd thrown down so carelessly on my way in: a half T-shirt and some wristbands.

"Get it?" he asked. "*Punchin'* out? Ha, ha!"

He threw the wet T-shirt into the rolling hamper and left the room. Obviously he'd heard about the fight. He laughed so hard that I didn't even hear him say "filthy animals" once, the whole time.

Thirteen

My teammates were still at work on the practice field when I finished dressing. Lou would expect to see me after what had happened out there, but screw him, I thought to myself. He'll be lucky to see me tomorrow before meetings. The fight notwithstanding, I was still seething over his reluctance to diffuse the whole situation by ordering Bobby to cool out. At the moment, I wanted nothing to do with Lou or the goddamn team. I just wanted to get out of there as fast as I could and get far away from anything and everything that reminded me of the place. The only problem was, I had nowhere to go.

Salvi's wasn't what I was looking for. Everything about his restaurant reminded me of my job. I was surrounded by it at the Point.

I needed to simply relax instead. I needed to forget about football for a while, forget who I was for the rest of the afternoon. Maybe see what life was like away from this game. The end was coming soon enough. I'd be driving away for real one day. Maybe it was time to make a practice run.

I'd never been tossed out of practice. I'd never driven past my teammates working behind the blue fence. And I'd definitely never left the stadium parking lot with this much time on my hands. I needed to continue this trend by going somewhere I'd never before been. Somewhere I was sure to know no one, and no one knew me. I also had a powerful thirst on, the kind that no cooler of Gatorade could quench.

I could hear the sound of thudding pads and blowing whistles from behind the blue fence. The list of potential watering holes in which I could drown my sorrows without attracting attention was short—indeed, nonexistent. Don't fret, I said to myself. Just drive.

I searched for an exit I'd never taken and guided the Monte Carlo out of the Meadowlands and onto the streets of New Jersey, bent on discovering a place I'd yet to see. This wouldn't be difficult, since despite being a resident of the Garden State for the last eight years, I knew only the stretch of road leading from my motel room to the stadium, and from the stadium to Salvi's. Everything besides that was virgin territory. Needless to say, within twenty minutes I was hopelessly lost in an industrial wasteland of scrap heaps and oil refineries. Places like this I'd seen from the safety of the turnpike but had never delved into firsthand.

Although a lot of activity obviously took place in this area, actual people were few and far between. Driving for miles on these soot-filled back roads, my only human counterparts were the drivers of the passing tractor trailers, cement trucks, and rolling garbage scows. These were in abundance, as well as dump trucks and front-end loaders filling them with scrap metal, junk pieces, or just plain dirt. Rusted barrels were stacked in pyramids everywhere I looked. God knows what sort of toxins and chemical death those barrels contained. I raised my T-shirt to my mouth and used it as an air filter. Nowhere in my observations did I see trees, bushes, or the slightest hint of vegetation. The morning's substantial snowfall had mysteriously disappeared from this patch of earth, while the rest of the metropolitan area remained buried. Rumors of radiation in this pocket of New Jersey constantly circulated through the locker room. This afternoon, I was seeing for myself the source of the scuttlebutt.

It wasn't long before I came to Newark. The factories and junkyards gave way to rows of businesses and tenements. Soon a sign appeared at the entrance to an Erector-set-looking bridge directly in front of me: WELCOME TO IRONBOUND. An appropriate name, I thought, as I drove over the iron structure that seemed to be the only entrance (or escape, depending on how you looked at it) for the now visible inhabitants of this enclave of three-storied row houses.

I felt as if I were driving into my grandfather's old neighborhood. The place looked, smelled, and felt the same. The houses lined the streets with no apparent breaks and were done over in the same eccentric shades of blue, red, pink, and purple aluminum siding. Telephone wires crossing the narrow streets and broad avenues displayed the same discarded sneakers dangling by their shoestrings and swaying in the breeze. Old men on street corners wore hats and smoked cigars. Young men beside them donned baseball caps and puffed on cigarettes. Small restaurants, delis, bakeries, and bread shops sent their delicious aromas into the emerging twilight and through the half-opened windows of my car. I forgot where I was and what I'd become since the days of my youth. No longer was I the man who'd grown to become a football player. Now I felt like a child on the way to my grandparents' apartment. I thought about the dinner that awaited us. I thought of the Mass that would have to be attended first. I thought of my grandfather grabbing me in a headlock and demanding a report of the week's athletic events and how I'd fared in them. I actually began salivating as I would have done, riding with a hungry belly in the backseat of our car.

But differences began to emerge through the nostalgia, the most telling of which was the language adorning the storefronts. I wasn't familiar with it, and no matter how I tried to decipher it, I couldn't figure out its origin or meaning. I couldn't read the Italian signs of my grandfather's neighborhood either, but I knew what language it was when I saw it. These words in Ironbound, on the other hand, left me clueless.

I drove for a while soaking in everything. So this was the real world, I thought. The sidewalks were crowded. It was five o'clock and the sun was down. People were coming home from work. Traffic was picking up. I remained in the neighborhood, circling particular blocks, not wanting to leave. I liked it here. It looked even better with the lights on.

My stomach began to rumble and I knew it was time to eat—and drink. Luckily, there was no shortage of eating establishments. But just what food was being offered was hard to tell. The last thing I wanted was to walk into a place specializing in sheep's liver or yak's tongue, so I kept driving until something looked familiar. And then I saw it.

CAFÉ FÁTIMA the sign read. The words offered no hint of the kind of food being served, but the name was familiar enough. Fátima was a small town in Portugal where three young children had been witness to an apparition of the Virgin Mary. Catholics everywhere honored Our Lady of Fátima with pictures and statues in their homes and churches. I'd sat with the figures of Mary and those three children in the courtyard of my grandfather's home, where I'd watched him lift his wine-filled glass, time and again, to salute the three visionaries and the Virgin herself. Just seeing this name over the door assured me that, if I was to enter any foreign establishment in the heart of this gritty stepcity of Manhattan's, Café Fátima was the place.

It was little more than a corner bar, and the entrance sat flush on the diagonal of the intersection, with two long plate-glass windows hung on either side of the triangle. Both were adorned with the name of the place, and both were so grimy that I couldn't see the interior. I steeled myself before opening the door. If it didn't look right when I walked in, I was walking right back out. That's how you had to be in the real world. Decisive. There was no training table loaded with food waiting for me. Either this place would do or it wouldn't.

Inside, I was greeted by dozens of Giants posters and paraphernalia littering the walls behind the long wooden bar. Strangely, this didn't deter me. Despite yearning for anonymity, my plunge into the real world made these articles seem like old friends. I hopped onto a tall metal barstool, welcoming the sense of security they provided, and took my seat at the well of inebriation. I knew the place had to be frequented by Giants fans. But I wasn't overly concerned with being recognized. I wouldn't know anyone here, and most people only knew my face when it was under a helmet. Regardless, I kept my sight focused on the bar and avoided eye contact with the handful of patrons beside me.

In the past, being recognized could mean anything from having to sign an autograph to having to sit through a recount of the entire season, including a breakdown of my performance in every game. Autographs I didn't mind, but report cards from fans weren't always punctuated with gold stars.

Even more disconcerting were the fans who heaped unwarranted and excessive praise upon me. Who was I to be treated with such overt respect? Why should they buy me a drink when I was making more money in a week than they made in a year? All I did was catch balls and get tackled. They were the ones working jobs and producing for society. Such behavior made me uncomfortable. That's why the Point in Connecticut and the double-burner hot plate in my room were the only places I dined at besides the lunchroom at the stadium.

As the minutes passed, however, I realized that no one in the place seemed the least bit concerned with sports. No televisions blared the latest sports news nor broadcast any heated discussions of our most recent loss. None of the patrons wore Giants attire nor any other NFL apparel. In fact, no one spoke English.

I took the opportunity to sit up and straighten my neck and back. It felt good. I took a long, unhindered look at my surroundings.

Behind me in the dining area were half a dozen small tables, few occupied, scattered throughout the building in no organized manner. Smoke hung over the room like a fog even though only three men at the bar with blackened fingernails were smoking. Each seemed lost in his own glass. They couldn't have cared less about me. Still, I didn't look too long at any one person.

Waitresses supported heavy trays of food and drinks with their skinny arms and slender shoulders. I admired their strength and wondered whether I could do the same without sending the whole pile of ceramics crashing. I doubted that I could and found it amusing that although I was a professional football player earning thousands of dollars a week, I'd have trouble holding down a job paying a couple of bucks an hour, plus tips. But before I could delve too deeply into the subject, I heard the bartender confront me with a question. He didn't address me in English.

"Excuse me, I don't understand," I said as politely as I could.

"Oh, you ain't Portagee?" the bartender asked, making the transition from Portuguese to English as smoothly as my Monte shifted from first to second gear.

"No."

"Don't worry about it," he said good-naturedly. "You just look Portagee, that's all."

I tried to look flattered.

"Whattaya'talyon?" he asked.

"Yeah, I'm Italian."

"Awright close enough." He smiled. "What'll ya have?"

"C.C. on the rocks."

Whenever I was in a strange place, I skipped the manhattans and went right for the whiskey. No chance of getting a lousy drink that way. And when I was drinking straight whiskey, I went for Canadian Club. It was sweeter than VO.

"Here ya go." I watched him glug a quarter of the bottle into the tumbler before me. The glass he poured into was thick and strong and filled to the top with ice. It looked as tough as its surrounding neighborhood. Drops of Canadian Club slid down the outsides of the glass and flowed slowly onto the translucent bar. A small puddle formed and the glass seemed to hover above it. This guy knew how to pour a drink, no question about it. No metered shots for him.

I swished my glass around, encouraging the whiskey to flow in and over the ice cubes. The pool of Canadian Club on the bar widened. Mine was by far the biggest drink on the counter, and I downed a good portion of it as I scanned the memorabilia behind the bar. Helmets, jerseys, chinstraps, mouth guards, sweatbands, cleats, and footballs adorned the cheap paneling. There were posters of most every starter on the offense and defense, past and present, including one of myself, and all were autographed to "My good friend, Manny." I didn't remember signing a poster to anyone named Manny, but I must've signed thousands of those things over the years.

"You got a lot of stuff back there," I said to the bartender, motioning to the back wall.

"Yeah, a friend of mine gives it to me."

"So you're Manny?"

"The one and only."

"Big Giant fan, huh?"

"Not really. Just makes the place look good."

"That's some valuable stuff, ya know," I pointed out.

"Yeah, I know. That's what Red tells me anyway."

"Red?" I said, bracing myself for one of life's strange coincidences.

"Yeah, Red. He works over at the stadium. Comes here all the time. And guess what? He drinks Canadian Club, too. 'Cept most of the time I think he's drunk by the time he gets here."

That's my Red all right. I hid my surprise as best I could, but Manny noticed my shock.

"You know him?"

"Yeah." I hesitated. "Yeah, I know him. We sort of work together."

"Over at the stadium?"

I nodded.

"Them's good jobs if you can get 'em. My brother-in-law was working over there a couple of years ago. He cleaned up after every game. Took him and fifty guys a week to do it. Pickin' up trash, sweeping the aisles, hosin' down the seats. There's eighty thousand of 'em, you know. The pay was decent but the fringe benefits was what he liked. Big football fan, my brother-in-law. Loved the Giants. He said that towards the end of the season the practice field out in the parkin' lot froze over solid. So's they practiced on the artificial grass inside the stadium. Artificial grass! What the hell is that all about? Anyways, my brother-in-law says he was able to watch the whole thing as they cleaned up. Pretty excitin' if you're a Giants fan, I guess."

"He don't work there no more?"

"Nah, the dumb bastard was a drinker. When the team came in to practice, he'd sneak off to the upper tier, grab a seat, pull out a bottle, and watch the guys play like it was a Sunday and he was at a game."

He stopped to laugh. I laughed, too. I used to watch those guys clean up during practice. It did take them all week. They worked their asses off so everyone could trash the place again the next week. I felt sorry for them because I knew they weren't getting paid squat. But the funny thing was, I think I remembered the guy Manny was talking about.

"It wasn't long before they caught him. It was his own fault, though," Manny said. "If he coulda just kept his mouth shut and not cheered and booed like some fan at a game, he woulda got away with it. He loved the Giants as much as his booze, and in the end they both led to his gettin' fired."

I remembered the day they carried that drunken worker out of the stadium. He was yelling obscenities at us for not covering that week's spread.

"What's he doin' now?" I asked.

"Oh, don't worry 'bout him. He's over at the airport loadin' baggage. The pay's decent over there, too. But again, it's the fringe benefits that keep him going."

"Fringe benefits?"

"Yeah. He's loadin' and unloadin' stuff all day, hundreds, maybe thousands, of things. So who's gonna know if one or two bags get *lost,* you know what I mean? One or two out of a thousand ain't bad. That's like a ninety-nine percent success rate or somethin' right?" Manny dried a glass as he talked. "By the way, you don't need no golf clubs or anything, do ya? He's got a great set of Pings, hardly been used, just itchin' to get out on the course."

I shook my head.

"I didn't think so," he said. "You don't look like the golfin' type." He sighed at the lost sale. " 'Nother drink?"

"Sure."

Manny walked away to tend to business, leaving me with my thoughts and another glass of whiskey. He left the bottle. Red. Red. Red. When the hell did he get all this stuff? And our stuff, too. "Filthy animal" stuff. He never asked anyone to sign anything. Hell, he never *talked* to any of us unless he was torturing us over a shoelace. He must've gotten Angelo, his assistant, to do his dirty work. Angelo was always going around the locker room making us sign stuff for this coach, that player, or some friend of the owner's. We all thought that was his job. Autograph boy. Who would've believed that some of that stuff was for Red? Red, who hated and despised us. Red, who couldn't stand to look at us unless he was making us squirm. Who in the world, least of all in the locker room, would think Red was proud enough of us to attach any value to our signatures or likenesses? I drained about half of the C.C.

The place was beginning to fill up. Manny was gone, tending

to the dinner rush. The C.C. was kicking in and my head was glowing. Football was far away. No one had come up to ask for an autograph. No one had volunteered an unwanted opinion on the team. No one had even looked at me once, never mind twice. I was totally invisible.

Only Manny had acknowledged my existence (and probably because as the bartender, he had to). At the moment, I was a regular joe, out on a Tuesday night looking to blow off a little steam after a rough day. I swished the whiskey in my glass and smiled. So this is what life was going to be like without football, I thought. Not bad. Not bad at all. This was turning out to be an all right day. A good one, in fact. The booze was hitting me just right and I was definitely in a good mood. Suddenly, I thought of Emma. I always did when I felt like this.

Without questioning this sudden break in my misery, I decided to call her. I knew I had to hurry before despair clouded over this bright patch of euphoria. I didn't know what I'd say to her. I didn't know if she'd even talk to me. But I knew I'd ignored her long enough. If I hadn't been drinking, I would've realized what a stupid idea this was.

Punching her number into the pay phone by the restrooms, I saw Emma's face in my mind's eye. She was a little out of focus because of the Canadian Club, but she looked beautiful. And so she should. It wasn't that long ago that we'd parted. The season had just begun the last time I'd seen her.

"Dom, we need to talk," she'd said at the beginning of our last conversation. We'd just finished some Chinese takeout in my room at the Regal Motor Court. Excitement was in her voice. I figured it was the MSG.

"Can't right now, honey. I gotta go in for treatment."

"Tonight? You just got back from practice two hours ago."

"I know, but the season opener is this Sunday. I gotta make sure my knee's ready."

"Dom, I've hardly seen you all summer, can't we spend one

night together without football getting in the way? I had something special planned."

"Sorry, hon. Football comes first. Always has. Always will."

"Excuse me?" she said, a bit miffed.

"I didn't mean it that way." I tried to appease her. "But I gotta do everything I can to get ready. You know that."

"You weren't so uptight before last season's opener."

"I wasn't hurt last year. This is the worst injury I've ever had. A lot of people are betting I'm through. If I'm gonna prove 'em wrong, I've gotta make sacrifices. You know I'd love to stay with you tonight. But I *gotta* get treatment. We've gone over this a thousand times. You understand, right?"

She didn't answer. Instead, she asked, "What if those people are right?"

"Right about what?"

"About this being the end of the line."

"Don't talk like that, Emma." I put on my coat.

"I'm serious. What if you're done? What then? Where do we go from here?"

"We?"

"Yes. *We.*"

"I don't know. I can't think about that right now."

"You can't play this silly sport forever. Haven't you *ever* thought about life after football? Haven't you ever thought about *us* after football?"

"No . . . I guess not," I said, thinking about Jimmy waiting for me in the training room.

"We've been together for two years now. We're way past boyfriend-girlfriend. I've given a big part of myself to you. Are you telling me you've never envisioned our future together?"

"I've never envisioned the future, *period.*"

"Never? What the hell *do* you think about?"

"Football," I said honestly.

"Football?"

"Yeah. That's what I get paid to do."

"Football?"

I was getting angry. "What's wrong with that? Don't forget, football was around long before you. And it'll be here long after—"

I caught myself. But much too late.

"I'm sorry," I tried to apologize. "I didn't mean that."

"Please," she said, holding up her hand. "You said exactly what you meant. If there's one thing I've learned about you, it's that you're honest. For good or bad, you're always honest."

"Listen. Let's not have this conversation right now. I want to sit down and talk about things . . . about us, about the future, I really do. You deserve that. But not right now. I got the season opener to worry about."

I braced myself for what I was about to say. I didn't want to say it, but I knew I had to. Her behavior lately had brought me to it.

"Maybe we should slow things down," I said forcefully, as though I were wading into the cold North Atlantic. You had to do it appendage by appendage. Jump right in and you might give yourself a heart attack. "Not permanently, mind you. Just temporarily. I don't know what you'd call it. Something like a vacation, or a break . . . or a, a respite. Yes, that's it! A respite. I think our relationship needs a *respite.* We can resume this conversation about the future, well, sometime in the future."

I spit it out and stood my ground, but I was not at all confident she was buying what I was selling. I wasn't even sure, myself, what I was selling.

"Whatta ya think?" I asked.

Emma stared at the broken clock radio on the bureau. She stared so long, I didn't think she'd ever talk again. Finally, I heard her say softly, to herself, "I can't believe it. I can't believe I've been such an idiot this whole time."

She looked to be carrying on an internal argument. She was calm. Composed, even. But she was angry. Very angry. I almost cowered into a corner when she rose up from her seat. Her look suggested she might scratch my eyes out. But all she did was gather up her things and head toward the door.

"There's champagne on ice in the bathroom sink," she said, as she walked past me. "You and your career have a drink on me. You two make a wonderful couple. I hope you're happy together."

"C'mon, Emma." I reached out to her. "Don't be like that. Look, I'll stay for a few more minutes. Didn't you say you wanted to tell me something?"

"Piss off!"

We hadn't spoken since. I wasn't sure how I would break the ice now. Something clever would have to come from my mouth to prevent her from hanging up on me. But I didn't have anything like that on file, so I flipped the receiver down and retrieved my coin.

Thankfully, I had carried my drink over to the phone with me. As soon as I hung up, I raised the glass to my lips and began pacing back and forth in the cramped hallway, hoping to find the right approach at the bottom of another C.C.

The buzz in my head increased. I recalled last night's conversation with Salvi. He'd had a funny look on his face when I'd brought up Emma. I swear he wanted to tell me something about her. There's no question he'd seen her recently. That he knew where she was and what she'd been doing did not escape me. What that meant, I wasn't sure. But I'd finally swallowed enough courage to pick up the phone again. Only this time, I did so with the nagging question of what it was that he had wanted to tell me.

"Hello?" I heard Emma say.

I froze.

"Hello?" I heard her say again.

My God, I hadn't heard her voice for so long! The sound of it brought tears to my eyes. Come up with something good, I said to myself. Something bright. Something funny. Unfortunately, my wit was lost in a vat of whiskey.

"Hey," I finally managed to spit out, as if I were getting back to her after checking call-waiting.

Real suave, I thought. That should win her back for sure. I waited for a response. This time, *she* paused. I took that as a good sign. At least she recognized my voice. When we first started dating, I'd always say, "Hey, Emma, this is Dominic Fucillo." But after she told me, "You don't have to say your name every time you call," I shortened it to just "Hey" and so did she.

"Hey," she responded after a moment.

"How ya doin'?"

"I'm fine. And you?" Her voice was cold.

"Great," I said halfheartedly.

"Where are you? I can hardly hear you."

"I dunno. Someplace in Newark."

"Are you drunk?" She wasn't asking, she was telling.

"I had a few drinks."

"What do you want?"

"N-nothin'," I stammered. "I just wanted to say hi."

She didn't respond. There was silence for a few moments. Finally, she asked, "Have you seen Salvi lately?"

"Yeah, the other night."

"Did he say anything?"

"About what?"

Visions of infidelity flooded my drunken mind. I knew that's what Salvi wanted to tell me. How could I have not seen it coming? I was so stupid! Emma had found someone else! How long did you think it would take a beautiful girl like her to rebound from a jerk like me? I punched myself in the head with my free hand, but barely felt it. That was not a good sign. A rush of jealousy swept over me. It filled my head and burst from within. This blow I felt all too well.

"What's going on Emma? Are you seeing someone?" I cried, losing control and dignity at the same time. All I could envision was that some guy was sitting beside her right now listening to the conversation. And worse yet, they were sitting on her bed! My stomach tightened in a knot. The green-eyed monster fueled on whiskey reared its ugly head and yelled to her, "Good luck tryin' to find someone as good as me! I'm the best thing that ever happened to you!" My voice cracked.

"Good-bye, Dom," she said, and the line went dead.

I went back to the bar, moist cheeks and all, where Manny, as if having overheard my conversation and reading my mind, had placed another tumbler in front of my still unoccupied seat. I sat back down as if I belonged there and stared at the glass. For the first time that night my vision blurred.

"Punchin' out early, Fucillo? Ha, ha! Get it? Ha, ha, ha!"

Short of some guy walking into the place and shooting me in the head, I couldn't think of anything or anyone that could possibly make my night worse.

"C'mon. You gotta admit that was funny," Red said with a laugh.

I turned slowly from my glass to face him. He was sitting on the stool next to me, drunk as I was. I stared at him in disbelief. How in the hell did he end up in here? A glimpse at the wall behind the bar refreshed my foggy memory.

"Got something in your eye, big guy?" he said derisively.

I hadn't done as good a job as I thought of wiping away my tears. I couldn't speak. I just stared and wondered what terrible thing I'd done to warrant the past seventy-two hours. It had to be the missed Mass. Everything was fine until that catechism slipup. Not only had it caused my current problems, it would probably wind up sending me to hell. Through Red, I thought God was offering a glimpse of what awaited me "down there." Red couldn't have looked more demonic if he'd had horns coming out of his head and was holding a pitchfork. He reveled in my misery as only an evil person could and drooled as he lifted his glass to his lips. We were both drinking C.C., except he had forgone the ice.

"C'mon, Dom, lighten up! We ain't in that dungeon no more. This is my place. This is the real world!"

He was either truly happy to be at the Fátima or truly happy to be away from the stadium. I couldn't figure out which.

"Lemme buy a drink," he slurred.

I continued to stare at him. First in disbelief, then with disdain, and finally in confusion. How had this miserable creature been transformed into such a happy and cheerful human being all of a sudden? Only this morning, he refused to replace one lousy cleat from the bottom of my shoes. Now he was offering to buy me a drink? The drink cost $4 and came directly from his wallet. The cleat didn't cost him a dime, and there were enough of them in his equipment room to provide traction for every Pop Warner team on the East Coast.

"I don't get you," I slurred right back at him. "What the hell is up with you? Where did you come from? Why are you here? What are you doing in *my* life, for crissakes? I just want to sit here and get drunk. Alone!"

I swallowed the remainder of my drink and held the empty glass up to Manny for another. The expression on Red's face didn't change at all. He still wore the same grin from his opening sentence.

"You wanna know what I heard about Moze?" he asked mischievously.

He could have said or done anything else and I would've ignored him. But when he brought up Moze, I turned back to face him.

"What could you possibly know about Moze?"

"Oh, ya talkin' to me *now,* are ya? What happened to all that 'leave me alone' stuff?"

I'd had a feeling he'd do that. "Screw you, Red. D'you hear something about Moze or not?"

"Maybe." He knew he had me, and he was making me squirm. One of his favorite pastimes. "First tell me why you was cryin'."

"I wasn't cryin', you jag-off," I shot back. "But if you don't tell me what you know about Moze, *you* will be."

"Awwwright," he said mockingly. "Calm down, animal."

Manny brought my drink. He brought Red one, as well.

"So you found each other," Manny said. "That's nice. Two coworkers out for an evenin' nightcap. Warms a man's heart to see such a thing."

The bartender's appearance changed Red's disposition in an instant. It must have dawned on him that I'd been there for quite some time and that Manny and I had been talking. I pounced on the opportunity as if it were a loose ball.

"Yeah, Manny, Red's the greatest," I said. "Everyone at the stadium loves him, especially the players. Ain't that right, Red?"

Red took a sip of his drink.

"Aww, Red don't have to blow his own horn in here. We all know how he rose up in the ranks over there. Look at the stuff on the wall. They wouldn't a give it to him if he was some miserable bastard. Right?"

"Absolutely," I said, disguising my sarcasm. Red detected it anyway. "You know, Red. You should bring some of those guys down here. They'd love it! They'd especially love to see how good all their stuff looks up on the wall."

Red lowered his face into his glass. He looked like a man exposed.

"Yeah," Manny chimed in. "You should do that, Red. Bring in some of the fellas! It'd be great for business."

Red was squirming now. He'd gone from obnoxious drunk to sullen fraud in a matter of seconds. There were a million things I would have liked to tell Manny about the Red we all knew from the Meadowlands. But I said nothing. It wasn't *my* place, it was Red's. I didn't belong here. He did. I might not have liked him all that much, but I wasn't cruel. Look at him, I thought. He's drunker than me. Manny was called away before Red or I had to say anything to keep the conversation alive.

"Thanks for not sayin' anything."

"Thanks for hidin' my playbook the other night."

We both sipped our drinks. It was as if he had suddenly become a real person. With all the booze flowing in my veins, I began to look at Red the way Manny presumed everyone at the stadium did. Why couldn't he be a good guy? I thought. Why did everyone hate him?

Red turned to me suddenly, as if reading my mind. Moving his drink from his lips, he said softly, "You know, no one ever said 'Thank you' to me. Not one time in over thirty years. *Not ever.*"

I blushed. The thought of saying thank-you to Red had never entered my mind. I suddenly felt sorry for him. All I'd ever thought about was how miserable he'd made *my* life. I guess I never really thought about how miserable I'd made *his.*

Maybe I should have said "Sorry" or "Thank you" at that moment, but I didn't. It would have seemed phony. Besides, I don't think he was looking for that. I think he was just telling it like it was.

"Do you really know somethin' about Moze?" I asked, breaking the uneasy silence between us. Red snapped out of his self-pity and welcomed the opportunity to focus on someone else's misfortune.

"He's in some *deeeep* shit," Red said in a low tone but with a smile back on his face. The way he said it made me nervous. You could tell he enjoyed being the bearer of bad news.

"What's going on?"

Red sipped his drink and made me wait. He had returned to his old self. My sympathy for him was gone. Not wanting to give him the satisfaction of seeing me hunger for gossip, I waited patiently. I knew he knew something. I also knew that he was so drunk that he'd tell it to me eventually.

"Let's just say that not only are his playing days numbered, but so are his living days."

"What are you talking about?" I asked, shocked into near-sobriety. Moze was our *defense*! "He's in his prime. His career's nowhere near over. And whatta ya mean 'his living days'?"

"I mean just what I said. His 'livin' days.' He's a walkin' dead man."

Red took another swig. I looked at him, trying to figure out if it was just the whiskey talking.

"You know Sammy Penrod?" he asked finally.

"Yeah. He's the guy who's always hanging around outside the locker room, having them big tailgaters in the parking lot and showin' up at all the charity fund-raisers the Giants have. He hosts that big golf tournament every year that I never go to. He's in insurance or somethin', right?"

"Yeah. He owns about thirty offices from here all the way up to New Hampshire."

"New Hampshire?"

"Yeah. He's from up there to begin with. He just comes down here cuz of the Giants."

"Sounds like a nut job to me."

"Well, that nut job is worth millions."

"Wow, I didn't know that. But what's he got to do with Moze?" I asked, not sure I really wanted to hear the answer.

"Moze plays full speed all the time. You know that. That means off the field, too. He can't go many places around here without everyone knowin' who he is. And the places he likes to go to and the things he likes to do ain't exactly what *respekabull* people prefer. Moze's reputation ain't exactly stellar, but he still don't want to bury himself with negative publicity. So's to avoid anything like that, he has someone else do most of his dirty work for him."

"Sammy Penrod."

"Exactly. Sammy's got all the connections. He's a shady guy. Just look at his business. Insurance, right?"

"Riggght," I answered, as if that meant something, which in my drunken head then it seemed to. "Waaait a minute. Why does

Sammy do Moze's dirty work? I mean, if the guy's worth millions, what in the world could he possibly get in return from Moze?"

"What does any jock-sniffin', wide-eyed fan get in return from befriending a player? An 'in.' A feeling of power! If they're providing the player with something he wants, or *needs,* there's a sense of ownership there, like he's staked out a claim or bought a piece of property. Any praise or adulation that's heaped on the athlete is heaped upon him as well. These kind of people can't just stand back and enjoy the sport. They have to own it. They have to corrupt it. They have to drag it down to their level."

"Jeez, Red. You sound like you almost respect the players."

"I used to. But not anymore. You guys are a bunch of showmen nowadays, seeing who can get their mug on television the most, running around crying poverty because they're only making a million dollars a year, and selling themselves to the highest bidder who'll tend to them like a servant. No one lifts a finger to help themselves anymore. I used to wash the uniforms of men. Now I wipe the asses of children. I still respect the sport, though. Football's a great game. But money's been ruinin' it. The more money comes into it, the more you see guys like Sammy Penrod. A guy like him says he hangs around because he loves football. Bullshit! I say he hates it. It's too good, and he's too rotten. He can't stand to see somethin' so good. It drives him crazy. So what's he do? He latches onto Moze, finds his weak spots, and digs in. Sammy's a spider and he's got Moze in his web. Moze can wriggle all he wants, but he ain't going nowhere. His time ain't up yet. The price for freedom is too expensive, and Moze can't afford it right now."

"Whatta ya mean, expensive?"

"You seen Moze this mornin' in the car, didn't ya?"

"Yeah." The bloody scene in the parking lot came back to me in all its horror.

"Like I said, expensive."

Red finished his drink and ordered us two more. I remembered him saying after our meeting with Lou that the only reason

Moze wasn't dead was because his debt wasn't paid in full. I got the shivers thinking that what I'd seen this morning was only a down payment.

"Red, are you sayin' Sammy done this to Moze?"

Red laughed at my question. "Sammy?! That piece a scum? He couldn't beat his way through an insurance form! Nah. He didn't do it himself, but you can be sure he's behind it."

My head was swimming and it wasn't from the whiskey. The conversation with Red had turned so intense that I didn't realize how hard I'd been staring at him until I had to peel my eyes from his as if they were two pieces of meshed Velcro. I almost forgot where I was. The dinner crowd had come and gone and the drinking crowd had moved on as well. It was a weeknight. All who remained were Red and me and a few alcoholics who couldn't let go of the bar. I'd come here to forget my problems and to get drunk. I'd certainly succeeded. My problems were the furthest things from my mind, and I was well past drunk. The clock on the wall read one o'clock. I had to sober up. So I ordered a light beer on ice. Manny brought it right away. It was cold and refreshing and cleared my head. Red came back into focus, as did our conversation.

It was obvious that Moze was mixed up in something bad, but I doubted it was as serious as Red was claiming. It couldn't be. He was being melodramatic, like an adult telling a child a ghost story. He said that's how he viewed us players: as children. I figured he was exaggerating circumstances to impress some life lesson upon me. However, the sight of Moze in his car this morning had not been exaggerated. The more I thought about that scene, the more I took Red's words to heart. Something had to be done.

"What can we do about it?" I asked Red.

"We?" he said incredulously. "Do about what?"

"About Moze! We can't just sit here and do nothin'!"

"Why not! What do we owe James Moze?"

Nothing that I could think of. Maybe Red was right. But my whiskey rage was going full force.

"C'mon, Red! He's my teammate!"

"I've done enough for him as it is" was all Red said.

"What have you ever done for him?" I asked skeptically.

"Nothing. Forget about it."

"C'mon, Red. Whatta ya mean?"

Red wiped his face with his hands and turned squarely to face me. "I've been pissin' in a cup for him for the last few years so's he wouldn't flunk his goddamn drug test. That's what I mean!"

Red looked sorry as soon as he'd said it. I didn't believe him, though. Those tests were too well monitored.

"Bullshit," I said. "There's no way you could do that without someone seeing."

"Who's gonna *see* anything when Lou *himself* hands me the cup and says, 'Fill it!' like I'm some kinda *piss boy*? And if I don't do it, guess who loses his job?"

"What?"

"You heard me."

I couldn't believe it. I knew Lou would do practically anything for Moze, but I always thought there were *some* limits. Red turned back toward the bar. I saw shame on his face. Maybe it was true. Moze had never flunked an NFL drug test despite being a known drug user. The incongruity had never hit me before. I was stunned.

"You really did that?"

"Forget it, I said."

Red ordered another drink. I sipped my beer and chewed on some ice chips. This was obviously a secret he'd never shared with anyone else. I didn't blame him. I'd no desire to dwell on the subject, so after a minute I attempted to change it.

"Getting back to Sammy Penrod . . ."

"Look, Dom," Red said softly, "Moze is a grown man. This is the life *he* chose. These are the people *he* wants to live it with."

"But . . ."

"But nothing. I've got my own problems and so do you. Moze is on his own as far as I'm concerned."

Red spoke with finality. But I wouldn't let the matter drop so easily. After an hour and a half of cat and mouse, he finally gave me a clue suggesting a course of action. It wasn't obvious, though. And if I hadn't sobered up on the beer, I might've missed it altogether.

"You're gonna see Salvi again, aren't ya?"

Fourteen

I headed for home on the empty roads of New Jersey. The absence of traffic made navigation easy. Within minutes, I was back in the Meadowlands. Although it had taken me over an hour to get to the Café Fátima, I discovered I was only five miles from the stadium. I laughed at my pitiful foray into the real world.

After some coffee and breakfast at an all-night diner, I drove directly to the stadium. Instead of returning to my room, I decided to sleep in my car until Red opened the locker room. The Canadian Club was wearing off and my head pounded fast from the caffeine. Depression set in after the whiskey high, and not even the sight of the approaching stadium brought me comfort.

The sport I loved so much had been exposed. Red had shone a light on it, and now its flaws were apparent. Sure, it was still running. But for how much longer? And come the day it broke down completely, how much damage would I suffer? How much damage might I inflict on innocent bystanders? Football, for me, was now tainted. I wanted to stay on the highway and keep driving, away from the broken-down wreck and everyone connected to it.

I did just that. Speeding past the stadium exit, I kept going on the New Jersey Turnpike. I was so flustered, I didn't know if I was heading north or south. But no sooner did I accelerate than I felt the tug of my master pull the collar around my neck and order me to heel. As if a bungee cord were pulling me tight, I braked, pulled into the breakdown lane, and went back to the only exit I really knew.

Whom was I fooling? I had nowhere else to go. Besides, what would I do if I ever got there (wherever "there" was)? I wasn't strong enough to survive without football. Not yet, anyway.

The exit ramp ended at the entrance to the parking lot. I stopped and stared at the open expanse. I didn't want to go in, but I didn't want to stay out. I didn't know what to do. Finally, a little voice in my head told me to step on the accelerator. Without hesitating, I stomped on the pedal as hard as I could. I thought my foot might go through the floor. Within seconds, the old Monte was shaking like an amusement-park thrill ride, and the speedometer needle pointed to numbers it had never before seen.

The concrete tollbooths guarding the lot came quickly into view. Tonight, they looked more solid than ever, and with my traveling at such high speeds, the gaps between them seemed impassable. Strangely, I didn't care. Whether I crashed or not made no difference to me.

I gripped the steering wheel calmly and braced for a possible collision. The barriers came up into my grill and I closed my eyes. In a flash, the booths were behind me and the surrounding swamp came fast on the horizon. It took all my skills to hold the Monte together and keep it from rocketing off the asphalt and into the reeds of the meadows.

My ears popped when I flew through the booths. Adrenaline had followed. And laughter now filled the car. I was exhilarated. That I hadn't plastered myself onto the concrete walls of the toll-booths pleased me. It proved that despite my problems I was glad to be alive. That in itself was a joyous discovery.

Almost instantly, I thought of Moze. Perhaps this was how he felt every night. Perhaps this was how he kept himself going, by infusing a jolt of life-bolstering adrenaline into his brain at the risk of ending it all with a simple slip of the wheel.

My breath was short. My heart pounded. I looked up into the black sky and caught sight of a shooting star.

After a lifetime's worth of dreams, I woke up in the front seat of my car. Some had been about Salvi, some about Red, some about Sammy. But most had involved Emma, and when I opened my eyes, I wasn't surprised to feel a tear running down my cheek. How had it come to this? I wondered. Why wouldn't she carry on a conversation with me over the phone? What had happened to the love we had shared?

I had needed to focus on my job. She knew that. It was imperative that I rehabbed my injured knee during the off-season. Why couldn't she understand that? And what was all the marriage talk about? One day she was the carefree girl I'd met at Salvi's; the next, she was trying to henpeck me into submission. I wasn't ready for *that,* not by a long shot. I'd seen guys come back from their honeymoons, happy and content, healthier-looking. But there was always something different about them. Something missing from their game, something gone from their eyes. They were never the same players they'd been in their prenuptial days. I refused to compromise my commitment to the game and to my teammates, and especially to Lou.

For the most part, I'd been successful. I'd overcome my knee injury and proved I could still play. I was an integral part of a winning team. But what had I lost along the way? Apparently, I'd achieved my victory at the expense of the only person I ever wanted to share it with. And after Dr. Bedrosian's revelation about my new affliction, the hollowness rang louder than ever. I was going to lose my career regardless. And I'd be left to endure its fallout in the circumstances wrought by my own hand, totally and utterly alone.

That's how I found myself this morning after my night with Red at the Café Fátima. Instead of resting peacefully in the arms of my loving Emma, I was utterly alone in the front seat of my car, cold and dirty, in the middle of a deserted parking lot, in the middle of a deserted wasteland.

If it weren't for Red tapping on my window, I might've sat there for hours staring into space. But the sound made me jump and forced me to face the day. Emerging from the car, a wave of nausea hit me. I stretched my stiffened body and yawned in the dull sunlight shooting out from behind the Empire State Building across the river. Red had already driven his bags of bagels and doughnuts down the ramp and into the stadium, and I was alone again in the parking lot. His waking me took me by surprise. I wondered if he'd known all along of my presence during these early-morning hours. Lately, I was learning that he knew a lot about a lot of things.

The nausea soon passed. So did the stiffness. Despite a headache, I didn't feel all that bad. I must've drank so much and slept so little that my body hadn't had the chance to develop a hangover yet. Undressing in front of my locker, I could still feel the booze flowing in my veins.

Surprisingly, no one mentioned my little outburst at practice the day before. I thought Lou would've taken his frustrations with me out on the rest of the troops by putting them through the meat grinder. But from what Jimmy told me, he'd actually lowered the intensity level after my departure, and practice had ended at near walk-through speed. Perhaps Lou sensed that I wasn't the only one on the verge, and that everybody needed a little break from "the routine." After all, that routine *was* the precursor to one of our few losses that season.

Lou was as superstitious as anyone else on the team. His office was proof of that. Alongside his crucifix and mounted Bible verses were right-side-up horseshoes and statues of elephants with their trunks pointed toward the sky. On the field, if we began a Tuesday practice session on the twenty-yard line and won the game on Sunday, practice would begin on the same spot the following Tuesday. If we lost, practice would begin anywhere *but* that spot. Practices would never vary from the previous week if we were coming off a win. But if we'd lost, there would be a mishmash of random drills and meetings as Lou tried to avoid repeating any action from the week before that might have been responsible for our losing. In Lou's mind, it wasn't so much what happened on Sunday that determined our success, but what happened during the *week*.

The day passed quickly under this new laid-back regime. Bobby Ward coasted along in cruise control, facial scars and all, apparently not forgetting the lesson I'd impressed upon him yesterday. Even Ramsey was happier than normal. So happy, in fact, that I thought he might even speak to Midland during our stretching period. I was mistaken, of course. But the day turned out to be a good one, nonetheless. I wasn't sure what was responsible for my good showing at practice, but whatever it was, I was tempted to conduct a repeat performance of last night, tonight and every night, until I found out.

But I was headed to only one place after practice today. Salvi's. What Red had told me about Moze and Sammy had been gnawing at me all day. So was my pathetic phone conversation with Emma. It was time to break my golden rule of ignorance and start asking some questions. But before I could hit the turnpike in search of explanations and information, I needed to do one more thing.

It was time to squat. This leg exercise was the most important weight-lift we did. It was also the most painful. Paulie was constantly admonishing us to go heavier and deeper. "Lower!" he'd scream. "Get those knees past parallel!" We could never put enough weight on the bar for Paulie or go low enough to satisfy him. But one guy could, our pass-rushing specialist, Charles Rosen. And that's who strode into the weight room as I finished my last repetition.

The big defensive end walked across the floor wearing a weight belt and a pair of sneakers. My legs burned and quivered like jelly, but I made sure to give him a wide berth since that's all he wore. It was a familiar scene, one that had been occurring for eight years. This particular moment was Charles Rosen's pregame ritual. Squatting naked was his superstition.

"Lower!" Paulie screamed as Charles took his place under the iron bar and began moving up and down. "Get those knees past parallel!"

Charles huffed and puffed. Veins on his forehead (and other areas of his body I should not have seen) bulged and trembled.

"*You . . . know . . . when . . . you're . . . low . . . enough?*" he grunted in between reps.

"When?" Paulie shouted on cue.

"When your balls hit the floor!"

According to Charles, laying his balls on the dusty rubber matting of the weight-room floor, while holding six hundred pounds of iron on the back of his neck, helped him play better. Who was I to judge? Sure, it was a strange superstition, but it was effective. Charles was our best pass rusher. As disturbing as it was to see him squat naked, it would have been more disturbing if he hadn't. We needed him to play his best. As soon as my quad muscles could function without collapsing, I left the weight room, comforted by the knowledge that the big defensive end was due for at least one or two sacks on game day.

Fifteen

The traffic on I-95 was horrendous. I was going nowhere fast. My Monte Carlo sat idling on the upper deck of the George Washington Bridge and reeled against the wind gusting down the Hudson River Valley. I put the car into park and leaned back to endure the delay. I felt I could hear and see every crack and flaw the bridge had incurred throughout its long history, the biggest among them being the lack of foresight for the future population of automobiles.

Even with two separate levels and six lanes going each way, the bridge was unable to handle the flow of traffic every morning and evening during the peak commuting hours. At the moment, it was little more than a parking lot, which left me thankful that I didn't have to subject myself to such a commute every day, week after week.

While sitting behind the wheel of my car usually brought

me comfort, being stuck in this kind of traffic brought me nothing but misery. Wherever my fellow travelers were going to, or coming from, the journey over this bridge was like running a gauntlet. A ride of thirty, twenty, or even ten miles could take as long as two hours this time of day if the bridge was a part of it.

And that's exactly how long it took me and dozens of other exasperated commuters to reach Salvi's exit. Sitting at the light at the end of the off-ramp, I looked at the bedraggled men and women in the vehicles beside me. They looked as if they'd just completed a day of double sessions with sprints thrown in at the end. Most of the men wore shirts and ties, the latter hanging loosely from their necks, like leashes to which they were bound. How did they do it? I wondered. Every day the same thing. Every week the same thing. Every year the same thing! I got claustrophobic just thinking about it. Still, next year this could be me. I shuddered, contemplating the possibility of impending reality. The thought of it made the tie of the fellow traveler to my right look less like a leash and more like a hangman's noose. Feeling entrapped, I stared at the red light above me, willing it to turn green. When it did, I stomped on the gas to escape this prophetic vision, and as I flew through the intersection, my speeding car nearly collided with another.

I hadn't seen the Buick crossing in front of me. It must have been pushing the tail end of its own yellow light. The near collision snapped me out of my trance like an ammonia capsule under my nose and set my heart racing. Like any good driver, I wasted no time in looking back at the LeSabre to signal with a single finger my displeasure at his driving skills, while shooting a glare of indignation that bellowed, "How dare you drive in front of me when I'm not looking!"

But the driver of the Buick had his eyes front so that my icy stares went unnoticed. At least his passenger wasn't oblivious. If I couldn't intimidate the driver, maybe I could scare his girlfriend. That was better than nothing. But if my heart was racing from the near miss, it raced even faster when I saw who was sitting in the passenger seat.

Emma!

What was she doing in that car? Whom was she with? Where were they going? And then just like the light I'd been sitting at turning green, a lightbulb of my own clicked on inside my head. Salvi! She must've been at the Point visiting with Salvi.

So he *had* seen her. I *knew* he had! And now it was certain that he'd known all along what she'd been up to. But who was that in the car with her? The "other" guy, perhaps? I wanted to go after them and beat the driver beyond recognition. But what would that have gotten me other than a lawsuit? It wouldn't have won Emma back, that's for sure. Besides, the car was gone now, indistinguishable from the dozens of other cars surrounding me.

A Buick LeSabre, huh? A reliable car. Conservative. Dependable. Certainly nothing to turn anyone's head. But good quality. The kind that would always be there when you needed it. The kind that never let you down. So, she'd finally found what she was looking for. A Buick of a man.

I couldn't argue with her choice. She deserved that, after all. But these noble thoughts brought me little comfort. In a flash, I was back at the Café Fátima, clutching the phone after Emma had hung up on me, fighting back tears of drunken sorrow and regret. Only now I wasn't drunk. There was no anesthetizing effect of the alcohol. Every twinge of pain hit home. It was the first time I'd ever stood in Salvi's parking lot, awash in the tantalizing aroma spilling forth from the Point, and felt not one pang of hunger, not one longing for an ice-cold manhattan, nor even one ounce of hopeful anticipation that Emma might be inside waiting for me.

Instead, I was on the verge of a breakdown. But to do it in the presence of Salvi, a man who'd hardly shed a tear at the sight of his missing leg, would have been tantamount to forfeiting all claims to the manhood I'd worked so hard to achieve.

Besides, too many people were coming in and out of the

restaurant with whom I had to exchange pleasantries. It was game time. I needed a game face to go with it. So I managed to wipe the agony off my mug and keep from collapsing.

One acquaintance in particular quelled my misery for the moment and replaced it instead with a strange mixture of shock and curiosity. The mere sight of this man brought me strength, the vindictive kind, and made me forget all about my heartbreak.

"Hey, Dom," Sammy Penrod said. "Whatta you doin' here on a Wednesday?"

I eyed him suspiciously. Thank God I didn't break down, I kept thinking. It would've hurt me if he had seen me in distress. As I said, I never liked the guy before, but now I harbored an intense repugnance toward him that bordered on all-out hatred.

"I come when I wanna come," I said.

"Don't get huffy," he answered. "I just haven't seen you here on a Wednesday night since you were nailin' that broad you used to go with."

It took all my restraint to maintain my composure. "Speakin' of not seein' me on a Wednesday night, whatta *you* doin' here? I didn't know you *ever* came here."

"I don't. I wouldn't eat this slop if Salvi handed it out for free. I stop in occasionally to see the old man, but believe me, four-star restaurants in Manhattan are the only places worth my time."

I believed him. The way he dressed and the way he was groomed told the world that he had nothing but the finest taste. Unfortunately, his tastes drifted toward the preppy, and his hairdo flirted with the disco era. He always sported a pair of loafers, no socks, green or navy-blue chinos, a Polo golf shirt, and a cashmere sweater thrown over his shoulders with the arms tied in a knot around his neck. A pair of Ray-Bans adorned his head, while the black cord hung off the back of his neck like a piece of jewelry. His hair was blow-dried, giving the impression that he'd just stepped off his yacht after an invigorating day of sailing. But in this premature winter weather, he looked more annoyingly preppy than ever. His loafers had been replaced with rubberized duck shoes, and his sweater exchanged for the newest L.L. Bean hooded parka. The sunglasses still sat unused upon his head, and his hair still looked as though he'd been in a headwind. I wondered why anyone in the world, never mind in the locker room, would want to associate with such a dork.

"I'm aware of your dislike for me, though I'm not sure why," he said, as if reading my mind. "You offend me by your repeated absence at my golf tournaments and your refusal to break bread with me at my postgame tailgaters. But that's all right. You do what you have to. I respect that. And your attitude towards me lessens not in the least my opinion of your abilities on the field. I wasn't sure that Lou knew what he was doing when he drafted you, but that's why he's the coach and I'm not. I want you to know that I think you've developed into a fine player over the years. I'm glad that you're part of our team."

If he knew why I didn't like him, he might've thought twice about speaking to me like that. Before I learned about the dark side of Sammy that Red had revealed, I'd always disliked him because of his misguided notion that he was a part of the Giants organization. I knew he contributed heavily to the team charities, that he wined and dined the coaches and the front-office staff, as well as the players. I knew he'd been around a lot longer than me, and that like Red he'd be around long after I was gone. But he'd bought his way into these inner circles, and that made me respect him even less.

"Whatta ya mean, *your* team?" I asked. "You got no say in what goes on with the Giants."

Sammy's feathers ruffled a bit, but he held himself together. "I have a lot more say than you might think," he said cryptically.

"Bullshit."

"Oh, yeah? You're not the only one to underestimate me, lately."

"Believe me, Sammy, I don't think I could ever underestimate you."

"Listen," Sammy said, returning to his syrupy self. "I don't know why we never hit it off, but all I want is to be friends. I really do. I could've made your time with us so enjoyable, and I know I still can. Why don't you come into the city with me right now? I'm having dinner at Lutèce. While we're there, we could get to know each other better. In fact, I believe you'll find we can be of great service to one another. Quit wasting time at this . . . this *pizza joint* and come with me. The game's passed by guys like Salvi. I'm where it's at now. I could unlock the future of your dreams."

He looked directly into my eyes as he talked. If I thought I had a future in the sport, I might've listened more attentively. As it was, I was overcome with the impulse to shout, "Get thee behind me, Satan!" But instead, I looked at him coolly and said, "In your dreams, dork."

Then I strode right by him, jostling him as I did. His Ray-Bans fell from his head and were saved from a trip to the parking-lot cement by the cord that hung around his neck. Too bad the glasses didn't weigh a hundred pounds, I thought.

"The scouting reports were right about you," he said admiringly. "You do have an attitude problem. Just remember, I'll be around here a lot longer than you will, and if you were smart, you'd start thinking about joining *my* team. All the people that matter already have."

"Keep talkin'," I said, as I made my way to the door of the Point. "That's about all you're good at."

Laughing confidently, Sammy got into his Jaguar and drove toward I-95 south. His personalized license plate read JINTZ-1 and I noticed the number 98 etched in detail onto the rear of his trunk. Ninety-eight was James Moze's number.

As he exited the parking lot, I turned my thoughts toward Salvi. The Point was crowded. Despite the commotion of the substantial dinner crowd, Salvi noticed my entrance right away. He looked surprised to see me.

"D-Dom! What are you doin' here? It's, uh, it's Wednesday," he said, looking at an imaginary calendar in his head.

His nervousness gave me strength. He couldn't have been caught more unaware if I'd walked through the door bare-assed like Charles Rosen walking into the weight room. My broken heart was temporarily forgotten. Tonight, I would settle for nothing less than complete answers for all the questions swimming in my brain.

"I felt like takin' a ride," I said coolly. "Nothin' wrong with that, is there?"

He shook his head.

"And I couldn't think of anyone else I'd rather see than my old friend Salvi."

He smiled faintly.

"You are my old friend, aren't cha?" I asked slyly.

"Of course! Siddown and take a load off."

I pulled up a stool while he went into the kitchen to order my meal. His son Frank plopped down a caramel-colored manhattan in front of me with two cherries floating on top.

"How'd ya know?" I said sarcastically.

"You looked like you needed one," Frank said. "Besides, when do you come in here and not have one?"

"Frank?"

"Yeah?"

"Was Emma just in here?"

I watched his hand as he poured.

"Who?"

"Emma. You remember her, don't cha? My old girlfriend."

"Oh, yeah," he said as if suddenly remembering her. "Cute girl. Nahh, she hasn't been here for a long time. As a matter of fact, the last time she was in here was with you."

"You sure?"

"Positive."

I would've believed him if he hadn't spilled a few glugs of whiskey on the bar as he poured.

"A little shaky there, Frank?"

Frank was never one to waste alcohol, under any circumstances. "Rough night last night, that's all."

"I bet."

I enjoyed my drink as best I could. Frank obviously knew something, but he wasn't about to open up. I knew it was useless trying to pry it out of him. Salvi had trained his boys well. They could do a lot of things that might bring dishonor to the family, but being a rat wasn't one of them.

Salvi returned from the kitchen and sat down next to me. The place was packed as usual with a lot of the regulars. We sat and drank while we waited for our food, and as we did, Salvi conversed with the patrons who made their way over to pay their respects and maybe ask a question or two of me about the Giants. We spent the next few hours saying hello to this guy or that family, signing a few autographs, taking a few pictures.

That was the problem with being a semi-public-figure. I couldn't mope around like the miserable bastard I was without a lot of people asking what was wrong. That's what I liked about the Café Fátima the other night. No one knew who I was and nobody wanted to know. I was just another suffering prick trying to cope with life. Nothing they hadn't seen before. But in the Point, I couldn't sneeze without twenty guys saying "God bless you" and another twenty asking me if my game was going to be affected because of it. If I had trudged into this place and slumped forlornly over my cacciatore, I would have been a spectacle. I had no choice but to put on a smile, answer every question, offer my insights, and try to enjoy my meal.

The evening wore on, and before long the last of Salvi's patrons were heading home. The place was quiet, and Salvi and I sat together at the bar. Frank and his brothers were closing up the place and making preparations for tomorrow's lunch crowd.

I hadn't had a chance to talk to Salvi alone. Someone else had always been around, and the conversation had consisted of only Giants talk or current events. Salvi had hardly looked me in the eye all night, and not once had his conversation been directed solely toward me. When Frank flipped the OPEN sign on the front door over to read CLOSED, and we were left with no further distractions, a distinct silence fell between us.

I had known Salvi long enough to recognize the kind of silence that wouldn't be breached. So I let it linger as I sipped on my drink and formulated my approach to chip into this rock of a man.

"Salvi," I said after a few moments, "why was Sammy Penrod here?"

"How'dju know he was here?" he asked, surprised.

"I saw him in the parkin' lot when I was comin' in."

"Oh," he said, almost in relief. "Nothin' important, just some insurance business I have with him. I bought a couple of policies from his company a few years ago, and he comes in every once in a while to update me on them."

"Can't he do that over the phone?"

"Sure. But he's always travelin' right by the place. So he stops in every now and then. Whatsamatta, you got a problem wi'dat?"

"No, I just don't like him, that's all."

"Well, good for you, cuz I don't like him either. If I didn't have these, ahhh . . . policies with him, I wouldn't talk to him at all. And you'd be best off if you did likewise."

Good, I thought. It showed me that he and Sammy weren't in cahoots with one another. I wanted to pursue the subject further, but I had more pressing issues on my mind. I said, "What the hell's goin' on with Emma?"

"Beats me." He sipped on his beer as though I were speaking rhetorically. "Why don't you call her?"

"I did."

That got his attention. He actually put down his drink and faced me.

"Well, what happened?"

"She told me to go fuck myself."

"She said that?"

"Well, no. Not in so many words. But that was basically the gist of her message."

"What did you do to make her say something like that?"

"I didn't do anything! I just asked how she was doin', and she freaked out on me!"

Okay, so I exaggerated a little.

"That's all she said to you? She didn't say anything else?"

"Nothin' . . .'cept was I drunk or not."

"Were you?"

"Why, you gonna give me a lecture on drinking?"

He looked at me with fire in his eyes but knew he was the last person who should criticize anyone for drinking. "That's all she said to you? She didn't *say anything else*?"

I was beginning to see a pattern forming. "You know, it's funny you keep saying that, cuz that's exactly what she wanted to know about you: whether or not you *said anything* to me."

I looked him straight in the eye. "There seems to be a couple of people I know who are very interested in whether either one *said anything* to me recently. Just what exactly do you suppose everyone's so concerned about my hearing?"

I waited for an answer. I waited for a lie. I waited for him to say anything. But he just sat and sipped his beer. Finally, I had to resume the conversation as if I were talking to myself.

"Salvi," I said almost pleading now, "what is it that I'm not supposed to know? Is there someone else? Has she found a new guy? Do you know or not? C'mon, tell me. I can take it."

So far, Emma's affair was something made up in my mind. Even though I'd seen her in the LeSabre, how did I know whom she was with? But if Salvi told me that my suspicions were correct, that she was indeed going around with someone else, well, then, I'd have to face reality. I'd have to admit she was no longer mine. And that, I wasn't ready to handle quite as bravely as I was claiming to.

He kept sipping his beer. He was in one of those you'll-never-make-me-talk modes that I'd seen before. I knew it was hopeless when he was like this, but I waited a few more minutes anyway before giving up and turning away.

I lowered my head in defeat. It was the first time that evening that I felt the booze. I'd lost track of how many I'd had, and for no good reason the drink in front of me suddenly looked unappealing. It was late. I had to leave soon. It was time to start sobering up. I went behind the bar to pour myself a cup of coffee. I needed a little pick-me-up before hitting the road.

Salvi sat still, staring at nothing in particular. I knew he was deep in thought because he didn't say anything as I poured. Normally, he wouldn't allow me to do such a thing for myself. I walked back with my filled mug and resumed my place at the bar.

"Call her again," he said softly.

"What?" I heard him, I just wanted him to repeat himself.

"Call her again. And this time make sure you're sober."

"C'mon, Salvi, cut the shit! What's goin' on?"

"Just call her again."

Frank came over to have a nightcap with us after he'd finished closing up. No one was here but us three. This was the time I loved most. Relaxing in an establishment at the most unconventional hour. You couldn't do this just anywhere or with just anyone. You had to be in the right place and you had to know the right people. At times like these I realized what I liked most about playing football. It wasn't the glory or the fame or the girls or even the money. It was how life could taste so good sometimes, especially after chewing on a day's worth of pigskin.

"Hey, Dad, d'you hear about Joey Delucca?" Frank said to Salvi, who just stared at him in silence.

"What happened to Joey Delucca?" I asked Frank.

"Joey Delucca runs a big book out of South Norwalk and—"

Salvi cut him off with a look that suggested he'd already said too much. But seeing that it was already out there, Salvi felt obligated to relate the facts according to himself, which, at the Point, was the only way that facts were ever related.

"And he picked up the tab for the whole lunch crowd today," Salvi said, finishing what Frank had started.

"How much did it cost?" I asked.

"Around three grand."

"That's an expensive lunch."

"Not when ya clean some dumb fuck outta three *hundred* grand!" Frank said.

"Three hundred thousand dollars?"

Salvi nodded, unimpressed.

"Do I know him?" I asked.

"Yeah, Dom. You've seen Joey around. He's usually here when you come in. As a matter of fact, he's bought you a few drinks over the years."

While I knew most of Salvi's patrons by face, I didn't always remember their names. In fact, I *never* remembered their names. As far as this guy Joey buying me drinks, well, everybody at the Point bought everyone drinks, so that clue didn't help me. I looked at Salvi with no hint of recollection on my face. Frank noticed this and put it in terms he knew I'd understand.

"Joey's the guy who's five feet tall and looks like Yoda from *Star Wars*."

"Oh, that Joey," I said. "Sure, I know him. *He's* a bookie?"

"One of the biggest around," said Salvi.

"How come you never told me?"

"You never asked," he said. "Besides, whatta you care? You wanna put some money down on next week's game or somethin'?"

"N-no," I stammered. "I just—"

"You just what?" Salvi cut me off. "You just wanted to know?"

"Yeah, I guess so."

"Why?" he demanded. "What in the world could you possibly gain from knowing that Joey Delucca is a bookie? Is that gonna change your life in any way, shape, or form?"

I hesitated at his ferociousness. He didn't normally talk to me like that.

"No!" he answered his own question. "So don't ask me why I never told you that Joey Delucca's a bookie. It's none of your goddamn business, that's why! Everyone who comes in here does something in life. They sit down and eat and maybe have a few drinks. They don't bother nobody, and nobody bothers them. Not in here, anyways. So stop worryin' about what other people do and just enjoy their company. Like my old man always told me—'Knowledge is not always a good thing. In fact, too much of it and you might wake up one morning and find yourself *dead.*'"

"Relax, Pop," Frank said. "He was only askin'."

"I know," said Salvi. "But sometimes it don't pay to ask so much."

I didn't care about Joey Delucca. I wanted information about Emma, not some midget crook. But since Salvi was mute on that subject, I was just trying to join in the conversation until my coffee was gone. Obviously, I'd hit a nerve. Salvi's reaction made me think of Red's words last night.

Suddenly, the appearance of Sammy in the parking lot of the Point, twice in the last few days, stopped seeming like a coincidence. So did the Joey Delucca story. Why after eight years of ignorant bliss was I learning that criminals frequented the bar of the Point and a man whom I despised was, if not a regular customer, then at least a familiar figure there? And all this a day after Moze was found beaten half to death in his car? The timing seemed odd.

I continued to sip from my cup, trying to drink the hot coffee as fast as I could. It hadn't been a particularly pleasant evening. In fact, after Salvi's scolding, it was time to leave.

"You in a hurry?" Salvi asked, when he saw me gulping down my coffee.

"It's time to go."

I guess I had a twinge of hurt in my voice because he picked up on it right away.

"Siddown and relax!" he ordered. "Frank, get him another cup of coffee and grab a cannoli out of the fridge."

"Salvi, really. I gotta go."

"Hold on, will ya! You'll go when *I'm* ready!"

How could you argue with that logic, especially since he wasn't coming with me. I resigned myself to not going anywhere unless our parting was amicable. Deep down, I didn't want to leave.

Frank freshened my cup and placed a giant cannoli before me, stuffed with sweet ricotta cheese and loaded with chocolate chips. The coffee was hot and strong, and the ricotta was cold and rich.

"Look," Salvi said apologetically. "The reason I don't want you askin' too many questions, and the reason I don't give you no answers, is because, like I said, knowledge is not always a good thing. You gotta remember who you are and what you do. Don't ever underestimate the position you're in or the number of people out there who'd love to sink their chops into you for one reason or another. Guys like Joey Delucca, for example. He comes around and buys you drinks and seems nice enough, and for the most part he is. But what you don't realize is how badly he wants to get in your head. To know what you know, especially all that information that's supposed to stay inside the locker room. He'd pay a lot of money for that. And if he could somehow get something over on you or find something that you were willing to pay a lot for, he might even be able to control you. Don't look at me like that! I ain't bullshittin' you."

I guess I *was* looking at him with an air of skepticism. But Frank nodded knowingly in agreement with what Salvi had just said.

"Whatta ya think, it's never happened before?" Salvi continued. "Ever hear of the Chicago Black Sox, or Pete Rose, or the Boston College point-shaving scandal? You remember when those

Packers and Lions got suspended for gambling? How about Art Schlichter? Don't tell me you still think the Jets winnin' the Super Bowl in '69 was legit?"

The look I gave him suggested nothing less.

"C'mon, Dom. Wake up and smell the coffee. There are guys like Joey Delucca all over the place. They'll treat you like a king, wine you and dine you till the cows come home. They'll give you anything you want. All you gotta do is name it. The more bizarre, the better. If they can become the only one to provide it for you, that puts you in their back pocket. You owe them. You belong to them."

"What can I give them?" I asked incredulously. "Besides tickets to the game, maybe."

Salvi gave me a look of disgust. As if he'd just drawn a picture that couldn't have been more clear and yet instilled not one drop of understanding in my brain.

"Who's the leading receiver on the team?" he asked.

It sounded like a rhetorical question, but I thought I'd better answer it just the same. "Me."

"Who's the go-to guy on third downs?"

"I am."

"Who has the most touchdown receptions when you guys get into the red zone."

"I do."

"And whose blocks determine the success of all those off-tackles and sweeps around the end that you guys run? Especially that one goddamn play you run all the time?"

"Slant Thirty-eight Boss?"

"Yeah, that's the one. My God, does Midland have no imagination at all? You guys run that play thirty times a game."

"It's an attitude play. Smashmouth football," I said.

"Yeah? Well, Midland's got the attitude of a moron, if y'ask me. Anyway, whose block is most important in that play?"

"Everyone's block is important, Salvi," I said humbly.

"Whose is *most* important!" he yelled.

"Mine, I guess."

"Now do you see how much influence that you, just you alone, have over the outcome of not only the game, but more importantly, *the score*?"

I had to admit, he was beginning to make sense. "I guess so."

"You guess so? All it takes is one dropped pass, one missed block, one less point, one more point, and you're talkin' about millions of dollars every week! Joey Delucca's a decent guy, but he'd use you for his own financial gain in a heartbeat. Why do you think you don't know him any better than you do? Because I won't allow it. That's why. And believe me, there's lots worse than Joey out there. *Lots worse.* There's guys who'd cut your nuts off without thinking twice about it. If you owe them a favor and you don't pay up . . . *fuhgedabowdit*!"

Salvi's eyes lit up. His whole countenance changed. Under his façade of disgust and anger, relish glowed. He was obviously speaking from experience. Moze's bloody and swollen face came to mind. Red's theory about foul play seemed more plausible than ever.

I sat in silence for a moment, or rather in disbelief. Could I have been that naïve? Was I so unaware of the outside world that I never saw any of the shadier sides of the game? Was I too stupid or just too wrapped up in my own world not to see the pack of piranhas circling the outskirts of the stadium? The more I thought about it, the more I realized that of all the pieces of meat in our locker room, James Moze was indeed the prize steer.

"Moze," I whispered to myself with regret and sadness. The poor guy, I thought. What in the world has he gotten himself into?

"Huh?" asked Salvi.

"Nothin'. I was just thinking about Moze."

The usual look of concern came over Salvi's face. "How's he comin' along? From his accident, I mean."

"I don't know. I haven't seen him."

"Shouldn't he be in the training room rehabbing or something?"

"Maybe, but I don't think he'll be rehabbin' for a little while just yet. He looked pretty beat-up."

"You saw him?" Salvi looked surprised.

"Yeah, in the parking lot. Red and I found him in his car."

Salvi's face lost its color. He looked me in the eyes as if searching for something. "What exactly did you see?"

"I saw him in the front seat of his car all beat to shit."

"Nothing else?"

"No, that's it."

Salvi wasn't satisfied. He kept looking at me. Glaring almost. He was probing for more, and his gaze made me uncomfortable.

"You know, Salvi, I don't think it was an accident," I said, offering him the only thing I had.

"Why not?"

"Well, there wasn't any damage to the car. No scratches, no dents, no dings."

"Nothing?"

"Nothing."

Salvi was silent.

"Hey, Salvi, can I get another cannoli?" I asked in the hopes of diffusing his laser-beam gaze.

"Sorry, Dom. That was the last one."

No more cannoli? The Point had never run out of anything before. Especially not for me. I kept my mouth shut of course, but looked over at Frank to see his reaction. Frank averted his eyes.

"How 'bout another espresso, then?"

"That's gone, too," Salvi said.

I'd never requested anything at the Point that wasn't given to me. Certainly, I wasn't used to being rebuffed. But Salvi kept his gaze fixed on me. And the look on his face said, "The night's over."

"Well," I said, wiping my hands nervously on my pants, "I . . . I guess I'll call it a night then."

"All right, Dom. Safe trip home," said Salvi quickly.

"Yeah, drive careful," Frank said. "I'll lock up, Pop. Why don't you get going, too."

"No, Frank. I'll take care of it tonight. Get outta here." Salvi fastened his prosthesis onto his upper thigh.

I was about to say something, but Frank motioned with his eyes toward the exit. He walked over to it himself and held the door open. Salvi got up from the bar and disappeared into a back room. He didn't even say good-bye. With nothing left to say, I walked through the door into the cold, dark night. Frank followed.

"Jeeezus, what's wrong with him?" I asked Frank in the parking lot.

"Don't worry. It's Joey Delucca that's bothering him, not you."

"What's the problem?"

Frank hesitated. "I shouldn't say anything, but Joey's not the sharpest tool in the shed. He's been running his business like an idiot lately."

"So what? Why does that bother your dad?"

"My father's a businessman. Let's just say he has a vested interest in the operation."

"Is that legal?"

Frank sighed. "Don't ask so many questions. I told you too much already. Just know that Joey's a fucking moron. He's been letting his personal feelings get in the way of business, and it's becoming a problem."

"For who?"

"For everyone involved." Frank nodded his head toward the Point. "*Capeesh?*"

Following his eyes, I saw Salvi through the storefront window. He had returned to the bar and was talking on the phone beside the cash register. From the looks of it, the conversation was not pleasant. He smashed a beer mug onto the floor as he shouted into the receiver.

"By the way," Frank said, getting into his Cadillac Brougham.

"You know the name of the dumb fuck who Joey took to the cleaners this past weekend?"

"Who?"

"Sammy Penrod."

The highway was deserted on the way home. Replaying the night back in my mind, I tried to make some sense of it. Like one big puzzle, different pieces were everywhere. Unfortunately, if there was one thing I truly stank at, it was putting together puzzles.

This trip had been a waste of time. I'd accomplished nothing. Only one solid conclusion could be gleaned, and that was that Salvi had a whole lot going on. More than I might ever possibly imagine.

How could he be connected with Emma, Moze, Joey Delucca, and Sammy Penrod all at the same time and still manage to cook the best chicken cacciatore that man has ever eaten?

I didn't know a lot of things at the moment, and I wasn't about to be enlightened anytime soon. But that was because the worst case of heartburn I'd experienced in recent memory was bringing tears to my eyes. As I entered the Bronx, thoughts of Salvi were replaced by a desperate search for a 7-Eleven or a Circle K so I could pull over for a bottle of Pepto-Bismol or at least a pack of Tums.

Sixteen

I was belching fire for the next three days and on the plane ride out to Chicago for our next game. A big, tough, veteran squad, the Bears were the top-ranked team in the league. They were also the reigning Super Bowl champions. Defeating them would make a major statement to the football world. A division title and home-field advantage in the play-offs were on the line as well. Emotions ran high, but confidence was tempered by the loss of our star linebacker. For us, James Moze was more than just an important player, he was our heart and soul. Not only were his spirit and his leadership missing, but his replacement was a kid. This'd be the toughest game Bobby Ward had ever played in . . . or would ever play in.

Offensively, we were in for a slugfest against Chicago's ferocious defense. They prided themselves on winning through physical beatings. I was going to need all my strength just to survive. As we touched down at O'Hare, my heartburn, among other things, was pushed aside by the pain in my leg. My knee hurt like hell. The missed Mass of last week and the nap at St. Basil's Tuesday morning were having their effect. God's help and protection couldn't have felt further away. In fact, His wrath felt closer. I was surprised the plane landed without mishap.

Walking into the lobby of the downtown Sheraton, my roomate, Jeb Watkins, was greeted by the outstretched arms of a slinky brunette. I picked up our room key and grabbed a snack box the team provided for us on a folding table by the elevators. I grabbed our punt returner's box as well. Jeb wouldn't want his. A ham-and-cheese sub, chocolate-chip cookie, and an apple were the last things on his mind at the moment. I wouldn't see him again until tomorrow's game. Every road trip was the same. Jeb would disappear with a different girl, and I'd take a long, restful nap alone, half-eaten candy bars and apple cores littering his empty bed. He was the perfect roommate.

Sunday morning's pregame Mass couldn't come soon enough for me. Entering the conference room twenty minutes early, I helped the visiting priest move some tables and chairs. I even slipped him a C-note for the poor box at his church. "I'm still rooting for da Bears," he said with a smile. I don't give a shit, Father, I thought. Just say the Mass. And he did.

This time, I stayed awake for the whole thing. The liturgy was music to my ears, every word medicinal. At its conclusion, I was certain that I'd set things right, confident that God was back on my side. The subsiding pain in my knee convinced me of it. Before Mass, I'd been in so much pain that an injection of lidocaine seemed like the only remedy. I'd been resolved to shoot up for the game. But after completing my sacrifice and fulfilling my superstition, I walked out of that conference room with a spring in my step. A Butazolodine and a couple of Percocets with my pregame pancakes and I felt downright perky.

Walking into the locker room for the Bears game, I happily bypassed the handful of guys waiting for Dr. Bedrosian to erase their problems with a needle. At the head of the line, Leroy Wilkins sat in a chair, topless. Obviously, his morning bowl of raisin bran hadn't been as effective as my Mass. Maybe he should convert, I thought, as I watched Doc stick a needle in his neck to numb a pinched nerve, and then another in his lower back to quiet a bulging disk.

The game progressed as expected. Hard-hitting, low-scoring, and cold. Wind whipped off Lake Michigan like jet-wash, and a mixture of sleet and snow blew through the face masks and ear-holes of our helmets. The temperature read low twenties, but the windchill brought it nearly to zero. That was cold for the regular season, especially since last week's game in Philly had been sunny and fifty-eight degrees. It took the entire first quarter for everyone, including the Bears, to adjust to the weather and begin playing with a semblance of normalcy. Still, neither offense did much. The score at halftime was tied at 7–7, but both touchdowns had been flukes. Chicago blocked one of our punts and recovered it in our end zone, and we'd returned the opening kickoff for a touchdown. Lou tore into us in the locker room.

"We came here to make a statement, fellas! Judging from the first half, I'm not quite sure what you're trying to say. These are the defending champions you're playing. Do you really expect that piss-poor effort to get it done? These guys are tougher than you. They're bigger, meaner, and nastier. I don't understand how the score is tied. You're being outplayed in every phase of the game. The only reason you're still alive is because of their mistakes. But these are the defending champions, guys. They're not going to keep making them. What the hell is wrong with everyone? You look scared out there. Where's the fire? Where's the emotion? Where's the effort? You have all the urgency of playing a training-camp scrimmage. It's embarrassing, fellas! Defense, you're dam's about to break. Offense, I don't know what to say. Watkins is the only one who's done anything right, today." I looked over at Jeb. He winked at me and smiled. He'd broken curfew, hadn't slept, and depleted his energy running laps all night in his girlfriend's bed. I smiled back, laughing that Lou was now holding him up as the perfect role model. Returning the opening kickoff for a touchdown was powerful stuff.

"It's embarrassing, fellas," Lou repeated. "I'm actually ashamed to be your coach. This isn't the team I built. I don't know who you guys are. If you don't want to play, then don't play. If you don't give a shit, then neither do I. I'm done. I refuse to be a part of this. Consider me an observer from now on. When I see some effort out there, I'll put the headphones on again. Until then, you're on your own." He took a step, then stopped. "One last thing. You can't win without me. You're not that good. I hope you know that." Then, walking out the door leading to the field, Lou said to Jimmy the trainer, "Get me a hot dog and some coffee. If I gotta watch this bullshit, I might as well have lunch."

No one spoke. No one moved. We just sat there and stared at the floor. This was something new from Lou's bag of tricks. He'd done a lot of things, but he'd never abandoned us before. The assistants weren't sure what to do, and neither were we. Typically, Moze or Hanes, being our captains, would say something in a situation like this, but they weren't here. As Lou said, we were on our own. Almost immediately after Lou's departure, the referee poked his head in the locker room and shouted, "Two minutes!" Like a cattle prod, the sound jolted us into movement, and we herded mechanically, and leaderless, through the door and back to the game.

The third quarter yielded no points for either team. It was only a matter of time, however, before the Bears offense broke the game wide-open. Moze's absence was glaring, and with every play our defense looked that much closer to disintegrating. Leroy Wilkins and Charles Rosen had their fingers in the dam, but Lou was right, it was about to break. In particular, Chicago's exploitation of Bobby Ward was beginning to pay dividends. They'd been running at him all game and the rookie was spent. Not only had fatigue set in, but so had confusion. Chicago's balanced offense was giving Moze's replacement fits. Play-action passes, drop-back passes, and hard-hitting runs kept him constantly out of position. Jack Pelham, the Chicago tight end, was having a field day with the kid. If he wasn't pushing the rookie all over the field, he was leaving him in the dust on his pass patterns. Bobby had watched the man assigned to him catch six passes for eighty yards. And there was still another quarter to go.

When the gun sounded the end of the third quarter, Chicago was poised on the border of our red zone, the twenty-yard line. In the midst of an eight-minute, seventy-yard drive, our defense had been less effective than speed bumps in a parking lot. Help was badly needed. I looked over to Lou for inspiration. Surely, he'd rally the troops, call some ingenious defensive scheme, maybe even force a turnover. But just as he'd promised at halftime, he remained a disinterested observer. With arms folded and pouting face, he watched the action before him as though it played on television.

As both teams began the long march to the opposite end of the field for the fourth quarter, the Chicago head coach huddled his guys together for some words of advice and instruction. When our guys passed by, Lou didn't move. No words of encouragement, no bits of advice. The only thing he offered was a look of disgust. When our defensive coordinator tried to intervene, Lou stifled him, shouting, "Keep your mouth shut!" Those were his first words since halftime.

My heart sank watching my teammates trudge by. They were exhausted, a cloud of defeat dogging their every step. Bobby Ward looked especially dejected. Charlie and Leroy and the rest of the defense sniped at him along the way.

"Bobby, you're killing us!"

"Do you know your goddamn plays?"

"Boy, you taking stupid pills?"

"We don't expect you to be Moze, but at least do your fuckin' job!"

Bobby's eyes were vacant. His bottom lip quivered. He looked as if he wanted to cry. The sight reminded me of practice earlier this week. Lou was right to step up the intensity level that day for the rookie. I was foolish . . . no, selfish for resenting him for it. The right thing to do . . . the team thing to do, would've been to cooperate and help get Bobby ready for today. That would've been more helpful than beating the shit out of the kid. I wanted to go over to Lou and apologize for my behavior, but I didn't. He wouldn't have known what I was talking about. At the moment, last week's practice might as well be last year's practice. Besides, he looked in no mood for conversation. Instead, I turned to Bobby.

"Hey, Bobby," I said, stepping onto the field to greet him. He didn't hear me. He was in a daze. "Hey, Bobby," I said again, reaching out and grabbing his elbow. My touch snapped him back to reality, but my face only deepened his despair. He was getting his ass kicked, and the sight of a guy who'd done the same thing to him just a few days ago only added insult to injury. He braced himself for a tongue-lashing; everyone else seemed to be giving him one. But I'd no intention of doing that. Instead, I remained silent and looked in his eyes. Amid the fog of defeat, I saw one last iota of anger. Good, I thought. There was still hope.

"Bobby," I said, "listen to me. Pelham's a punk. As far as tight ends go, he's average, that's all."

"Yeah, right," Bobby said. "He's kicking my ass."

"No shit. But he shouldn't be. You're a hundred times better than him."

"Thanks for the pep talk," Bobby said, uninspired, and resumed walking.

"I'm serious," I insisted, not letting go of his arm. "You should be kicking *his* ass, not the other way around. I know linebackers better than anyone, Bobby, and I'm telling you, you're a pretty damn good one. That might seem like a stretch at the moment, but a few more games and you'll believe it, too. You're going to look back on today and kick yourself for letting a guy like Pelham have his way with you. Don't forget, this is only your first *real* game. You don't know any better. Everything's distorted first time around. Guys seem better than they are, faster, stronger. Hell, my first game was a disaster, too. I should've told you that last week at practice. I should've helped prepare you better. I'm sorry I didn't."

"You prepared me better than you think, Dom. The pain and humiliation at practice was pretty much the same as today."

A hint of a smile was visible on his lips. I laughed and tapped him on the helmet with my hand. Tension seemed to lessen in his shoulders, and he kicked the dirt as he gazed at the ground.

"You really think I'm good?" he asked, his eyes still turfbound.

Bobby had been a college all-American and a first-round draft pick. He knew he was good. But hearing it from a newspaper or a fan was different from hearing it from another player. In the pros, compliments between players were rare. Confidence was as potent a weapon as your bench press or forty time. At this level, everyone was a threat to your livelihood, teammate or not. Letting anyone know you thought he was good gave him a mental advantage over you that could one day work to your detriment. Hell, I never told Moze I thought he was good. We were in the pros, that was sufficient acknowledgment. But Bobby was on the verge of catastrophe. A beating such as he was experiencing would leave irreparable mental scars if allowed to continue. And mental scars had turned many a first-rounder before him into a monumental bust.

"Absolutely," I said. "You'll be All-Pro someday, no doubt about it."

Bobby laughed. "Awright, that's enough."

"I'm serious. You're that good. There's no way Pelham should be doing what he's doing. But look, nobody in this league sucks. Get your head outta your ass and start believing in yourself. We need the guy we drafted. It's nut-cutting time. Forget these last three quarters. Your career starts now."

Life returned to his eyes. The fire rekindled. It was imperative Chicago stay out of the end zone, and Bobby was crucial to that. A field goal was manageable, but not a touchdown. At this juncture, seven points would create a breach we'd never be able to mend.

Bobby rejoined his teammates on the twenty-yard line, and the fourth quarter began. Chicago lined up and ran their first play: off-tackle right at Bobby. Pelham released off the line of scrimmage to block the strong safety. Bobby, thinking it was pass, turned to run with him. Before his third step, however, he stopped in midstride and turned back around. He sensed something. As he did, the Chicago fullback met him helmet to helmet; the crack echoed in the frigid air. Bobby absorbed the blow and fell backward, but not as quickly or as easily as before, when he'd taken four steps to correct himself. Chicago gained three yards instead of their usual five. Bobby was learning.

The Bears stuck with their game plan and pounded the rookie. On second and seven, they ran an end sweep to Bobby's side. Pelham jumped off the line and attacked Bobby's outside shoulder. If he could hook Bobby inside, the running back would have all the field to the sideline in which to maneuver. The hook was the hardest block for a tight end to execute. Chicago would never have asked, nor expected, Pelham to attempt it against Moze. But Bobby's lackluster performance and inexperience were too tempting not to give it a shot.

Pelham wedged one hand into Bobby's outside armpit, the other on his chest: textbook position for a hook block. Bobby was already beaten. The outside running lane was wide-open. By all rights, the play should've been a touchdown. But instead of giving up and letting Pelham kick his ass again, Bobby fought back. Like a grizzled veteran, he assumed contempt and disdain for his opponent. As best he could, he righted himself and started pushing back against the tight end. Although he'd been blown backward a good five yards, Bobby eventually regained his leverage and moved Pelham toward the sideline. With every step backward, he pushed

Pelham two steps sideways. By the time they were ten yards downfield, Bobby had reduced the outside running lane to no more than a yard. Eventually, the Chicago running back ran out of room once he met the back of Jack Pelham's block and was forced to step out of bounds. A big gain, but no touchdown. A victory as far as Bobby was concerned.

It was now first and goal at the four-yard line. Chicago called a time-out and ran as a unit to the sideline to confer with their coach. Lou remained stone-faced, his arms crossed and headphones off. The assistant coaches milled nervously about, not daring to attempt anything that might jeopardize their jobs. Jimmy the trainer was the only one who jumped into action. With a tray of water bottles, he jogged onto the field. Our defense met him halfway. I joined them to have another word with Bobby.

"Nice job," I said, handing him a water bottle.

"Are you kidding?" Bobby asked, squeezing a long stream of liquid into his mouth.

"No. You plugged up that off-tackle pretty well, and you saved the touchdown on the sweep. You already look like a different player."

"Well, thanks . . . I guess." He wasn't fully convinced. "Say, what's in this bottle?"

"Coke."

He looked at me curiously. "Why?"

"I put it on my towels." I pointed to two small towels hanging out the front of my pants. One was brown and wet, the other dry. "I soak my hands with this one and dry them with that one. When the sugar dries, it's sticky. Helps me catch the ball."

"I don't need sticky hands, Dom."

"I drink it, too. Gives me good spit for my hands. Again, nice and sticky, and lots of it."

"I don't need spit, either."

"Yeah, you do. In the next three plays, Chicago's going to try at least one play-action pass featuring Pelham. He's their hot receiver today, and they'd be stupid not to use him. The way you played that off-tackle run, it looks like you're beginning to understand the difference between his pass release and his run-block release."

"Yeah, I think so. His pass release is fast, like he's running away from me. That block release was slower, more deliberate, like he wanted me to follow."

"Good job. You're learning."

Bobby smiled, a bit of pride showing.

"Well, in the next three plays, one of his releases will be for a pass. It's important you recognize it. When you do, I want you to do something."

"What?"

"Hock a loogie through his face mask. Best-case scenario, it impairs his vision. Worst-case, it distracts the shit outta him."

Bobby laughed. "Spit? Isn't that illegal?"

"Probably. But it's been done to me, and I've never pressed charges," I said, laughing with him.

"I don't know, Dom."

"Just keep it in mind. You can't have too many weapons. Have another swig and get out there. Time-out's over."

Our defense huddled near our goal line as Jimmy and I walked back to our sideline. Amidst a sea of long faces, I saw Lou's looking at me curiously. He averted his gaze when our eyes met and resumed his menacing pout. I looked away as well and turned my attention to the field.

First and goal from the four. Pelham released off the line of scrimmage. It looked like pass to me. Bobby followed him, but then stopped after two steps. Chicago was running the off-tackle play again, and Bobby had read it. Turning around, he met the fullback coming out to block him. This time, he was in position. With head and shoulders lowered, he blew up the fullback in the hole and knocked the tailback behind him to the ground. A loss of a yard on the play. "Great instincts, Bobby!" I yelled.

Next, Chicago ran the sweep. While Pelham got his hands into Bobby and pushed him back a yard, he wasn't able to hook him.

Bobby stayed strong and strung Pelham out to sideline, never giving up the outside running lane, and never retreating more than that initial yard. The Chicago tailback eventually quit trying to go outside Bobby and cut back inside. Four Giants in pursuit greeted him with exuberance. No gain.

Third and goal, Chicago lined up in a balanced formation. It was fifty-fifty whether they'd run or pass. Pelham gave no pre-snap reads, his stance was neutral. Bobby fidgeted over him, his uncertainty and nervousness apparent. The ball was snapped and Pelham shot into Bobby full force. They collided violently, and Pelham began trying to hook Bobby once again. Sweep. Bobby fought successfully to the outside to secure contain. The tailback raced with the ball in an effort to turn the corner. But Bobby had the situation well in hand. The outside running lane was closing fast. The tailback was going to have to cut back inside as on the previous play, into the heart of the defensive pursuit. He slowed down in preparation to make the cut, but never did. Instead, he stutter-stepped to a halt and manipulated the ball in his hands so that his fingers were on the laces. At the same time, Pelham slapped Bobby with his inside hand, shoving him toward the sideline. Then he disengaged from Bobby and released downfield. That's when cries of "Halfback option pass!" erupted from our sideline. Bobby, finally realizing Pelham had let himself be beat, made one last grasp at the tight end before losing his balance and falling to the ground. Pelham broke free into the end zone and awaited the ball. Bobby got back up, took one step toward the tailback, then remembered he had Pelham in coverage and reversed direction. If he had looked incompetent throughout the day, he looked downright foolish at the moment. One step forward, two steps back, then a pitiful leap for the ball as it floated over his head into the arms of the uncovered Pelham.

The ball was as easy to catch as any pass ever thrown. A five-yard floater. Red snagged harder to catch T-shirts aimed at his laundry basket. But when I looked at Pelham, alone in the end zone, he only had one hand out for the ball. The other was thrust through his face mask, frantically wiping his eyes. "Bobby, you sweet son of a bitch!" I said.

As Pelham tried to cradle the pass into his chest with the one hand, the ball took an unexpected bounce off the chest plate of his shoulder pads. It then hung before his face like a floating balloon. He removed his other hand from his face mask and reached out with all ten fingers to grab it. But the extra second it took to secure the catch allowed Bobby to take the four steps necessary to join him. As Pelham's fingertips touched the ball, so did Bobby's helmet. The hard plastic sent the inflated leather flying away from Pelham's hands and straight into the stands. Not only did Bobby break up the play, but he delivered a blow to the tight end that he'd not soon forget.

Our sideline erupted. Pelham, after peeling himself off the turf, complained vociferously to the ref, pointing to Bobby, then to his eyes, then back to Bobby. The ref, however, turned a deaf ear. He hadn't see a thing. Pelham would've complained for hours but was forced to quit when the Chicago field-goal unit came onto the field. The score became 10–7, but that was better than being down by a touchdown.

Bobby came off the field giddy. "I can't believe it," he cried, "it worked!"

I grabbed him in a bear hug and laughed.

"Where's the Coke bottle?" he said. "My mouth's dry."

"Forget it," I said. "You won't have to do that again. Pelham will be flustered for the rest of the game. You play like you just did and you'll be fine."

"It was a gooey one, Dom. That Coke is really something."

"I wouldn't steer you wrong, rookie."

The goal-line stand was inspiring. Life returned to our sideline. Even Lou was impressed. This was the effort he'd been waiting for. As soon as the pass got broken up, he emerged from hibernation. "Field-goal-block team!" he'd shouted, even before

Chicago's kicking team came on the field. Arms unfolded, pout gone, headphones back on, he resumed control.

"Offense, listen up," Lou said. "There's time for maybe two possessions. We need to score on both of them. Touchdowns, field goals, whatever. I've been watching them and there's something we can do. Just do as I say, and we'll walk out of here with a win. You with me?"

Every one of us, to a man, thought Lou's behavior had been childlike and absurd. Normal men would've told him to shove it, after what he'd pulled. But not us. We ran back to him like a group of Moonies. With rapt attention, we nodded eagerly. Every one of his words bathed us in confidence. Pathetic.

Our huddle had heightened energy when our offense took the field. But the game plan remained the same. Pounding, pounding, and more pounding. Chicago played a 4-6 defense, meaning they kept eight men on or just off the line of scrimmage: the box, as we called it. With eight men in the box, it was hard to make progress running the ball. Our signature play, Slant 38 Boss, wasn't nearly the game-breaker it normally was. No matter how we schemed it, one defender was always left unblocked. Our tailback, Mark Lane, was continually brought down just short of breaking the big one. In the passing game, it was the same problem. We could pick up seven rushers, but they brought eight. Although this compromised their secondary, the tenacity of their blitzes left this weakness unexploited.

We started our drive on our own twenty-yard line after Watkins downed the kickoff for a touchback. Eight grueling runs later, we were on the fifty-yard line. Lou signaled for a time-out and called us over to the sideline. I enjoyed the break immensely. The 4-6 defense put two outside linebackers directly on my head, one on each shoulder. Every snap of the ball was a double-team. I felt I was being beaten with a baseball bat.

"Listen carefully," Lou said as we huddled around him. "Johnston, every time you pull, McMillen follows you." Johnston was our center. McMillen, their middle linebacker. "And Fucillo, every time you block down on the end, those two outside backers hit you, then let you go."

I nodded my head in agreement. The wheels were turning in Lou's head.

"Okay, so this is what we're gonna do. Johnston, I want you to pull to Fucillo's side. Fucillo, I want you to block down on the end. Ramsey, fake the handoff to Lane. Fucillo, give Johnston two seconds to pull past you. Once he does, leave your block and release over the middle. Ramsey, hit him as soon as you see him."

We envisioned our assignments for a moment, then the questions started.

"Who am I pulling for?" Johnston asked.

"What hole do I hit?" Lane asked.

"How deep is my route?" I asked.

"Where's my protection?" Ramsey asked. "You're leaving three guys unblocked."

Lou responded with disdain. "Johnston, just pull. I don't care if you run up into the stands. Lane, hit any hole you want. Dom, there is no depth. Get your head around as soon as you leave the block. And, Ramsey, you've got no protection. You're gonna get hit, so get rid of the ball as fast as you can. But not too soon. Now get out there and execute!"

In the huddle, we talked excitedly.

"Is this even a play?"

"What do we call it?"

"What do the rest of us do?"

Ramsey shouted, "Everyone, shut up! What's the problem? Sounded simple enough to me. Johnston, Lane, Dom, you all set?"

We nodded.

"Good. Then whatever the fuck it's called, let's run it on the first sound. Ready? Break!"

We got down in our stances. The ball would be snapped as soon as Ramsey uttered a sound. If he was going to get hit, he wanted it to be quick.

"Go!" Ramsey barked, and the play was set in motion. I blocked down on the defensive end. Derek Jones, not knowing what else to do, stayed to double-team with me. The two outside backers initially crashed down on me, but when they were convinced I was blocking, they turned their attention elsewhere. I put on a good show of effort, keeping one eye on Johnston as he lumbered toward me. "One one-thousand," I counted. "Two one-thousand." Lane smashed into the line pretending a ball was tucked into his belly. The noseguard over Johnston, left unblocked, charged toward Ramsey. The two outside backers blitzed as well. The other side of our line, because they hadn't seen the play drawn up on a chalkboard, blocked no one, leaving the whole Bear defense, with the exception of the defensive end Derek and I were double-teaming, free to sack Ramsey. Lou was wrong. Hoss wasn't going to get hit. He was going to get killed.

Johnston brushed past me when I finished my second one-thousand. Pushing off the defensive end, I stepped over the line of scrimmage. The middle backer chasing Johnston as he pulled to nowhere almost knocked me over. With his absence, the middle of the field opened into a vacant pasture. I hadn't see the light of day the entire game, and now I had more grass than I knew what to do with. Lou was a genius. Turning my head around, I saw Ramsey's arm already in motion. Surrounded by five Bears coming in from all sides, his eyes were as wide as silver dollars. They closed abruptly once the ball left his hand. Poor Hoss, I thought. Lou would've never sacrificed Hanes like that. I tried to focus on the ball, but the sight of him folding like a paper doll was too gruesome to ignore.

Once I caught the pass, I turned upfield. The bulk of the Bear defense was sitting on Ramsey. Only three defenders remained in their secondary. Before I knew it, I was on the forty-yard line, the thirty, the twenty. Not until the ten-yard line did a cornerback and a safety finally catch up to me. One jumped on my back, the other on my legs. Together, they dragged me down at the five-yard line. I groaned, seeing the goal line so near. It wouldn't look this close with a regrouped Chicago defense in front of it.

As I feared, the end zone proved to be too far away. Unable to punch it in after three plays, we settled for a field goal. Ramsey had been hit so hard, he was flying on automatic pilot. Barely able to find the huddle, he'd lined up under Derek twice for the snap. At least we tied the game.

Our defense, flush with the success of their goal-line stand, and playing once again under Lou's command, shut the Bears down with a minute left on the clock. As our punt-return team took the field, our offense prepared for a game-winning drive. Ramsey was halfway back from la-la land after inhaling four ammonia caps. He could now recognize faces, although he still wasn't sure whom we were playing. As he went over last-minute strategy with Midland, I huddled with the linemen, discussing blocking schemes with the O-line coach. Defensive players passed by anxiously, offering words of encouragement.

"Go get 'em, now!"

"It's up you to, baby!"

We were so absorbed with this last possession of the game, no one realized Jeb Watkins was returning Chicago's punt for his second touchdown of the day.

Inexplicably, the Bears' punt coverage had broken down. Watkins found a seam and hit it hard. North and south. Straight-ahead running, collisions be damned. We didn't even look up until he was halfway to the end zone. The scene was surreal. The stadium silent. I looked over to Ramsey talking on the phone with the coaches upstairs. He looked as if he'd just received a pardon by the governor.

Lou gave no postgame congratulatory talk. Instead, he strutted into the locker room shouting, "See? . . . See?" as if he'd known all along we'd win if we just followed him blindly. From our perspective, it seemed true. If he hadn't stepped in when he did, we would never have come back. As he said at halftime, we couldn't win without him.

Seventeen

It had been one heck of a turbulent week, from the Philly game to the Bears game. But with that last victory, things really calmed down. Our last three games of the season were played at home, and all three were against lesser opponents. Besides our losing the coin toss in the last matchup, none of the three was much of a contest. Statistic-wise, they were my three best games of the season. Catching twenty-five balls for 309 yards had padded my stats enough that I was named an All-Pro. More important, finishing with a 14-2 record, we had, just as Dr. Bedrosian had hoped, secured home-field advantage throughout the play-offs.

Confidence ran high. Winning was expected. The atmosphere in the locker room was electric. The bumps and potholes of that one week, when all my problems seemed to erupt, were forgotten.

Physically, my knee was still a concern, but the success I enjoyed convinced me that Dr. Bedrosian may have been mistaken about his original diagnosis. Pain increased by the day, but Doc kept it under control. Extra Butazolodine and Percocets helped, but the aspirations now kept me on the field. Without them, the swelling in my joint would've sidelined me. Sticking the six-inch, tubelike needle into the heart of my knee every few days to drain off the hot liquid was a godsend. Like popping a whitehead the size of your fist, the relief was incredible. Aside from Lou, no one but Doc and I knew what was going on with my knee. No one suspected anything was wrong. With the way I was playing, no one had no reason to.

Mentally, things were okay as long as I stayed busy. My problems only surfaced during the quiet times. That's when visions of Emma would flood my mind, tempting me to pick up the phone and, as Salvi had suggested, "just call her." But so far, I'd resisted any urge. My first attempt had been like electroshock treatment. I'd no desire for another go-around. Instead, I filled these lonely moments by lifting more weights, watching more film, and spending more time tending to parts of my injured body that needed particular attention.

The Monday following our last regular-season game, a 34–7 romp over the Green Bay Packers, I was alone in the sauna afterhours, sweating out the memory of Emma, when Moze returned to the stadium for the first time since the day of his accident. I'd heard from Jimmy that he was scheduled to return for the playoffs, but was still surprised to see him when he entered the hotbox and sat down next to me.

"How ya doin', Dom," he said, wrapped in a towel and looking no worse for the wear. The angles were back on his face and his features looked sharp as ever. It was hard to believe he was the same guy I'd seen beaten to a pulp a few weeks ago.

"Good, Moze. How you feelin'?"

Jimmy had told me that most of Moze's injuries had been easily remedied lacerations. A few dozen stitches saw to that. Internal bleeding had been controlled, and the multitude of bruises had disappeared. Besides a concussion, there was no lasting damage. But a concussion was no big deal for a guy like Moze. It wasn't the first one he'd ever had, and the way he played, it wouldn't be his last. The scars on his face, however, were obvious, and it was hard not to stare.

"I'm good, I'm good," he said, smiling cockily, revealing a shiny new gold tooth that replaced the one I'd seen lying next to him in the passenger seat of his Mercedes. "I see you guys have been holdin' down the fort while I was away."

There was no shortage of confidence in James Moze. We *had* been holding down the fort in his absence, but knew we couldn't hold out much longer. As well as Bobby Ward had filled in, he'd be a liability against play-off-caliber teams. If we were to succeed in the postseason, we needed reinforcement. Moze's return was the bugle call from the approaching cavalry we'd all been waiting for.

"We've been managing," I said.

"Hell yes! You guys have been doing great!"

His tone of voice startled me. Moze was not stingy with compliments, but they'd always come across as condescending. Whether that was his intention or not, that's how I always perceived them. I knew Moze's worth to the team, and he knew it, too. No matter how humble the guy tried to be, his aura and ability were so fantastic it was almost impossible for him to be modest. But "You guys have been doing great!" was different. It was humble. It was sincere.

That the team hadn't fallen apart without him might have had something to do with it. It must've made him realize that we *could* win on our own. Maybe it had finally dawned on him that while he might be a significant piece in the Giant machine, he was nonetheless just a piece.

Or maybe it was his "accident." Maybe that had helped him see just how vulnerable he really was.

"Thanks, Moze."

"No. Thank you," he said, patting my shoulder.

"You doin' all right?"

"Sure am," he answered, a bit surprised. "Why do you ask?"

"You just seem different, that's all."

I wasn't sure where I was going with this. Personal talk wasn't the norm around the sauna.

"Funny you say that," Moze said with a smile. "I've been feeling different lately."

I paused for a moment, then asked, "The accident have anything to do with it?"

"No, not at all." He ran his fingers over the scars on his forehead. "I've only been feeling like this for a little while now, ever since the autograph appearance I did when I got out of the hospital. My agent thought it'd be good for me to face the public before getting back on the field. So he set up a card show at the Hasbrouck Heights Marriott. Something happened there that changed my life. Man, it was like getting hit with a bolt of lightning."

I said nothing. He looked as if he was going to continue talking, so I kept my mouth shut and my ears open. Maybe it was the confession-booth-like atmosphere of the sauna, but whatever he was about to say, it looked as if he'd been wanting to tell it to somebody for a while now.

"A boy asked me for my autograph. Nice kid, too. About twelve years old. Reminded me of my nephew back in Oklahoma. He's really not my nephew, though. I just call him that. We met during a speaking engagement I did at my old elementary school a few years ago. He was a fatherless kid I took a liking to. I've been sort of his surrogate uncle ever since. Anyway, this kid at the autograph show looked just like my nephew back home. Dressed the same, too. Untucked shirt. Baggy jeans. Baseball cap on backwards. Something about him hit a nerve with me, so I asked him if he wanted to come sit with me while I finished signing pictures for the rest of the line.

"He said great and comes around to the other side of the table to take a seat. He starts telling me about his life and how I'm his hero and everything. He's got my posters and pictures hanging on his walls, reads every article in the papers about me, and every night, before he falls asleep, he prays to God to be just like me. A little scary, don't cha think? Anyway, people are coming up and I'm signing everything for them. I start to notice a pattern forming. Every third or fourth guy not only has a picture in hand, but something stupid to say as well. And they said them right in front of the kid like he wasn't there. Never paid him any attention. I guess having the kid sitting next to me, I was more aware of it than usual. I don't know. But I couldn't believe what came out of their mouths."

"Like what?"

"All kinds of things. Dom, you wouldn't believe how little class some people in this world have. I had guys coming up to me, drunk as shit, handing me a flask full of booze. They wanted to have a 'shot' taken with me. A few offered joints. And a couple of losers even asked if it was okay to spread some lines out on the table."

"Cocaine?" I asked.

"Yep."

"That sucks. If I had to sit through that crap, I'd a felt like a bolt of lightning hit me, too."

Moze shook his head. "The people weren't what hit me. I see them all the time. Hell, everyone knows my reputation. I can't hide it or pretend I'm offended. It's too late for that. It was the kid sitting next to me. He was watching and listening to everyone who come up to the table. As the show was ending, he says he's gotta take a leak. Fine with me, I say. I'm running the forty-yard dash outta here, though. So don't take too long or you won't get to say good-bye.

"Twenty minutes later, no kid. It was time to leave so I left. As I'm walking out of the hotel, I see a ruckus going on outside the door. The police had two guys handcuffed and were putting them in a cruiser. I recognized them. They were the two guys with the blow. Before I can even ask what's going on, I see the kid being shoved into another cruiser. His hands are in cuffs, too. 'What's going on?' I ask one of the cops. 'Drug bust,' the cop says. 'Who?' I ask. 'Those two morons with your jersey on. But the kid, too. We found a bag of coke on the two guys along with some marijuana cigarettes. The kid had a couple of joints in his possession as well. My partner saw the transaction.'

"I couldn't believe what I was hearing. The kid was only twelve. Sloppy dresser, but clean-cut, smart. I never would have suspected. But there he was, hands behind his back with the old steel bracelets on. 'What were you thinking, kid?' I asked him. 'What the hell were you trying to do?' "

"What'd he say?" I asked incredulously.

"Here comes the bolt of lightning, Dom. The kid looks up and says, 'I wanted to get high with you, Moze. Like everyone else. I've never done it before and I wanted you to show me how. I want to be just like you.' "

Moze's eyes were moist. "I felt my heart hit the cement. I thought I was going to puke. Watching the kid drive away in that cruiser, I felt like some doped-out scumbag. I kept thinking about my nephew and all the other kids out there. Is this the example I've been setting for them this whole time? Have I been influencing them to do shit like that all along?"

He spoke rhetorically. Good thing, I thought. Because I wasn't sure how to answer.

"Wow" was all I could say.

"Yeah, wow is right. Like I said, man . . . a bolt of lightning. Come to think of it, a bolt of lightning wouldn't of hurt as much. It couldn't have." He paused, sighed. "Anyway, it was a wake-up call. You are looking at a new man, my brother. A new man. All my habits and vices are gone. I've quit everything cold turkey and I've never felt better."

"Must be tough, though."

"Not at all!" he said with a big smile. "That's the funny part. Sure, it ain't easy. And it's gonna get worse. But right now the pain feels good. I deserve it, and more. Besides, the memory of that kid hurts so much that everything else pales. I've been such a selfish prick, worrying about my own pleasure, my own good time, and nothing else. And practically advertising it, like it made me some sort of big shot. I never thought of the kids. It never occurred to me that they were watching how I lived as well as how I played. What a dipshit I was! But let me tell you, it's over. You think I seem different? You don't know just how different I am. And I ain't ever going back."

He fingered the gold tooth in his mouth.

"That's great news," I said, wanting to keep him talking. "Sammy Penrod's gonna be disappointed, though. Sounds like he's losing his wingman."

"Fuck him!" Moze said violently. "He can kiss my ass. But that's another issue, entirely."

"What happened? I thought you guys were tight."

"Me, too. But things went bad for him and his true colors came through. He's all screwed up."

"How so?" I was prying now.

"He's an addict, like me, but worse. On top of the booze and drugs, he's a gambler, too. He craves the action more than anything. It rules his world, and it's about to bury him. He's got himself in a major jam and now expects me to help him fix things. He's out of his fuckin' mind. Like I owe him?"

"Don't you, though? He's done a lot for you, no?"

"He has. But keeping me stoned out of my mind for ten years ain't the kind of thing I feel indebted for. Besides, he got his money's worth from me. Now that I can see straight, I realize we were never friends. I've been nothing but his dog all these years. He led me around the city on a leash like I was his fuckin' pet. The thought of it makes me sick. I don't owe him shit. I'm through with Sammy. In fact, I hope I never see him again."

"But if he's in trouble . . ."

"Hey, just because we partied together doesn't mean I'm responsible for him. He made his own bed. It ain't got nothing to do with me. Whatever mess he's in, he'll have to get himself out. Besides, he needs something I can't give . . . something I *won't* give. He's shit outta luck as far as I'm concerned."

He had stood up when Sammy's name was mentioned and paced the sauna as he spoke. The subject clearly agitated him, and he was sweating more profusely than the sauna warranted. As he uttered this last sentence, he opened the door and stepped out before I could ask another question. But before leaving for good, he looked back and said, "Hey . . . I mean it about how you guys have been playing while I was out of action. I'm really proud of everyone. And I want you to know that I'll never let you guys down again. Never."

The door slammed shut and I heard him yell from the other side, "See ya tomorrow!"

"Yeah, Moze. See ya tomorrow."

And take care of yourself, I thought. Through the small window in the door, I watched him walk away, wishing I'd asked more questions. He'd opened up pretty good about the kid, but he still wasn't revealing something about Sammy. What did he want from Moze? What was the truth behind his accident? I thought about it for a second. The incident seemed so long ago. So did my conversation with Red at Café Fátima. In comparison, the play-offs were a much bigger concern. Despite my curiosity with Moze's plight, I realized I wasn't as interested as I had been. The Los Angeles Rams, having won their division, were coming to town in two weeks, and they were bringing with them the highest-scoring offense in the conference. We were going to have to put up a lot of points to beat them. Despite Red's notion that Moze's accident wasn't over, that's exactly what it appeared to be—over. Nothing further had happened since that fateful day in the parking lot, and listening to Moze describe how he'd cleaned up his act, I doubted anything further would. Moze was fine. In fact, he never seemed better. I just hoped his newfound attitude wouldn't lessen his play and that with him back in the lineup our defense could keep the Rams from catching fire.

The second Sunday of January was a bright, clear, mild day. Temperatures hovered in the thirties, and the Meadowlands was ominously still. The American flag and other pennants adorning the stadium hung lifeless from their poles in the dead calm of the afternoon. There wasn't a hint of tension in the air. But our locker room was full of it. Jay Stanton, the Rams quarterback, and his elite corps of wide receivers were averaging forty points a game. We'd been counting on the Northeastern elements to sap the spirit of these California boys and keep their scoring to a minimum. Lou had even gone as far as banning the use of heated benches on the sidelines to heighten their discomfort. But Sunday came and it was so nice that none of the Rams even wore long-sleeve shirts. Without the swirling winds of the Meadowlands and the icy temperatures of January, we took the field with trepidation.

Aside from the weather, the next biggest worry on everyone's mind was James Moze. How would he perform after such a long absence? He'd looked okay in practice, but Lou started Bobby Ward, playing Moze only sporadically. Surprisingly, Moze complied without objection. On the sideline, he rooted wholeheartedly for Bobby and conferred with the rookie at every break in the action. Waiting patiently by Lou's side, Moze went on and off the field when ordered, not one complaint to be heard. He didn't even ask to go in, no begging, no whining. After all the years of watching him dominate the playing field, it was the first time he looked like part of the team instead of his own franchise.

Lou never altered this arrangement, not even when Los Angeles scored fourteen unanswered points in the first quarter. Stanton had led one long drive down the field for a score, then hit a long bomb for another. Bobby continued to take the bulk of the snaps. While the rest of us questioned his judgment, Lou never wavered. He couldn't have looked more undaunted. I wondered where his confidence came from. Our offense fared well against the weaker Ram defense, but it still took the whole first quarter for us to score a touchdown. I knew we'd score more, but doubted we could match the Rams' ability to put points on the board. At this rate we'd lose the game 56–28.

What I didn't know was that Lou's defensive game plan was slowly turning the tide. On his orders, our secondary punished the Rams' wide receivers whenever possible, personal fouls and late hits be damned. Penalty flags were of no consequence. Everyone had a green light for violence. It wasn't long before alligator-arm disease infected their receiving corps. Balls began dropping left and right. Some passes were never reached for at all. Apparently, their receivers decided that receptions weren't worth the price they had to pay for them. A discouraged Stanton lost faith in his teammates. He hesitated to throw the ball unless a guy was wide-open. This fraction of a second delay was all Charles Rosen needed. Our big defensive end had been giving the Rams' left tackle fits all day. Now with Stanton's indecision, Rosen was getting his hands on the quarterback. By halftime, Rosen had three sacks and an untold number of hurried throws. Along with Wilkins plugging up the middle and Bobby securing the corner, the Rams' running game, entirely dependent on their passing game, became nonexistent.

Our offense continued its slow roll to victory, tying the game at the end of the half, 14–14, then pulling away by the end of the third, 28–14. Los Angeles didn't score another point after the first quarter, and after a physical beating at the hands of our offense and defense, Rams players were openly discussing off-season vacation plans with six minutes to go in the fourth quarter. While the rest of us celebrated the end of the game, Lou never smiled. His demeanor was something more than stoic. He actually looked preoccupied. What could've been on his mind was beyond me. We'd just won our first play-off game ever. We were one game away from the Super Bowl. Not even Emma, my knee, or my career could distract me from that.

Eighteen

Older veterans had told me through the years, "There's no better town to be a winner in than New York City." I never doubted their words, but judging from past experience, I wasn't convinced that I'd ever be part of a team successful enough to prove them right. New York wasn't like Boston or Green Bay, where just being on the team was enough to earn you celebrity status. In New York, you had to do something impressive before you were shown any special treatment.

Now people from all walks of life started wearing "Giant blue." I'd never seen so much interest in football. At my motel, people who'd never bothered to say hello before stopped to talk to me about upcoming games. Even the chambermaids, who despised my sloppy ways, were affected. My room was cleaner than usual when I came home at night, and a small bouquet of fresh flowers began making a daily appearance on my bureau.

Leroy Wilkins's mug now graced the box of raisin bran he ate every morning, thanks to a promotional deal with a local grocery chain. Charles Rosen signed on with a local retailer to design a line of workout clothes. We awaited the unveiling with much interest. Jeb Watkins had more female fans than he could handle. And Hanes, despite his inactive status, was appearing in half a dozen radio and television commercials. He'd also been invited to provide color commentary and weekend anchoring for a sports channel. Ramsey, meanwhile, was imprisoned by Lou in the quarterback meeting room and sentenced to scour the playbook with Midland during every waking hour. Appearances, fame, and glory were strictly forbidden him. Lou didn't want anything corrupting what he considered an already imperfect mind.

Despite Ramsey's unavailability, the average citizen couldn't get enough of the rest of us. The same held true for the businesses headquartered in Manhattan. Requests poured in from across the river for paid player appearances at all kinds of company functions. Since my paychecks had slowed after the Philly game, I was happy to reach out to our swollen fan base. I had to make cash wherever I could. So along with our big lineman Derek Jones, I headed to the offices of Avco & Associates one afternoon a few days before our second play-off game.

Derek and I parked in a Midtown garage and walked up Sixth Avenue with coats and ties on. Buildings rose up around us like granite mountains. Traffic flowed past in torrents. Wind screamed down the valley of skyscrapers like arctic gales and blew our ties up over our heads. It was noon and a sea of people bumped and jostled one another on the concrete sidewalks as they made their way to lunch. Turning a corner, we were greeted by a howling mob being held back by police barricades.

"What the hell's going on?" Derek asked.

"Beats me!"

Hundreds of people were gathered, holding signs and shouting incomprehensible slogans at the top of their lungs. The placards in their hands were so weathered they were illegible. Obviously, these were veteran troops of many former battles. We stood there, puzzled.

The more we watched, the more it became evident there was not one mob, but two, and that they weren't yelling at us, but at each other. Only the cops and their barricades seemed to keep them from tearing each other to pieces. The emotion, the passion, the restrained violence, was hypnotic.

"Hey, ain't you Dominic Fucillo?" a voice piped up from behind us. It snapped us back to our surroundings.

"And ain't you Derek Jones?"

We turned to find a young man barely out of his teens dressed in a wrinkled dark blue business suit. He looked at us in awe, totally unfazed by the commotion before us.

"Yuze guys comin' up to the office, or what?" he asked.

We looked at him quizzically.

"Avco and Associates," he explained. "The boss said yuze guys was comin' up to give a speech or somethin' and then maybe sign a coupla autographs, too."

"Right," I said, suddenly remembering the reason for our trip into the city. The spell of the mob might have been broken, but our curiosity lingered.

"What's goin' on over there?" Derek asked.

"Oh, that," the kid said casually. "They come here every second Tuesday of the month. A bunch of fanatics, you know, whatta ya call 'em, ahhh, pro-lifers. There's a women's clinic in the same buildin' as us, and they come here every month to protest outside."

"Why are they yellin' at each other?" I asked.

"They ain't yellin' at each other," the kid said. "The group that's facin' 'em is what you call, ahhh, pro-choicers. Although I don't think they're too wild about choosin' what the other guys stand for."

"A women's clinic?" Derek asked. "As in abortion? Aren't they supposed to be in some back alley?"

"I dunno," said the kid. "But this one's right here in my buildin' and they must be doin' a good business cuz the rent is sky-high in this part of town."

I always thought of myself as a good Catholic and knew abortion had been a hot issue lately. But I never thought it applied to me. I mean, I always took precautions. Besides, the whole matter riled me. I didn't like how people talked so publicly about such a private matter. As far as I was concerned, when it came to abortion, ignorance was bliss. Why should this issue be any different from anything else in my life?

"C'mon, I'll walk yuze guys up," said the kid.

We followed him like two country bumpkins visiting the city for the first time. I was glad we had a real New Yorker to escort us in, even if he was a kid.

I looked over the crowd. It was difficult distinguishing one faction from the other. But the longer I stared, the less concerned I became with the rabble and the more preoccupied I grew with the feeling that someone familiar was in the mass of humanity before me. I stopped at the door. Derek and the kid kept walking. I looked again. There, on the corner! Emma!

I dove into the crowd of screaming flesh. Protesters jostled me from every side as I pushed my way through. Some told me I was going to hell. Others spat on my shoes and called me a chauvinistic pig.

"Get the hell out of my way!" I yelled, plowing through the crowd as if I were scrambling for a first down. It may have been one of my best performances yet. Bodies flew everywhere.

Within seconds, I burst through the madness and emerged into daylight. And there she was, walking back and forth along the sidewalk as if she was lost and in need of help. She didn't even see me coming.

"Emma!" I yelled.

My voice scared the bejesus out of her. She jumped backward before she saw who it was, and when she did, I saw that her face was full of torment.

"Dom?" she said softly.

"Yeah, it's me! How'd you know I'd be here?"

"Huh?"

She scrunched her face as if I were speaking a foreign language. I didn't care that we hadn't spoken in months, or that I thought I'd seen her with another man. All I knew was that she was here and I had a chance to make things right.

"C'mon, hon! Don't be embarrassed. I'm glad you came. If I ever coulda figured out where you were, I would of done the same. But this is perfect. I'm about to make two grand . . . cash. We'll go out and celebrate. A nice dinner, a bottle of wine. Just like we used to. God, I've missed you so much."

It was as if I'd just been with her yesterday. It never crossed my mind that she might not feel the same.

"C'mon!" I said again, grabbing her arm through the thick winter overcoat she had on. "Let's go! I gotta go upstairs and do this thing, then I'm all yours!"

She stiffened at my touch. "Let go of me!" she said emphatically. She was strong for such a petite woman and had no trouble pulling free from my grasp.

"How dare you!" she yelled. "You can't just come here and do this to me! I have reasons for being here, which, believe it or not, don't concern you!"

"What are you talkin' about? You came to me." The look in her eyes suggested otherwise, prompting me to feebly add, "Didn't you?"

"Did Salvi tell you? Did he put you up to this?"

There she goes again with Salvi, I thought. What was this big secret that I wasn't supposed to know about? Why did Salvi seem to be in the middle of everything lately? I saw tears forming in her beautiful eyes, reducing me to the Neanderthal that I was.

"I'm sorry. I didn't mean to grab you. I just haven't seen you for so long and I missed you. Don't be angry. Please. Just let me look at you for a second. I can't believe you're really here."

She seemed to relax, though she refused to look me in the eye. I didn't care. She was such a sight to behold. I stepped back to take a good look. She was so beautiful. So lovely. So strong. So . . . so . . .

"Pregnant?!" I blurted out.

"Wow, a regular Sherlock Holmes," she said sarcastically. "Took you long enough."

I was stunned. Floored. Speechless. With that big coat on her, I hadn't noticed. My jaw kept moving but no words came out. Eventually, I regained control of my vocal cords and uttered something that suggested I was on the verge of completing a sentence.

"H-h-how? W-w-where? W-w-why?"

Breathing came hard. Her composure recovered at the loss of mine, and her tears dried up. I knew this meant she was returning to normal, and seeing this, so did I.

"When did this happen?" I finally managed to spit out.

"I'd say about five months ago," she said condescendingly, measuring her protruding stomach with her hands. I reflexively did the math in my head. Counting out change at the drugstore was a major challenge for me, but in less than a millisecond I calculated that five months ago was the beginning of August. I'd been with her almost every day that month.

"Oh, thank God!" I blurted out. "It's mine!"

Did I say thank God it's mine? Yeah. Wow, I thought. In one day I'd not only found Emma again, but discovered I was to become a father. We were going to be a family. On top of that I was about to make two grand. For a moment I dared believe that my luck had turned. In fact, only one thing seemed to be standing in the way of my believing it wholeheartedly: Emma. She didn't look at all happy to see me. And come to think of it, she hadn't since I'd arrived.

"Dom, you've no idea why I'm here, do you?"

It was as if she were waiting for me to turn on the little light-bulb that was supposedly tucked away in some long-unused corner of my brain.

"Keep your rosaries off our ovaries!" the crowd roared.

Click. The lightbulb went on. "No," I shouted. "Not that!"

"You've got nothing to say about it," she countered.

"You're showing for crissakes. Isn't it a little late for this?"

"It's never too late," she said coolly. "All you have to do is find the right doctor."

"But you can't," I cried.

"Why not?"

"I don't know. You . . . you just can't, that's all."

"Why do you care? Whoever said it was yours?"

"Don't say that," I responded, full of hurt.

My knees almost buckled at the thought of her giving herself to another man. The hard look that accompanied her words was obviously meant to wound me. But I don't think she knew just how lethal the combination had been. As soon as she saw the blood leave my face, she softened, replacing spite with a measure of tenderness. She was a tough woman, but she wasn't cruel. Her next look assured me that of all the things that had passed between us, infidelity wasn't one of them.

This crack in her coldness filled me with as much hope as a ray of sun slicing through the clouds of a monthlong drizzle. I saw this chink in her armor and made a dash for it. I approached her with arms outstretched, wanting only to hold her and tell her how much I loved her. But the break in the weather passed faster than the eye of a hurricane, and before I reached her, the outstretched hand of her slender arm stopped me dead in my tracks.

"You have to go now," she said calmly, but with the force of a tempest.

"Emma, I love you," I said softly.

My tears got hers started again.

"It's too late," she sobbed. "You weren't there when I needed you."

"Emma, I'm sorry," I said weakly, knowing my apology was long overdue. "But I'm here now. I'm yours now."

"I don't need you *now*!" she cried. "I can take care of myself, *now*." Her voice grew louder. "I've *been* taking care of myself, ever since you left. Ever since you chose football over me!"

Her last words almost brought me to my knees. The thought of her on her own, enduring pregnancy by herself, going to work every day and lying awake every night wondering what to do, wondering how to manage, alone and scared, with no one to turn to, no one to hold her, no one to love her and tell her it'd be all right, pierced my heart. The thought of her suffering erased any pride I'd just felt about becoming a father. It made me see what a rotten piece of scum I really was. I was paralyzed. I'd never be able to make this up to her and didn't think she'd ever let me if I could. I was struck with the fear that she'd never love me again. And for that, I couldn't blame her.

But still, I tried, if only reflexively, like a corpse that continues to twitch after death, to reason with her.

"Emma . . . ," I said searching for words, but coming up with nothing. "Emma . . . ," I repeated, as if I were grasping for the precious air that had been knocked out of me.

"Go away!" she cried, finally letting loose with all her emotions. "It's over! I begged you, Dominic . . . *I begged you!* But you made your choice!"

"I didn't know . . . ," I said, still trying to catch my breath. "I didn't know."

"What was there to know? Why should the baby have made a difference? Wasn't I enough for you? You could have had *me* . . . you could have had the baby . . . you could've had football. You could've had everything. But you chose what you truly loved, and you threw away everything else. You sacrificed me for a stupid *game*, just like you've done with your body, your education, and your future. I wouldn't take you back now if you begged me like I begged you last summer. I need a man, not a boy. And right now, I don't need anybody, especially not you. You made your choice, and now it's time for me to follow through with mine."

I didn't know what to do. I couldn't find anything to say. She was right. I was wrong. I just didn't know I'd been *this* wrong. I didn't know I'd treated her *this* cruelly. I had a job to do. My teammates were counting on me. *Lou* was counting on me. I thought I did what I had to do for everyone involved, including her! Why didn't she tell me what was really going on?

I looked at her with pleading eyes, not realizing I was walking toward her. She backed up with every step I took. I was as numb as I'd ever been from any hit I'd ever taken. I saw her mouth moving, but heard no sound coming out. I knew I was in the middle of the city, but nothing was moving. It was as though I were in a dream, running. Running toward her while she moved farther and farther away from me.

"I didn't know, Emma. I *didn't* know!"

People were beginning to stare. I saw two women wearing yellow armbands with the word ESCORT written on them. They heard Emma's cries and came over to us.

"Do you need help, honey?" they asked her tenderly.

She looked at me before answering. Her face was set, her jaw rigid. She looked at me and I knew I'd lost her.

"Yes, please . . . take me in."

I looked at her one last time before she disappeared through the crowd and into the building. I would never see her again. Not in this lifetime.

I stood motionless. People had yelled at her as she passed by, but I couldn't make out the words. The look on their faces told me it wasn't anything I wanted to hear, nor anything Emma should have had to bear. She didn't deserve this. I did.

I heard a man say to me, "You and that whore are going to hell, mister!"

And it was like Dirty Rivers coming at me all over again. I reflexively turned and grabbed the man by the throat. His feet dangled off the ground and I squeezed his esophagus until I could feel it about to snap. Ten policemen converged on me instantly and pressed their billy clubs up around my own throat. Surprisingly, as Moze had said in the sauna, the pain felt good.

The clubs diffused my anger and made me realize whom I was really mad at. Myself. Regardless, I held on to the man. One of the cops raised his club over my head. The thick piece of wood reached its apex and hovered directly above my face. I hoped for a direct hit between the eyes. I deserved that and more. But the cop stayed his arm. I could see it in his eyes. He recognized me.

"Holy shit, it's Fucillo! Stop now, Dom, and walk away. Before it's too late!"

His words *too late* made me think of Emma again and reminded me of my guilt. I became as weak as a child and let go of the stranger's neck. A woman dressed in a woolen serape with a long, hand-knit scarf and hat squeezed between two of the cops and blasted a noisemaker directly in my face.

"Officer, Officer, arrest this man!" she screamed. "I saw him trying to prevent a young woman from exercising her legal rights!"

The cops quickly decided to hustle me out of there. I seemed to have incited the rage of the entire mob. Both sides joined in an effort to get at me.

Two cops dragged me around the corner, while the rest covered our retreat by fending off the crowd.

Back on Sixth Avenue, the two policemen let go of my arms. Actually, they didn't "let go" as much as they tossed me onto the sidewalk.

"Beat it, Dom. You don't want to get caught up in this!" one said. "Besides, we need you this Sunday."

"Yeah. Yeah, sure," I said, rubbing my neck.

The two cops hurried back to the mob. They had no time for me. They didn't even ask what I was doing there in the first place.

That's when I remembered my paid appearance. Derek was up there by himself. He had to be fuming at being left alone. I went to the next cross-street and entered the building from the back. In the offices of Avco & Associates, I was met by Giants banners and pennants adorning dozens of cubicles. Derek was in the middle of the room looking miserable, surrounded by employees, a corned beef on rye in his hand.

"Hey, it's Dominic Fucillo!" the office manager shouted. Cheers and applause followed.

"Where the hell you been?" Derek asked.

"Later," I said, bracing myself for the onslaught of pictures and footballs being thrust in my face to sign.

"You're the best!" said one worker.

"Your mother must be so proud!" said another.

"I wish my boyfriend would work out like you!"

"You don't know how happy you've made us!"

"We've waited so long for a championship!"

"My kids worship you!"

"God bless you guys!"

"Thanks for coming!"

"Have some deli!"

Once again, I was the center of a mob's attention. I laughed at the irony. It was better than crying.

Nineteen

I didn't have a lot of time to think about Emma and what had happened. Before I knew it, the Bears' defense was in my face again, double-teaming me at every snap of the ball. Despite our victory over them a month ago, Chicago had won their division along with their first playoff game. The only thing standing in the way of their shot at a second consecutive Super Bowl ring was a rematch with us. Jack Pelham, the Chicago tight end, entered the stadium seeking retribution from Bobby Ward, but was instead met by James Moze. Lou had reinstated our captain as the starter. With Moze back in stride, Pelham was reduced to the average player he was, and Chicago's offense was even less effective than it had been during our last meeting. By halftime, they'd only managed to score two field goals, and as the clock diminished in the second half, so did their number of offensive plays. They made no first downs the entire third quarter.

Offensively, we fared much better than before. Although the Bears' defense was still formidable, Lou and Midland had had ample time to review our previous shortcomings and had devised a way to crack the dreaded eight-man front. Unfortunately, nothing innovative or labor-reducing had been forthcoming other than a refined version of Lou's original sandlot play, the one he'd improvised in our last game. The verbal instructions relayed to us on the sideline of Chicago's stadium had been committed to paper, and everyone now had an assignment that could be seen and studied. The play was called 337 COB Pop. Pass protection was installed for Ramsey so that he'd no longer be hung out and left to dry. There would still be contact, but he'd only get hit by one defender instead of five. And since the play was essentially a play-action pass, Lou and Midland drew up a complementing running play that gave the play-fake legitimacy: 37 COB. *COB* stood for "center on backer." Now when Johnston, our center, pulled to the outside, he did so with an objective; to kick out the end man on the line of scrimmage (the outside of the two outside backers lined up over me). Derek and I still doubled down on the defensive end, but now we combo-blocked for the middle backer who chased Johnston as he pulled. If the backer went inside, Derek would peel off the double-team to get him. If he went outside, I would. And Chris Smith, our fullback, would block the inside of the two outside backers on my head. It was a hard-nosed play, nothing fancy. Similar to our meat-and-potatoes play, Slant 38 Boss, except that our center pulled for the linebacker instead of the fullback blocking the strong safety. The design wasn't meant to be especially effective. It was merely intended to disguise the play-action version that popped me over the middle for a pass. This running play, like all our running plays, faced the same problem from Chicago's eight-man front. Namely, there were only seven of us to block eight of them. One defender in the box would always be left unaccounted for. Lou's solution to this was simple: brute force.

"They don't have guns, fellas," he'd said during our scouting-report meeting. "They can't kill you. They can only beat the shit out of you. Or you can beat the shit out of them. One or the other." In other words, despite the imbalance of X's and O's on the line of scrimmage, we'd be running the ball. Exploiting their weakened secondary through the passing game with quick releases, three-step drops, and shortened routes was the logical thing to do. But it was also the expected thing to do. Lou's game plan was to pound the snot out of the Chicago front eight while taking shots with the pop pass to me over the middle. They couldn't defend both. We'd either gain big chunks with the pass, or small chunks with the run.

By the end of the third quarter, Lou was looking like a genius, although no one had ever thought differently. I'd already caught six passes for over a hundred yards, and Lane, our running back, was closing in on 150 yards of his own. He was doing a great job against the eighth, unblocked defender. Although Lane hadn't creased one for a big gain, he made positive yards every time he touched the ball. And that was disheartening to such a good, solid defense. With basically two plays, we controlled the line of scrimmage as well as the clock. Johnston, our center, never pulled so much in his life. But despite our success, the game was not in hand. We'd only scored one touchdown and three field goals. The score was 16–6 with a quarter left. There was plenty of time for anything to happen.

At the sound of the fourth-quarter gun, I unbuckled my chinstrap and walked to the other end of the field. As we were on our own forty-three-yard line, it didn't take long. As I walked, I heard Tony McMillen, the Bears middle backer, yelling in frustration at his defensive squad.

"They're only running two plays, for crissake! What's the fucking problem here?" He was pissed. No one had an answer for him.

He was right. Our game plan fit on an index card. We ran other plays to keep the defense honest, but we didn't need more than our two new ones to be effective. The code to their defense had been cracked. We were beating them with a play that Lou had originally drawn in the sand. I laughed as I passed by.

"Frustrating day, huh?" I said.

"Fuck you," McMillen snapped. "And quit holding me, you prick!"

Translated into English, *Quit holding me* meant "You're kicking my ass and there's nothing I can do about it." After years of dominating the league, McMillen was finally learning what it was like to be a loser. His lack of composure irritated me.

"Stop whining, you fucking baby," I said.

"Seriously," he said. "Quit holding me or I'm gonna fuck you up."

"I don't need to hold you, douche bag. You're the worst linebacker I've ever played against."

I could've said the F-word to him all day and called him every name in the book and not have made any impact. But when I critiqued his performance as a player, he went ape-shit.

"Fuck you!" he snapped again. "Who the hell do you think you are?"

"I'm nobody. That's what makes you so bad."

I laughed again. He didn't. Instead, his fist came flying into my face mask. My head reeled back from the blow, which nearly knocked me to the ground. I stayed up and swung back with a haymaker. His head ricocheted off my fist and his mouth guard flew into the air. Turning his face back toward me, his eyes bulged. He was livid. None of those guys on that defense had ever experienced a beating like the one we were giving them. It was driving McMillen mad. And all because of two plays. I chuckled as I ducked his counterblow and slammed my fist against his ear-hole again. It was funny.

McMillen threw a couple more punches. One landed, jarring

my vision for a moment. I sidestepped a third and raised my arm for another roundhouse. Before I could throw it, however, Derek Jones grabbed my wrist from behind.

"Not this again," he said, holding my arm in place.

Suddenly, whistles blew and zebra-striped arms waved. The refs were just now paying attention to our little scuffle. They hadn't seen any punches thrown . . . yet. Looking back at Derek, my arm in his grip, I said, "Thanks." Actually, I only said "Th—" because before I could complete the whole word, McMillen lunged at me with his body and delivered an elbow to my chin that went under my face mask and bloodied my mouth. That's when I saw a yellow flag bounce off his helmet and heard the ref shout, "Personal foul. Chicago. Number fifty-eight!"

McMillen went crazy. Jumping up and down and flapping his arms, he looked as though he'd attack the ref. His teammates subdued him, however, before he could.

"Hey, ref," I said, wiping the blood from my face. "How 'bout an ejection? He just coldcocked me."

"Get back to your huddle, Fucillo. Knowing you, I'm sure he had a good reason."

"That hurts." I smiled.

McMillen, in the grip of three teammates, yelled to me, "I'm gonna fuck you up, Fucillo. I'm gonna fuck you up, bad!"

"Fuck you," I said.

Once the penalty had been walked off, play resumed. Lou, never one to fear going to the well too often, called 37 COB. Johnston snapped the ball. Ramsey handed it off to Lane. Chris Smith plowed into one of the two outside backers. And Derek and I doubled down on the defensive end. I kept one eye on the end, and the other on McMillen to see which path he'd take in pursuit of the pulling Johnston. But he took no path at all. He stayed right where he was. With no one to peel off for, Derek and I remained on the double-team. Lane hit the hole and was met by the unblocked strong safety. Before hitting the ground, he dragged the defensive back for a three-yard gain.

I looked at McMillen, wondering why he hadn't pursued. He looked back, pointing his finger at me, and said, "Fuck . . . you . . . up!" real slow. That's when I realized he was waiting for the passing version of the same play, 337 COB Pop. He was going to stay right where he was, right in the path of my pass route. He knew we'd call it sooner or later, and he was going to be there to carry out his threat. I went back to the huddle and told Ramsey about my alarming discovery.

"Hoss," I said, "we'd better not call 337 COB Pop anymore. McMillen's gonna be sitting there waiting to jump it."

"I don't call the plays, Dom."

"I know, but if McMillen doesn't clear out of the middle, things could get ugly."

"All right, I'll tell Midland when I can."

A few plays later, the refs called a television time-out and Ramsey went to the sideline.

"Don't forget, Hoss," I said.

He nodded. I saw him talking to Lou. Returning to the huddle, he had an exasperated look on his face. "Okay, guys," he said. "Next play is 337 COB Pop. Let's run it on *two,* on *two.*"

"Hold on!" I said. "Did you tell him what I told you?"

"I sure did."

"What'd he say?"

"He looked at me like I was trying to tell him what to do and said, 'So what? Run the fucking play.'"

"It ain't gonna work," I said. "I'm gonna get my head taken off."

"Are you questioning our fearless leader? Of course it'll work. Lou's never wrong," Ramsey said sarcastically.

I looked out of the huddle and over to McMillen. He was staring at me with those crazy eyes. Ramsey said, "Don't worry, I'll call an ambulance for you."

Johnston snapped the ball and pulled. McMillen didn't move. I blocked down on the defensive end with Derek and tried my best to make it look like a running play. McMillen didn't move. I counted, one one-thousand, two one-thousand, then pushed off the block and popped over the line of scrimmage into the middle of the field. McMillen didn't move. He just stood there, salivating. Turning my head back to Ramsey, I had to fight every impulse not to keep my eyes focused on McMillen. I knew I was running right toward him and that he was waiting anxiously for my arrival. But I was a professional. My job was to catch the ball, and I kept my eyes glued to it as it sailed through the air. Little more than a twelve-yard throw, it wasn't a hard catch to make. Expecting to get hit, I was surprised when the ball hit my hands with no interfering contact. McMillen made no effort to break up the play. He's letting me catch it, I thought. The bastard! He's gonna kill me. Unable to control myself any longer, I took my eyes off the ball before tucking it away and turned my vision frontward. Only inches from my face, McMillen's eyes were the last thing I saw before he lowered his head. The glee in them seemed to say, "I told you I was gonna fuck you up!" That's when the *doinnnggg* of the concussion rang in my ears and the January sun of the Meadowlands turned to black. A familiar sound, the *doinnnggg* was the same as I'd heard in any Saturday-morning cartoon collision. It was a funny noise when the Road Runner dished it out with impunity, but it lost its humor when I assumed the role of Wile E. Coyote.

For the moment, all was forgotten. The ball, the game, McMillen, my knee, Emma, everything. Gone. I once hit an opposing linebacker so hard that he'd admiringly said, "Nice hit, you knocked me into yesterday." But McMillen hit me so hard that he knocked me back to infancy. After the initial blackout, I opened my eyes and was met by a brilliant whiteness. Sun streamed through a window as I lay on my back, alone in a quiet room, toying with a musical mobile floating above my head, suspended from the ceiling.

Everything was fresh, new, and clean. The bars of my crib rose up around me, and the tingling of the metal charms rang in my ears. It was spellbinding, the sound reaching deep into the depths of my month-old soul. Flicking the mobile with my hands, I giggled in ecstasy. An indescribable sense of warmth and peace enveloped me. It was the happiest I'd ever felt.

Unfortunately, a few more flicks of the mobile, and a few more goo-goos and ga-gas was all the happiness I'd get. An ammonia cap under my nose snapped me back to reality. How I'd gotten back to the sideline and on the bench was a mystery. Dr. Bedrosian stood over me with a handful of ammonia caps. A couple of broken and discarded ones were on the ground.

"Dom," he said sternly. "Where are you?"

I'd no idea. Searching my surroundings, I finally said, "In the stadium."

"Who are we playing?"

Again blank. But then I looked onto the field and saw the Bear uniforms. "Chicago."

"Okay, you're all right." He breathed a sigh of relief. "I'll go tell Lou."

Derek came over. "You okay?"

"I think so. What happened?"

"McMillen knocked the shit outta you."

"Oh, yeah," I said, remembering.

Derek's face turned sour. "You fumbled."

"Really?"

He nodded.

"Shit!" I said.

"Don't worry, they didn't get far. Lane made the tackle right away."

"Who recovered?"

"McMillen."

"Shit!" I said again. That motherfucker.

I saw Doc talking to Lou. He was telling him the good news

that I was okay. But Lou just looked disgusted. I dropped my head. I was disgusted myself.

Looking at the scoreboard, I saw Chicago had the ball on our forty-yard line. With seven minutes left in the game, the score was still 16–6. McMillen had given his team new life. Luckily, Moze and the defense held Chicago to just a field goal, and after Jeb Watkins returned the kickoff to our thirty, I was back on the field with five minutes left to play. As I listened in the huddle, my head still reverberated from the hit. Ramsey entered the fold and smiled at me. Nausea rose in my throat.

"Three thirty-seven COB Pop on *one*," he called, laughter in his eyes and in his voice.

"Are you shittin' me?" I said.

"On *one*," he repeated.

Walking up to the line of scrimmage, I avoided making eye contact with McMillen. At the snap of the ball, the play unfolded. Doubling down with Derek, I watched the middle backer. Again, he ignored Johnston's pull. He stayed home, right in the path of my route. After two seconds, I gritted my teeth and left the double with Derek. Ramsey threw the ball. Only four yards over the line of scrimmage, McMillen allowed me to make the catch again. He was waiting for me to turn around. Snatching the ball out of the air and keeping my eyes on it until it was safely tucked away, I braced for a collision. This time, however, I refused to turn around and instead backed into the awaiting assassin. My spine exploded with pain, but at least I stayed conscious. More important, I held on to the ball. Three yards later, I was on the ground.

"I ain't through with you," McMillen said in the pile that had formed on top of us. "I'll be here for the rest of the game. I hope you have good insurance."

"Oh, was that you who hit me?" I said, trying not to grimace in pain. "I thought the mosquitoes were out early this year."

He laughed. But not nicely. I didn't know how many more hits like that I could take. Anger welled up inside me. Something needed to be done.

Next play, Ramsey called 37 COB. I doubled down on the end with Derek. This time McMillen pursued, chasing the pulling Johnston. This was my chance, I thought. Peeling off the double-team, I went after the middle backer, flames shooting from my eyes. As our paths crossed, I ducked low and cut his knees. He went down like a sack of potatoes. I heard a *pop!* followed by a high-pitched scream. Rolling back onto my feet, I looked down at McMillen. He was writhing on the ground, both hands holding his right knee. Even with his hands obscuring the view, I could see from the distorted angle of his shin that his knee had been dislocated. The sight turned my stomach. I'd meant to hurt him, but not like that. I was hoping for a bruise or a little cartilage at best. His teammates tried to calm him, but he kept screaming, his leg bending sideways. One Bears player came up to me and said, "You piece of shit!"

"Fuck off," I retorted. "This ain't soccer. People get hurt."

"Bullshit!" he responded, shoving both hands into my chest.

I swung back, catching him in the face mask. And as if that were the signal for the start of a rumble, both teams lit into each other. Even Ramsey got in on the action. The benches cleared. Half the guys were swinging, the other half were trying to break things up. After ten minutes of chaos, the refs finally restored order.

McMillen had to wait for the storm to end before being carried off. I watched from the huddle as his leg dangled over the side of the injury cart.

"Damn," said Derek. "You see his knee?"

"Sick," said Chris Smith.

"Don't worry, Dom," Mark Lane said. "These things happen. It's not like you meant to do it."

"Yeah, right," I said.

With McMillen out of the lineup, our running game kicked

into gear. The unblocked strong safety, who'd been tackling Lane all day, finally broke down. Without McMillen propping him up, he was barely getting our running back to the ground. Lane increased his yards-per-carry with every play.

When we'd moved inside the Bears' twenty-yard line, Lou called 337 COB Pop. The new middle backer had no clue it was coming. When I popped across the line of scrimmage, the middle was wide-open. Catching Ramsey's pass, I turned upfield and plowed through the free safety defending the goal line. Touchdown! After we kicked the extra point, two minutes were left on the clock and the score was 23–9. For all intents and purposes, the game was over. We were going to the Super Bowl.

After the game, I saw McMillen being loaded into an ambulance. Running over before the doors closed, I asked the attendants, "What's going on? Where are you taking him?"

"Into the city," one of them said. "His knee needs to be reset. They gotta knock him out for that. He'll probably stay in the hospital for a few days until the trauma quiets down."

I looked over to McMillen. I wanted to say good luck or tough break or something. But his eyes were glazed and I realized he was under heavy sedation. Christ Almighty, I thought. I didn't mean for this to happen.

"Nice hit, by the way," the attendant said.

"Thanks."

Our first day of practice as a Super Bowl–bound team was no different from our first day of practice in July, with one exception. After we'd lined up in our stretching rows, Lou came over to Ramsey and me as Paulie shouted out instructions. Lou had never wandered past the first two rows of the stretching formation before. Not since I'd been there, at least. I assumed he wanted to talk to Ramsey about strategy or maybe even congratulate him for leading the team this far in place of Hanes. I thought this might be the day Lou actually treated Ramsey like a first-string quarterback.

"Lou's coming," I said in between grunts to Ramsey as he pushed my legs apart like a wishbone. Ramsey's back was to the approaching coach.

"What's he doin' comin' here?"

"Dunno. Maybe he wants to shoot the shit with ya."

"Yeah, right," Ramsey spit out. "That'll be the day when that ass-wipe treats me like Hanes."

"Well, I know he ain't comin' over to talk to me. We've hardly made eye contact all season."

I could see in Ramsey's face that he thought I might be right. Maybe Lou was coming over to talk to him, just as he used to do with Hanes. Lou's face appeared over the back of Ramsey's head.

"How you fellas doin' over here?"

"Good, Coach," I answered.

Ramsey said nothing. But Lou wasn't Midland. The silent treatment didn't work with him. Lou rapped his knuckles on the back of Ramsey's helmet.

"Hellooo! Anyone in there?"

Ramsey flinched. "I'm doin' all right, Lou," he said hesitantly.

I could never call him Lou. He was always "Coach" to me.

"That's what worries me," Lou said. "As soon as you think you're doing 'all right' you're in trouble. I had Midland break down film from the past few Super Bowls. Watch them and see how real quarterbacks perform under pressure. You might learn a thing or two."

Ramsey's face filled with hurt and anger. He'd led us to two play-off wins while earning the admiration of the team, the city, and the league. But the person whose opinion mattered most refused to give him credit.

"Whatever you say, Lou," Ramsey said with a frown.

Lou smiled cockily, then said, "Listen, Dom," suddenly shifting his attention to me. "Say hello to Salvi for me. Make sure you tell him he's welcome here anytime as my personal guest."

"Sure, Coach," I said.

And then Lou walked away, whistling as he went. Whistling! We continued to stretch, silent in disbelief—Ramsey at the blatant snub, and me by his mention of Salvi. How the hell did Lou know Salvi Rossini? And how did he know that I knew him well enough to relay a message like that?

I watched Lou walk back to the front of the stretching formation. Reaching the first row, he stopped in front of Moze, sitting upright with legs outstretched. They exchanged a few words, then both laughed. It was strange seeing Lou so jovial. Ever since Moze had returned, Lou had been a new man. We were all happy Moze was back, but Lou was downright euphoric. Not once had he lost his temper or even berated us. It was as though his best friend had returned from the dead and nothing else mattered. Watching him bend down with a big smile to tussle the hair of his favorite son, I wondered why he couldn't spread around such goodwill a bit more evenly. I was going to need some of it myself after the Super Bowl, and Hoss could sure as hell use some right now.

Looking at Ramsey, I saw him observing the playful antics between Lou and Moze.

"Maybe I should wrap my car around a lamppost and go into rehab," Hoss said. "That seems to be the only way to get any respect around here."

I laughed. "Lou's just happy, that's all. He's a good coach. He cares about his guys."

"Lou's a jackass," Ramsey said. "And you're a jackass for believing that."

I whistled a couple of notes to lighten his mood. He responded with his biggest pout ever. Name that tune was out of the question.

Twenty

Salvi and I sat at the bar of the Point having our last home dinner of the season. It was a somber meal. I was preoccupied with Emma. He was preoccupied with his own thoughts. I twirled my fusilli absent-mindedly with my fork. Salvi hadn't taken one sip of his beer.

"Whatta ya thinking about?" I asked him.

"Nothing. You?"

"You know what I'm thinking about. I still can't believe you didn't tell me."

"Emma told me not to. She made me swear."

"C'mon, Salvi."

"Hey, don't get mad at me. I didn't even know until the Philly game. She hid it well. Besides, I told you to call her a hundred times after that."

"I know."

"She's a grown woman. She made her choice. Let it go."

I could never let it go. But it was useless getting mad at Salvi. It wasn't his fault. I should've called Emma a long time ago.

"I'm finished," I said, pushing the full plate away from me.

"All right, take care. I gotta go see someone," said Salvi, getting up. "Good luck next week. Stay healthy."

He didn't notice that my plate was still full, or if he did, he didn't care. He was in a world of his own.

"Thanks," I said. "See you in California. Pick out a good spot for our pregame meal."

"Sorry, you're on your own. I ain't going."

I was shocked. "You've been to every Giant game for the last twenty years, but you're not going to the Super Bowl?"

"No. See ya."

I watched, dumbfounded, as he walked out the door.

Frank came over with a manhattan. "If you're not gonna eat your dinner, at least have a drink. The cherries are loaded with carbs."

"What's up with your dad? Why isn't he going to the Super Bowl?"

"Let's just say, he's disillusioned with the sport."

"Huh?"

"I told you all about it the week following the Philly game. Remember?"

"The Joey Delucca night?"

"Absolutely."

"You didn't tell me anything that night except Sammy Penrod lost money to that midget bookie."

"Well, that's it."

I looked at him skeptically. "What does one bet, over a month ago, have to do with your father acting so weird tonight? I've seen him five or six times since then and he's been nothing like this."

"That's because it wasn't just one bet, one month ago. It's been hundreds of bets over many years. This thing between Joey and

Sammy has been going for decades. Millions of dollars have changed hands. Their bets are like slaps to the face. Depending on who wins, they keep trading blow after blow. They hate each other's guts."

"So what's the problem?"

"The problem is, Joey let things get out of hand. Sammy's been getting his ass kicked all year. He's been hemorrhaging money. The Philly game was the third time he welshed on his bets with Joey. That was strike three. Things came to a head that week."

"Did Yoda send Luke Skywalker to break Sammy's thumbs?"

I laughed at my own joke. Frank didn't.

"That's not Joey's call. His boss handles that stuff," he said gravely. "Fortunately, Sammy was able to sell his insurance business to get to level before anything had to be done. Everyone thought that was the end of it. But then Joey went and fucked things up again. He's been betting with Sammy these last few weeks after being ordered not to, and now Sammy's in the hole again."

"Why doesn't he just pay up? Sammy's supposedly worth millions."

"Not anymore. He's broke."

That was shocking. I couldn't believe someone could lose so much money gambling. I wondered if this was the jam Moze had mentioned in the sauna.

Frank shook his head slowly, drying a highball glass with a towel. "It never should've come to this. It's bad business."

"Not for Joey," I said.

"If Joey stopped when he took Sammy's last dollar, I'd agree with you. But he didn't. He kept giving him a chance to redeem himself."

"Sounds like Joey was doing him a favor."

"Letting someone dig their own grave ain't a favor. He took Sammy's action, but with conditions. The line he gave him was doubled compared to everyone else. It was practically impossible for Sammy to win."

"Joey can do that? I thought the line was the same for everyone."

"It usually is. But this was personal, remember? Unofficial business between him and Sammy. Joey could give whatever odds he wanted."

"Why did Sammy take it? Why didn't he just go to another bookie?"

"He couldn't. Everyone knew he was broke. These guys don't take bets if there's nothing to collect. Joey had him locked up."

"Why wouldn't Sammy just stop?"

"Cuz he's a degenerate gambler. He couldn't help himself. It's a disease."

"So what's Joey's story? Why would he take bets if he knew Sammy couldn't pay?"

"Because he's a sadistic prick and he hates Sammy. He'd love to bury him. He's been waiting for an opportunity like this for years. He figured if Sammy was into him deep enough, his boss would step in and take care of the problem once and for all. But that was a mistake. Joey'd already been warned to stop dealing with Sammy. His boss, thinking the situation had been resolved after Sammy made good by selling his insurance company, went ballistic when he learned that Joey had put Sammy back in the hole."

"Why'd the boss care?"

"Because it was a stupid thing to do. Joey put him in an awkward position. It's important for your clients to have money in their pockets. Taking bets that can't be collected on is idiotic. Joey's a fucking moron. If a guy's tapped out, he's tapped out. What's the boss supposed to do? Breaking thumbs can't get blood from a stone. Besides, break too many thumbs and you're liable to send some scared asshole running to the cops. Worse yet, dispose of a problem like Sammy and you might as well invite the Feds to come investigate you yourself. Forget that shit. No one's worth that kind of trouble, no matter what he owes."

"How does Sammy's money get collected then?"

"It doesn't. Joey fucked up, so his boss forgave Sammy his debt."

"All of it? You mean Sammy's in the clear?" I was disappointed.

"Not exactly. The boss forgave the debt to his business because of Joey's incompetency. But he can't forgive the debt altogether. Only Joey can do that."

"Did he?"

"Hell, no. Sammy owes him a shitload of money."

That made me feel better. I didn't want Sammy getting off free and clear.

"So, what happens now?"

"Who knows? We're talking about one crazy midget here. Joey's hell-bent on erasing Sammy one way or another. Now that his boss took a pass, it wouldn't surprise me if he took matters into his own hands."

"Is Joey capable?"

"Of course! He may be small, but he'll pull the trigger."

My eyes widened. I didn't like Sammy, but I didn't wish him harm.

"Don't worry," Frank continued. "The whole thing'll probably blow over."

"How so?"

"The boss brokered a last chance for Sammy to come clean. He knows he can't keep Joey from going after Sammy. But he doesn't trust him to take care of the problem without bringing unwanted attention to his little enterprise. So he arranged one last bet between the two to resolve the matter once and for all. No inflated point spread, any venue Sammy chooses. Sammy wins, the debt's gone for good. He loses, and the boss agrees to take care of things the right way."

"I thought nobody was worth that kind of trouble."

"No one is. That's why the boss is making sure that Sammy wins."

"He fixed the bet?"

"Nothing's a sure thing. But it's as close as it'll ever get."

"What are they betting on?"

Frank smiled and shrugged his shoulders. He was through talking.

"Fine," I said. "But what's all this got to do with your dad's shitty mood?"

Frank smiled and shrugged his shoulders again. I knew I couldn't force him to speak. Sitting back, I drained the last of my manhattan, absorbing all that he'd said. Moze wasn't kidding when he said that Sammy had a gambling problem. I'd no idea it was this serious. Moze's drug problem seemed mild in comparison. I thought about practice the other day and how Lou had come up to me in regard to Salvi. I knew Frank wouldn't reveal anything more, but I had to ask a couple more questions.

"Anyone else involved here besides Sammy and Joey?"

"There's always other people involved," Frank said, declining to elaborate.

I popped a maraschino cherry into my mouth. Last question.

"This boss you keep talking about. Who is he?"

Frank laughed and slapped the bar towel he'd been drying glasses with over his shoulder. "The answer to that, my friend," he said with a gleam in his eye, "would fall into the category of *too much knowledge for your own good.* Bar's closed. Good night."

Twenty-one

My conversation with Frank had been interesting. If I'd heard it a month ago, I would have been more intrigued. But I just couldn't rouse much curiosity. If Dr. Bedrosian was right, in another week Moze and Sammy wouldn't concern me anyway. I'd lost interest in the whole affair. Besides, since my encounter with Emma, I'd been consumed with my own predicament. Despite being on the threshold of the Super Bowl, I could no longer ignore that my life was a failure. The girl I loved was gone. The child we'd conceived was gone. And the career I'd built was as good as gone. Thirty years old, I was about to enter the real world with little to my name and no means of survival. Besides a few trophies and some money in the bank, I had nothing. If it weren't for the upcoming Super Bowl, I might apathetically have driven my car off the George Washington Bridge on my way home that night.

The week following the Chicago game had been hard. The nights in my bed grew longer and more restless. Sleepless, I thought of what could've been and what *should've* been, if only I'd been more aware of Emma's feelings and less concerned with my own. I was also kept awake by images of McMillen writhing in agony on the field, his knee twisted in a knot.

Regret, contrition, and self-loathing were my constant companions. Any rest obtained was the result of the whiskey kept by the side of my bed. But the alcohol didn't always work, and more often than not I'd jump into my car and drive, hoping to leave these unwelcome guests behind. Trips through the Delaware Water Gap, some seventy miles away, became routine. The procession of highway markers rolling by my eyes hypnotized me into numbness. A stomp on the accelerator was my only relief from despair. But I couldn't drive forever, and no matter where I set out for, I always wound up in the same spot—the extreme end corner of parking lot B, sipping on coffee and waiting for Red to open the doors of the stadium.

Since Moze's accident, I'd yet to see him fly through the empty tollbooths, swerve around the trash barrels, and screech into his parking space. No longer was he the first one there to claim that spot each day. It was now a space of no significance, open to anyone who pulled into it first. Not since that uneasy morning when he lay half-dead in his Mercedes had Moze arrived to work early. I missed him terribly. If the lot had been a lonely place before he burst into it, it was lonelier now, knowing that he wouldn't. His presence had made me feel not so alone in my need for the locker room or for the game. But now his absence made me despise myself for depending so heavily, and so foolishly, upon them both.

The city was awash in Super Bowl fever. Banners, logos, and posters were everywhere. Anticipation was tangible, excitement contagious. But to me, the Super Bowl was merely the last game of my life and simply the beginning of a bleak future, one Dr. Bedrosian had created for me when he'd uttered those two horrific Latin words in the middle of the season. Nothing made sense anymore. The future? I didn't want it. The way I'd been behaving, I didn't deserve one.

On the eve of our departure for California and the Rose Bowl, the silence of the Meadowlands almost did me in. As I pulled into the parking lot from a trip to Allentown, my mind raced wildly unchecked into near madness. The road trip had done nothing to ease my mind. Voices rang in my head, loud and strong: Emma's, Lou's, Red's, Salvi's, Doc's. Anxiety engulfed me. I lifted my hands to my ears, but nothing could suppress the clamor. Putting the car into park, I jumped out and screamed into the black sky, *"Stop!"*

But the uncaring meadows' response simply buried my plea in the silence of its swamps. My anxiety continued unabated as the last echo of my voice was lost in the reeds. Leaning face-first onto the hood of my car, I clung with outstretched arms to the only thing left in my command.

"I quit," I said with exhaustion, not knowing to whom I was conceding. "I quit. No more. You win."

The warmth of the engine soothed my face, and that small comfort allayed the cacophony in my brain. A concession for my surrender, perhaps. A drop of cold sweat fell from my brow onto the grime-covered hood. Suddenly, above the muffled din in my head, one voice asserted itself.

"Believe and live your faith," it said. I didn't know whom it belonged to, but it wasn't in my head. It was right next to me. Startled, I looked around. No one was there. Those words, I thought. Where had I heard them before? All was silent but for the ticks of the Monte's engine as it settled. "St. Basil's," I said aloud, remembering. My grandfather had spoken them in my dream the morning I fell asleep during Mass. He'd been on his deathbed and had held a prayer card in his hands. A prayer card for the souls in purgatory. The priest who'd awoken me had given me one just like it. I pulled it out of my wallet where I'd kept it and looked at it. On the front was a figure engulfed in flames, a halo over his head. On the back, a prayer read, *May the Divine assistance remain always with us. And may the souls of the Faithful Departed, through the Mercy of God, Rest in Peace. Amen.* As I looked at the card, the voice spoke again: "Pray for me." This time I recognized it. Like my grandfather calling me to church on a peaceful Sunday morning, I knew where I had to go.

St. Basil's was quiet when I arrived. The door seemed locked tight, but opened easily with the gentlest of pulls. I wasn't sure why I'd come. I didn't know what I was hoping for. I just felt the need to be here, as though the building itself held the answer to my problems.

As I walked down the main aisle, my shoes squeaked loudly on the floor and echoed throughout the empty chamber. This time, the noise didn't bother me. No one was there to hear it. I walked all the way down to the first row and took a seat. The altar looked different from this vantage point. Up close, I saw how big and ornate it truly was. Carvings of saints and disciples were etched in its marble, and massive candelabra protected both flanks. It was beautiful.

My breath blew white and frosty in the cold air, and I watched it ascend to the darkened ceiling. With every breath, my mind emptied. Soon, relaxation took hold, and out of habit I slid off my seat and onto the kneeler at my feet. Raising my hands in front of me, I assumed a praying position. But I'd nothing to say. I could've prayed for help and protection on the field, but my next game wasn't for a week. I didn't need that kind of help at the moment. Besides, I never really *prayed* for that, I just sort of expected it as a result of my attendance at Mass. Putting football aside, I thought about my personal life. That's where I needed help the most. But the more I thought about my actions lately, the less I felt I deserved any. Remembering Emma, our baby, McMillen, Bobby Ward, and everything else, I cringed. Staring at the magnificent altar before me, I felt dirty and unworthy. Unworthy of help. Unworthy of a second chance. I wanted to ask God for forgiveness, but I didn't believe forgiveness was possible. Despondent, I was convinced that God wouldn't help such a miserable creature as myself. Still, I was there on my knees with my hands folded, the body of Christ alive in the tabernacle. I ought to say something, I thought. So with little faith to say anything else, I recited some childhood standards ingrained in my memory. "Our Father, who art in heaven, hallowed be Thy name . . ."

As I spoke, tension rushed out of my body like flowing water. Each word brought a new level of peace. Over and over, I repeated the same prayers: Our Father, Hail Mary, Glory Be. Soon I was calm, bordering on sleep. Entering the church, I'd noticed a chapel in the back. Heat had been coming from it, and its small confines looked like the perfect place for a nap. Barely able to keep my eyes open, I walked back to it and lay down on one of its three pews. Moonlight shone in from the only window in the room, and under the shadow of obscured paintings and statues, I closed my eyes and fell asleep.

If I dreamed, I'd no recollection. I only knew I'd slept for a long time. When my eyes opened, the sun had replaced the moon and beams poured through the narrow window, lighting the room on fire.

I soaked up the sunlight and reveled in its warmth. I couldn't have been more comfortable if McMillen had knocked me back to my infant crib again. I felt wonderful. Even my knee had stopped throbbing.

With the light, I could see the icons and statues of the small chapel. Everywhere were images of the Vision of Fátima. Statues of the three children knelt before the snow-white figure of the Virgin Mary, and above their heads were inscribed the words REPENT AND FORGIVE.

Repent and forgive. These words struck a chord.

Suddenly, a voice sounded behind me: "Can I help you with

anything?" A priest stuck his head into the little chapel. It was the same priest I'd spoken with last time I was here.

"Hi, Father," I said. "No, I'm fine. Thanks. I was just resting . . . I mean, praying."

"Oh, it's you," he said, recognizing me from our last encounter. "H-how did you get in here? I didn't see you come in."

"I came in earlier. I snuck back here because I was cold and the chapel was heated."

"This chapel isn't heated, my son." He stared at me.

"It isn't?"

"No. None of St. Basil's is heated. We can't afford to heat a building of this size."

"But it was warm in here last night."

"You've been here since last night?" he asked with a mixture of anger and surprise. "I'm the only one who can open the door to the public." He seemed huffy.

"I'm sorry, Father, the door *was* open, and I didn't think anyone would mind."

"I don't know how that could be. I unlocked the door myself this morning."

Obviously, something weird had happened last night. But I hadn't done anything wrong and I felt as though the priest was accusing me of something inappropriate.

"Look, Father, I came in here to pray. The door was open. I didn't break in, if that's what you think. I didn't come in here to get off the street. And I didn't come in here to spend the night. My name is Dominic Fucillo and I have an apartment in town and a job. I just came in here for a little peace of mind and some prayer time. Now if you'll excuse me, I'd like to get back to what I was doing, unless of course you're in the habit of harassing worshippers simply because they got to church *before you.*"

I couldn't believe I was talking so flippantly to a priest. I wasn't sure what my outburst would yield, so I played it cool by turning to face the small altar of the chapel and piously got down on my knees to pray like a holy man. What he didn't know was that I was praying for him to leave.

"Dominic Fucillo?!" he exclaimed. "You know, I thought that was you! But the way you're dressed, and the way you . . . well . . . *smell,* kind of threw me off. I didn't recognize you before. Holy Mother of God! Dominic Fucillo of the New York Giants. Right here in St. Basil's. Can you beat that?"

He looked around as though he wanted to tell someone. But no one was in the church besides us.

I couldn't believe it. The priest was acting like any irrational Giants fan. I didn't know priests cared about things like the Super Bowl. I looked at him and wondered what else he had in common with the rest of us. But as I did, a strange yearning overtook me, the same yearning that had compelled me to come to St. Basil's in the first place. I couldn't make sense of it last night, but now it was obvious. Suddenly, I understood why I was here.

"Father," I asked him almost involuntarily. "Would you hear my confession?"

My stomach turned as I spoke. I hadn't been to confession since my First Communion in the second grade.

"Of course, my son. I'd be honored," the priest said, transitioning seamlessly from a rabid fan to a man with the power to forgive sins. As he sat down next to me on the pew, our knees touched.

"Shouldn't we go into a booth or somethin'?" I asked nervously.

"No need, my son. We can do it right here. It counts just the same."

Too late now. I wanted the shelter of the screen, but figured he knew who I was already, so what difference would it make?

"Awwwright," I said apprehensively. But it wasn't as difficult as I'd imagined. In fact, my confession almost came out on its own. There was no shortage of material, that's for sure. Beginning slowly, I picked up steam until I was unloading years of sin with as much force and emotion as when I unloaded punches on Dirty

Rivers and Bobby Ward. Everything and anything I could think of came rolling off my tongue. Swears, cheating, sexual misconduct, lies, impure thoughts, gluttony, envy, pride, drunkenness, licentiousness, cruelty, greediness, violence, fights both physical and verbal, sins of commission, sins of omission. They had seemed like small things at the time, but balled together they were frightening. Especially the fights. The number of times I'd lost my temper was alarming. But the biggest admissions were how I'd treated Emma, along with the fate of the child for which I was responsible. Those confessions did not come easy.

By the time I finished, the sun was headed for the West Coast, the very place we were bound for early this evening. I was exhausted. Sweat dripped from my forehead. The priest offered me his handkerchief. If he'd been horrified by what I said, he sure didn't show it. Instead, he was calm and relaxed. What a pro, I thought.

I was transformed. Never did I think that confession could be so liberating. It was like casting off physical locks and chains.

"In the name of God, my son, your sins are forgiven," the priest said gently.

Simple words, indeed. But it was beyond me how I'd lived so long without ever hearing them.

"You have a clean slate now, Dominic," he said with a smile.

I knew that was a cliché, but the funny thing was, I felt clean. Looking on my past, I marveled at how grimy my life had been. I'd been so entrenched in filth that I didn't know what being clean was. I felt as if the priest were a master mechanic performing a major overhaul on my soul.

"Your anger however, Dominic, must be controlled," he said.

Like any good mechanic going over the list of problems he had found, he gave me a few words of parting advice.

"God has given you great physical gifts, but don't forget that your physical skills are driven precisely by your temperament.

Without the proper attitude, these physical tools can be wasted, or at least not used to their potential. Just as you've mastered your body to perform at your command, so, too, must you forge your temperament to reflect the dictates of your moral conscience.

"Remember, Dom, 'sin' means anything less than perfection. It's not quite the 'evil' thing that it's come to depict. It simply means you missed or fell short. But that in no way signals the end of the contest. You will sin or fall short of perfection every day. The man who admits his failings and gets back up to try again is the man who truly loves God. Life is a race that's run to the end. The Church gives us Communion and confession and the rest of the sacraments as pit stops in our journey. They are meant for cleansing, refueling, and preparing for the next round of events. The ultimate and *only* goal for any of us is to make it to the next world with our *faith intact.* There is nothing here on earth that can ever be more important than this. Remember, the real evil is not sin. The real evil is the abandonment of faith, for without faith we cannot be saved."

"What about Emma?" I asked. "And my baby? Can God really forgive me for that?"

"God can and will forgive anything, *if* you ask Him. The real question is, will you forgive yourself? Will you forgive Emma?"

I hesitated. I honestly didn't know the answer.

"Remember our Lord's Prayer. 'Forgive us our sins as we forgive those who sin against us.' We are all our own little gods. The way the one true God will ultimately deal with each of us is the way that we have dealt with one another."

I nodded, deeply moved.

"Emma did what she did under duress. And I might add, that duress came about as a result of your sexual actions. The Church states very clearly its position in this regard."

"But, c'mon, Father. I'm human. You can't expect me to . . ."

"*I* don't expect anything. The rules are the rules, designed as signposts leading to heaven. If a man were expected to abide by these rules without deviation, there would be no need for confession, would there? There would be no need for purgatory, either. Yet, there they both are, given to us by the Almighty, specifically because *He* doesn't expect us to be perfect.

"The Lord never gives up on us. We're the only ones who do that. I've already told you, the worst tragedy in God's eyes is losing hope, losing faith. Life goes on here as well as in the next world. You have to decide where you want to spend your eternity, and then you must prepare for it. I can absolve you of your sins, but it's up to you to accept forgiveness. It's up to you to accept God."

The priest's voice was soothing. His words were like drops of water on a barren plain. My soul devoured them greedily.

"And now for your penance," he said.

The thought of the potential punishments made me cringe.

"You asked about purgatory the first time we met. I explained how we should pray for the poor souls. In addition to prayers, we can also endure sufferings here on earth that their sufferings may be alleviated. In your line of work, the opportunities for such sacrifices are endless. The penance I give you is simply this: offer those sufferings along with your prayers for the poor souls."

Easy enough, I thought. Things could've been much worse. Breathing a sigh of relief, I nodded with acceptance.

"Great," the priest said. "We're through then."

I sat still, basking in the glow of my newfound cleanliness. I felt so good, I didn't want to leave. Not until the priest reminded me of my trip to California was I able to peel myself from the worn wooden pew of the chapel. Even then, I didn't want to leave. But the priest said he was counting on me. He had a bet on the Super Bowl with the rabbi from across town. So with a final blessing from his hand and a sincere thank-you from my heart, he hustled me out the door and into the fading light of an early New Jersey sunset.

"Remember, Dominic," the priest said, "believe and live your faith!"

Those words again. I thought of how much turmoil I might've avoided if I had taken those words to heart when my grandfather had uttered them so long ago on his deathbed. Pulling out the card the priest had given me earlier, I recited the prayer on the back. "From now on," I vowed to my grandfather, "every suffering I endure will be offered up for you, Pop, and for the souls in purgatory." It was probably my imagination, but I thought I heard someone whisper, "Thank you," in my ear.

Arriving back at the stadium with only minutes to spare, I jumped onto the team bus as it left for the airport. My mind was quiet and my body rested. I felt elated, as if I'd been given a new lease on life. Visions of Emma flooded my head. Anger and regret no longer accompanied them. Forgiveness had taken their place.

Twenty-two

Super Bowl Sunday arrived without incident, in a season that for me had been full of them. The way the game started, it appeared the hand of fate was about to pen yet another disappointing entry onto my already miserable résumé. By the end of the first quarter we were down by seven points. Seconds before the half-time gun, we trailed by seventeen.

I couldn't have asked for a better day, a beautiful, warm afternoon. A soft wind was lazily gliding across the field of the Rose Bowl. I unsnapped my chinstrap and pushed my helmet back as far as I could without its falling off.

"Damn!" I mumbled, as I looked at the game clock: 3 . . . 2 . . . 1 . . . *Ccccrackkk!*

The smoke from the referee's gun drifted toward the fading sunlight. The first half was over, and both teams headed for their locker rooms. I watched the Miami Dolphins run off the field and wondered how we'd managed to fall so far behind what I considered an inferior team. Moving the ball against their defense had been no problem, but a big fat zero was still on our side of the scoreboard.

I slipped from the reality of the stadium and onto a windswept beach filled with bikini-clad California girls and coolers of ice-cold beer. I decided to stay for a while. The surf was up and a brunette with piercing green eyes was beckoning me to join her in the waves. If I could just stay on this beach for a few minutes, I might hasten my recovery from the first half. Just a few more minutes, one more drink, and a last final dip in the ocean. That would do the trick, I thought. Concentrate and relax, I told myself. Forget about where you are, forget about the game for just one more minute.

"Hey, Fucillo! You *suuuccckkk*!" An obnoxious voice with a Bronx accent jerked me back to reality.

Opening my eyes, I saw two half-naked men, slathered in blue body paint, leaning over the railing that separated the stands from the field. They certainly weren't the California girls I'd been thinking about. Instead of bikinis, they both had the word GIANTS plastered over their bare chests in white lettering, and each held a twenty-four-ounce plastic cup of beer in one hand and a foot-long bratwurst sandwich in the other. Mustard overflowed from their rolls and fell in globs onto their exposed stomachs, creating a kaleidoscope of yellow, white, and black and blue body hair.

"Fucillo, you *suuuccckkk*!" the same voice repeated, as one of the slobs pointed his sausage at me with one hand and spilled his beer with the other. As soon as I made eye contact, fat slob number two decided to throw in his two cents' worth.

"Fucillo, what the hell you doin'? Stop daydreamin'and get your ass in the locker room. You're the only one out here, for crissakes!"

I looked around. He was right. I was the only player left on the field.

"Get your act together, Fucillo! You look like shit!" said fat slob number two. "I got a lotta money ridin' on this game! If you don't score some points, someone's gonna pay!" He sprayed bits and pieces of half-eaten bratwurst as he shouted. "Believe me, I can make you pay!" he yelled ominously.

I kept moving toward the locker room, trying to ignore the two idiots, and passed a stadium security guard.

"Don't mind them. Just a couple of my fans."

"Good thing they're on your side," he shot back, rolling his eyes.

Yeah. Good thing.

I thought of Joey Delucca and Sammy. Perhaps a much bigger game than I could imagine *was* being played off the field, the consequences of which were just as dangerous, if not more so, than anything that might happen between the goalposts. Before my conversation with Salvi, I would've laughed when the fat slob said he could "make me pay." Now, I wasn't so sure. My teammates and I *did* have an awfully big part in the outcome of the game, just as Salvi said, and as I looked around the locker room, I eyed everyone with suspicion. That fat slob in the stands was right. We should've scored at least a couple of touchdowns by now. We shouldn't be losing this game. I had a bad feeling about it all. Common sense told me I was paranoid, but my experience these last few months, especially the memory of James Moze in the seat of his bloodied Mercedes-Benz, suggested otherwise.

The locker room had always been a sanctuary for me, whether at home or on the road. But with these new thoughts running through my head, and with us on the verge of losing the most important game I'd ever played in, the relief I longed for was nowhere to be found. Instead, I walked into a cauldron of energy and chaos.

"Let's go, you buncha mothafuckas!" James Moze shouted. "We're getting our asses kicked out there! Defense, you're playing like a bunch of pussies! Offense, you gotta score some points!"

"Take it easy, Moze. It'll be all right!" an anonymous voice peeped up from the back.

"Fuck you!" Moze shot back, faster than he could run the forty. "I don't know about you assholes, but I didn't bust my hump all year just so we could *lose* the mothafucka!"

Tears of rage were in his eyes. Some guys joined in, trying to snap the team out of its funk by hurling invectives. Swear words flew throughout the room like pieces of hail in a midsummer day's thunderstorm.

The guys who weren't swearing were too busy hustling here and there, making adjustments to their uniforms. Missing cleats needed replacing. Air pads in helmets needed replenishing. Loose face masks needed tightening. Players ran frantically back and forth, in and out of the training room, hoping to procure the taping services of an unoccupied trainer. Tape jobs tight enough before the game to cut off circulation now hung loosely off the body, torn to shreds and drenched with blood and sweat.

Trainers worked like madmen, slapping tape on guys so fast, the naked eye couldn't follow them. Equipment men, including Red, with power drills in hand, screwed and unscrewed cleats with such rapidity, and pumped air into helmets so furiously, they looked like pit crews at the Indy 500.

A game of "musical chairs" played out around the toilets provided to serve the eighty people in the Giants entourage. The trainers had poured an abundance of fluids into our bodies to prevent dehydration. Now, whatever we hadn't sweated out was banging violently on the doors of our bladders screaming to be released. Players were yelling at one another "Hurry up!" and "Piss or get off the pot!" Some just let loose in the showers and sinks. Urine vapors stung my eyes. Anarchy ruled. No one was in charge of anything.

Since the only piece of equipment I cared about was intact (my helmet), and no tape in existence would have adhered to my sweat-drenched body, and I didn't have to go to the bathroom, I went directly to my locker and plunked my sweaty behind down on my stool to await the arrival of the boss.

Lou came bursting through the locker-room door with urgency on his face.

"Offense, over here! Defense, over there!"

Everyone stopped what he was doing, and the room, for a moment, turned even more chaotic than it had been, as offensive and defensive players plowed into each other trying to get to their respective ends of the room.

"Listen up!" Lou didn't wait for our attention. He knew he had it. "Get your heads outta your asses! This is the biggest game of your lives and you're pissing it away! You couldn't beat Hackensack High playing like that, never mind the Dolphins! This is the Super Bowl, goddammit! How many times you think you're gonna get here? If some of you don't start playing better, I'll tell you what, you sure as hell won't make it back as a New York Giant, that I guarantee! Now get with your coaches and find out what the hell's goin' wrong out there!"

The assistant coaches, as if on cue, launched into their own expletive-filled assessments of the first half and began drawing elaborate hieroglyphics that only they could decipher.

After about fifteen minutes, one of the game officials poked his head through the door and shouted, "Two minutes, Coach!"

Lou retook center stage. This time he was more subdued. "Listen up, fellas."

Everyone fell silent, hoping for some words of encouragement.

"I want you all to know that this is the best team I've ever coached. I don't think there's anyone out there who can beat you when you play like you're capable. Hell, I don't think there's *ever* been a team that could hold a candle to you. You have the chance, right now, to do something that most people only dream of. The chance to achieve something that the great majority of your peers never will. *You have the opportunity to be champions of the world!*

"The only things standing between you and the record books are yourselves and the Miami Dolphins. And let me tell you, fellas, *they're not that good!* They're really not. So that leaves *you.* It's there if you want it, guys, it really is. I promise you, I'll do everything I can to give you a chance to win this game. You just do what *you're* supposed to do and they'll be fitting us for rings when this game is over. *Now let's go out there and play some New York Giant football!*"

The locker room exploded. "New York! Let's go, New York! Kick some ass! Thirty minutes, baby! Thirty minutes to the ring!"

Fresh energy surged throughout the room. Lou had done it again. But that was no surprise.

The team burst out of the locker room and took the field like a bunch of wild animals. I was so revved up I didn't notice the two fat slobs. I didn't notice the Dolphins either, as they ran onto the field. And I especially didn't notice that the sun had now sunk below the horizon.

My teammates were hopping up and down on the sidelines, anxious for action. Guys were hitting each other with fists, elbows, and helmets. Some were crying in frustration that they weren't able to take the field right away and act out their aggressions. Others paced the sidelines quietly like heartless assassins, waiting patiently to perform their services.

I was of the latter persuasion. Wasting strength on meaningless displays of emotion had become too costly lately. Besides, we were kicking off so I had no choice but to be patient.

Our defense took the field and dug in as if they were building a trench for the Battle of the Marne. Miami, up by seventeen, figured to run mostly time-consuming running plays, so our defense had eight men up on the line of scrimmage. But to our surprise, on the first play from scrimmage, Matt Devers, the Miami quarterback, went for the home run. He fired a missile downfield that caught our defense and everyone else in the stadium completely off guard.

A wave of panic struck as I watched the ball sail over the head of every Giant defender on the field. A lone Dolphin receiver ran down the sideline, completely uncovered. Nothing stood between him and the goal line. It looked to be a sure six points. My heart sank. All of Lou's pep talks rolled into one could never shake off this impending knockout blow. A seventeen-point lead would require a comeback of monumental proportions. A twenty-four-point lead was insurmountable.

The pass from Devers hit its apex and began its descent. I looked back to see if any of our defenders had a shot at a tackle. Not a chance. In seconds, we were going to be in a hole that might as well be our grave. All the confidence that Lou had instilled in us minutes earlier was about to be destroyed.

"That's another six points," said Jimmy the trainer morosely, standing at my side. He flung a water bottle to the ground in frustration. The sideline waited for the inevitable. Everyone in the stadium assumed it would be a completion. Only I knew better.

My eyes weren't trained for many things, but they could spot an overthrown pass when they saw one.

"It's long," I said.

"Bullshit," Jimmy responded.

Instead of maintaining his stride, the Miami receiver left his feet and stretched the length of his body parallel to the ground. He reached his hands for the ball as far as nature would allow, and in the blinding flash of a thousand camera bulbs, we watched the pass fly inches from his fingertips and fall harmlessly to the ground.

Incompletion.

"Told ya."

If there was a moment when you could feel defeat turn into victory before it actually happened, this was it. In the four and a half seconds that it took for the ball to leave Devers's hand and overshoot its target, the whole Giants team was galvanized.

The confidence we'd carried from the locker room at halftime was not only intact, but was stronger than ever. Likewise, the confidence the Dolphins had possessed a moment before had suddenly, irreparably been damaged.

The Dolphins tried a running play. Our defense stuffed them. On third down they tried another pass. Sack! James Moze. Fourth down and fifteen, they had to punt.

Jeb Watkins caught Miami's punt and looked upfield. I watched as he cradled the ball in his arms, and I heard him let out a "Waahoooo!" as he ran straight into the mass of eleven Miami defenders. Our guys blocked their hearts out for the banshee. They buried a few Dolphins in the dirt and blindsided others. Bodies were flung recklessly through the air.

Jeb never really looked for a seam to run *through* as much as he searched for the right person to run *into*. Yet, he kept running and the Dolphins kept missing. They whizzed by him like aqua-green-and-white blurs, and he ran untouched, from our twenty-yard line to the thirty . . . to the forty . . . to the fifty . . . We were going crazy. There was only one Dolphin to beat!

Bradley Andrade was Miami's biggest and meanest linebacker, and he stood at midfield drooling like an ogre, waiting for his dinner. One of the most feared players in the league, he had already ended his share of careers. Watkins, on the other hand, was a diminutive special-teamer who weighed 160 pounds. And as he drew closer to Andrade, it became obvious that he wasn't planning to run around the bigger and much stronger linebacker.

Andrade might've been a trained killer, but he wasn't the most agile guy on the field. All Jeb had to do was give him one little juke, one little head fake, one little hip shake, one little wiggle, and he'd be off. But it wasn't going to happen. I'd seen him in this situation before. Times like these were what kept Jeb from being the leading punt returner in the league. Like me running at Dirty Rivers, Jeb just couldn't help himself.

Five yards from Andrade and he was at the perfect distance to give a move and blow by him. Everyone in the stands expected one. Andrade sat back on his heels so that he could move in either direction. But Jeb's only move was to lower his head and catapult himself like a jet fighter off the deck of an aircraft carrier straight into the mouth of the big linebacker.

SMAAACCCKKK!

Everyone in the stadium felt the impact of *that* hit. Even I let out an "Oooohhh." Our sideline exploded as we watched the invincible Bradley Andrade, Dolphin Pride personified, hurtle through the air and land flat on his back, his cleats pointing toward the sky.

Both players were on the ground, but only one was conscious. Watkins jumped up like a pogo stick and stood over the groggy linebacker. He grabbed the towel that hung from his belt and began to run aimlessly around the field, waving it over his head and screaming, "Woohoooo!" over and over until his teammates chased him down.

"That's one crazy little mutha," Jimmy remarked.

"No kiddin'," I said.

We'd all have preferred the six points of a touchdown, but the hit Watkins put on Andrade did more to inspire us than any touchdown ever could. A touchdown was just points. A hit like that was magic.

I buckled my chinstrap, feeling that I'd been released from a cage. Stepping onto the soft grass of the Rose Bowl, I made my way toward the huddle forming at midfield.

Trotting out, I felt like a dinghy leaving the safety of shore, bobbing its way to the main ship already afloat in the sea of grass. In all my years of playing, I'd never left the sideline without feeling vulnerable and exposed. In the middle of the field, everyone knew who you were. Large white numbers on the front and back of your jersey, to say nothing of the bold lettering of your name, saw to that.

While there was only one way to trot out to the huddle, there were three ways of returning to the sideline. On the wings of victory. In the ashes of defeat. Or strapped down to a stretcher. I made the sign of the cross over myself in the hopes of avoiding scenario number three.

"Get in the fuckin' huddle!" Ramsey shouted.

We looked at him admiringly. Ramsey had become the man, no question about it.

"Time to get our act together," he said. "We need some points and we need 'em now!"

He looked to the sideline for the play. Midland signaled it in with his hands like a third-base coach giving the runner on first the sign to steal.

"Awright . . . Slant Thirty-eight Boss," Ramsey interpreted for us. "Now look, fellas, let's run this pig right down their throat till they choke! It's time to take control of this game! No more foolin'around!" He paused a moment for effect, then gathered himself. "Awright, let's go! Zero Strong Zip Slant Thirty-eight Boss on *one,* on *one*. Ready . . . break!"

We clapped our hands in unison and broke from the huddle. Ramsey strutted confidently toward the line of scrimmage while we stepped quickly around him to our own positions. Walking like a gunfighter in the Old West, he looked ready to engage in a showdown with the Miami defense. Within seconds we stood motionless on the line of scrimmage, poised to attack at the command of our leader, whose arrival under the center coincided perfectly with the completion of our deployment.

My heart was pounding. My lungs grew tight. The first play from scrimmage was always the hardest. The only way to ease back into the violence of a football game was to jump in with both feet. So I methodically squatted into my three-point stance and prepared to fire out on the snap of the ball.

Leaning forward on my grounded right hand, I rested the other on the thigh of my bent left leg. In all the years I'd played, I had never gotten used to this position. Even now I felt uncomfortable. The thing I hated most about it was how restricted I felt. No matter how I tried to lift my head to look at my opponent, I was never able to see anything more than the pair of cleats on his feet in front of me. It was almost claustrophobic.

Look at the size of those feet, I muttered to myself, as I beheld the strange new shoes in front of me. They gotta be a good size seventeen. Look how clean they are. This guy hasn't been on the field all day. Who the hell is he?

I strained my face upward to try to identify him, but the back of my shoulder pads prevented my helmet from moving far enough. "Friggin' pads!" I mumbled in frustration.

Who is this guy? Why aren't his shoes dirty? Why are they putting him in the game now? Why are they putting him in over me? And why can't I see anything in this goddamn stance?

"Blue Fifty-four! . . . Blue Fifty-four! . . . Set! . . ."

Ramsey's voice snapped me back to the situation at hand. All right, I said to myself. Enough. Get your head in the game.

I was back. But the damage was done. In my wonderings, I forgot the snap count. Did he say on *one* or on *two*?!

"Hut one!" Ramsey barked, answering my question. All hell broke loose. The time for thinking was over. Before I could get out of my stance, the mysterious man in the clean shoes jackhammered me under the chin with one of his fists. My lip split open, my mouth filled with blood. His other hand, meanwhile, grabbed control of my shoulder pads.

Holy shit, this guy is *strong,* I thought.

He was no linebacker, that was for sure. This guy weighed forty pounds more than me. A defensive lineman. I was headed in the wrong direction. The Miami player had beaten me to the punch and was making the most of his size advantage as well as my late start off the ball. I wasn't used to this. I was supposed to be the one dishing out the punishment, not the one *receiving it.* I hadn't always gotten off to perfect starts in the past, but I'd always managed to recover. This time, however, no matter how hard I tried, I simply didn't possess enough firepower. I was being beaten, plain and simple. It was embarrassing.

A moment's hesitation off the line of scrimmage had cemented my defeat. If I'd been standing on a map of the United States, looking at Canada, with my feet in Oklahoma, and my job was to block my man in the direction of Maine, then I was in trouble, because I was heading for South Beach—in a hurry!

Our fullback, Chris Smith, who was searching for an opening in the line, decided that he spotted one in the middle of my back and plowed into me from behind like a runaway train. I was crushed between the 240-pound fullback and the 300-plus-pound defender. Mark Lane, our running back, plowed into all three of us, and the sad, sorry debacle of a play was finally ended.

Giants fans yelled obscenities. Miami fans cheered. I lay on the bottom of the pile with more than a ton of human flesh suffocating my aching body and bruised ego. The Miami defender and I remained locked in a hostile embrace. His helmet pressed against mine. If not for the steel rods of our face masks, the weight on top of us would've melded our faces together.

As it was, the sweat from the defender's face and the spit from his foaming mouth fell unhindered. His stinking, hot breath filled my nostrils and gagged me as I struggled to free myself. But it was no use. I was just going to have to wait until everyone piled off. In the meantime, I looked into the eyes of the man who'd just beaten me. I couldn't avoid them, they were right there in front of me. They were a little too wide and a tad too jittery for him *not* to be hyped up on some type of amphetamine. But then I could've figured that out by the sheer display of strength he'd just exhibited. It felt superhuman.

"It's over, little man!" he shouted into my face. "I just kicked your ass, Fucillo! You ain't nothin'!"

It seemed as if we were stuck there for hours. Neither wanted to be the first to let go, so we continued our warlike embrace. He kept ranting and raving and spitting sweat and drool into my face.

"So much for big, tough Dom Fucillo!" he continued. "I guess it was all just hype. You've been pushing around our outside linebacker all day, but that's over now. He shouldn't a been in here to begin with. He's a freakin' pussy, lettin' your sorry ass drive him off the ball. This is a place for men. You hear me, boy? Men! Right now you ain't much of a man, Fucillo. Right now, you ain't nothin' but my bitch! And you're gonna keep on bein' my bitch for the rest of the game. I'm gonna embarrass you straight into the parkin' lot."

On and on he went, spouting insults and invectives meant to burrow under my skin. A week ago, such verbal attacks would've caused me to swing away. I wanted to rip his helmet off and beat him with it as it was. But remembering my confession at St. Basil's and the words of the priest, I decided to harness my anger instead and use it to my advantage on the next play.

At long last, the weight on top of us subsided and I was able to look at the yard markers. We lost six yards on the play. Disaster! Slant 38 Boss had gotten stuffed before, but never for lost yardage. This wasn't the message Lou wanted to send the Dolphins, and I knew exactly whom he'd blame for our poor showing. I could do nothing but get up, wipe the spit and drool off my face, and head back to the huddle.

"Hey, shiny shoes," I called to my attacker. "Hope you enjoyed it, cuz it's the last time it'll happen."

"Screw you, punk! You ain't nothin'!"

Man, was he wired. I hurried back to the huddle to get the next play.

"What happened?" Chris Smith asked.

"I forgot the snap count," I mumbled.

"C'mon, Dom," Ramsey butted in. "We can't afford that shit now."

"I know. It won't happen again."

"Don't worry," Mark Lane said kindly. "Just do your best and I'll make the adjustments."

I appreciated Lane's kindness and my teammates' restraint. But I wasn't too worried about them. The only person who worried me was the guy standing on the sideline. Even though my back was to Lou, I could feel his irresistible force beckoning me from that direction. Sheepishly, I looked over my shoulder. Bingo! There he was, staring me down with hatred in his eyes and his face beet red with anger. A thousand insults from my teammates I could endure. But one stare like that from Lou and I felt like the most incompetent football player who ever donned a helmet.

It was second and sixteen. We were in a deep hole. A big play was needed. A pass. Maybe I could make a big catch and make up for the lost yardage. Ramsey read the play from Midland's hand signals.

"Looks like Lou's giving you a chance to redeem yourself," Ramsey said to me. "Awright, fellas, this one's for the coach's pet. Same play with a different look. Zero Up Slot Slant Thirty-eight Boss Don't Screw It Up This Time, Fucillo, on *two*! On *two*!

"On *two*!" he repeated, looking solely at me. "Ready . . ."

"Break!" we all yelled in unison.

With the clap of our hands we dispersed from the huddle. Ramsey was right. Lou *was* giving me a second chance. But not out of kindness. Rather, he was challenging my manhood. He was saying, "Perform . . . or else!"

This time nothing went through my mind but the play and the snap count. I got down in my stance expecting to see the shoes of the ape from the last play. Instead, I recognized the familiar cleats of the linebacker I'd been punishing for the majority of the game. I was disappointed. I wanted another shot at the loudmouthed lineman. But a Miami defender called for a shift, and the linebacker's shoes were replaced by the ones I wanted.

There was no mistaking those feet. "I'm back, punk," the lineman said. "And I'm gonna kick your ass some more. Just like last time."

I'd be lying if I said I wasn't intimidated. As far as I could figure, he was some third-stringer who'd been pumped full of black beauties and sent to pull a Dirty Rivers on me. Maybe he was trying to make me lose my cool and get me thrown out of the game. If that was the plan, I wasn't going to fall for it.

"Hey, good to see you," I said in a friendly manner. "I'm glad you're back cuz we're runnin' the same play and it's on *two* this time. Good luck, ass-wipe!"

The lineman's feet shuffled and he was silent.

"Blue Eighty-two! . . . Blue Eighty-two!" Ramsey said as he began the cadence.

"You still there?" I said to the pair of shoes.

There was no response.

"Set!" Ramsey continued.

"S-screw you, man!" the shoes finally said, a little confused.

"Not yet," I responded.

"Hut one!"

"Okay, *now* here we go, big boy!"

"Hut two!"

I sprang from my stance and fired into the big goon with the force of a lion. Even I was surprised at my explosiveness. The lineman froze for an instant, not knowing if I was telling the truth about the snap count and the play or if I was just trying to psyche him out. The moment of hesitation that had been my downfall the play before was now about to lead to his.

First, I stunned him with a preemptive head butt to the face. I got him good and knocked his head and shoulders up in the air. This gave me perfect hand position on the breastplate of his shoulder pads. Second, while he reeled from the blow to the head, I pushed against him with my arms and legs as though I were pushing over a wall. This threw him back on his heels.

Now I poured it on. Churning my legs as powerfully as I could, I could feel the big man begin to move. I pushed and churned and churned and pushed, and pretty soon I was driving him straight to Maine for a vacation.

I felt Chris Smith whoosh by me in search of the strong safety as he hit the hole I'd just opened. A second later I heard the *crack!* of another defensive back's face being emblazoned upon the helmet of my favorite fullback. The roar of the crowd and the silence of the referee's whistle told me Mark Lane had broken free and was running in the open field. I felt and heard these things, but could see nothing since my face was buried under the lineman's chin.

One nice thing about blocking a big lineman, I thought, was that once hand position and leverage were established and he was back on his heels, he was more likely to *stay* blocked than the more athletic linebacker. In fact, once I got this jerk going, I switched over to automatic pilot. My block was so fundamentally sound that it had taken on a life of its own. I didn't even feel that I was working. Normally, I'd disengage at this point and run downfield to try to help Lane gain even more yards. But this time was different. This *guy* was different. He was a trash-talker. So I took it upon myself to teach him a lesson in humility.

Figuring we were near the sideline by now, I decided to end the block with a bang. The lineman was moving backward so fast that it was like pushing a wheelbarrow full of rocks down a hill. I had to pump my legs as fast as I could just to create some tension between us. Doing so, I gave one last mighty heave with my whole body and sent the big dumb-ass sailing into the Giants sideline.

Landing face-first in the dirt, I kept my eyes on the big mouth as he flew through the air, past my teammates. They opened a wide swath for him to pass through. No one felt obliged to slow him down. He was headed for the benches when I let go, but somehow he landed in the middle of the water station, which was even better. Plowing into the folding table full of drinks, he sent cups and liquid spraying everywhere. One big Gatorade bucket flew into the air and came down directly on his head, submerging him in a waterfall of sticky-sweet energy drink.

When the Gatorade settled, my teammates pounced on him like a pack of wild hyenas, jawing every insult and obscenity imaginable.

Finally, the whistle blew, signaling the end of the play. I got up and ran back to the huddle. But not before I felt Lou pat me on the ass for a job well done. I was back in his good graces and could once again play with peace of mind.

The next play, the dirty cleats of my old linebacker friend returned in front of me. I wouldn't see those clean size seventeens for the rest of the game. His moment of Super Bowl glory was over.

Lane gained twenty yards on that play and we had a first down on the Dolphins' thirty-yard line. A few running plays later and we were on the goal line. Momentum had swung in our favor, and for the first time all day we were able to score. With the third quarter half over, the score was Miami 17, Giants 7.

Our defense turned into a stone wall. Devers couldn't complete a pass. The Dolphin running game disappeared. Moze was having a hell of a game. If we could pull out a win, he'd most likely be named MVP. All my paranoid thoughts in the locker room at halftime about hidden agendas disappeared. We were rolling.

For the next hour we put together several impressive drives. Unfortunately, they all stalled in the red zone, but not before setting up three field goals that cut Miami's lead to one point. The score was now 17–16, and with the way Moze and the defense were playing, it looked as if one more Giants touchdown might break the Dolphins' back for good.

Our chance came toward the end of the fourth quarter. Again, we advanced the ball into the red zone and stood on the brink of six points. First and goal from the eight, a touchdown seemed inevitable. A holding penalty on first down, however, set us back ten yards. What a momentum-killer. Before we knew it, we were facing third and goal from the fourteen. But we still had one more shot at the end zone before having to settle for a field goal. A field goal would give us the lead, but two points was no safe margin for victory. We needed a touchdown—a pass or reverse or something designed for the end zone. The play came in from the sideline. Dive 23. Dive 23 was a hard-hitting play right up the middle. It was designed to gain a yard or two, no more.

I'd been playing under Lou for so long and had seen his genius in action so many times that I never questioned his strategy before. None of us had. But this play call shocked me. He was settling for a field goal without even attempting to score a touchdown. That didn't make sense.

"Dive Twenty-three?" I repeated in astonishment when Ramsey called the play.

"That's what Midland sent in."

"Bullshit!" I yelled. "We don't need two yards, Hoss. We need a touchdown!"

He shrugged. "That's the play, Dom."

"Maybe Lou's just positioning the ball in the middle of the field for Sergio," said Derek Jones.

Sergio Manuela was our field-goal kicker.

"Why the hell we settling for a field goal?" asked Chris Smith. "We'll only be up by two points. You've seen what Devers can do in the last minutes of a game. At least make him have to score a touchdown instead of just a field goal. Hell, he burnt us last year with one of those 'miracle comebacks,' remember?"

"Yeah," I added. "This is our chance to ice the game. We score here and it's over. You know it. And *they* know it."

I pointed to the exhausted Miami defense facing us. They were on their knees, panting like ragged dogs. Some even had their helmets off, trying to cool down before we broke the huddle.

"Besides," said Mark Lane. "What guarantee is there that Sergio's gonna make the kick? If he misses and Miami runs the clock down, we're screwed. They don't even have to score. I like Sergio, but I've been playin' too long to let the biggest game of my life be decided by a soccer player from Brazil."

"Whatta ya want me to do?" asked Ramsey. "Change the play?"

"Yes!" I said.

"Are you crazy? I can't do that!"

"Why not? This is the Super Bowl, Hoss. Did you come here to win or to just come close? Forget Dive Twenty-three! We're on the fourteen-yard line, for crissakes. Take a shot. Call Double Seam and go for the score. You know it'll work."

I could see he agreed with me. The look in his eyes told me he was thinking about it.

"But the play's Dive Twenty-three," he said. "Lou might bench me for the rest of my career if I do something like that."

"Let's face it," I said truthfully. "Even if you win this game, Hanes will be the starting quarterback next season."

Ramsey's face reddened with anger. He knew I was right.

"C'mon, Hoss," I coaxed him. "Do it!"

"Yeah, right. I'll catch hell!"

"Do it!" I yelled.

"Why do *I* have to do it?"

"Cuz you're the *number one,* bro!" I said.

Ramsey liked that. "I won't be for long if I change the play."

"Do it!" we all yelled.

"Awright, screw Lou. Two Slot H motion Seventy-six Double Seam F check swing, on one!" Ramsey said with conviction.

"And you better catch the son of a bitch, Dom," he added.

"Don't worry," I assured him. "I gotcha covered."

We ran to the line of scrimmage like a bunch of naughty boys disobeying our parents. An emotion surged through all eleven of us as we broke the huddle, a feeling that most of us hadn't experienced in a long time. It was called fun.

"Red Eighteen! . . . Red Eighteen! . . . Set! . . . Hut!"

I fired off the line and headed downfield. Miami had quickly switched into a pass defense when they saw our formation. Their scouting report had obviously showed our tendency to throw Double Seam when we lined up like this, especially when we were in the red zone. They'd be foolish to think we wouldn't run it now.

The play called for Chris Smith and me to streak downfield between the numbers and the hash marks, or the seams, as we called them. If only one safety was covering the middle of the field, he'd have to commit to one of us while leaving the other uncovered. If two safeties were splitting the field playing Cover 2, then Chris was supposed to bend his route into the middle between them. I liked this play because it was one of the few passes that let me run past the brutal linebacker zone and into the land of the munchkin defensive backs.

As I ran downfield, I tried to avoid the big linebackers. Their job was to harass me before moving on to their assigned man or drop zone once they read pass. I got held up longer than normal since the play held bigger consequences than usual.

Once free of the linebackers, I looked up to see if there was one safety in the middle of the field or two in the seams. Before I could determine that, however, two defensive backs pounced on me.

Double coverage.

Uh-oh, I thought. Although we hadn't run Double Seam all game, the Dolphins were prepared for it. I had to hand it to them, they were in the perfect formation to defend against it. Maybe that's why Lou had hesitated to call the play. Suddenly his play selection in the red zone stopped appearing so suspicious. The Dolphins had a scouting report detailing our tendencies. Lou was simply bucking his trends. He was trying to catch Miami off guard. Maybe he knew what he was doing after all. And maybe, I thought as I mentally kicked myself in the ass, that's why he was the head coach and I wasn't!

I hated to think what was going through Lou's mind as he watched us line up to throw a pass. This could be ugly. *Very* ugly. You don't blatantly disregard the head coach like that, no matter who you are or what the circumstances are. Not even Hanes would do a thing like that.

Nothing short of a touchdown would prevent Lou from benching Ramsey on the spot. If anything disastrous happened,

Red would be more likely to quarterback the offense on our next possession than Ramsey.

The two defensive backs accompanied me down the field, stride for stride, almost effortlessly. Unlike the linebackers, they didn't harass me; they didn't have to. There was no way I could outrun them. And unless I made a move or two, I couldn't lose them.

The pattern called for me to run straight down the field, in between the numbers and the hash marks. No cuts. No stops. No turns. Just straight out running. As long as I did that, the backs would be with me every step of the way. I was already on the five-yard line. If I didn't do something quick, I was going to run through the end zone and into the stands. If that happened, I might as well just stay there and have a sausage and a beer with the two fat slobs. That would be a lot less painful than having to face Ramsey again . . . or Lou.

The only thing I could think of was the middle of the field. I knew it didn't belong to me, but it was my only chance to escape the double-team. Peeking between the two defensive backs as I ran, I checked to see if it was open.

It was.

Chris should have been in it by now, but he wasn't. He'd either slipped, fallen, or effectively been delayed. Ramsey must have been cursing me up and down for making him change the play. The hell with it, I said to myself. If Chris wasn't going to take that plump, juicy middle of the field, then I was.

I wasn't the fastest runner in the league, but I could stop and change direction with the best of them. Slapping one little defensive back with my hand, I sent him flying ahead into his partner. I ducked underneath both of them and shot into the vacant middle, hoping Ramsey had seen the adjustment. The sight of a brown flying object sailing over the heads of the big guys up front told me he had.

Ramsey threw such a bullet that I didn't have time to ponder the importance of the catch. It would be my biggest highlight or my deepest regret. Either way, I'd never forget it. In a flash, the perfectly thrown ball line-drived into my gut and my arms cradled it like a baby.

The ball and the goal line arrived at the same time. Before I could turn around, the painted grass of the end zone began staining the bottom of my cleats and the referee signaled to the world:

TOUCHDOWN!

The stadium erupted. New York fans, who had watched their beloved team lose season after miserable season, opened the floodgates of their souls and emptied the emotions they'd stored away through the years. Cheers and energy spilled onto the spot where I now stood and washed over me in wave upon wave of exquisite gratitude and joy.

I felt their emotions join with mine. A light show of countless flashbulbs blinded me as I gazed into the frenzied stands. Like the delayed effect of three shots of whiskey in a row, the gravity of the moment hit me. My joy turned to confusion. My head swam and my knees wobbled. I'd imagined doing so many things if I ever got to this position, but I couldn't remember any of them.

The moment was so big, perhaps, that deep in my heart I knew I couldn't claim it as my own. All I did was run down the field and catch a ball. A lot of people could've done that. But for some reason *I* was the one to do it.

In total awe, I dropped to one knee and closed my eyes. The moment I'd dreamed of all my life had finally arrived, and all I could do was kneel down and say thank-you.

Unperturbed by my piety, my teammates assaulted me with slaps and hits of congratulatory joy. While still on my knee, I joined the collective group hug and yelled at the top of my lungs like everyone else.

"Woohooo!"

Holding my teammates as tight as I could, I hoped to make the moment last forever. Rejoicing in their company, I drank deeply from the waters of pride and satisfaction that poured from their camaraderie. I felt the hard plastic of their equipment. I breathed the scent of their sweat. Perspiration beads, drops of blood, and sprays of spit all merged into one as we held on to one another in triumphant celebration.

The party got even bigger when we went back to the sideline. Everyone was jumping up and down, even Red. I never knew that he *could* jump, but there he was barely getting the soles of his shoes off the grass.

Ramsey jumped on me from behind. "Nice catch," he said, eyes wide.

"Nice throw," I answered.

We both laughed, joy and relief spilling from us like water. That's when I remembered Lou and that we'd changed the play. I looked to see what *his* reaction was.

Normally, he'd be busy keeping everyone's head in the game by tempering our enthusiasm. Instead, he was silent. His headphones hung limply off his head, and he was staring at the scoreboard. He didn't seem angry at the audible, but he didn't seem happy about the touchdown, either. Ramsey walked right by him. Lou didn't even look at him. He was preoccupied as I'd never seen him before.

I went over to the water table for a drink. The skidmarks from the Miami lineman with the size seventeen shoes were still there. I laughed as I looked at them. That'll teach that blowhard to keep his mouth shut, I thought. I drank feverishly. The water leaked from the corners of my mouth and spilled beneath my shoulder pads. Cold rivulets made their way through my steaming undershirt and sizzled against my burning skin.

What a glorious sensation! After all my years of playing, I was still amazed at the pleasure little streams of dribble could produce. I was transported to the heights of ecstasy as Jimmy slapped an icy, wet towel over the back of my neck. Cold inundated every pore of my skin. It was pure heaven!

"Thanks, Jimmy!" I crooned.

"No. Thank you, bud," he said sincerely.

"Come sit with me."

"Can't. I play the *whole* game. No breathers."

And he was off. He was responsible for fifty guys on the sideline. He worked the whole game. He never sat down.

I, on the other hand, played in spurts. And for the moment, I was spurted out. The oxygen tank was behind me, but only Red had the key. He was in charge of turning the knob to release the flow. No one else was allowed to do it. I don't know why the tank needed a knob turner. We were all capable of the appropriate wrist action.

Perhaps because some of the rookies were a little too adept at it had led to the rule. I knew a few of those guys were always looking to get a head start on their postgame festivities. But whatever the reason, no one got oxygen unless Red gave it to him. Unfortunately for the winded, Red held oxygen in the same light as shoelaces. You already had some, so why did you need more?

I signaled Red. Surprisingly, he came right away.

"Red, can I get a shot?"

"Hell, Dom. I'll buy you all the shots you want!"

Red was ecstatic. I'd never seen him happy before. He noticed my surprise at his new attitude but didn't say anything.

"You all right, Red?"

"Yep," he said, turning the knob of the tank. "Why?"

"I've never seen you smile this much."

"Well, let's just say my faith's been restored."

"In what?"

"In you guys."

"Whatta ya mean?" I asked suspiciously in between pulls through the plastic breathing cup.

"I know how to read Midland's signals," Red said, prudently cutting me off from the tank. "He sent in Dive Twenty-three, not Double Seam."

I smiled. "Good thing Ramsey called that audible."

"Yeah, good thing. Lou say anything?"

"Not yet, but I'm sure he will."

"No, he won't," Red said disdainfully. "Look at him over there. He's scrambling."

I looked. Lou continued to stare at the scoreboard. I'd never seen him so removed from the action, especially in the middle of a game.

"Looks like he's zoning out to me," I said. "He better snap out of it before the time-out's over. What's he think he's gonna see up there?"

"He's studying," Red said.

"Studying what?"

"The score."

"It's Twenty-three to seventeen. What more is there to know?"

"The point spread is four. Your audible threw a wrench in his gears. He called Dive Twenty-three because he wanted a field goal. A field goal would've put us up by two points. And two points keeps him within the spread."

Good ol' Red, I thought. Crazy as ever. Still, I had to admit I'd been suspicious, too, when Dive 23 came in from the sideline.

"C'mon, Red. You don't really think Lou's capable of that, do you?"

"Eyes and ears, Fucillo. Eyes and ears," Red said, walking away.

Last year, I wouldn't have given Red's words a second thought. Hell, last year I wouldn't have asked him for oxygen. But I'd come to learn that Red knew more than it appeared. Playing for a field goal was out of Lou's character. Already today, we'd run a fake punt and had gone for it on three fourth downs. These were not the actions of a conservative play-caller. Maybe the pressure had gotten to Lou and he believed a field goal and a two-point lead was better than taking one risk too many. I doubted that was the case. Lou had balls the size of grapefruits, there wasn't a chance he wouldn't take. Maybe Red was right. Instead of playing conservative, maybe Lou was taking the biggest chance in the history of the sport. Manipulating the score of the Super Bowl was as ballsy as it got. But why would he do such a thing? He was one of the most respected coaches in the league, one of the highest paid as well. I could think of no reason for him to act this way. I must be as crazy as Red, I thought, to think like this. Then I remembered Salvi. Lou had told me to say hello to the old man for him. They knew each other. Salvi had told me about Joey Delucca. Frank had told me about Sammy and "other people." Moze had been to the Point. And Red knew about everyone. Eyes and ears?

I looked at Lou. His attention had left the scoreboard, and he was now giving our defensive captain last-minute instructions before taking the field. Whatever he was saying was not sitting well with Moze. They looked as if they were arguing. Lou had a pleading look on his face. Moze had an I-don't-give-a-damn look on his. I couldn't make out any words, but I was able to decipher Moze's last response.

"No fuckin' way!" is what I translated.

Nearly two minutes were still left in the game. Miami may have looked like a defeated team, but they were still professionals. And this was still the Super Bowl. We had to remember we were ahead by only six points. The game was not a lock, not with Devers on the field. A touchdown and extra point, and victory was theirs.

I got up to watch the kickoff. I'd rested enough. If the defense played the way they'd been playing, I'd be back on the field shortly. I went over to Jimmy, who was making a last-minute adjustment to Moze's wrist tape. Moze seemed entranced by Jimmy's moving hand. I nudged Jimmy. The interruption in his rhythm broke Moze's meditation. He looked up. His face was sad, but his eyes brightened when he saw me.

"Hey, Dom. Beautiful catch, baby! Beautiful!"

The soil of the Rose Bowl was caked on him from head to toe. Tape hung loosely from his fingers, his uniform was in tatters, and blood flowed from his exposed flesh. He looked like hell, but his spirits were high. He really was, as he'd said in the sauna, a changed man.

"Thanks, Moze," I said. "You're having a hell of a game yourself. Best I've ever seen you play."

"Well, you know, if you're gonna go out, you might as well go out with a bang!"

He smiled. I smiled back, but wasn't sure what he meant. Go out with a bang? Where was he going? I thought I was the only one going anywhere after this game.

"Well . . . keep it up," I said, not knowing what else to say.

"I'm tryin', man. But it ain't easy."

"I know what you mean."

"Oh, no, you don't." Moze ran toward the field. "And I hope you never do."

I looked at Jimmy. "What's up with him?"

"I don't know. He keeps talkin' like it's his last game or somethin'," Jimmy said. "Maybe he's gonna retire."

"Moze? Why would he retire now?"

"I don't know," Jimmy said, obviously not too concerned. "You know him. He's always talkin' crazy. That's Moze for ya."

I don't know, I thought. I knew Moze was crazy, but I'd never heard him talk like this before.

"By the way," Jimmy said. "Moze ain't the only one talkin' crazy. I just heard Lou telling Moze to *let* Miami move the ball down the field."

"What?" I said in shock. "Why would he do that?"

"He said to give up the short stuff, nickel and dime 'em, and make them use up the clock."

Prevent defense. I hated that formation. All it seemed to prevent was victory for us.

"What if they score?" I asked.

"That's what Moze asked."

"Well?"

"Lou said don't worry. In the event that happens, Miami would never make the extra point. He said that was all taken care of."

"What does that mean?" I asked.

"I don't know. Maybe he's got some secret play he's been hiding up his sleeve."

That might be true. The special teams were their own separate units. I wasn't on the field-goal/point-after team, so if they had a secret play, I wouldn't have known about it. Maybe Lou had come up with a foolproof scheme to block the extra point. It sounded awfully risky. Hell, a touchdown would still tie the game. Even if we did block the extra point, this strategy was no guarantee for victory. It was only a guarantee for overtime.

I searched for Red. He was filling paper cups with Gatorade, a big smile on his face.

"Red, let's talk."

"Shoot."

"I'm beginning to think you might be onto something with Lou and the score."

"Aww, forget about that. We're up by six. Miami hasn't scored a point all half. They ain't gonna do it now, not with the way Moze has been playing. Whatever Lou had going on is over."

"I wouldn't be so sure," I said, disbelieving I was now trying to convince Red of foul play. "Jimmy just overheard Lou telling Moze to let Miami move down the field and don't worry about giving up a touchdown. He said the extra point was 'taken care of.'"

Red's eyes lit up at the mention of the extra point. His smile disappeared. "Chalmers!" he said softly. "I should've known."

I barely heard him. "What?"

"Never mind. What was Moze's reaction?"

"I don't think he was too happy."

"Are you sure?"

"I'm only guessing. I was watching from a distance."

"Hmmm" was all Red said.

"Whatta ya think?"

Red scowled. With an angry swoosh of his arm, he cleared the table of the paper cups he'd just filled with Gatorade. Liquid flew everywhere.

"A touchdown ties the game, a missed extra point puts us into overtime, and a winning field goal by either team ends the game within the spread." Red's face was red with bitterness. "Whatta ya think I think?!"

I groaned. Could this really be happening? Was the biggest game of my life in the hands of a madman? Was Moze in on it, too?

I grabbed Red. "C'mon. Let's see how this shakes out," I said, pulling him to the sideline. "I hope we're just crazy, Red. I'd hate to have to kill the prick."

"Who? Lou or Moze?"

"Both."

With one minute fifty seconds left on the clock, Miami lined up in Two-Minute formation: four wide receivers and one running back. Matching them, our defense deployed into Prevent mode: Moze, Wilkins, and Rosen as rushers, the rest staying back in pass coverage. Gains would come in five- or ten-yard increments only. I may not have liked it, but Lou's decision was sound. Miami needed a touchdown, not a field goal. His cavalier attitude should Miami reach the end zone was what bothered me. Having that much faith in your PAT-block team was bad football. No matter what the scheme, blocking an extra point was hard to do.

Devers began the drive at his own twenty-yard line. Play after play, he dropped back and picked our coverage apart with precision throws. He was making progress, but it was slow. Every play cost Miami precious seconds. Moze, Wilkins, and Rosen, meanwhile, rushed the passer as best they could. Fighting double-teams every snap of the ball, they were exhausted when the Dolphins crossed midfield. By the time Miami reached our red zone, they could barely stand.

Red and I watched in horror.

"Why doesn't Lou switch it up, for crissakes?" I said. "Call a blitz, or jump the underneath routes. We're not even playing Prevent anymore. We're in some sort of Hail Mary defense. Hell, those shallow receivers are so wide-open even I could get the ball to them."

"At least give Moze, Wilkins, and Rosen a break," Red added. "Look at 'em, they can't even breathe. If Lou gets his way and this game goes into overtime, they're gonna be useless."

Goddammit! I thought. He's giving the game away! I made a move toward Lou.

Red held my arm. "Where do you think you're going?"

"I can't watch this. I gotta do something."

"Don't be stupid. You already did whatever you could when you guys called that audible. You're done. This is Lou's world now."

"But, Red . . ."

"But nothing. We don't have any evidence, just a lot of suspicions. There's thirty seconds left, we're still winning. Like you said, let's see how it shakes out."

Play resumed and Miami lined up in regular formation just inside our twenty-yard line. Our defense made no adjustment. Moze hunched over with his hands on his knees. Leroy and Charlie did the same. I couldn't believe Lou was keeping them in, but I held my tongue.

Miami's formation raised a red flag. A screen play was coming. Like Double Seam for us, screen plays were their red-zone bread and butter. I looked to Lou, expecting to hear shouts of hysterical warning. But he said and did nothing. Instead, a wry smile appeared on his lips.

I couldn't help myself. "Screen! Watch the screen!" I yelled at the top of my lungs.

Lou turned sharply toward me and gave me an icy stare. True hostility was in his eyes.

"Moze, watch the screen!" I yelled again. Screw Lou, I thought.

Devers took the snap from center and dropped back to pass. Wilkins and Rosen engaged the Dolphin linemen. Despite their exhaustion, they made good penetration. It looked as if the linemen were letting them by. Moze had the running back in coverage but started to rush once he saw him set up to block. The running back ducked low and cut Moze's legs out from under him. Moze fell to the ground in a heap. Wilkins and Rosen busted through their double-teams and headed toward Devers, who took a deeper drop than usual. The linemen disregarded the two pass rushers, regrouped, and headed toward the flat. The running back rolled back up to his feet and leaked out to the flat as well. Devers lobbed the ball to him over a prostrate Moze. The five linemen turned upfield, and along with the four receivers already in the secondary, they visually latched onto the eight remaining undersize Giant defenders.

Screen!

Devers's pass floated lazily over Wilkins and Rosen, who chased him in vain. The Miami blockers began hunting their victims. The running back awaited the ball, which was now passing over our depleted captain lying on the ground. All the back had to do was catch the ball and there was little hope of keeping him from the end zone.

"Jesus, Moze, I told you to watch for the screen!" I yelled with tears of frustration in my eyes. "You dumb-as—!"

But before I could complete my insult, Moze shot up off the ground. I don't know where he got the strength. I would never have thought it possible. In a last act of desperation, he stuck his hand in the air and tipped the ball as it passed over him. The ball wobbled straight toward the heavens and seemed to float in the California sky. While it bobbed in the air and began its descent, Moze regained his composure in time to catch it before it fell. He clung to the ball as though it were life itself and sprinted downfield toward the Dolphins' end zone.

The Miami running back was on him in an instant, but after his pitiful attempt at a tackle, Moze shook him off like a flea. I watched in shock as he ran past our sideline. Pure joy covered his face. No one could catch him now. After he crossed midfield, no one even tried. Every Dolphin held his head in defeat. Approaching the Miami goal line, Moze slowed down and looked up at the game clock. Timing his steps accordingly, he walked into the end zone as the last second expired. I fell to my knees in disbelief. We had won the goddamn, freakin' Super Bowl!

The flight back to New York was the best I'd ever experienced as a member of the Giants. In the past, losing flights home were much more common than winning ones. Frustration and regret were our flight attendants then. But even victory flights had been tempered by the stress of the following week's game. While Lou made sure we never got too down on ourselves after a loss, neither did he allow us to think too highly of ourselves after a victory. Celebrations of our biggest road-game triumphs were always subdued and tempered. But this flight home was different. There was no game the next week. We had won it all. The season was over. We wouldn't even watch the film of this game. There would be no regrets for past actions, no frustration at blown plays, no dread of impending chastisements in the classrooms of the locker room. Nothing stood in the way of our celebrating our achievement, not even Lou, who never left his seat in first class to check on our behavior.

Alcohol had something to do with our raucous ways I'm sure, but not much. Most of the champagne in the locker room was poured over our heads, not down our throats. We still had a booze-free flight policy, so not many bottles were smuggled aboard, either. We were riding an emotional high, the kind that needed no additives. Any drinks taken were strictly to mark the occasion. No one seemed interested in numbing his senses on this night. Euphoria and accomplishment were meant to be felt with every nerve ending in our bodies. We had achieved the ultimate. Our flag was now planted firmly in line with those of past champions on the summit of Mount NFL. The impact of such a feat was intoxicating. Only an idiot would alter that feeling by getting drunk.

I wanted to savor not only the victory, but my last moments together with the guys I'd just won it with. This was the first championship team I'd ever been a part of, and would probably be the last. Hell, I might never even see any of the guys again once the plane landed. No breakup meeting was scheduled. Lou, despite his attention to detail, had failed to plan beyond the end of the game. As far as I could tell, we were free to go as we pleased, wherever we pleased, once we touched down at Newark Airport.

Even if a formal good-bye were scheduled, I wouldn't have been able to attend because of my bone-graft surgery, scheduled for the next day. Dr. Bedrosian, after rolling the dice for a couple of months, wanted to do it as soon as possible. His sense of urgency concerned me. It made me wonder how unstable my knee had really been this whole season.

When the plane landed, I went straight to my motel room to pack and grab a few winks before heading to the hospital. Ironically, my knee never felt better. I didn't even have to ice it down on the plane ride home. I wondered whether the operation was even necessary. But when I woke up a couple of hours later and could barely walk to the bathroom, I knew the Vicodins Doc had given me had merely masked the pain.

I looked around my room. It seemed barren. Nothing in it was mine except the suitcase and the dirty laundry on the floor. I wasn't planning on coming back after the operation. After today, I would never sleep here again. Sadness filled my heart at the thought of it. Everything I'd done, and everything I'd been, for the last eight years would be wiped away as quickly as the maids could change the bloody sheets on my bed.

I longed to call Emma. To hear her voice. To see her face. To wallow in her love. But she was gone and there was no one to replace her. I was all by myself, just me and my beloved championship. In the backyard of the biggest city in the world, I couldn't have been more isolated, or more desolate.

Twenty-three

Wearing a backless hospital gown and little cotton socks resembling slippers, I lay flat on my back in an operating room of the York Orthopedic Hospital on the Upper East Side of Manhattan. Dr. Bedrosian lopped off pieces of my hip with a hammer and chisel and stuffed them into the dreaded hole in my knee. My head tilted downward toward the cold, sterile linoleum floor, and blood rushed unmercifully to my eyes. My skull throbbed forcefully under the onslaught of my own corpuscles. It hurt like hell. The pounding in my head kept pace with the clanging of the doctor's hammer.

A wall of fabric had been erected around my head so that I couldn't see what Dr. Bedrosian was doing to my body. I was better off that way. But it prevented me from focusing on something by way of distraction, to take my mind off the pain.

The anesthesiologist had wanted to put me to sleep from the beginning, but I'd opted for an epidural catheter instead. It was helping, but every twinge of pain announced that the procedure had not been wholly effective. The catheter, a needle and tube inserted into my lower spine, wasn't as strong as general anesthesia. It didn't seem to render my knee and hip quite insensitive enough. But I was wide-awake and lucid, and that's all I really cared about. The pain, I could handle. The going under, I could not.

Being knocked out would leave me ill for days. That was something I could *not* live with. Especially not now. It was imperative that I stay awake for this surgery more than any other.

Nobody would be waiting for me after this operation. No trainers would be catering to my needs. No ride would return me to the locker room for rehabilitation. Caring hands and concerned faces would be absent. As soon as I could walk out of post-op, I was on my own. I needed my wits about me. To end this chapter of my life properly, I was going to need a clear head for the next day or so.

It was supposed to have been a quick operation, sixty minutes or less. The clock on the wall, however, told me we'd entered the third hour.

"Don't do it that way!" I heard Dr. Bedrosian say to a subordinate.

"It's coming along just fine," the underling responded.

The pounding in my head intensified as I listened to them argue. The heart monitor near my head beeped loudly, exposing to everyone in the room my rapidly increasing anxiety. The anesthesiologist noticed it immediately.

"You all right, Dominic?"

"Yeah, Doc. I'm fine, just fine."

"You want a little medicine?"

Why not just offer me a cup of rat poison, I thought. "No thanks, Doc. I'm fine, really."

"You're the boss," he said innocently. But I heard him fumble around behind me with his assortment of sedatives, nevertheless.

"Leave him alone, for crissakes! He's been through worse than this!" Dr. Bedrosian shouted over the clanking of the hammer.

A rush surged through my body. The anesthesiologist had slipped me something. I cringed at the sensation. I didn't want any medicine. I'd already told him that. But he obviously wasn't interested in my desires.

A scene from high school flooded my mind. I'd dislocated my elbow the first game of the season, my senior year. At the emergency room, the doctors knocked me out to reset the bones. When I awoke, the pain in my arm paled in comparison to the pain in my head. A hangover like I'd never had before, or since, drove me mad for three days. I thought I was going to die and actually looked forward to the escape. In between heaving my guts out, I vowed never to go under again. No matter what the operation, no matter how bad the pain. Stay awake at all costs. That was my motto.

In this current operation, my motto rang louder than ever. Stay awake, I chastised myself. Don't let this disgruntled anesthesiologist send you back to that place from high school. Get your mind off the operation and concentrate on something else! But that's hard to do when two guys are chopping you to pieces.

I tried to make sense of how I'd wound up on this operating table. On top of the world before the season began. Buried six feet under at the end. I just didn't get it.

I replayed every significant event that had taken place in my small world. As moment after moment ran through my mind, the pain lessened. Even the sounds of the operating room faded. Scenes from bygone days passed before my eyes until I became firmly entrenched in the past. The rehab from my original knee surgery. My breakup with Emma. The ejection from the Eagles game. The fine from the commissioner. Moze's plight. Red's situation. My conversations with Salvi and Frank. Emma in the city. My despair. My confession. The Super Bowl. The end of my career.

As an impartial observer, I viewed my life as though it played on a movie screen, a process no doubt elevated by the drugs seeping into my brain. Ironically, I began to see things clearly.

Sure, there had been some bad breaks. It's true things could've worked out better. But overwhelmingly, as I reviewed the past six months, the cause of my problems became painfully obvious. So much so that I stopped hearing the clanking of the hammer and chisel. The pain throughout my body ceased to exist. And I was left with only myself. My problems were no one's fault but my own. I guess I had known it all along. But it felt good to finally admit it.

Dr. Bedrosian's voice snapped me back. "We're just about finished, Dom."

Thank God, I thought. I was running out of memories. The dizziness was making a comeback and I was starting to gag. The anesthesiologist had certainly given me my money's worth of narcotics. The bastard.

"Let me just sew you up and we'll be all set."

A little past noon, I was wheeled into the post-op room. I figured I'd be out of there with pair of crutches before the afternoon rush hour. My leg required no brace or cast, so as soon as I could feel my legs again, I'd be able to slip my pants back on and head over to the stadium to settle my affairs before leaving for the off-season.

I needed to see Lou and hear from his own lips what my status on the team would be from here on out. Also, I wanted to take some things from my locker while it was still mine, in particular, the slide-able nameplate that said FUCILLO. It didn't mean all that much to me, but the thought of its being tossed in the garbage was tough to bear.

I needed to see Salvi as well. He was my link to Emma. Even if she never wanted to see me again, I still loved her, and I had to ask for her forgiveness one more time. I doubted that would mend our broken relationship. But I wasn't going to leave New York without a last try.

In post-op, my idle mind turned toward the Super Bowl. In all the excitement of victory, I'd forgotten my crazy suspicions at the end of the game. Red had really stirred things up in my head. Why did I listen to that old coot? Sure, things looked bleak at the half, but the game was well in hand by the end. We were a bigger, much stronger team than Miami. In time our physical, methodical play would wear them down. So Lou settled for field goals. So he let Miami run the clock out on the last drive. So what? It all worked out. We won the game. Point spread or no point spread, there was never anything to worry about. I laughed at myself for ever thinking there was.

What an idiot I'd been. I'd always heard that no one leaves the NFL smoothly. But I wondered if everyone's departure had been as bizarre as mine. Probably each in his own way thought it had been. After all, how does one die while not really dying?

Still, Jimmy's words suggesting that Lou had told Moze the extra point was taken care of continued to bother me. What had Lou meant? Had Jimmy heard him correctly? What could Lou have possibly known? How could he have risked six months of hard work on such a gamble as Miami missing a routine extra point? One slip of the cleats, one miscommunication between any of the eleven players on the extra-point-block team, and Lou's secret play was ruined. And our efforts to win the game would be destroyed. A person would have to be crazy to attempt something so risky. Lou Gordon wasn't crazy.

"How are you doing, Dominic?" Dr. Bedrosian asked.

I was semi-sitting-up in a bed with my left leg elevated. My knee was wrapped tightly in cotton dressing and covered with an Ace bandage. Doc had been able to fill in the hole in my femur through arthroscopic surgery. Only two small holes requiring three stitches apiece lay underneath all that dressing. He told me I would never feel much pain in my knee. My hip, on the other hand, was going to be a major source of agony. That's where he and his fellow had pounded and hammered pieces of bone for over two hours. The good news: the scar would be minimal, maybe two or three inches long at most. I couldn't see where they'd cut me. Cotton bandages wrapped around my waist covered any evidence of blood or trauma. It would be another hour before the epidural wore off. Until then, he said, I'd feel as if nothing had happened. As soon as I could move my legs freely and the anesthesiologist's sedatives were out of my system, I would be free to go.

"Can you move your legs yet?"

"Just about," I said weakly. "They feel like pins and needles."

"Good. You should be able to walk soon, and then you can get out of here. But you have to promise you'll get in touch with Jimmy. He'll give you a list of instructions on how to take care of that leg. Remember, you have to stay off of it completely for three full months. That's very important. And no strenuous running for at least a year. I know that's a long time, but you have to give that bone graft every possible chance to fill in. If that happens, your knee will be as good as new."

My eyes lit up at his words.

"Well, as good as it was after last year's reconstruction," he clarified. "Which, come to think of it, wasn't really that good, was it?"

"It was good enough to play on." I shrugged, trying to give him a little encouragement.

"And play pretty darn well, I might add," he said, pride in his voice.

"Thanks, Doc."

He sighed. We'd been together in this hospital a dozen times in the last eight years. Each time, he made it possible for me to go back on the field. Without him, my body might've been better, but that was a small price to pay for those moments inside my helmet.

"I'll sure miss you, Dom," he said tenderly. "They don't make them like you anymore." His eyes moistened.

I felt like crying myself, but didn't. "Let me ask you, Doc. If I sit out a year and the graft takes, my knee will be stable, right?"

"Technically, yes."

"Then what's to stop me from playing again?"

"To be honest? Nothing."

He wasn't in the locker room anymore. He was in *his* element now. Hell, he was the chief of surgery. Lou might have reigned supreme in the Meadowlands, but he held no sway in a hospital on the other side of the river.

"Well, what if I sit out the year without getting paid. Why can't I come back the following year and rejoin the team?"

"Lou won't let you. In order to get out of paying you next year's salary, he's forcing me to declare you incapable of playing again, which to be truthful is really how I feel about your condition."

"You really don't think I can come back?"

"I really don't. Nor do I think you should try. Remember, the knee isn't your only problem, it's merely your *latest.* Don't forget your shoulder, your other knee, your ankles, your feet, your hands and fingers, and your jaw. Call it quits, knee or no knee. You just won the Super Bowl, what more do you want? What more can you get? The game has gotten as much as it deserves, and more, *out of you.* It pains me to keep sending you back out there. Enough is enough."

He paused for a moment and seemed to reflect on my history.

"But if anybody can come back from this, it's you. And I won't be surprised if I see you back in the league two years from now. Unfortunately, it won't be in a Giants uniform. I'm releasing a statement tomorrow declaring my unwillingness to give you medical clearance based on the damage you've sustained, and that I'm doing it for the sake of your own health."

"How thoughtful." The pain of his words was devastating. Lou's stance on the issue was no longer a mystery. "I guess once you do that, you can't let me play again without looking like a hypocrite, huh?"

"Exactly. It's a business. Lou has an opportunity to save the club a bundle of money. Unfortunately for you, that bundle is yours."

I couldn't argue with him. Still, the air was tense.

"Gosh, how about that game last night," he said suddenly. "Was that great or what!"

"It sure was."

"And what a finish! Moze made a great play there at the end. If he didn't intercept that pass, it would've been a Miami victory, for sure."

That's not what Lou thought, I thought to myself.

"It would've been ironic if Chalmers had kicked the winning extra point, don't you think?" Like Red last night, he was referring to the Miami placekicker.

"I don't know about weird. More like nerve-racking, if you ask me."

"I mean *weird* in light of Chalmers being a former Giant."

"Chalmers was a Giant?" A shock went up my spine.

"Sure. He was here long before you. Between you and me, I think he has a drug problem. At least he did when he was here. That's what got him kicked out of New York."

Former Giant, drug addict, placekicker. It felt as though I'd accidentally tripped over the dog in the living room and saw the missing pieces of an unsolved puzzle beneath the couch. A question shot to the front of my brain like words from a Tourette's patient.

"You don't by any chance know Sammy Penrod, do ya?"

"Sure. A great guy. There's no more loyal a fan. He gave my wife and me a Christmas gift. Does it for all the coaches and staff. Great man. Very successful. Funny you should mention him. Chalmers and he were good friends. When Chalmers went off the deep end with the drugs, Sammy did everything he could to help him out."

"They still friends?" I asked, my ears ringing.

"I assume so. I saw them out together last week in California, having dinner. It's nice to see people keep in touch like that. I hope we can do the same."

He stood and patted my shoulder. He looked worn-out. Physically and emotionally. "I'm going home. Everybody was making such a racket on the plane last night, I hardly slept. I'll call Jimmy in a few days to make sure you're all right. There's really nothing to do but rest and heal up. As long as you take it easy, you should be fine. I wish there was more I could do for you, but I can't. You're going to have to find a new doctor to see you through this rehab. The sooner, the better. You understand, don't you?"

Sure. He was the Giants' doctor. I was no longer a Giant. I could never trust him again, since it would be in his best interest if I never fully recovered. I understood perfectly. We shook hands.

"See ya, Doc. It was fun while it lasted."

"Good-bye, Dominic, and good luck. It's been a pleasure."

Twenty-four

Fluorescent yellow lights inside the hollow tube of the Lincoln Tunnel whizzed past my taxicab. The pounding effects of the hammer and chisel in my hip grew stronger as we drove, and by the time we pulled into the stadium parking lot, I could feel the effects of every blow from Doc's handiwork.

As soon as I paid the cab fare, I popped open my jar of Percodans and chewed up two of them with no water. Mercifully, by the time I hobbled down the ramp of the tunnel, they'd begun to take the edge off.

I wanted to see Lou before he disappeared. The off-season had officially begun, but I figured he'd be here today. He was a creature of habit. Rarely did he go on vacation the day after the season. His office was upstairs with the rest of the corporate staff's. But I was in no mood to exchange high fives with the suits and skirts sitting at their desks, so I entered the stadium the way I did every other day, down the ramp and into the tunnel.

Pain accompanied me every step of the way. It was a manageable pain, though, and with every jolt and sting, I thought of my penance and my grandfather.

The upstairs offices had a back entrance. A staircase in the rear of one of the maintenance rooms led directly to them from the tunnel. This was how the coaches and staff traveled back and forth to the locker room. Only those who knew the five-digit code to the stairwell door had access.

Jimmy had given me the code a while back. He'd shown it to me the day they'd bestowed him with its knowledge. He'd been so excited that he'd made me watch him open the door just to prove that he knew the combination.

One, two, three, four, five. That was the combination. Yeah, real special, Jimmy, I remembered teasing him that day. Next, they'll let you pick the first-rounder in the upcoming draft. Jimmy, as usual, took no offense. He was good like that. I was going to miss him, I thought.

Normally Lou espoused an open-door policy. But today his door was closed. Voices conversed on the other side. Strange. I put my ear to the door and listened intently. It would be embarrassing if Lou caught me eavesdropping, but the hell with it. What was he going to do, cut me?

"You've really screwed things up," I heard Lou's voice, filled with panic.

"How?" James Moze.

"I told you not to worry about Miami scoring a touchdown. I told you they never would've made the extra point."

"What does it matter now? Game's over. We won. Remember? Besides, how could you know something like that?" Moze laughed incredulously.

"I just know."

Lou's tone gave Moze pause. He was silent for a moment before asking warily, "What's going on?"

"Look, I know about everything. I know about you and Sammy. I know he had you beaten when you wouldn't help cover his bets."

"What?" Moze said in shock.

"Salvi Rossini tipped me off."

"The guy who owns that restaurant in Connecticut?"

"Same guy. He owns the bookie Sammy's in trouble with."

"Joey Delucca? Salvi owns that midget?"

"Among other things."

"Jesus. I'd met Salvi at the Point a couple of times when Sammy had business with Joey. But I didn't know Salvi was the boss. I just thought he was a good cook."

"Not quite." Lou laughed. "Salvi's pretty connected. I met him years ago up in Saratoga when I used to follow the horses. Big Giants fan. He warned me back then about Sammy's gambling problem. He knew you guys were friends, and he always believed that if Sammy got desperate enough, he'd take advantage of his relationship with you. In fact, he'd heard Sammy brag more than once as to how you were his 'ace in the hole' in case he ever got into a jam. When Sammy's debt to Joey coincided with your 'accident,' Salvi put two and two together and gave me a call. He figured Sammy was playing his trump card."

Moze sighed. "Sammy said I owed him. He said if I didn't help him, he'd kill me. I told him to go fuck himself."

"And so the beating."

"Yeah. Sammy said that was just a taste of what would follow if I didn't play along." Moze paused. "I don't wish harm on anyone. But if Sammy owed so much money, why didn't Salvi or Joey take care of the problem?"

"Joey wanted to, but Salvi wouldn't give his permission. Dead people, he explained, were not good for his business. But considering the hatred between Joey and Sammy, Salvi doubted whether

Joey would restrain himself. That, coupled with the realization that Sammy was putting your life in jeopardy because of Joey's pressure, led him to come up with a solution to diffuse the whole mess before it blew up in his face."

"The Super Bowl bet?"

"Yes. But he needed a fix to make sure that Sammy won. That was the only way to keep anyone from getting killed."

"What fix?" asked Moze. "I told Sammy I'd take a bullet in the head before doing anything like that."

"I know. That's why I cooperated instead. In return for Sammy cutting ties with you forever, I promised to do everything I could to keep the score within the spread. But it wasn't easy. There's so many different factors and extenuating circumstances that I had to wait until near the end of the game before trying anything. On our last possession, we were supposed to kick a field goal to go up by two points. That would've given us the lead and the cover."

"But Ramsey hit Dom for a touchdown. That put us up by six."

"They acted against my orders. Those two changed the play I called and they'll pay for that. That's why I needed Miami to score that touchdown at the end. They would've missed the extra point and the game would've been tied."

"You keep saying they would've missed the extra point. How could you be so sure of that?"

"Chalmers," Lou said. "He's still a junkie, and he's into Sammy deeper than you. He was doing everything in his power to help Sammy, too."

"He would've thrown the game?"

"Not thrown it. Just kept it within the spread. Missing the extra point would've sent the game into overtime. After that, it was every man for himself. A field goal from either side in overtime would've ended the game and covered the bet. But I was confident that we would've scored first."

"What if Ramsey never changed the play and we went up by two, like you wanted, instead of six? Miami would've only had to score a field goal in regulation to win outright. They had plenty of time and firepower to do it."

"True. But I didn't think they would. I would've called different defenses, sent pressure, man-zoned, any number of things. Devers was through. The only reason he moved the ball at the end like he did was because I let him. It was a risk, I know. But it was one I was willing to take. I never had any intention of losing. I just wanted to fulfill my end of the bargain with Sammy. Unfortunately, none of that matters now. Your interception put an end to that."

Moze's jaw hit the floor. It was lying next to mine.

"What the fuck, Lou?" Moze spoke as if the wind had been knocked out of him. "Why would you do something like that?"

"For you," Lou said tenderly. "I wouldn't be here if it wasn't for you. They were going to fire me a few years ago. But then you came along, and you . . . well . . . you turned it all around. I owe you. Besides, James, I've always thought of you as sort of . . . a son."

Lou's voice cracked as he said it. He was a lifelong bachelor. No one ever saw him with anything even resembling a female. He was all football, period. His life had no room for anything but X's and O's. I guess somewhere along the way his paternal instincts had welled up inside him until they finally burst out and fell upon the best player he'd ever developed. James Moze was the closest thing he would ever have to a son, and he was protecting him just as he would his own flesh and blood. In a strange way, I was impressed.

No one said anything for maybe a minute. I leaned harder on the door. Every time they fell silent, I half-expected one of them to open the door and send me toppling onto Lou's carpet.

"Well, what do we do now?" Moze finally said. He sounded dazed. Not one hint of his normal aggressive nature was in his voice. He talked like a defeated man. And that was a tone I'd never heard come from his mouth.

"I'm not sure," answered Lou. "Sammy's screwed, that's for sure.

And I'm afraid he's gone off the deep end. About nine o'clock this morning, I got a phone call from someone in California. Chalmers never made the flight home last night. No one's heard from him. All I can believe is that Sammy's up to something and that he'll be looking for us next."

I'd heard enough. In fact, I was beginning to think like Salvi and suspect that I may have heard too much. My head was swimming. My hip was pounding. I wanted to open the door and scream, "Are you guys outta your goddamn minds?!" But I didn't. I wanted to talk to them but didn't want them to know I'd been listening, so I crutched down the narrow corridor and out into the main reception area.

Lou's secretary turned her head when I came through the door. So did the heads of a few other office workers sitting at their desks.

"Hey, Dom," they shouted. "We did it!"

"Yeah, we sure did," I responded, high-fiving them as they approached me, one by one.

"Wait a minute," Lou's secretary said. "How did you get up here? Players aren't supposed to use that staircase."

"Jimmy gave me the combination—Dr. Bedrosian's orders. He wanted me to see Lou right after the operation, but his door is closed. Is he here?"

"Yes, but he's asked not to be disturbed."

"I don't want to bother him, but . . . Doc's orders."

"Hold on, take a seat."

I went over to the couch while Lou's secretary picked up the phone. She spoke into the receiver, but I couldn't hear what she was saying. I was more curious as to what Lou was saying to her.

Just then I spied Ron Hanes walking down the hallway from the direction of the owner's office. He looked preoccupied as he stopped and lit a cigarette. Surely, he'd just had a personal meeting of some importance with the head honcho. Perhaps a frank discussion of the new pecking order on the Giants had taken place and a smoothing over of ruffled feathers had been in order. Ramsey was now a Super Bowl–winning quarterback and a serious threat to Hanes's position on the team. How the mighty have fallen, I thought. Perhaps my original assessment of Hanes's exalted status had been wrong. Perhaps he might discover, after all, what it was like to be cast adrift like the rest of us dead weight. The irony made me chuckle.

But my enjoyment was premature. Entering a conference room, Hanes was met by a flurry of flashbulbs and voices greeting him at the door.

"Ron! Ron!" they yelled in unison. "Is it true that Ramsey's been traded to the new expansion team?"

"No comment, fellas. No comment," I heard him say smugly as he shut the door behind him.

I should've known better. Hanes was the franchise. All the wishful thinking in the world would never change that.

"All right, Dom. Mr. Gordon will see you now," Lou's secretary said, snapping me back to my own plight. I laughed at how she referred to him. The name Mr. Gordon reminded me that Lou was not only the head coach, but also the general manager of the team, a dual title held by no other coach in the league. Many thought it foolish to entrust budgetary responsibilities to a football coach, but under Lou's management, the Giants had become the most efficient and profitable franchise in the league. That was no surprise to me. Lou was the only coach I knew of with an Ivy League MBA.

Crutching into his office, I wondered who would greet me, the passionate, hot-blooded strategist who reveled in conquering indomitable defenses (preferably with a loyal, if somewhat damaged, tight end), or the cold, calculating businessman who thrilled in constantly streamlining his successful financial enterprise.

The secretary foreshadowed what to expect. Looking in every corner of his office, I braced myself for turbulence. Moze was nowhere to be found. He must have gone down the secret staircase.

"Looking for something?" Mr. Gordon said defensively, in lieu of a greeting or even a "How you doin', kid?"

The general manager sat behind his desk in an oversize leather chair, the kind that swivels, looking like the chairman of the board, with hands folded on the mahogany desk and a look of control in his eyes. It was his most formidable "Lou" look and would normally have reduced me to silence and submissiveness. But not today.

"Just you."

"What can I do for you?" Lou said impatiently. Obviously, he had other things on his mind at the moment.

"Relax, Lou, this'll only take a second."

He bristled at my flippancy, but kept silent. He wanted me out of there fast, and after what I'd heard a few minutes ago, I didn't blame him. I'd lost most of my respect for him, I realized. His standing by Moze might have been enough to overcome my disillusionment, but he'd betrayed me. My teammates, too. I was aware of a little sibling jealousy. While I admired him for standing by Moze, I was jealous that he was refusing to do the same for me.

"My future with the Giants needs to be addressed," I said. "I keep hearing things from Dr. Bedrosian. But I need to hear them from you." I stared unwaveringly into his eyes. "I want to know, are you going to stand by me or are you going to cut me loose?"

"That's not up to me, Dom. That's the doc's call," Lou said coldly. He could lie with the best of them.

"Cut the shit," I shot back. "You know the risk I took for you this year. You know about the rehab I'm facing from this surgery, the missed time and all that. But you also know there's a chance I can come back. All it's gonna take is your okay. One word to the doc and he'll pass me on my physical. One word from you and I can stay. Are you gonna stand by me, or are you gonna screw me?"

Lou didn't like what I said. But he kept his composure. "I'm not going to *screw* you. Your contract specifically states that if you can play the game, we'll pay you. If you can't play, then we're no longer obligated. You're the one who signed it, not me. And secondly—"

I didn't want to hear any of this legal stuff. "That's the standard contract everyone signs in order to play in this league. What choice did I have? And sometimes you have to go beyond what a piece of paper obliges you to do. Sometimes you have to do what your *heart and soul* tell you to do. I wasn't obligated to play with my jaw wired shut a few years ago, was I? I wasn't obligated to play with my shoulder hanging out of its socket that one season, was I? I wasn't obligated to finish this year with a knee that might have imploded at any moment, was I?"

"That's got nothing to do with anything," he said, brushing my words aside. "And secondly, I got you into this league, son. Don't forget that. No one wanted to touch you coming out of college. So don't start telling me what *you've* done for me. I've given you a job for the last eight years. Where's my thanks for that?"

He was talking to me like a third-stringer who should've been happy to just be there. Before he'd even had time to put a question mark on his sentence, I lifted one crutch into the air and slammed it down on his desk. Lou jumped in his seat, and the look of control jumped with him, right off his face. I swept the crutch back and forth on the desk and wiped all the contents onto the floor. Pens, pencils, picture frames, elephants with raised trunks, lucky horseshoes, stacks of videotape, a clock-trophy with a pen holder. Everything onto the floor. Then I pushed the end of the crutch into his chest.

"Here's my thanks! Can't you feel my gratitude?"

He didn't answer. I kept the crutch where it was. Surprisingly, no voice in my head tempted me to run him through. Instead, my mind was peaceful. I wasn't angry. It suddenly dawned on me that Lou had never asked me for anything. It was all my own doing. I'd sacrificed myself all on my own. My mistake was thinking he'd be grateful.

"Wow, Lou," I said, suddenly deflated. "I've been in awe of you since the day I met you. Turns out I've been lookin' up to an asshole all along."

My submission was quick and apparent. He sensed it immediately, like a dog smelling fear.

"Who the hell do you think you're talking to, son?" he said, swatting the crutch away, outrage in his voice.

I thought about it for a second. "I guess I'm talkin' to my *ex*-coach."

His face was unmoved. Oh, sure, there was emotion beneath the surface, but that was only in response to my behavior. He felt no regret at my departure. It was just business to him. My price/earning ratio no longer made sense. I was fiscally inept. The company's portfolio had no room for me anymore.

I turned to go. There was nothing else to say. My career was over.

"And, oh, yeah," I said over my shoulder. "Just mail me my ring when it comes in. I won't be back for the ceremony."

Red had warned me I'd be treated like any other player who'd outlived his usefulness to the club. He'd been right. It wasn't that I hadn't believed him. It was just that I'd clung to a sliver of hope that I might somehow be different. Foolish.

As I left Lou's office, I realized I wasn't upset. Rather, I was relieved. A burden had been lifted. The past few months I'd been trapped in a sport I loved, while being kicked out of it at the same time. The irony had almost driven me mad. Now that I'd seen Lou, I could move on to the next phase of my life, whatever that was, regardless of whether I really wanted to or not. My purgatory was over.

I headed toward the locker room to get my helmet and nameplate before Lou had Red commandeer them. The stairs were harder to navigate going down. Pain filled my body. Again, I thought of my grandfather. Reaching the bottom landing, the air of the tunnel made me gag. Anxiety crept slowly over me. I was reminded of the night I'd gone back for my playbook. There was no sign of life anywhere. No players, no security guards, no workers. Other than a few dim bulbs placed thirty feet high and twenty yards apart, there was no light. Everything was shadowy. The pills and my weakened condition sparked a mild panic. I couldn't have felt more vulnerable.

A sharp sting on the left side of my chest forced me to stop and adjust the pad on top of the appropriate crutch. The silence that followed engulfed my head like a blanket. Despite this, it seemed I could hear every tick and crack of the old stadium, as though my hearing had turned supersonic. Somewhere down the tunnel, water dripped from a spigot, and the winter wind howled through portals and crevices. I stood motionless. It touched my soul. It sounded as though the tunnel itself were moaning in agony. The noise slowly changed as if in response to my attention. Gradually, it became more like that of a cat crying sorrowfully in some far-flung corner of an enormous alleyway. I stood transfixed, its echo effectively masking its source. Then the wails became less feline and more human, the most pitiful cries I'd ever heard.

Following the noise as best I could, I came upon a rusted door in the tunnel wall. I knew it well. It opened to a storage facility for the tackling dummies we used out at practice. The sobs were louder than ever. Opening the door, I poked my head into the darkened room.

"Hello?" I called. "Are you all right?"

The noise stopped. I felt around for a light switch. With a click of my finger, the room was as bright as the sun.

"Shut if off!" a voice yelled.

I did so immediately. But I'd seen enough to recognize the occupant.

"Moze? Are you okay?"

He didn't say anything. I assumed he was trying to compose himself.

"Moze, come on out. It's all right."

There was no sound of movement, nor any indication that he was going to speak. I stood silent for a moment, as uncomfortable stumbling upon him as he probably was at being discovered. But then, as if guided by some inner force, I decided to confront him.

"Moze, I know about last night."

His breathing stopped. "Whatta you talkin' about?"

"I heard you and Lou talking a few minutes ago. I was listening outside his office door."

Silence. It seemed he was afraid to speak.

"C'mon, Moze, I heard everything. The point spread, the touchdown at the end of the game, Chalmers, Sammy Penrod."

"Everything?" he asked weakly.

"Yeah, everything."

I heard him punch one of the dummies in the room, the sound as loud as a gunshot. He began wailing again like a wounded animal. It was heart-wrenching to hear such sounds from him. They aroused all the feelings of loyalty I'd had that night with Red at the Café Fátima when I'd been so adamant about protecting Moze from Sammy.

"Don't worry," I said soothingly. "Don't be afraid. I'll stay here with you."

"I'm not *afraid.*"

If it weren't for his tone of voice, I'd never have believed him. But he truly didn't sound frightened at all.

"Then why are you so upset?"

"I fucked everything up. I let people down. I betrayed *the game.* Betrayed it like a goddamn Judas!" He spoke in between fits of tears.

"You didn't let anyone down," I said quickly. "You stayed true. We won, didn't we? And we won *because of you.* Lou was the only one who flirted with that abomination."

"Maybe so," Moze said, trying to compose himself. "But my behavior. My lifestyle. That was the root of the whole thing. If it wasn't for me, none of this would've happened. *I made* Lou do what he did. He never would have acted that way if I wasn't in trouble." The huge man emerged from the shadows. "Look, I know you're trying to help. But forget it. I'm too far gone. It's over for me. Once people find out what happened, they'll never forgive me. Hell, I don't think I could ever forgive myself. If I didn't think Sammy was gonna kill me, I'd jump off the third tier of the stadium and splatter myself all over the parking lot. I can't go on like this. I . . . I just can't live like this."

The despair in his voice made my gut tremble. "Believe," I said quietly. "Believe and live your faith."

It just came out. Like a reflex action. The kind that makes your knee jerk when the doc hits it with his rubber mallet. Only in this case, the rubber mallet was Moze's despair, the knee my gut, and my words the reaction.

"What do you mean?" he asked curiously, even hungrily. "Tell me, Dom."

Without mentioning my own confession with the priest at St. Basil's, I relayed to Moze everything that had been ingrained in me about forgiveness and hope. Moze drank in every word as if he were dying of thirst and I were feeding him drops of water.

By the time I finished, he was standing in the dim light of the tunnel, bathed in an aura of peace. His soul at rest. The tears he cried, when told that all is forgiven for those who ask, were different from the tears he'd cried only moments before in his despair.

I was compelled by that same inner force to move closer to him. We joined like two magnets in an embrace of forgiveness and hope. The pain seeped from his body and sorrow filled his grasp.

Maybe if we'd stayed in each other's arms a little longer, it might have turned uncomfortable. But suddenly, the peace and joy of our secular act of reconciliation was shattered by the sight and sound of a runaway car speeding down the ramp from the parking lot and barreling headlong into the enclosed quarters of the stadium tunnel.

Moze and I recoiled. We froze like statues as the car halted in front of us about thirty feet away.

For a minute, nothing happened. But then tumbling out of

the discount rental car like a blind and confused weasel came Sammy Penrod.

The darkness of the tunnel made him hesitate, his eyes obviously adjusting to the lack of light. He looked as though he'd just gotten off the plane from California. His clothes were wrinkled and he was missing his customary Ray-Bans. Despite the cold, he wore nothing heavier than a pullover windbreaker. The logo of a charity golf outing was emblazoned upon the upper left breast of the jacket: SAMMY'S GIANT DAY FOR THE KIDS. Those kids had enjoyed their last free meal on Mr. Penrod, I thought.

Obviously he'd had no time to groom himself before coming to the stadium. Obviously, too, he was drunk. What a slob. His slovenliness looked exaggerated in light of his usual impeccable appearance. But it wasn't a major concern of mine. Rather, the sight of the gun in his hand commanded my attention.

"There you are, you son of a bitch!" he said, rubbing his eyes.

I assumed he was talking to Moze, but it was dark in the tunnel and Moze and I were only inches away from each other. Sammy aimed the wobbling gun back and forth between us as if not sure two people were in front of him.

"Do you know what you've done!" he cried. "Do you have any idea who you're dealing with?"

"Fuck you, Sammy," Moze said calmly. His eyes were clear and his mind at peace.

"Fuck me? Fuck me? No. Fuck you, Moze. I'm gonna blow your goddamn head off. And do you know what I'm gonna do after that?"

I didn't venture to guess.

"I'm gonna go upstairs and give Lou his share of the winnings, too. Right between his lyin' eyes." Sammy laughed drunkenly. "And then I'm gonna finish up the job by blowin' my own lousy head off. And you know why?"

Again, I figured it was a rhetorical question.

"Because I'm a dead man. Y'understand? A dead man!" Sammy shouted. He raised his arms up in the air. "I already took care of Chalmers. And now I'm gonna take care of you!" He fingered the trigger and pointed the gun back in our direction.

"Hold on, Sammy!" I shouted. "Hold on a second now. Listen, it's not too late. There must be a way out of this. You just gotta live your faith, that's all."

Nothing compelled me to talk. I just figured I was on a roll with that phrase, so why not give it a shot.

"Who is that? Fucillo?" Sammy said, finally realizing that he wasn't seeing double. "Hell, I might as well take care of you, too. Why not? You always were a pain in the ass. Too good to hang around with ol' Sammy, huh? Well, now we'll all take a nice little trip together after all." He laughed.

Nice going, Holy Roller, I told myself, but at least the interruption seemed to sidetrack him from shooting us. Instead, he decided to spew forth a drunken monologue.

"You couldn't just play along. Could you, Moze? You had to be Mr. Football Hero. The great James Moze! Too pure to help out an old buddy. You'll shove a bag of coke up your nose and go to bed with any whore that'll have you, but you won't drop one ball or miss one tackle on purpose because it violates the sanctity of the game! Hell, you're more screwed up than I am. But I figured I could count on Lou. The look on his face when I told him you were going down with me was priceless. Agreeing to shave points in the Super Bowl was easy for him. He would've done anything to save his boy. The only problem is, he didn't come through, and more importantly, you ain't Lou's boy . . . you're mine!"

"You don't own me, you pathetic piece of shit!" said Moze.

"Oh, but you're wrong, Mr. All-Pro. I *do* own you. You signed on a long time ago. You *belong* to me. There's no escapin' that. And now we'll be together forever. Cuz I'm gonna take you with me . . . to *hell*!"

I saw Sammy's hand tighten on the pistol and watched as his eyes and body prepared for the recoil of the impending explosion. I knew he was close enough not to miss. Dropping my crutches, I lunged at Moze. The blast of Sammy's gun coincided with my tackle and we hit the ground hard. My body exploded with pain. Immediately, I knew something had gone wrong. But I couldn't tell if my misfortune was from Sammy's gun or if the wounds from Dr. Bedrosian's knife had ripped themselves open when I hit the hard concrete of the floor.

"Dom! Are you okay?!" Moze shouted.

My insides were on fire. The bullet from Sammy's gun had found its mark. But my head remained clear. I saw Sammy walking toward us.

"You didn't have to do that," Sammy said. "I have enough bullets for both of you. I would've taken care of you next!"

I could smell the alcohol on his breath.

"But seeing as how you're almost done, let me just finish you up."

Sammy pointed the gun in the direction of my head. Poor Moze, I thought. He was trapped under my body. In my attempt to defend him, I'd actually rendered him helpless. I didn't know what to do. We both just lay there, me on top of him, as he cradled me in his arms. He didn't even try to move.

I could think of little else but Moze. It was as though he'd been my responsibility, my assignment on a play called by Lou. I'd blocked one bullet for him. But the whistle hadn't blown. The action still raged. More bullets were on their way. All I could think was "How am I going to get him out of this mess?"

Sammy loomed over us. Drool fell from his drunken lips. His eyes glowed with bloodlust, wide in anticipation of the kill. I braced for the end.

Suddenly, a door opened behind him. A familiar voice shouted, "Who the hell's out there?"

Sammy swung around.

"Look out!" Moze yelled.

Sammy fired blindly down the tunnel. The bullet ricocheted off one of the support beams and the door closed shut. Sammy's gun still pointed in the direction of the voice, searching for a body to go with it. Moze began to struggle out from under me. The voice must have awakened his fighting spirit. He was just about free when the door swung back open.

Red!

He stood there with a dark stick in his hands. When fire shot out from the end of it, I realized he was holding the shotgun he'd greeted me with the night I knocked on his door to retrieve my playbook.

The *boom!* of the shotgun dwarfed the *pop!* of Sammy's pistol. Sammy was blown back a good five yards. He fell. All was silent. I craned my neck to look. His body lay motionless. Moze scrambled to his feet and ran over to him.

"Shit, Red. I think you killed him!"

"I did?"

Red made his way over to Sammy's body. I tried to talk, but couldn't. The pain was overwhelming. Again, my penance came to mind.

"Oh, yeah, Pop," I whispered to myself. "Here you go. I offer up this pain for you."

Resting my head on the floor, the muscles in my neck relaxed and my head felt as heavy as if I'd been wearing my helmet. The sensation brought me comfort, and despite the pain, sleep beckoned. Listening to Moze and Red converse over by Sammy's body, I closed my eyes and began to drift away. In an instant, I was back in my old dream standing by my grandfather's deathbed. This time, however, he wasn't in it.

"How ya doin' kid?" a voice said happily. Turning, I saw him. No longer pale and shriveled, my grandfather was young and vibrant. Tattoos full and tight, his muscles bulged beneath his shirt. "Thank you," he said to me. "Your sacrifice fulfilled my penance. Your offering unlocked my chains."

"Huh?" I said dreamily.

"From purgatory," he said, his eyes glowing with satisfaction at having endured and overcome such a tribulation. "Now follow me. I've come to take you home."

"Home?"

"Paradise."

He held out his hand. I hesitated.

"Come with me or go back," he said. "Choose wisely."

I don't know why I hesitated. The choice wasn't hard. The life I'd known was gone. Paradise sounded wonderful. Extending my hand, I reached out for his. A smile appeared on his lips. But moving toward him, I was stopped, as though something held me in place. The harder I pushed forward, the stronger I was pulled back. Lowering my head, I saw a thread tied to my waist, stretching into the darkness behind me.

"You can break it if you want," my grandfather said. "It's your choice."

He seemed to be right. The thread looked fragile and easily breakable. Grabbing it with both hands, I prepared to snap it. But when I touched it, I realized it was more than just a thread. It was my last hope left on earth: the hope that I'd somehow reconcile with Emma. Even in my dream, I couldn't escape her. Every pull of the thread was like a plea from her to return. The pressure wrenched me backward, forgiveness accompanying every tug. As I filled once again with earthly desire, the prospect of paradise waned. My love for Emma was too great. I'd ignored her pleas once. I refused to do so again. My decision was made.

"If you leave, you must begin anew," my grandfather warned as if reading my mind. He spoke ominously and in perfect English. "Your soul will be constantly at risk. Paradise is never guaranteed. Every day, you must believe and live your faith."

Emma was worth such a risk. I nodded with understanding. "Thanks, Pop. I'll remember that always." And then I turned and followed the thread back to life.

In a quiet hospital room somewhere on the Upper East Side of Manhattan, a young woman struggled to rise from the hard recliner she'd been sleeping on for the past few weeks. A strange noise had awoken her. She went to the bed in the middle of the room and stared in disbelief at the patient. The young man was covered with tubes and wires.

"Doctor!" she called out into the hallway. "Come quick, he's waking up!"

The doctor rushed in, checking vital signs and listening to the incoherent mumbles coming from the young man's mouth.

"Who's 'Pop'?" he asked her.

"His grandfather," she said. "He's been dead for years."

"Well, his heartbeat is faint but steady. The rest of his vitals are satisfactory. Now that he's regaining consciousness, he may just make it." The doctor paused for a moment as he looked at the young woman. "Who would've thought?" he mused.

"Thank God," the woman cried in relief.

She stroked the brow of the patient's forehead with one hand and rubbed the curve of her swollen belly with the other.

Twenty-five

I remember the first rays of sunshine that streamed into my hospital room the morning my second life started. I knew the York Orthopedic Hospital by smell, but I thought I was there recovering from my bone-graft operation. The East River roiled past my window, and the glare off the cars on the FDR was blinding. The grind of the workday had begun, and the city looked as dirty and grimy as ever for mid-February. But it all looked wonderful to me, as if I were seeing it for the first time. And in a sense, I was.

Seconds after my eyes opened, nausea and pain welcomed me back to this realm of flesh and blood.

"Nurse, come quickly," I yelled suddenly. "And bring a bucket!"

Too late. Heavy footsteps approached and my eyes

welled in embarrassment at the mess I'd made. Blinded by the sun, I felt a cool cloth wipe my face and mouth. The moisture replenished my dry, chapped lips. I yearned for mouthfuls more, but the thought turned my stomach. The damp towel would have to do. My head pounded and my body burned.

The nurse continued to clean me up. Her touch was gentle. I knew she would've done it for anyone, but I was weak and helpless and was overcome with gratitude.

"Thank you," I said fervently.

"Anytime."

Stroking my cheek, she rubbed against me as she continued to clean. Stepping in front of the blinding sun, she cast a shadow over my eyes. My vision focused and I could see her face for the first time.

"Emma?" I gasped.

I couldn't believe what I was seeing. Was it really her?

"Hey" was all she said.

Suddenly my memory opened like a sieve. Everything after the bone-graft surgery came flooding into my mind. The ride back to the stadium. The conversation between Lou and Moze. My own conversation with Lou, and then Moze. Sammy Penrod. Red. Even the dream of my grandfather. It all came back as clear as a bell.

I looked at Emma's beautiful face and stared into her loving eyes. The pain and nausea disappeared. Reaching out with a weak and trembling hand, I whispered softly and meekly, "I love you, Emma. My God, how I love you."

"I love you, Dom."

"How'd you know I was here?"

"Salvi."

Her stomach protruded onto the bed. I noticed in disbelief.

"I thought you . . ."

"Shhh," she whispered, putting her finger to my lips.

"I'll never leave you again, Emma."

"You mean you'll never leave *us* again," she said, lifting my hand to her stomach and rubbing our baby inside . . . for me.

It was a few days before Emma had a chance to explain her change of heart. All conversation prior to that consisted of "Bucket, please" and "Hold still while I wipe your face." That's all we could muster due to my nausea. But on the fourth day after awakening, I swallowed a milk shake and nothing happened. No bucket. No cleanup. No embarrassing noises. That's when the wheels starting turning in Emma's head and she began formulating her explanation for being there. I could see her muttering to herself as she moved around the room, absentmindedly arranging flowers and dusting furniture. She was prideful and a fierce competitor. Her resolve to live without me that day outside of Avco & Associates was so strong that her presence here, as well as her condition, could only, in her mind, be seen as a defeat and an embarrassment. Her discomfort was obvious. Her shoulders drooped with a hint of shame. Of course, I didn't see it that way. Her return carried no shame in my eyes. I was overjoyed with her presence. If she had never shown up at the hospital, I would gladly have crawled back to her on my belly. That's what I was planning to do before I got shot. But none of that mattered to Emma. In her eyes, she was the one who caved, and I could see it was eating her up inside. Beautiful Emma. Her fiery temper was exactly why I loved her. Even though she considered herself the loser in this battle, she wasn't going to let me feel like the winner. I smiled inwardly as she prepared to explain herself because, despite her intentions, I *was* the winner. Not the winner in a battle of wills as she supposed. But a winner because the woman I loved, the woman I'd thought I'd lost forever, was sitting beside me holding my hand. And more than that, she looked as if she planned on staying.

"As you can see, I never went through with the procedure," she blurted out with the tone of a teacher lecturing a student, or a prosecutor instructing a jury. "Halfway up the elevator I changed my mind. The whole thing was wrong from the beginning. I was an angry woman. Angry at you for our breakup. Angry at your indifferent silence. Angry that you continued to play your stupid games in complete oblivion to my situation. I went to that clinic to get rid of *you,* not my baby. When you showed up with your stupid know-nothing grin and started telling me what I could and couldn't do, I was more resolved than ever to proceed with my original plan. You should have known better than to have talked to me like that. You know what kind of temper I have."

She paused and raised an eyebrow. I stared back motionless, petrified to move.

"Anyway," she continued, "I calmed down in the elevator. You're right about that music; in the right circumstances it can be relaxing. Looking at the escort beside me, I realized I didn't need her help. I was a strong, independent, self-sufficient, grown woman who didn't need anyone's help, especially not the doctor's who she was taking me to see. I was happy to be pregnant. I'd been happy all along. I wanted that child inside of me and I wanted to be a mother. As soon as the elevator doors opened, I headed straight to the stairwell and walked down seven flights of stairs without a break. On the way, I berated myself for letting my anger get the best of me. I couldn't believe I'd come so close to doing something so wrong. If I hadn't calmed down, I would've regretted it for the rest of my life."

She smiled for the first time. "Once I made my decision, I felt better. Most of my anger melted away. I'd put you behind me and was ready to move forward. But as the days went by, my misery grew. At first, I thought it was the pregnancy. But then Salvi called to tell me what had happened, and my heart nearly broke. Just the mention of your name brought tears to my eyes. That's when I realized I still loved you. Despite everything you did, and didn't do, I still wanted to be with you. I couldn't help myself. Life alone was unbearable. Looking back, I realized I hadn't been happy since our last dinner together. I hadn't laughed or smiled in over six months. You're a big jerk sometimes, but I know you're a good man. And I know you'll make a wonderful father. I know, also, that you love me," she said, speaking nearly in a whisper and running her fingers through my hair. "I want us to work. I'm swallowing my pride right now for both our sakes. I made the first move because, left up to you, we'd never get back together. Somehow, you'd find a way to screw it up, and you know it. That's why I don't care how it looks or what you think about my being here. Go ahead and gloat if you want, but we both know that contrary to your drunken rant from the barroom pay phone that night, *I'm* the best thing that ever happened to *you.*"

I blushed at the memory of my embarrassing performance at the Café Fátima. "I agree wholeheartedly," I said, "and I'm not gloating. I'm just grateful for the second chance. Thank you for coming back, Emma. I promise you, I won't blow it this time."

Man, we were a perfect match. No one ever got the best of Emma. She'd never let them. How I ever let football almost ruin our relationship was inconceivable to me at the moment. The accomplishments of this season paled in comparison to her presence by my side once again. All the Super Bowl rings in the world could never match the satisfaction of winning the love of such a woman. I held her tighter than any pass I'd ever caught and vowed to never let her go. She did the same. Putting my head on her stomach, I pondered the life inside. The potential of our two sets of genes comingling was awe-inspiring.

"Holy smokes," I whispered to our baby, "I can't wait to see you. You're gonna be some piece of work."

It was weeks before I started feeling normal again. The bullet from Sammy's gun had passed cleanly through my body, causing a whole lot of bleeding but leaving little permanent damage. I'd lost so much blood that I actually passed away, if only briefly. I might not have had the chance to come back if Red hadn't immediately called Dr. Bedrosian. He ordered the hospital's emergency helicopter to get me, and within twenty minutes I was across the river, in a bed, and stabilized. From that point, it was just a matter of my will to live. The doctor in charge of my case could give no explanation, nor take any credit, for my recovery. He wasn't a religious man, he'd said, but if he had to guess as to why I came back from the dead, he'd simply point to Emma.

"It was probably her tears and prayers that did it. They sure would've worked on me."

After the first few days of consciousness, the nausea passed and I began to enjoy my stay in the hospital. I'd been unconscious for more than a week, and Dr. Bedrosian said it would be at least another month before he'd release me. Besides the gunshot wound, he was worried about the bone graft in my knee. He wasn't happy that I'd jeopardized his handiwork only hours after the operation. This time, he wanted me under his supervision to make sure I stayed off my feet.

Salvi sent runs of food down from the Point almost every evening, every meal accompanied by his finest bottle of red. He never came himself, for reasons I could understand, but Frank and the rest of the boys made regular visits. I missed Salvi, but I guess we both needed time to heal.

The whole matter was hushed up of course. As far as anyone knew, I was in the hospital for a bone-graft operation. Besides Jimmy, Red, and Moze, none of my teammates came to visit. Most of them had left for the off-season, and my annual postseason surgeries had become so commonplace they elicited little sympathy or interest from anyone. Besides Dirty Rivers, who sent a get-well card with the inscription "My appointment with your knee has been postponed until you're feeling better," no one even called. But I didn't blame them. They had their own problems. Besides, who needed them? Emma was at my bedside every day.

Moze came in one day with some interesting news. "I'm gonna learn how to coach," he declared. "I figure I'm with

Lou nearly every day as it is, I might as well learn something while I'm there."

I laughed. "You want to be the next Lou Gordon?"

"No," he smiled. "I'm going to be better than Lou. Lou just teaches X's and O's. I'm gonna teach responsibility, too." I looked at him curiously. "You've gotta hold guys accountable," he explained. "Just because someone's good at playing a game doesn't mean he can do anything he pleases. Like it or not, this game's a *business.* And no business in the world would've put up with an employee like me. Lou should've punished me a long time ago. He should've benched me, or suspended me, or even cut me. At the very least he should've sat me down and explained how much of a jackass I was."

"Would you have listened?" I asked skeptically.

He laughed. "That's a good question. I honestly don't know. But one thing's for sure; if I'd been held accountable for my actions, you wouldn't be lying in this hospital bed right now."

I nodded. He made sense. Moze's newfound maturity was impressive.

"When I came to New York," he continued, "I was an unknown with barely any money in my pockets. Within a month, I had millions and was a household name. You know who my closest advisor was throughout that transition?"

I shook my head.

"Sammy Penrod," he said.

"That's screwed up."

"No shit! And Lou never objected. He probably thought Sammy was good for me, you know, helping me to blow off steam or something."

"Lou's a prick," I said. I'd forgiven Lou, but I'd never forget.

Moze shook his head. "No, Dom," he replied. "I was a grown man. I should've known better. Holding my hand wasn't Lou's job. But instilling discipline, and enforcing rules, *was.* Covering up my stupidity benefited no one. While he's teaching me the finer points of the game, I'll try to make him understand that. After all that's happened, I've come to realize that personal responsibility is the bottom line. If we don't give a shit about ourselves, then we shouldn't expect anyone else to either. Depending on other people for our well-being will only lead to frustration and regret, maybe even disaster. Lou's going to cut me someday, just like he did to you, and just like he's gonna do to all of us. It's inevitable. We need to realize that and plan accordingly. That's why every dollar I make from here on out's going straight to the bank. I've flushed so much money down the toilet that I'd be broke in three years if I stopped playing today. But if I'm smart with the few seasons I've got left, I should be able to secure at least a decent future for myself."

Moze's talk of the future reawakened the anxiety I'd felt when Dr. Bedrosian had first told me about the hole in my knee. He had a few seasons to get his act together. My moment of truth was upon me now.

"I hear you," I said, disconcerted. "I could've avoided a lot of misery myself if I'd been more responsible. And I'd sure as hell be more prepared for what's awaiting me once I leave this hospital."

"Shit, Dom," he said, noticing my discomfort. "You're sitting pretty, man. You got the most important thing you can have: a good woman. That's money in the bank. Emma's not going to let you fuck up your future. She'll kick your ass before that ever happens."

He had a point. Emma was as tough as Lou. Whatever I ended up doing, she'd see to it that I'd do it well. We both laughed at the thought of her putting me through my paces. Inside, though, I lamented the time Moze and I had wasted. If only we'd been this smart years ago.

Red visited every couple of days. It was nice to get to know him for who he was, sober and outside the confines of the stadium. He'd show up with a bottle of Canadian Club anyway, and we'd share a few shots for old times' sake. But he was beginning to stop at one or two.

"You're welcome back anytime," he said one day. "I hope you know that."

"Thanks," I said. "Do me one favor, will ya?"

"Name it."

"Can you bring me my helmet and nameplate? I want to keep them to remember."

"I'll bring you your helmet, Dom. No one will want to use that stinky piece a shit again. But no nameplate."

"Why not? Don't tell me you already threw it away. My locker's not even cold, for crissakes."

"I didn't throw it away. I got it taped on the wall above my desk."

I thought of the handful of nameplates I'd seen in his room the night I went back for my playbook.

"Why?" I asked, stunned.

"Because I want to remember, too."

Jimmy came in one morning as excited as the day he was given the combination to the coaches' stairwell.

"You'll never believe it!" he cried. "You'll never guess what just happened to me."

"You got the head trainer job with the new expansion team in Jacksonville," I said nonchalantly.

His face fell. "How the heck did you know?"

"Dr. Bedrosian told me." I laughed. "Congratulations."

His smile returned. "They're not going to be active for another year. We've got the whole upcoming season to put the team together." He said it as if that meant something.

"So?"

"The doc can't recommend your health to anyone, but I can. I can verify to the new coach that you'll be fit in another year or so. With a year's rest you can let all those old injuries heal. You'll be as good as new. Well, as good as old. And now that I'm the head man, I'll see to it that we save you a spot on my team."

"*We?*" I said. "*My* team?"

"Get used to it, rookie," he said with authority.

Jeez, I thought. I might just have to.

"What's more," he said, "guess who the new head coach is gonna be?"

"Who?"

"Midland!" Jimmy shouted. "Can you believe it? He already signed Dan Ramsey to a contract. They're gonna announce everything this afternoon."

Wow, good for them, I thought. They deserve it. But could I play again? Or better yet . . . did I really want to?

These three regular visitors, along with Dr. Bedrosian, were the only people from the team present in the hospital room when the priest from St. Basil's joined Emma and me in holy matrimony. It wasn't the most elaborate of weddings, but it was the smartest move I'd ever made, or would make, in my life.

By the time I was able to leave the hospital, Emma was on her way in. If I was ever nervous before any of my games, I was more so the morning she dug her fingernails into my arm and delivered into the world our new little girl, whom we named Fatima.

Shortly thereafter, Emma, Fatima, and I left New York. On our way out of town, we pulled into the parking lot of the Point. Salvi was sitting at the bar as usual, going over the day's lunch receipts. It was around two o'clock and the crowd had gone back to work, full and satisfied. I crutched in alone, as Emma and Fatima waited in the car. This wouldn't take long, I told them.

"Hey, Salvi," I said, hobbling my way along.

"Dom!" Salvi shouted, surprised. "How you feeling?"

"Doin' all right. Doin' just fine."

I had looked to him as my dearest friend at one time. But new revelations made me hesitate. I realized I didn't really know him at all. It was hard to be so familiar with him. But I tried.

"It's good to see you," I said.

"It's good to see you, too."

We were both ill at ease. Finally, he must just have said screw it and began acting like his old self.

"C'mon, siddown and eat somethin'. Didn't they feed you nothing in that hospital?"

"I only ate *your* food. You sent me three meals a day, for crissakes."

"Well, eat anyway. You look like hell."

"I can't. Emma and the baby are waitin' for me. I gotta get goin'."

"Oh."

He didn't argue the way he normally would. I didn't expect him to.

"I just wanted to say thanks," I said. "You were like family to me while I was playing. It meant a lot."

"If I hadn't almost gotten you killed, I'd say you're welcome."

I reached out to embrace him. Instead of his bristling and calling me a twat, he hugged me back. We held on to each other for a moment before separating.

"Well, I gotta get goin'," I said.

"Where are you headed?"

"I'm going back home for a bit, see some family and friends, take it easy for a while."

"What are your plans for the future?"

"I don't know."

"Would you please call Johnny Marotta, you dumb ass," he said, smiling.

"Enough with the Johnny crap. I don't need a job," I responded right on cue, though less vehemently than usual. Perhaps I should get Johnny's number after all, I thought.

"Seriously, what are you going to do now that football's over for you?"

"Who says it's over?"

"The Giants. I read it in the paper."

"Don't believe everything you read," I said. "And whatever you do, don't ever bet on it."

We both laughed.

There were so many questions I wanted to ask him. But I knew I didn't want to hear the answers. I loved Salvi. I would never have survived my time in New York without him. But it was different now. Too much information had come to light. I wanted our relationship to be the way it'd always been. I wanted to be ignorant again. But it was too late. Avascular necrosis had set in. Our friendship had been compromised. In time it would completely collapse. We both knew it was over. Moisture clouded our eyes as we said good-bye for the last time.

Falling into the Monte, I pulled out onto my beloved highway. The roads were quiet and I floated above the rest of the workaday world, sailing smack-dab into a future filled with uncertainty. I wasn't scared, not sitting behind the wheel of my car.

I mumbled a prayer of thanks and stepped on the accelerator with an ecstatic foot. I was finally free. The white stripes of I-95 passed so fast beneath my car they became one solid and continuous line. The speedometer needle hit eighty-miles an hour in no time, then continued to climb. The dread was gone. The anxiety nonexistent. My head was clear, my body unfettered. I felt unburdened. The chains of football were broken and it felt wonderful. I wanted to push the Monte so hard that it might take off into the atmosphere like a jet.

But the fingernails in my arm, and the crying in the backseat, anchored me firmly to the realm of this sweet earth. Letting up on the accelerator, I looked over to Emma and our baby and slowed to just under the speed limit. That was just fine with me. I realized I had no choice anymore. Even if I did, I would've made no other. I was driving for three now.